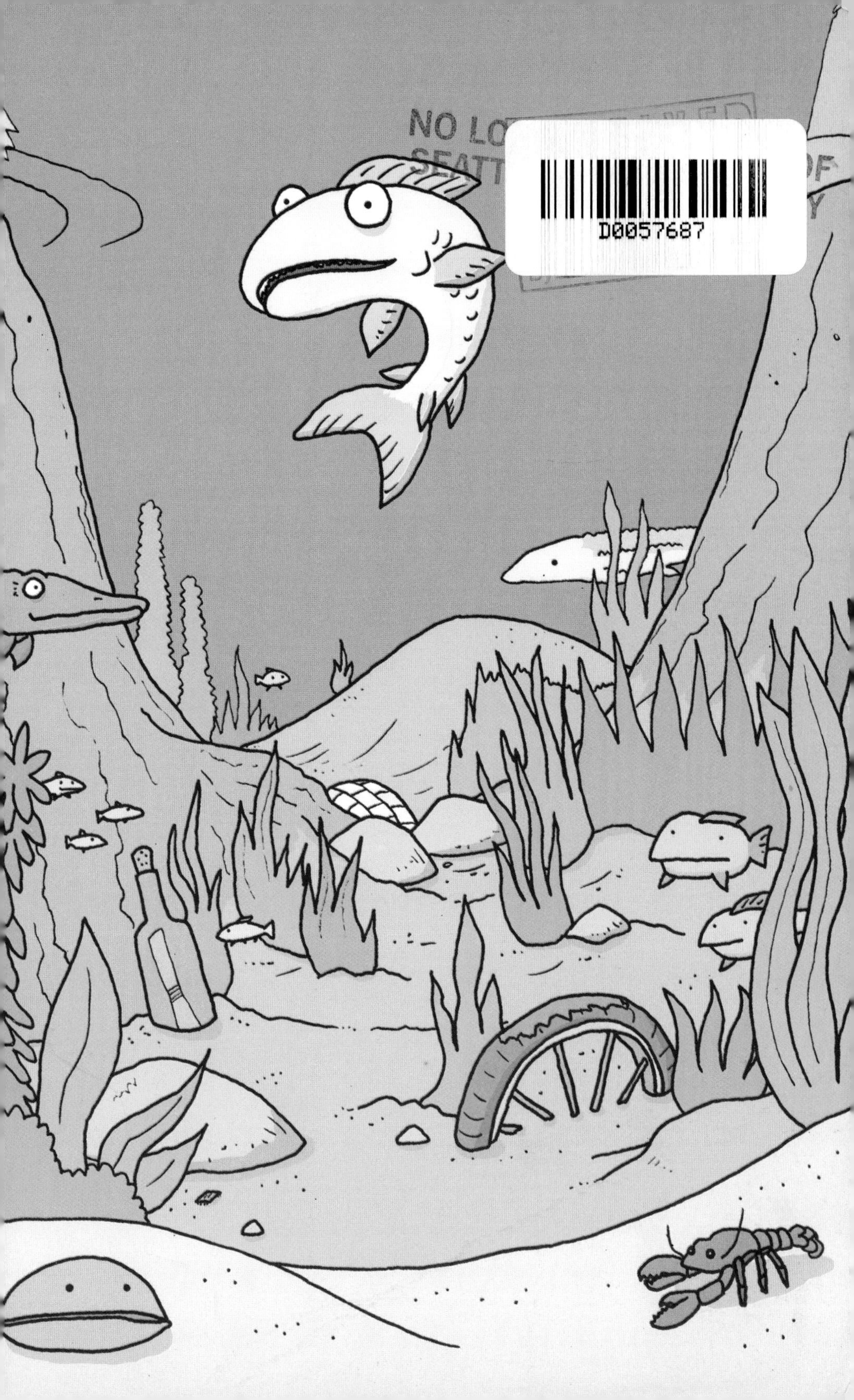

LASER MOOSE AND RABBIT BOY: TIME TROUT

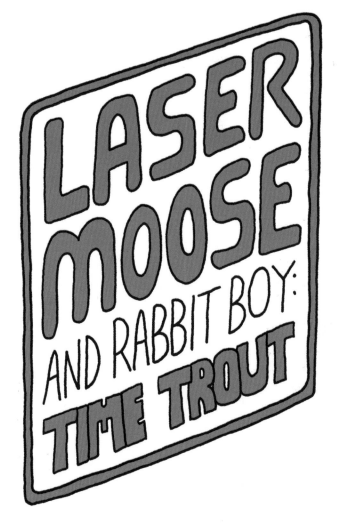

DOUG SAVAGE

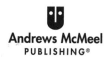

Andrews McMeel
PUBLISHING®

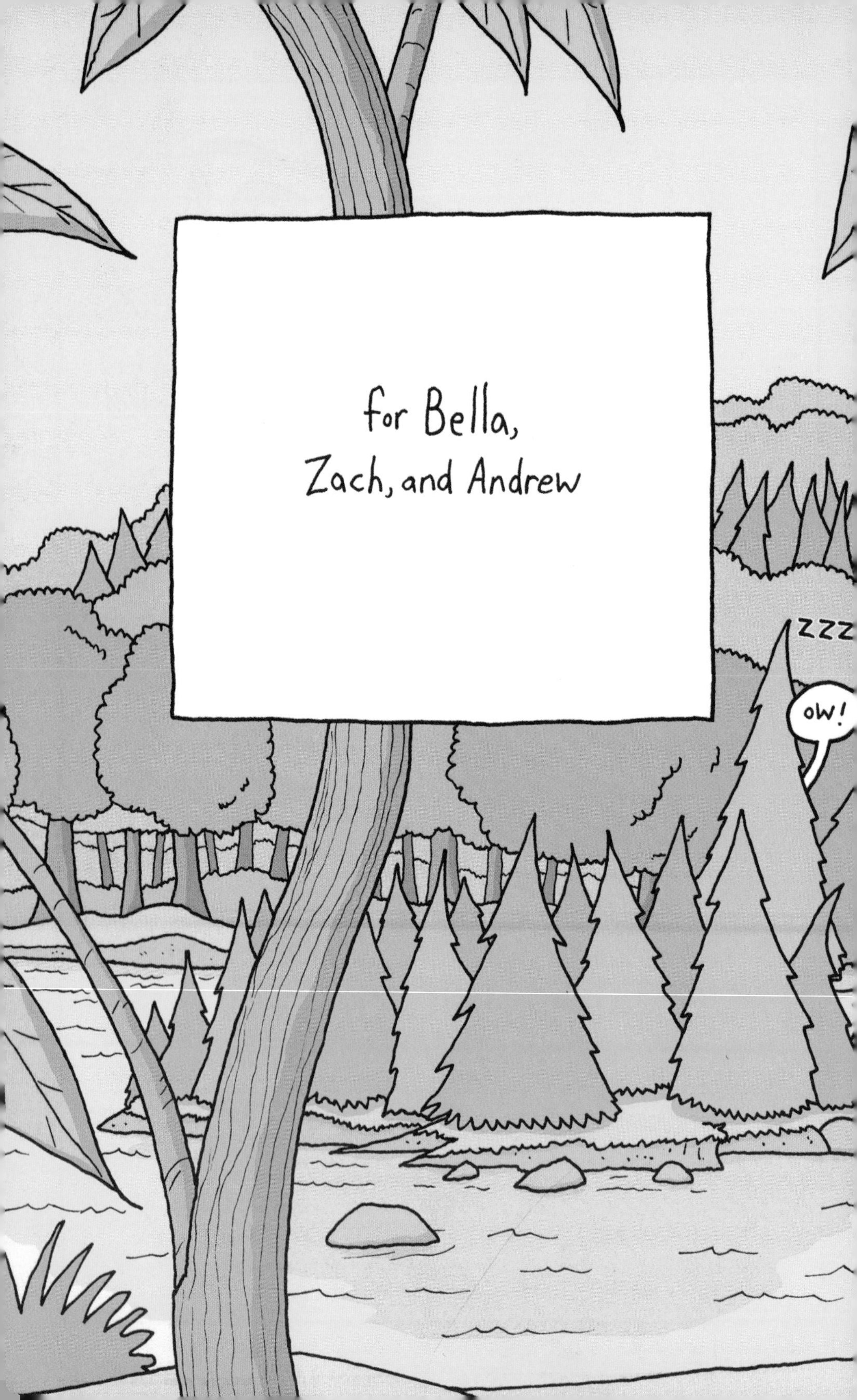
ZZZ
OW!

for Bella,
Zach, and Andrew

CONTENTS

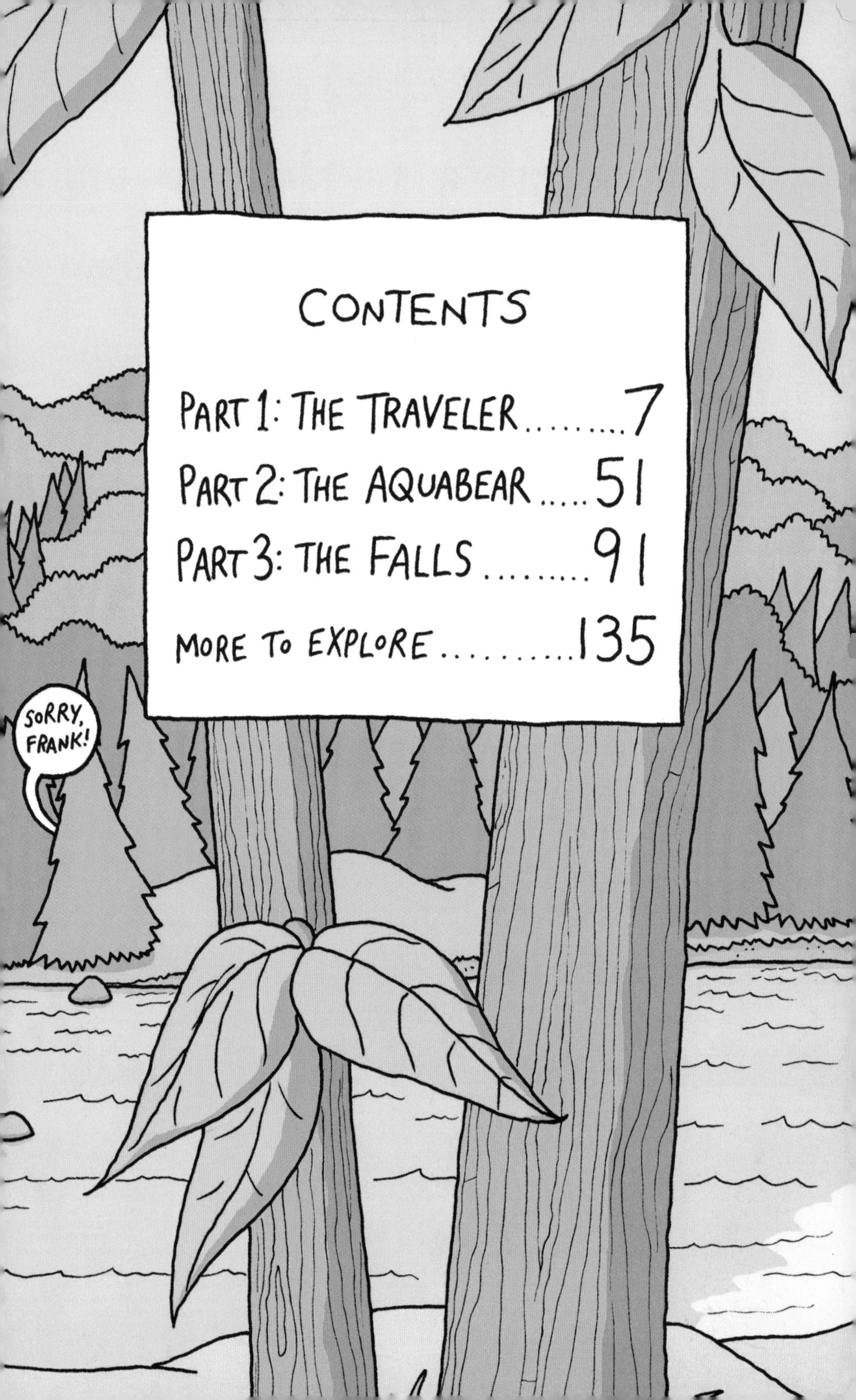

SORRY, FRANK!

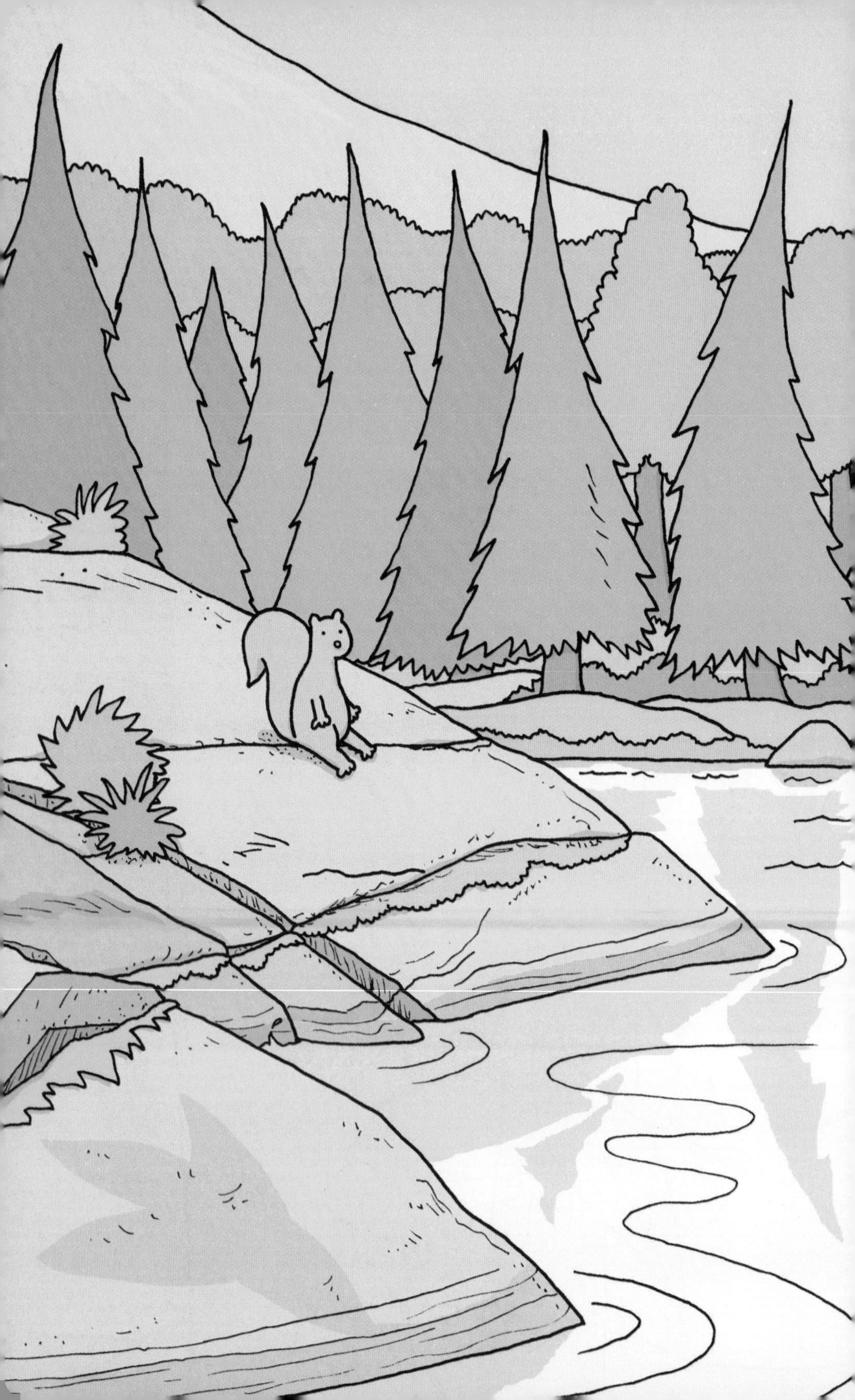

PART 1: THE TRAVELER

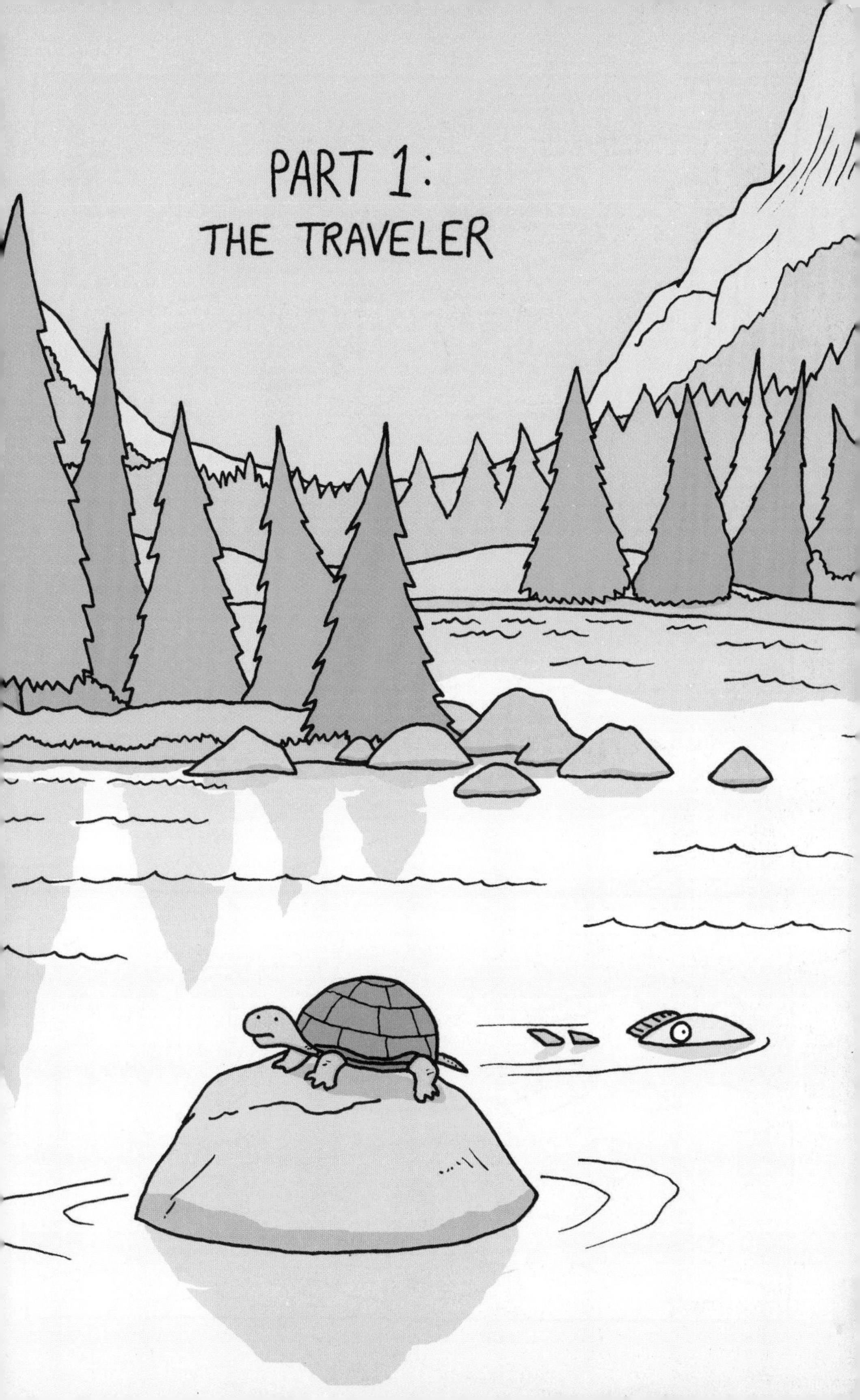

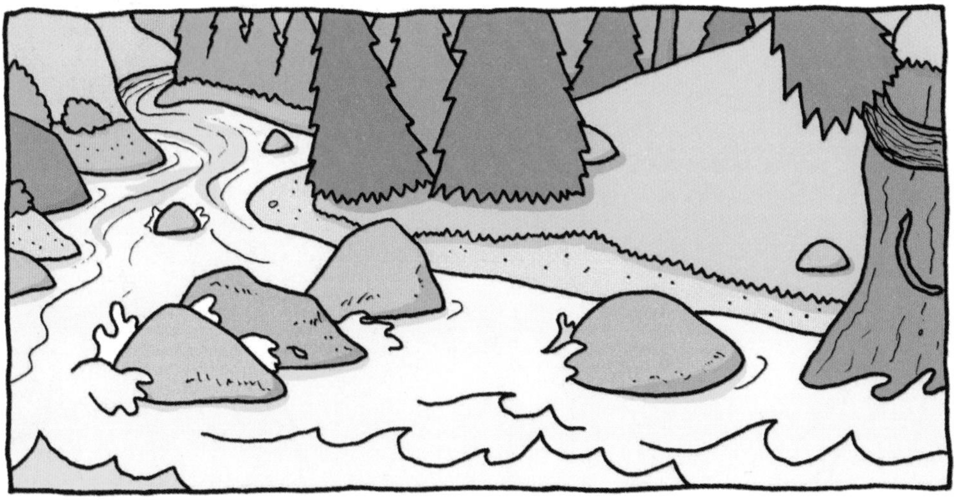
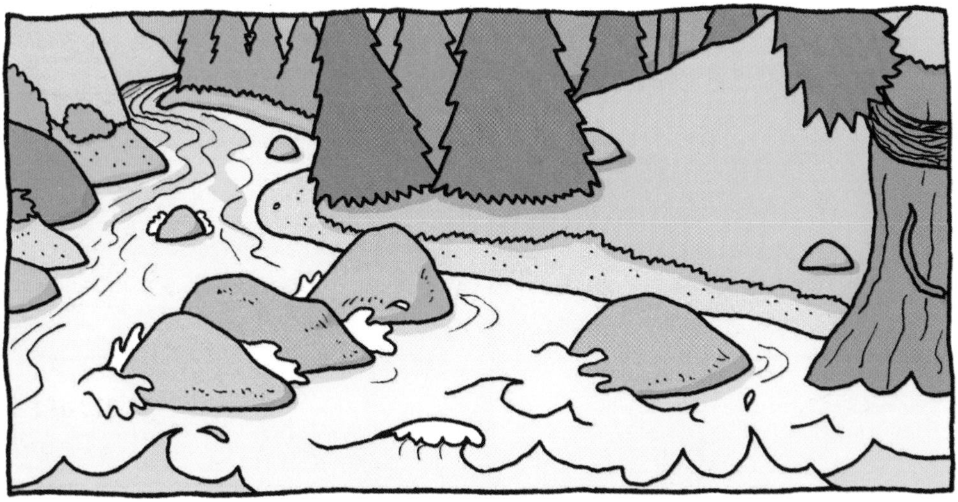
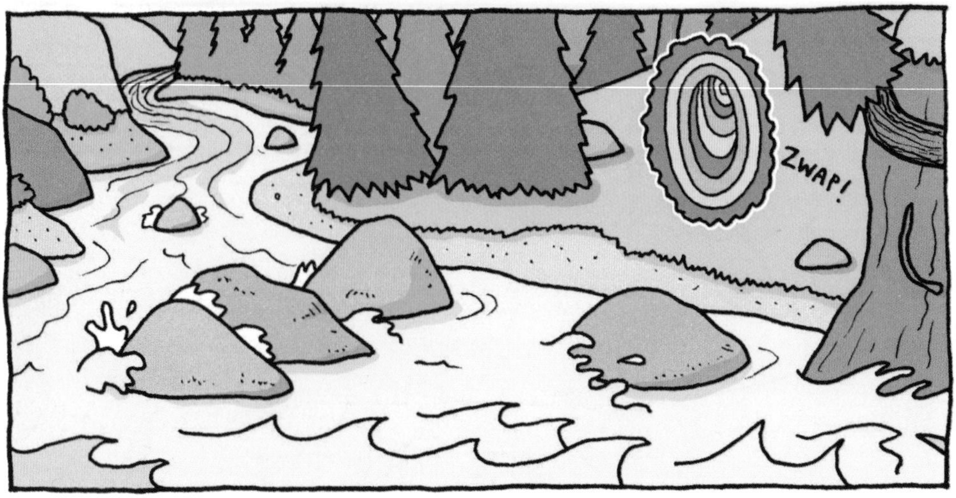
ZWAP!

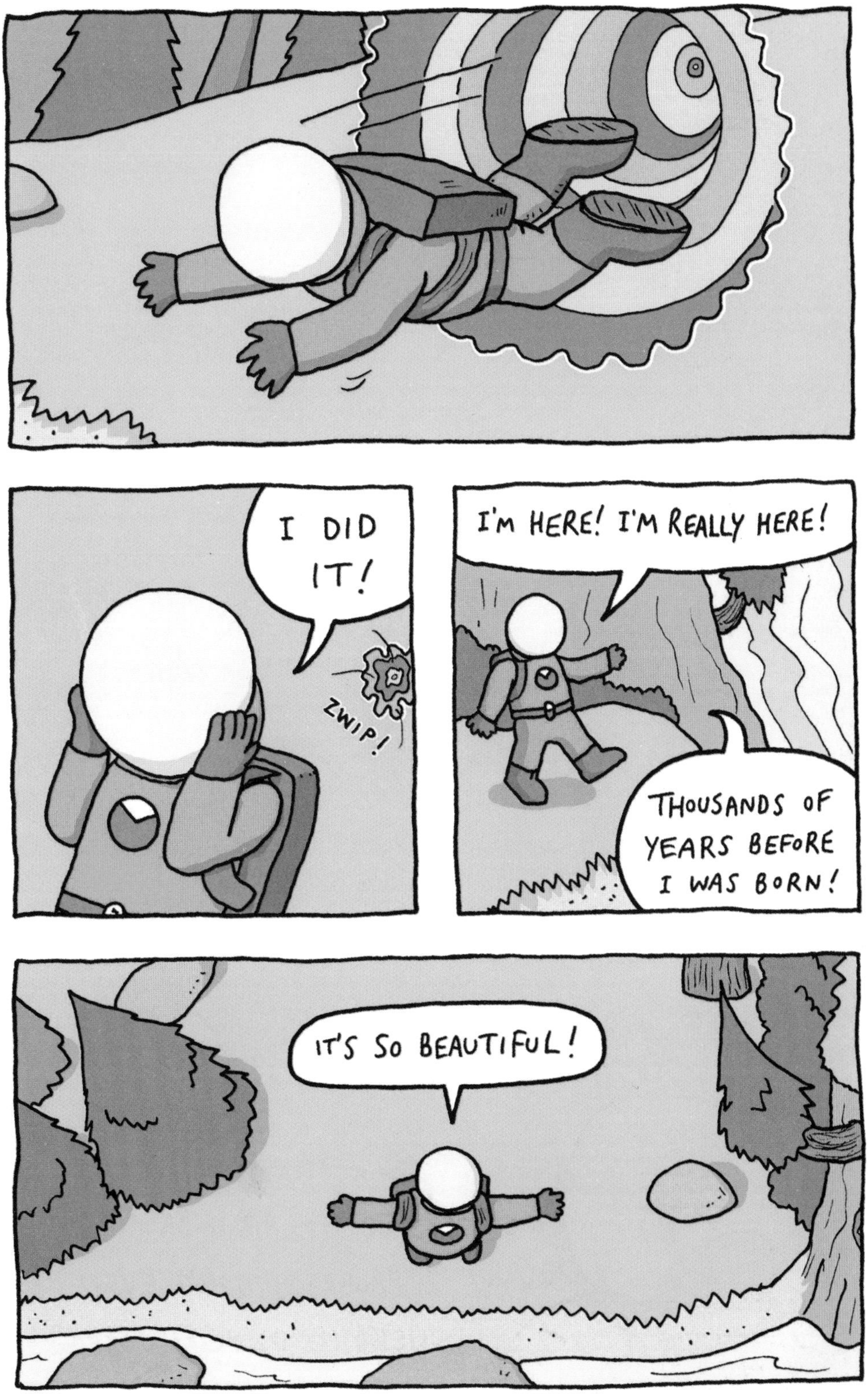
I DID IT!
ZWIP!
I'M HERE! I'M REALLY HERE!
THOUSANDS OF YEARS BEFORE I WAS BORN!
IT'S SO BEAUTIFUL!

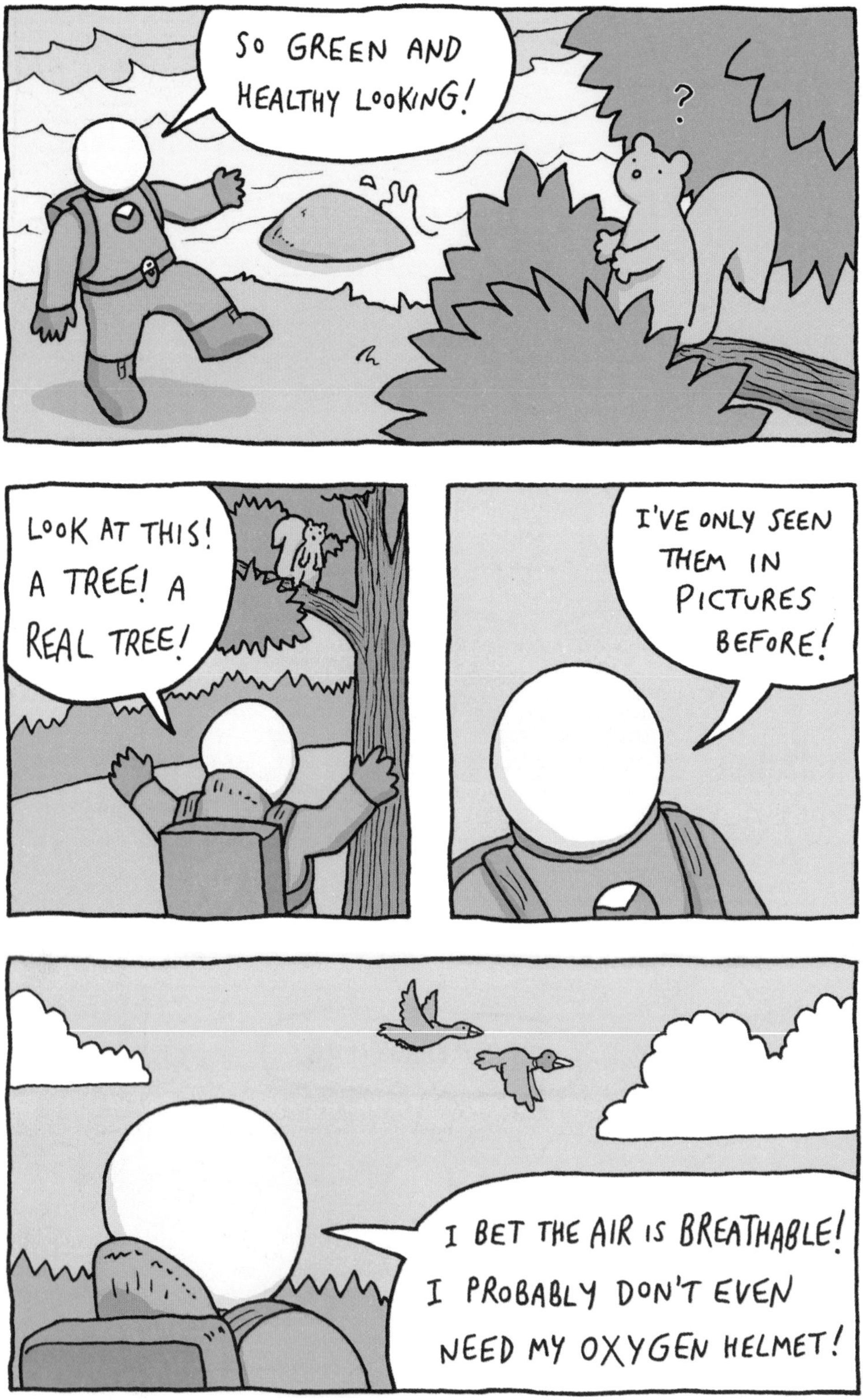
SO GREEN AND HEALTHY LOOKING!
?
LOOK AT THIS! A TREE! A REAL TREE!
I'VE ONLY SEEN THEM IN PICTURES BEFORE!
I BET THE AIR IS BREATHABLE! I PROBABLY DON'T EVEN NEED MY OXYGEN HELMET!

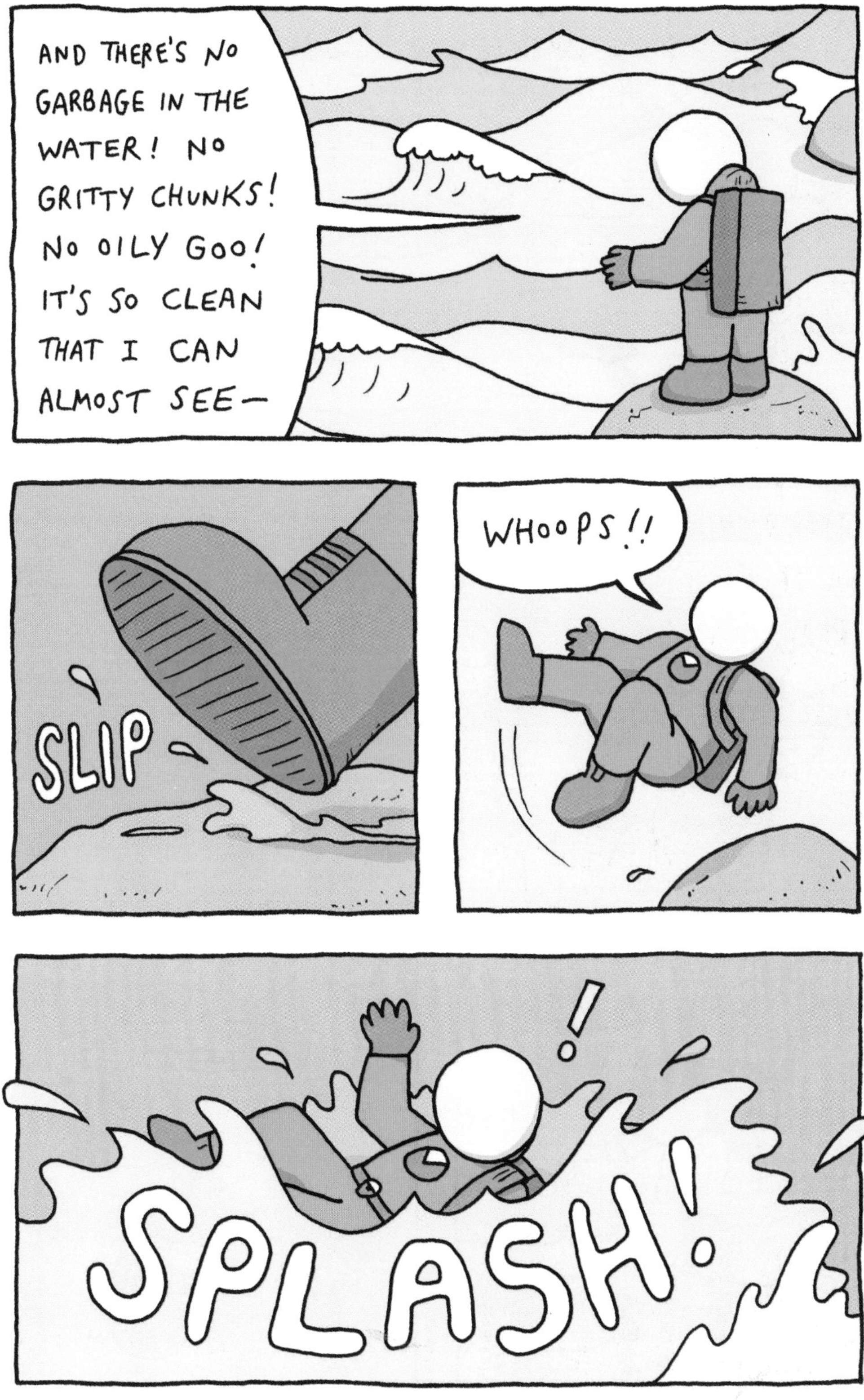
AND THERE'S NO GARBAGE IN THE WATER! NO GRITTY CHUNKS! NO OILY GOO! IT'S SO CLEAN THAT I CAN ALMOST SEE—
SLIP
WHOOPS!!
!
SPLASH!

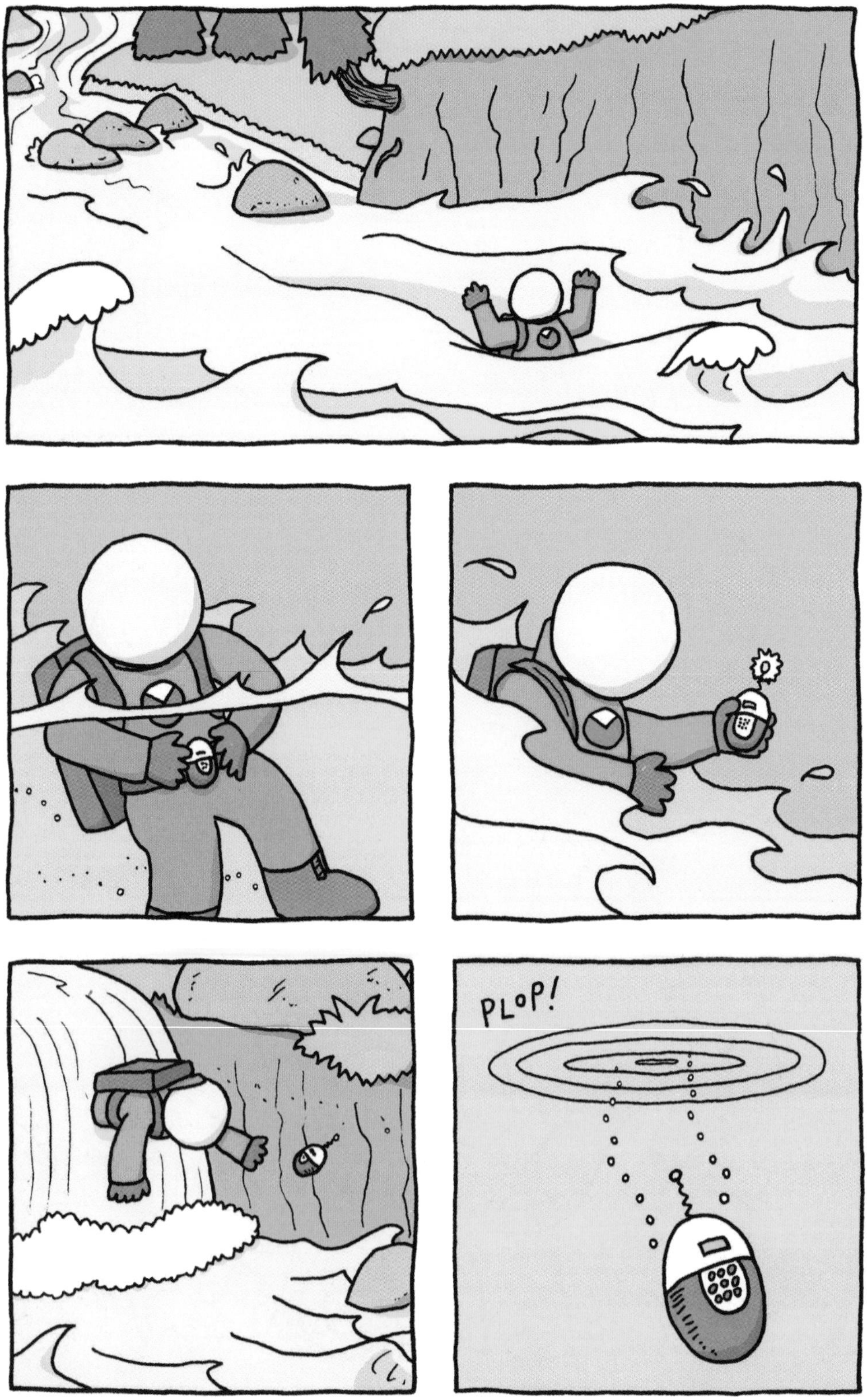
PLOP!

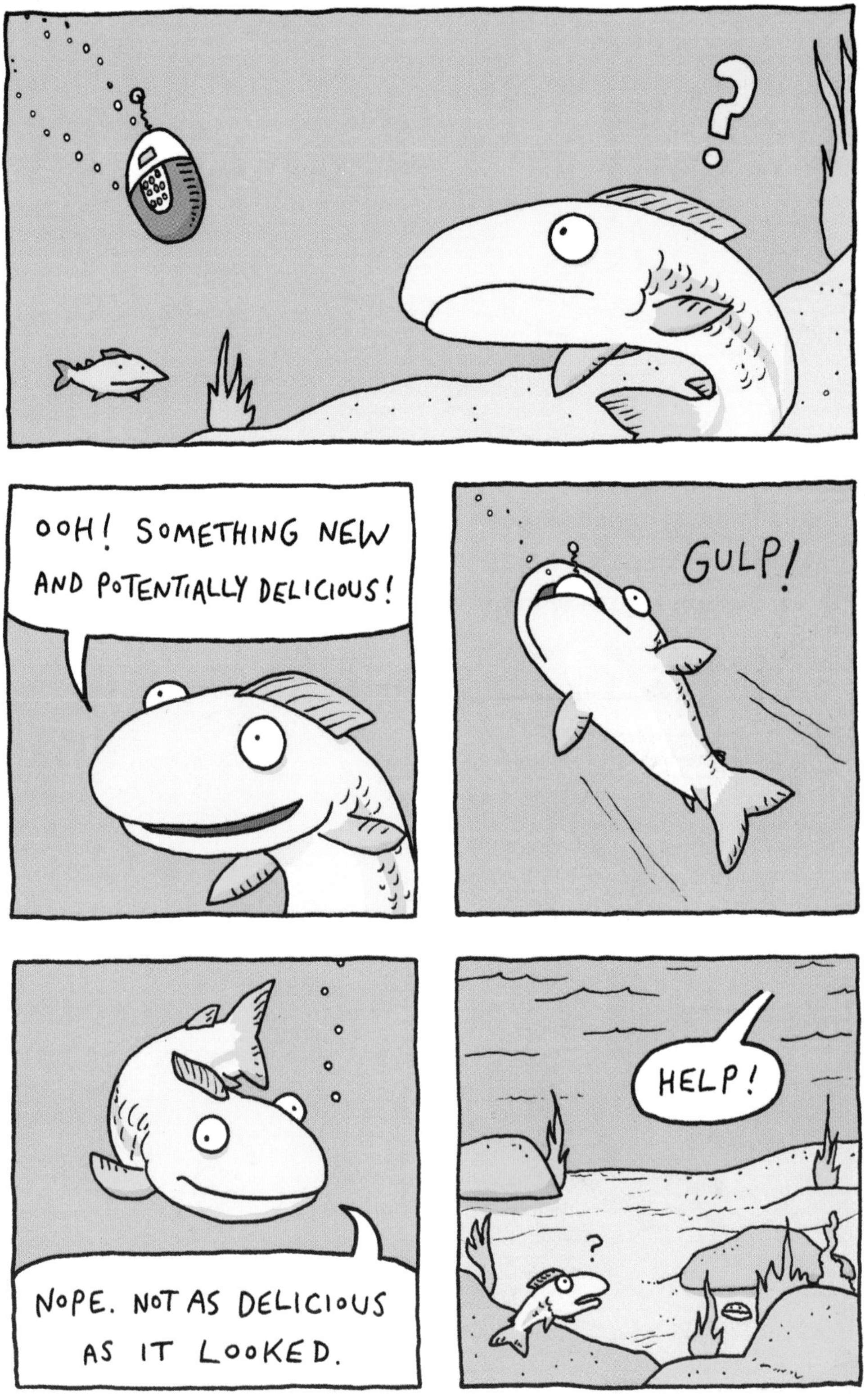
?
OOH! SOMETHING NEW AND POTENTIALLY DELICIOUS!
GULP!
NOPE. NOT AS DELICIOUS AS IT LOOKED.
HELP!
?

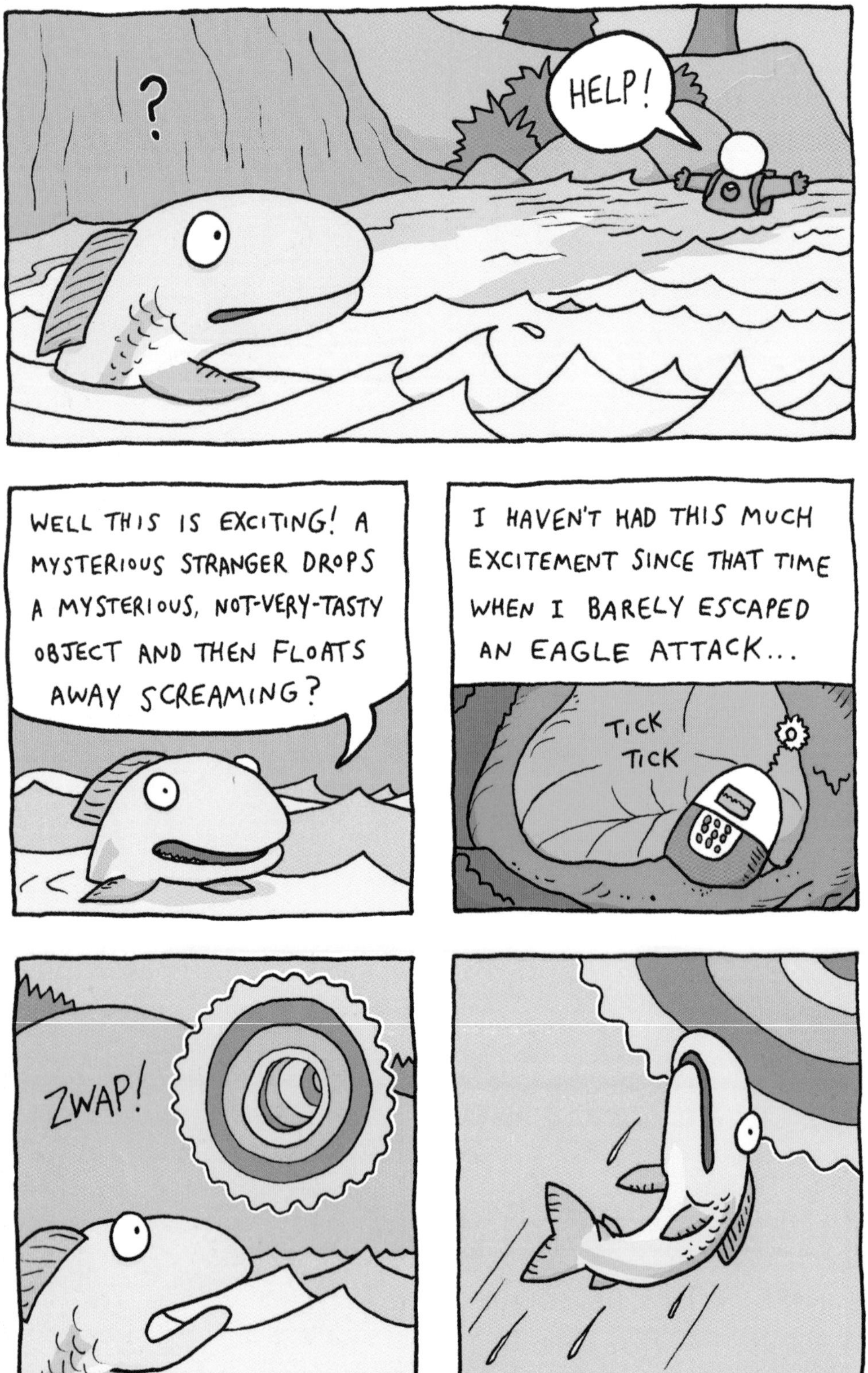
?
HELP!
WELL THIS IS EXCITING! A MYSTERIOUS STRANGER DROPS A MYSTERIOUS, NOT-VERY-TASTY OBJECT AND THEN FLOATS AWAY SCREAMING?
I HAVEN'T HAD THIS MUCH EXCITEMENT SINCE THAT TIME WHEN I BARELY ESCAPED AN EAGLE ATTACK...
TICK
TICK
ZWAP!

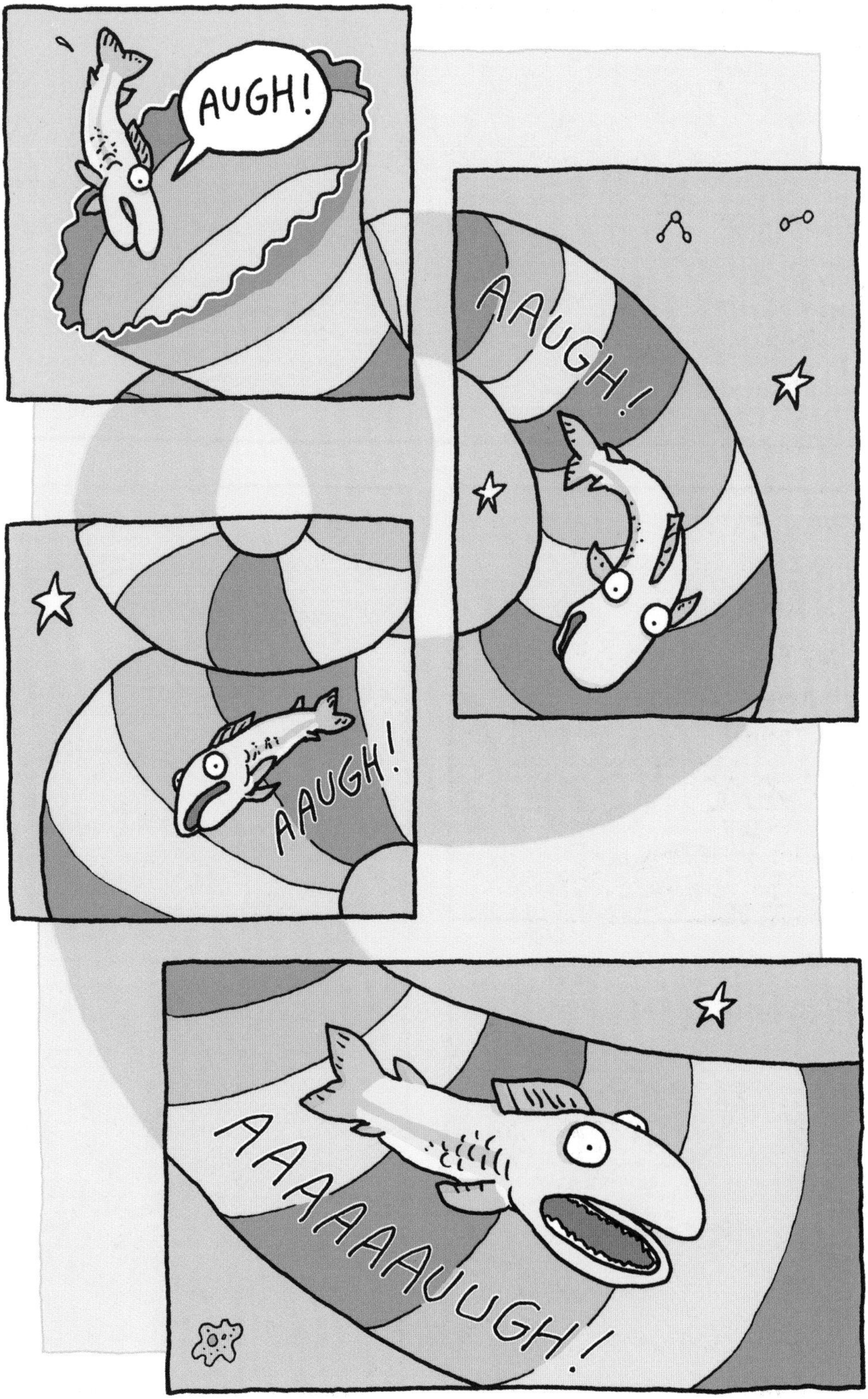
AUGH!
AAUGH!
AAUGH!
AAAAAAUUGH!

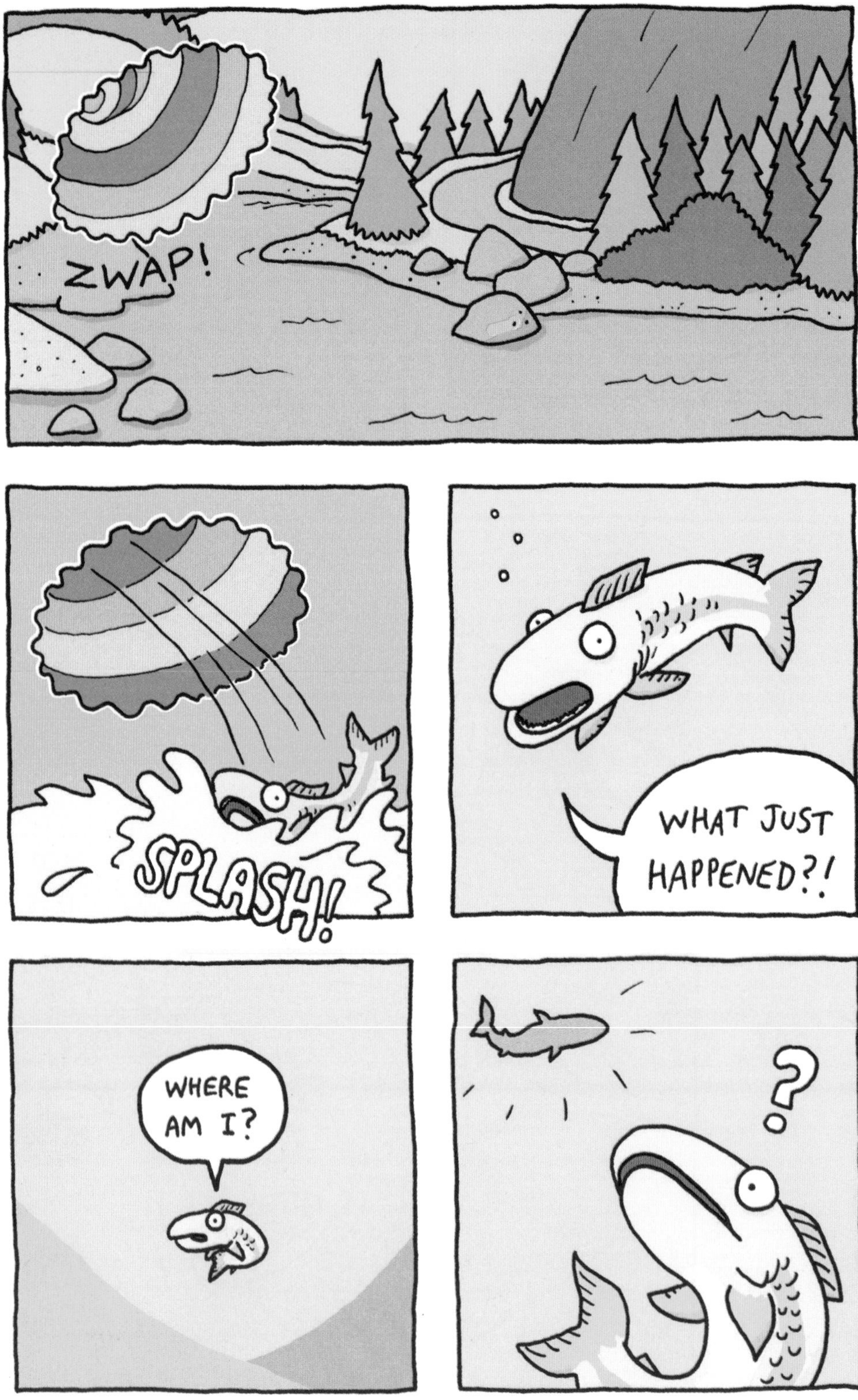
ZWAP!
SPLASH!
WHAT JUST HAPPENED?!
WHERE AM I?
?

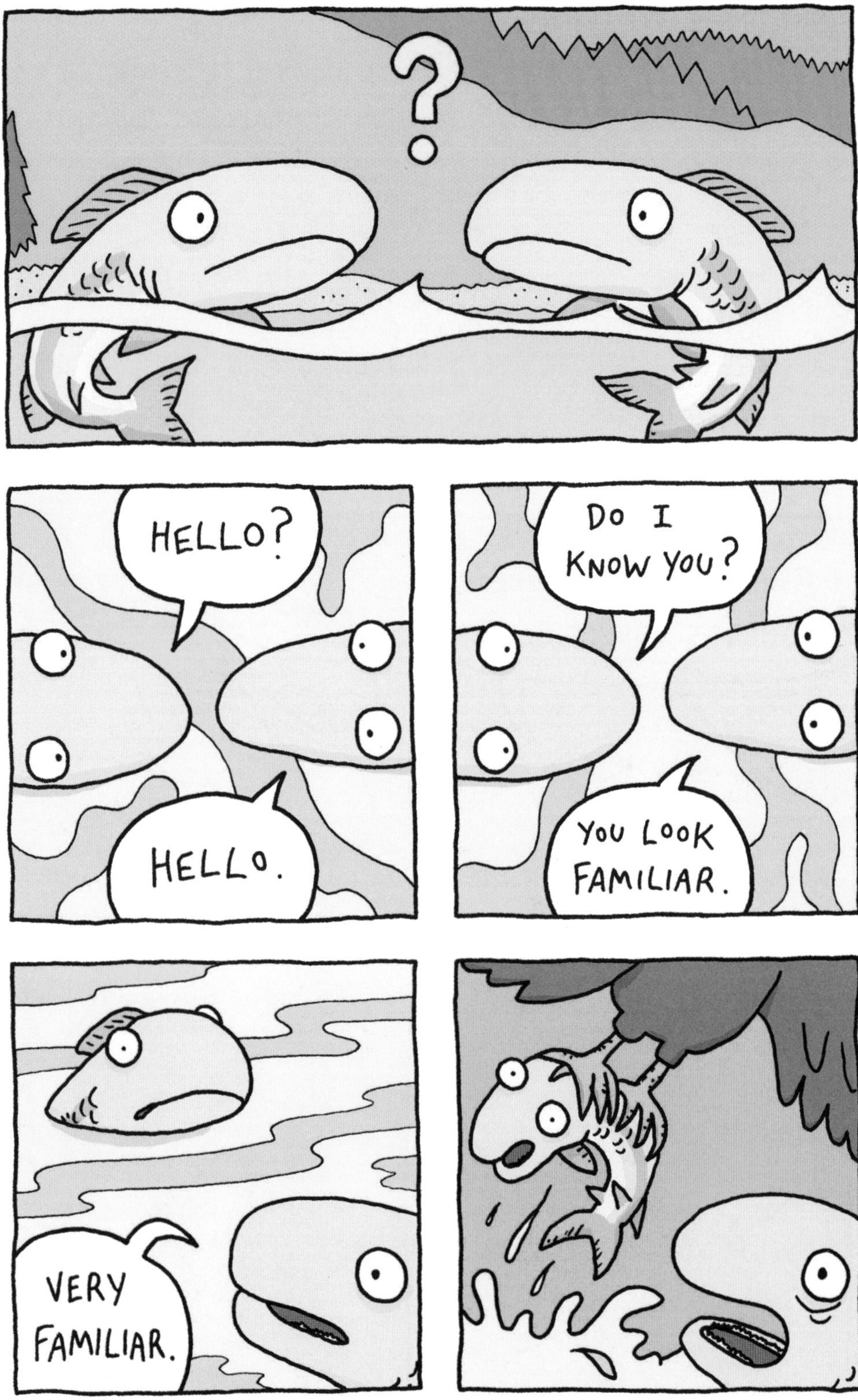
?
HELLO?
HELLO.
DO I KNOW YOU?
YOU LOOK FAMILIAR.
VERY FAMILIAR.

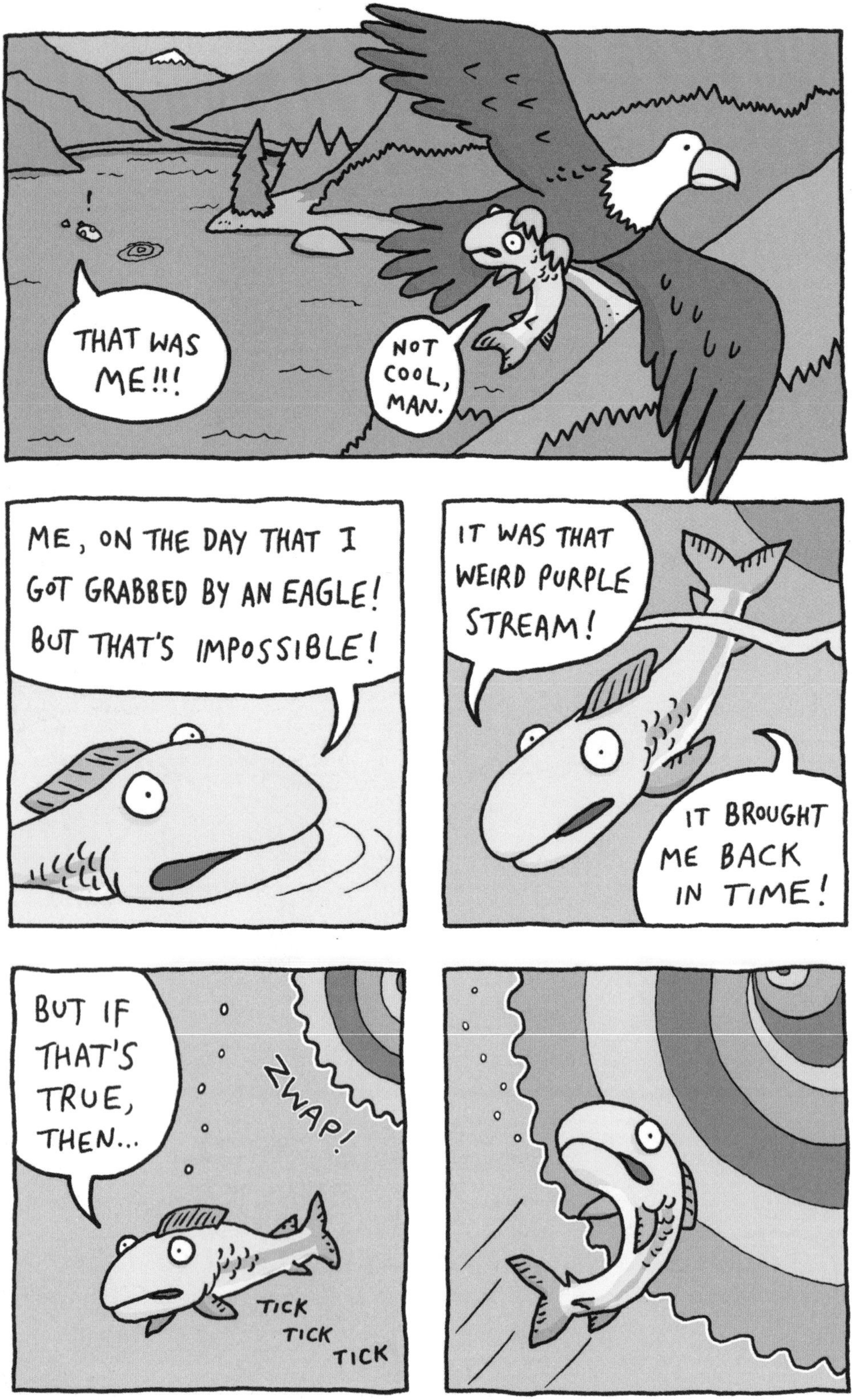
!
THAT WAS ME!!!
NOT COOL, MAN.
ME, ON THE DAY THAT I GOT GRABBED BY AN EAGLE! BUT THAT'S IMPOSSIBLE!
IT WAS THAT WEIRD PURPLE STREAM!
IT BROUGHT ME BACK IN TIME!
BUT IF THAT'S TRUE, THEN...
ZWAP!
TICK
TICK
TICK

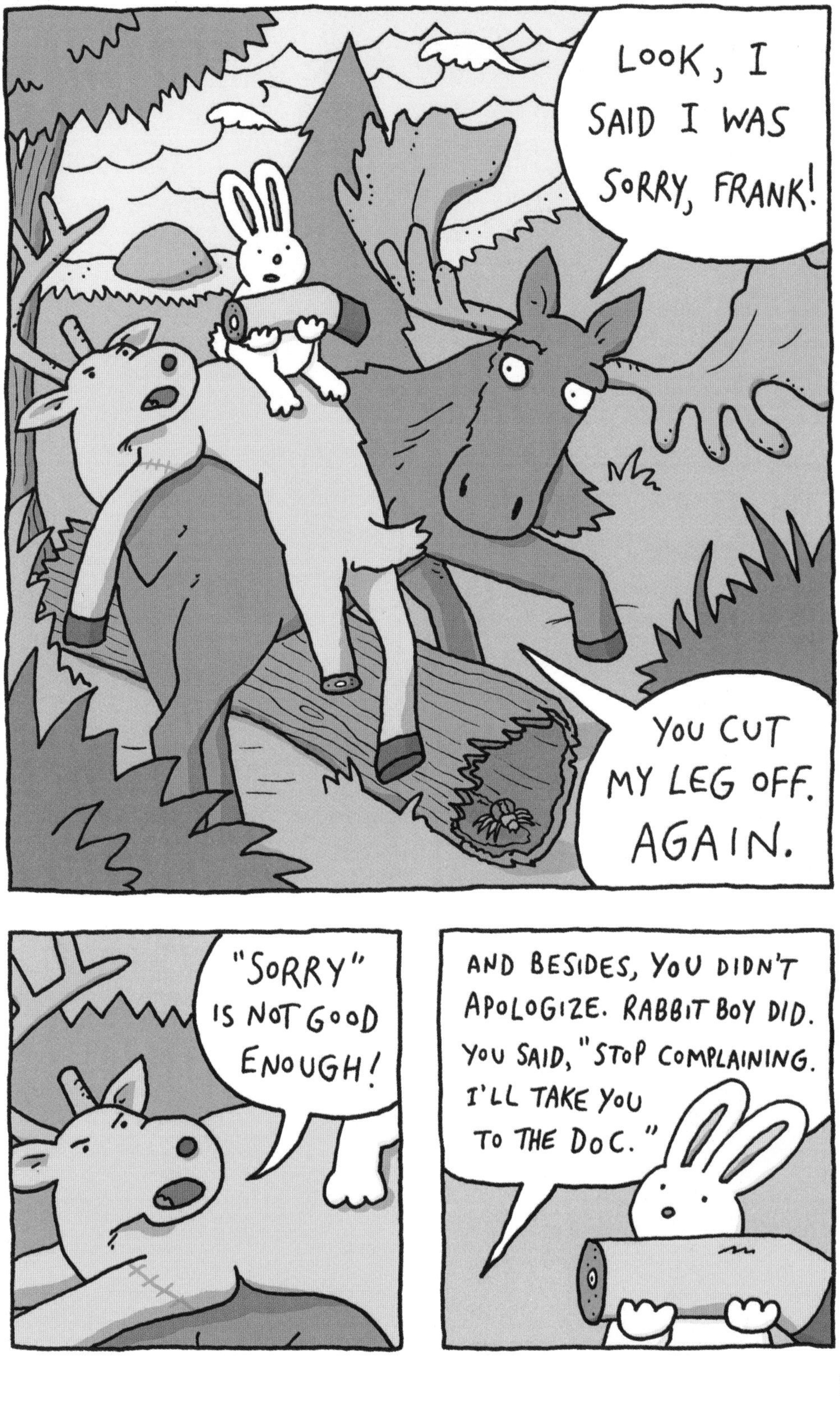
LOOK, I SAID I WAS SORRY, FRANK!
YOU CUT MY LEG OFF. AGAIN.
"SORRY" IS NOT GOOD ENOUGH!
AND BESIDES, YOU DIDN'T APOLOGIZE. RABBIT BOY DID. YOU SAID, "STOP COMPLAINING. I'LL TAKE YOU TO THE DOC."

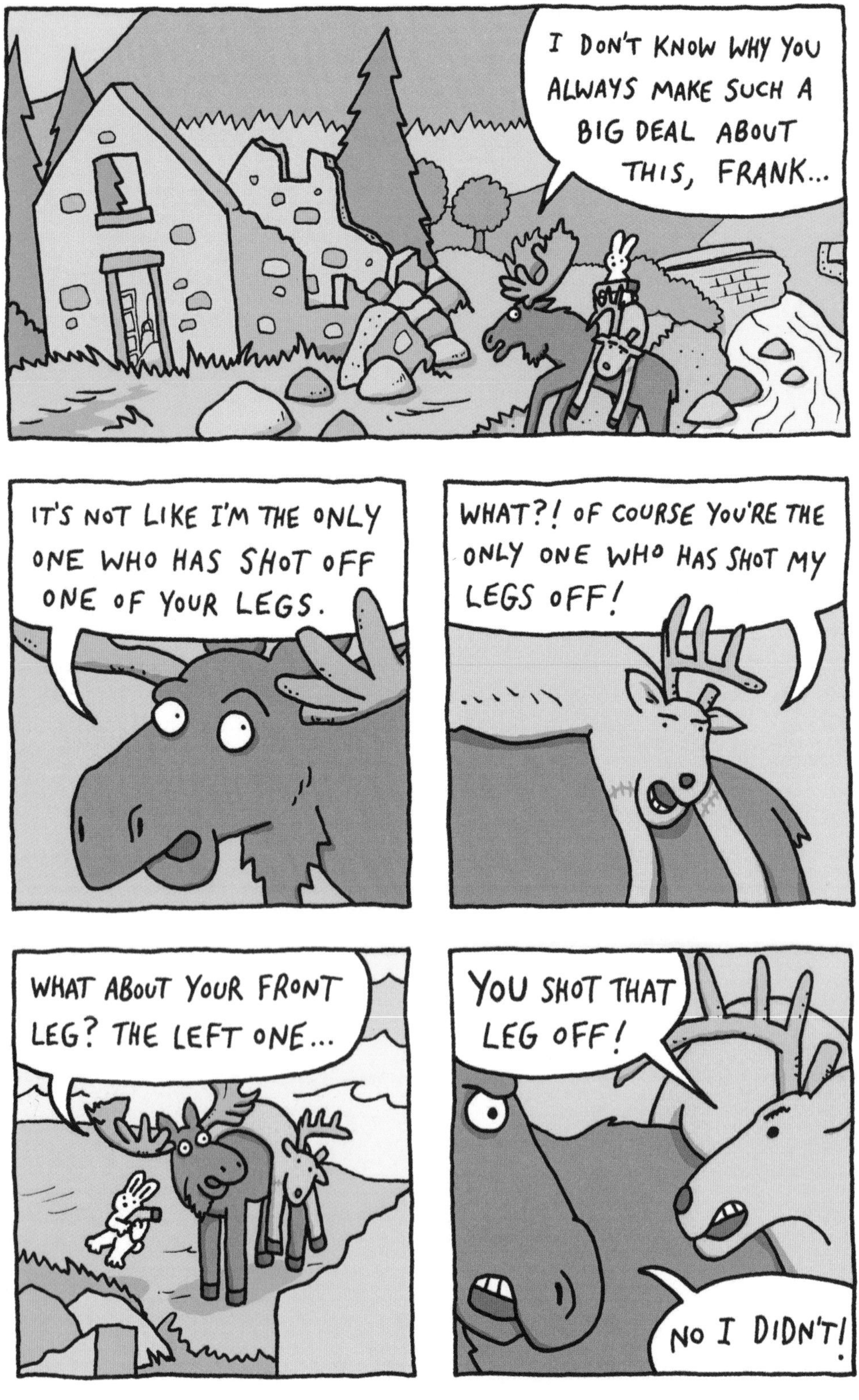
I DON'T KNOW WHY YOU ALWAYS MAKE SUCH A BIG DEAL ABOUT THIS, FRANK...
IT'S NOT LIKE I'M THE ONLY ONE WHO HAS SHOT OFF ONE OF YOUR LEGS.
WHAT?! OF COURSE YOU'RE THE ONLY ONE WHO HAS SHOT MY LEGS OFF!
WHAT ABOUT YOUR FRONT LEG? THE LEFT ONE...
YOU SHOT THAT LEG OFF!
NO I DIDN'T!

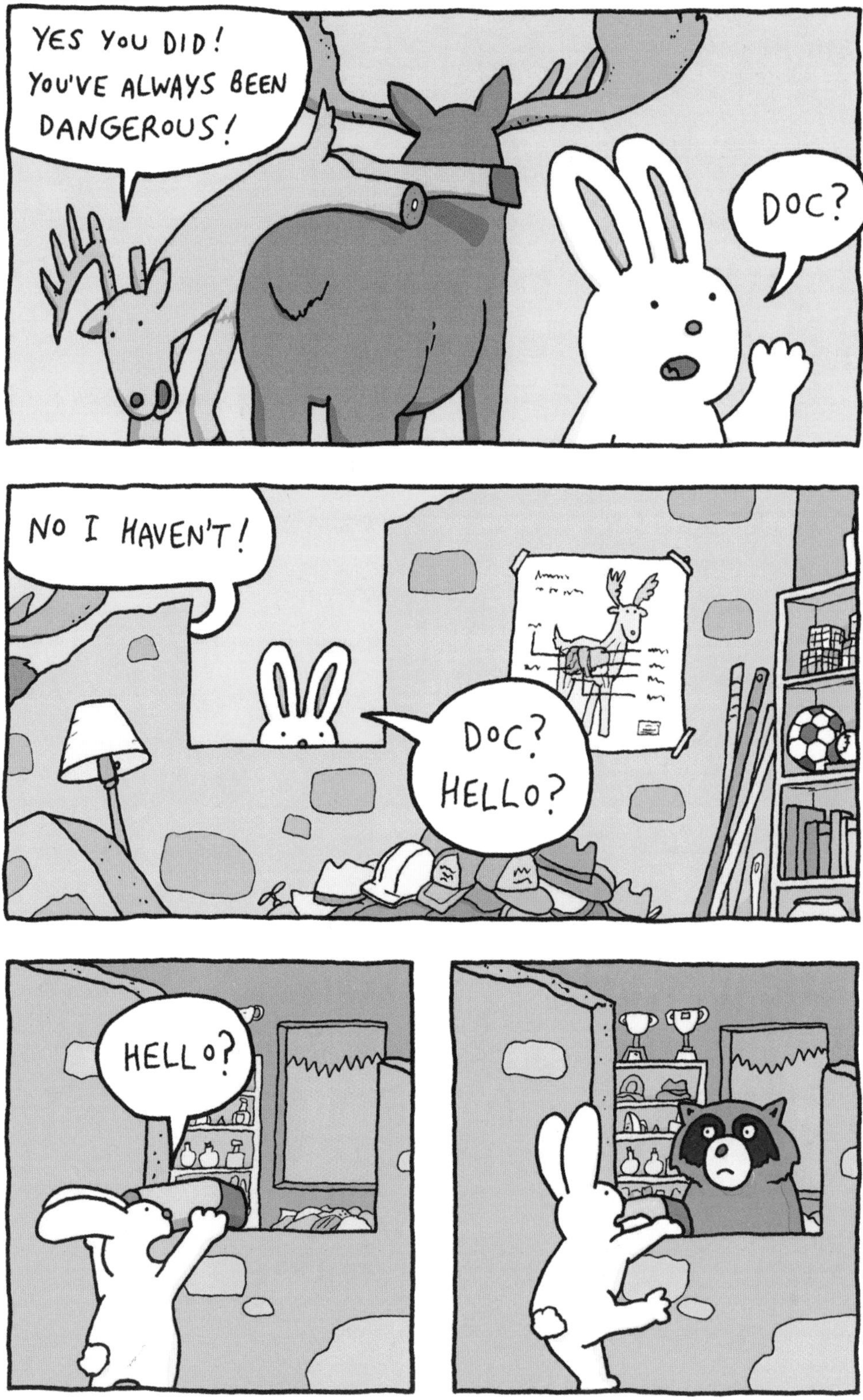
YES YOU DID! YOU'VE ALWAYS BEEN DANGEROUS!
DOC?
NO I HAVEN'T!
DOC? HELLO?
HELLO?

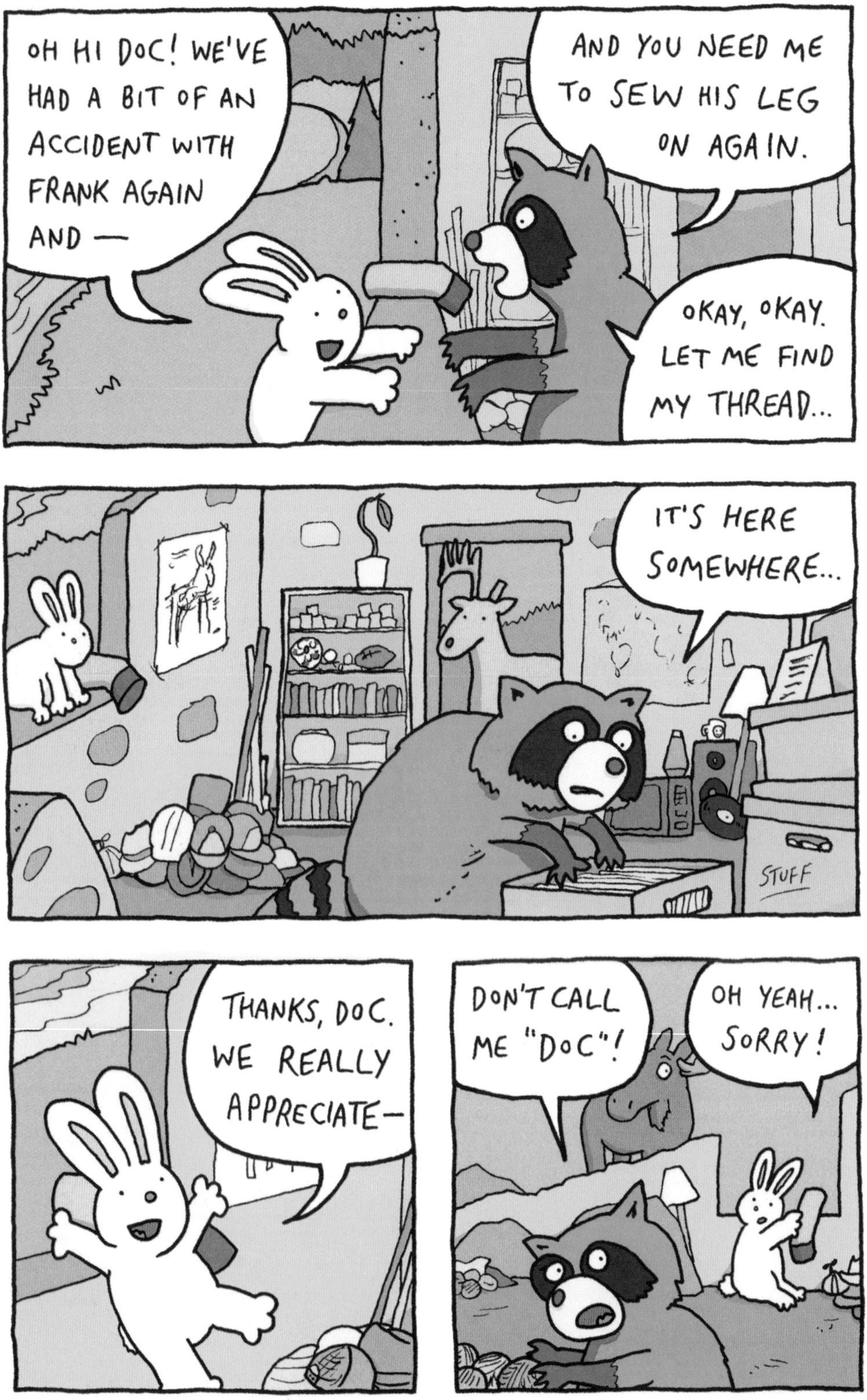
OH HI DOC! WE'VE HAD A BIT OF AN ACCIDENT WITH FRANK AGAIN AND —
AND YOU NEED ME TO SEW HIS LEG ON AGAIN.
OKAY, OKAY. LET ME FIND MY THREAD...
IT'S HERE SOMEWHERE...
STUFF
THANKS, DOC. WE REALLY APPRECIATE—
DON'T CALL ME "DOC"!
OH YEAH... SORRY!

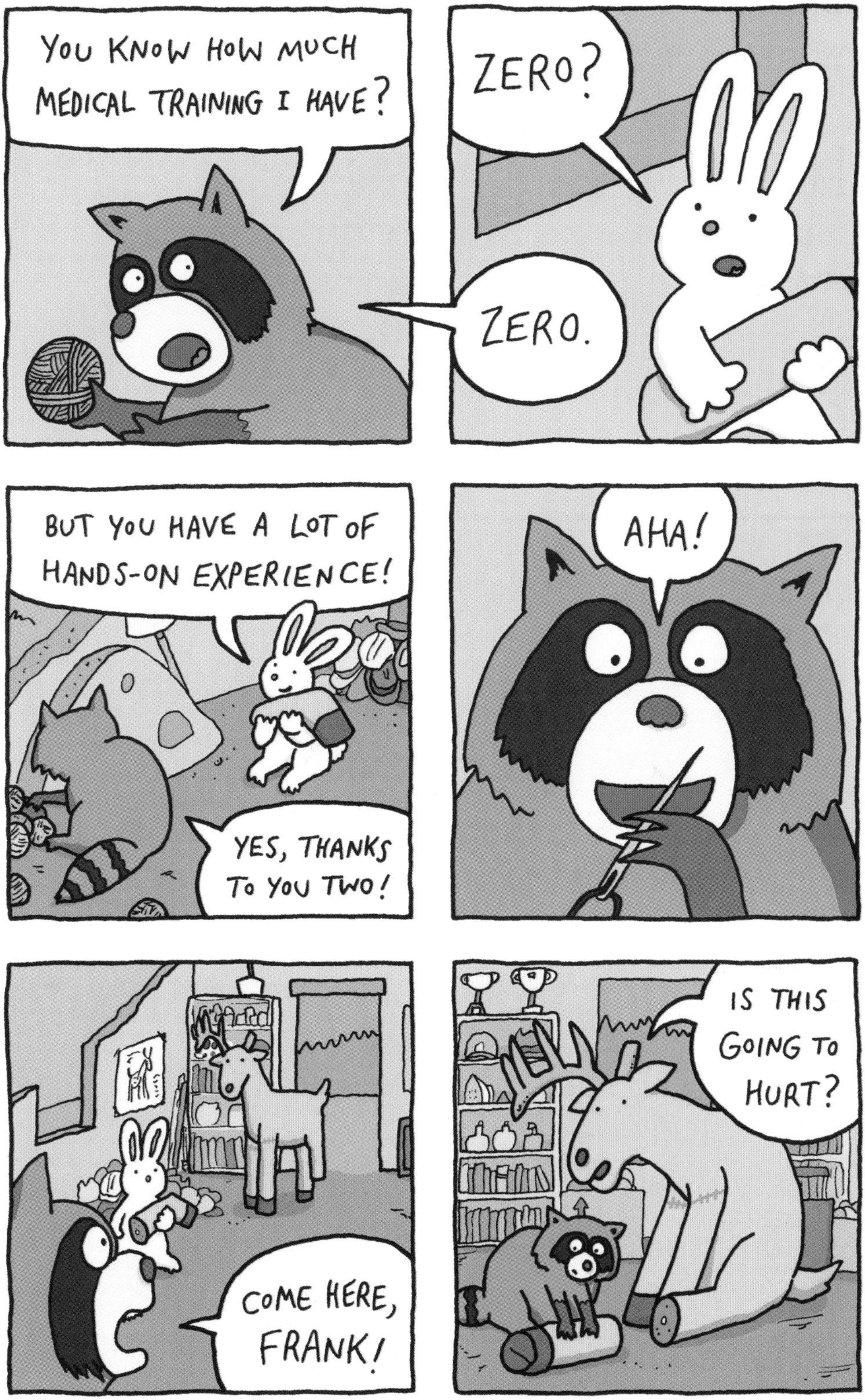
YOU KNOW HOW MUCH MEDICAL TRAINING I HAVE?
ZERO?
ZERO.
BUT YOU HAVE A LOT OF HANDS-ON EXPERIENCE!
YES, THANKS TO YOU TWO!
AHA!
COME HERE, FRANK!
IS THIS GOING TO HURT?

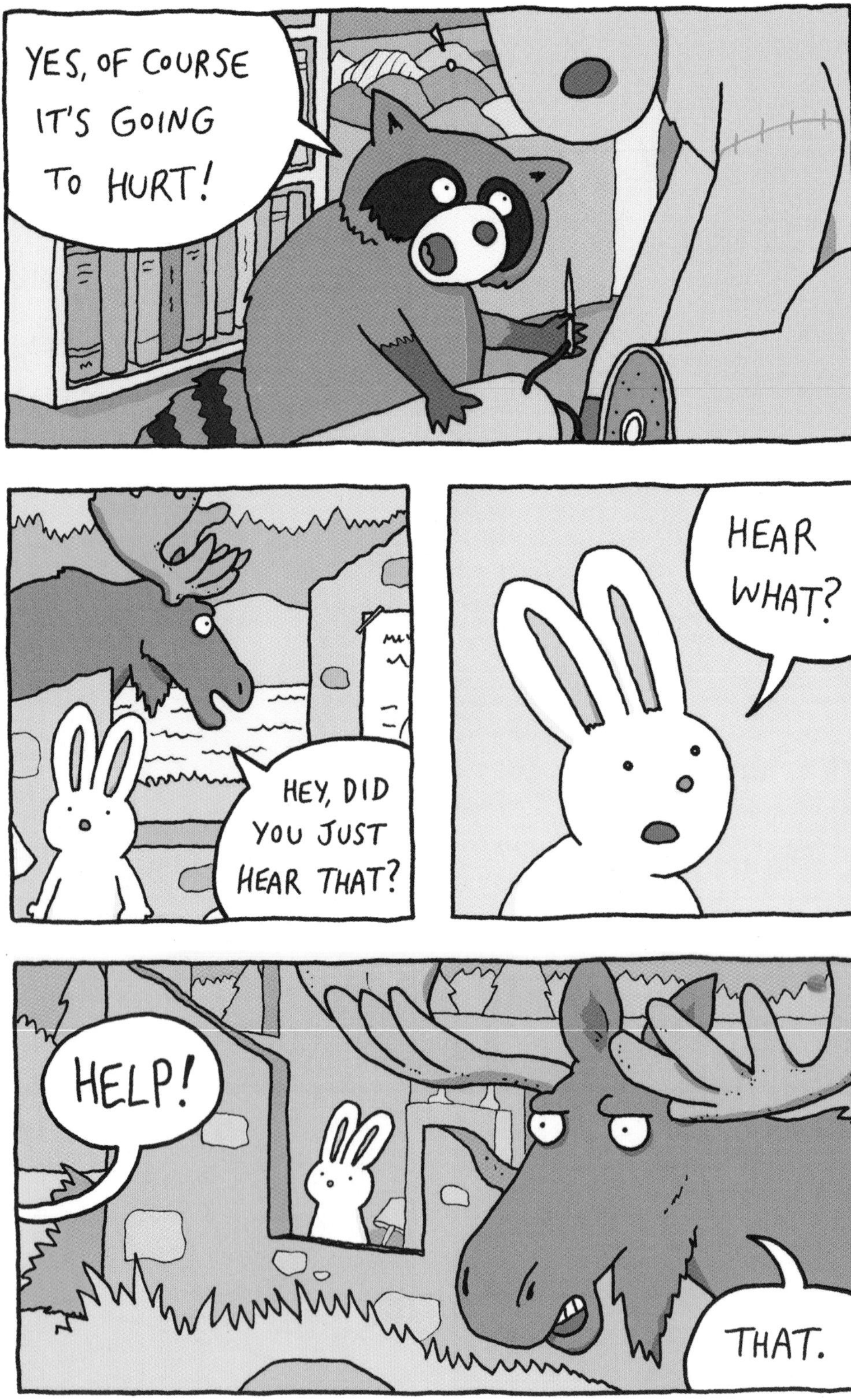
YES, OF COURSE IT'S GOING TO HURT!
HEY, DID YOU JUST HEAR THAT?
HEAR WHAT?
HELP!
THAT.

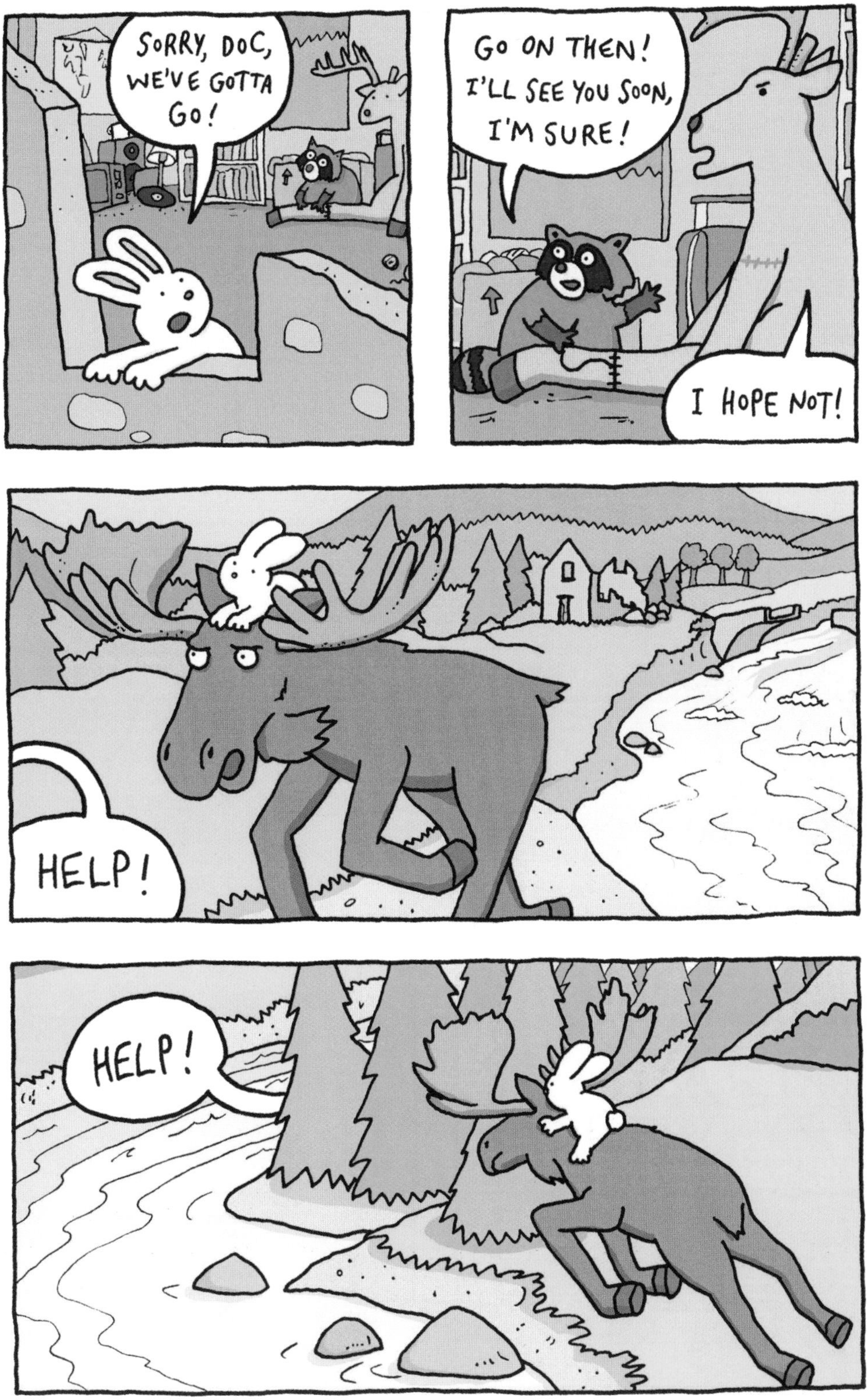
SORRY, DOC, WE'VE GOTTA GO!
GO ON THEN! I'LL SEE YOU SOON, I'M SURE!
I HOPE NOT!
HELP!
HELP!

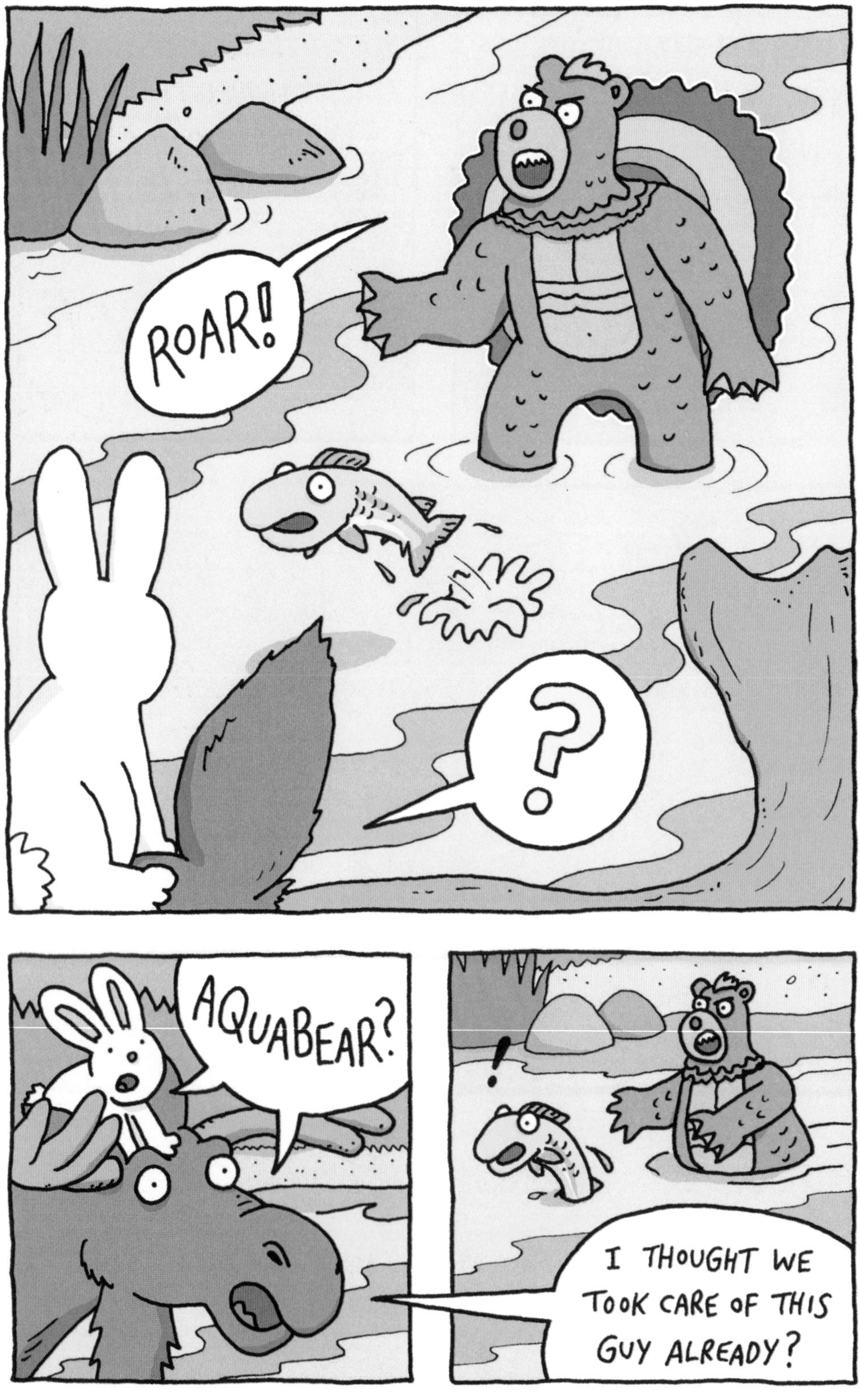
ROAR!
?
AQUABEAR?
!
I THOUGHT WE TOOK CARE OF THIS GUY ALREADY?

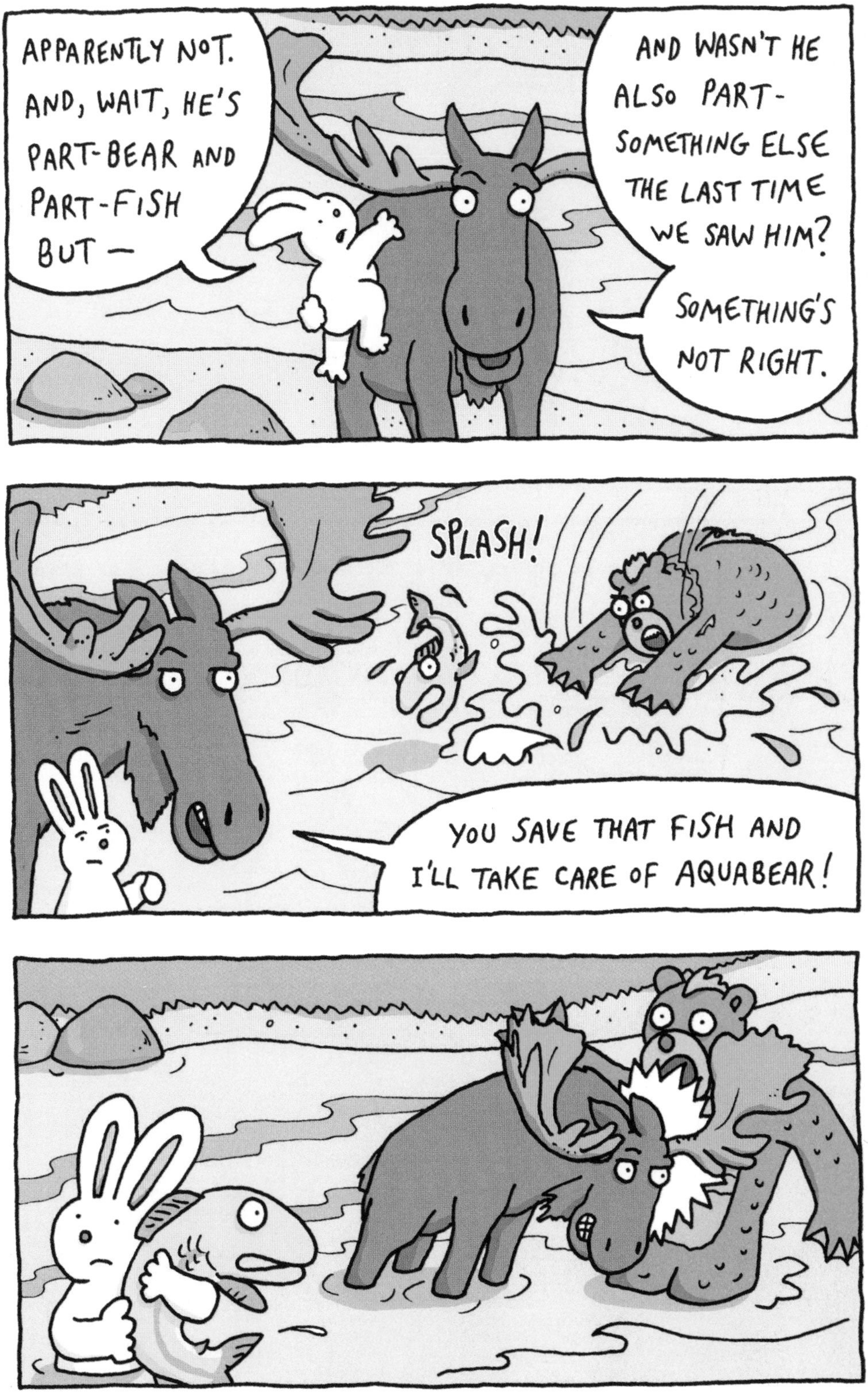
APPARENTLY NOT. AND, WAIT, HE'S PART-BEAR AND PART-FISH BUT —
AND WASN'T HE ALSO PART-SOMETHING ELSE THE LAST TIME WE SAW HIM?
SOMETHING'S NOT RIGHT.
SPLASH!
YOU SAVE THAT FISH AND I'LL TAKE CARE OF AQUABEAR!

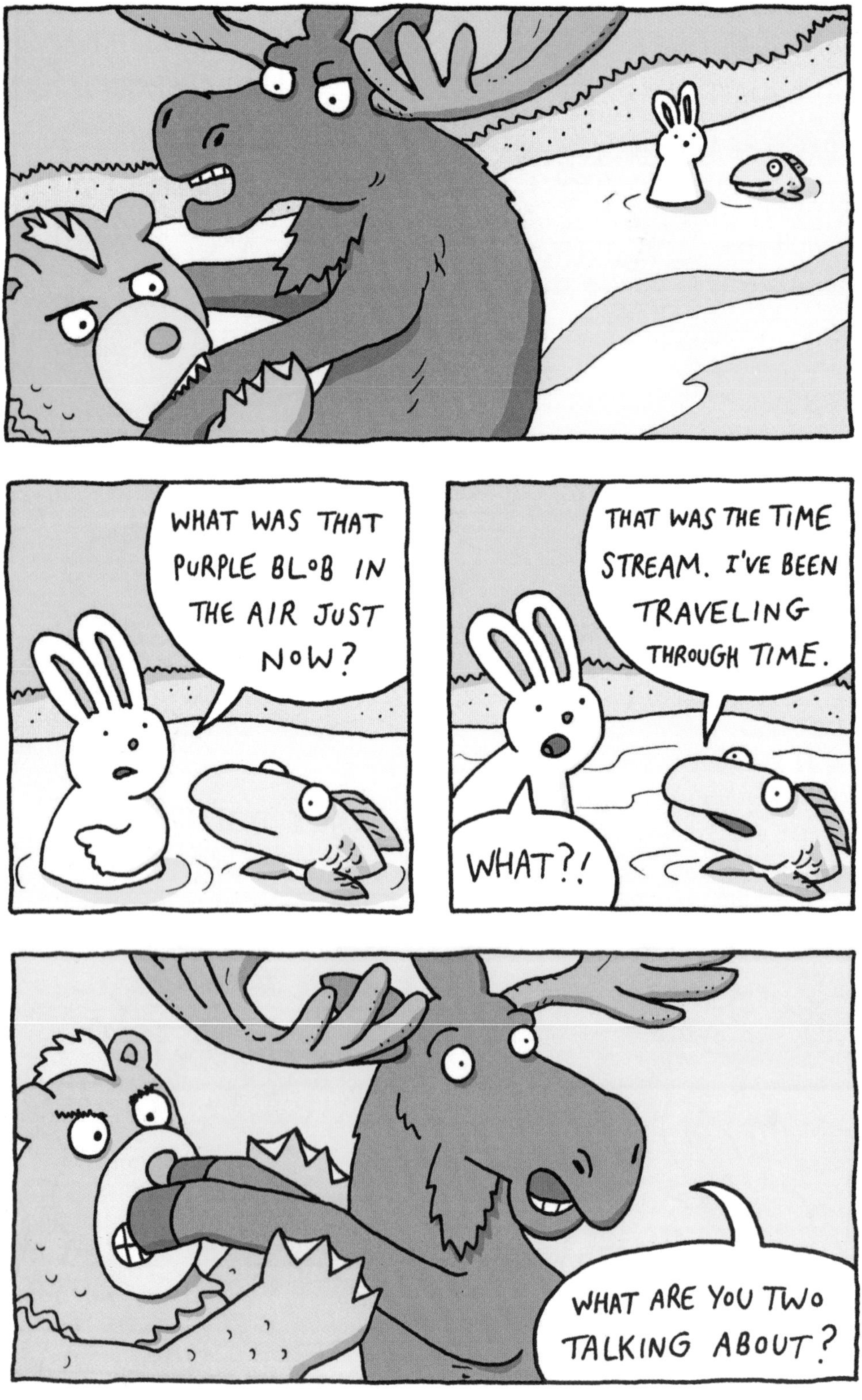
WHAT WAS THAT PURPLE BLOB IN THE AIR JUST NOW?
THAT WAS THE TIME STREAM. I'VE BEEN TRAVELING THROUGH TIME.
WHAT?!
WHAT ARE YOU TWO TALKING ABOUT?

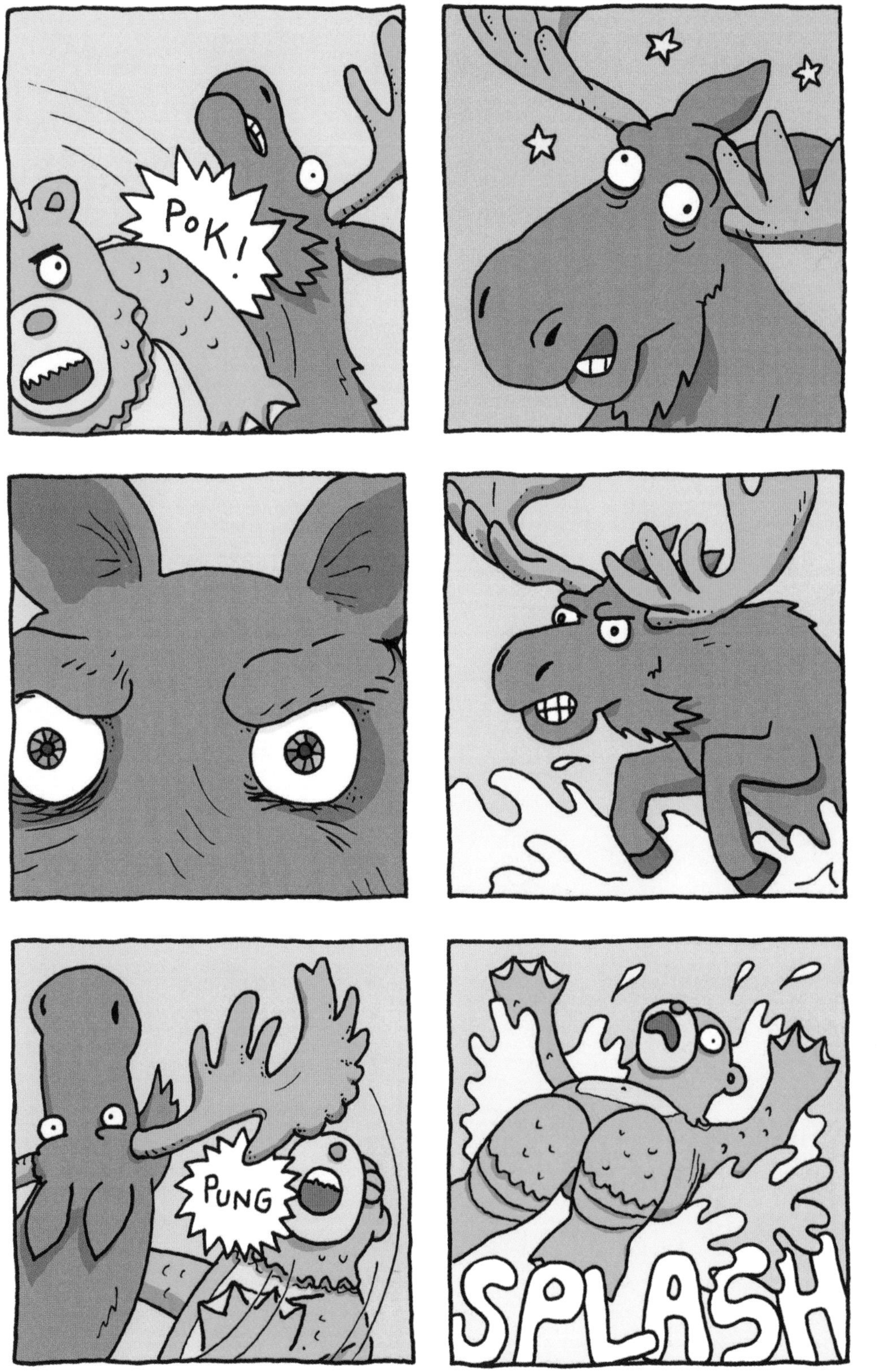
POK!
PUNG
SPLASH

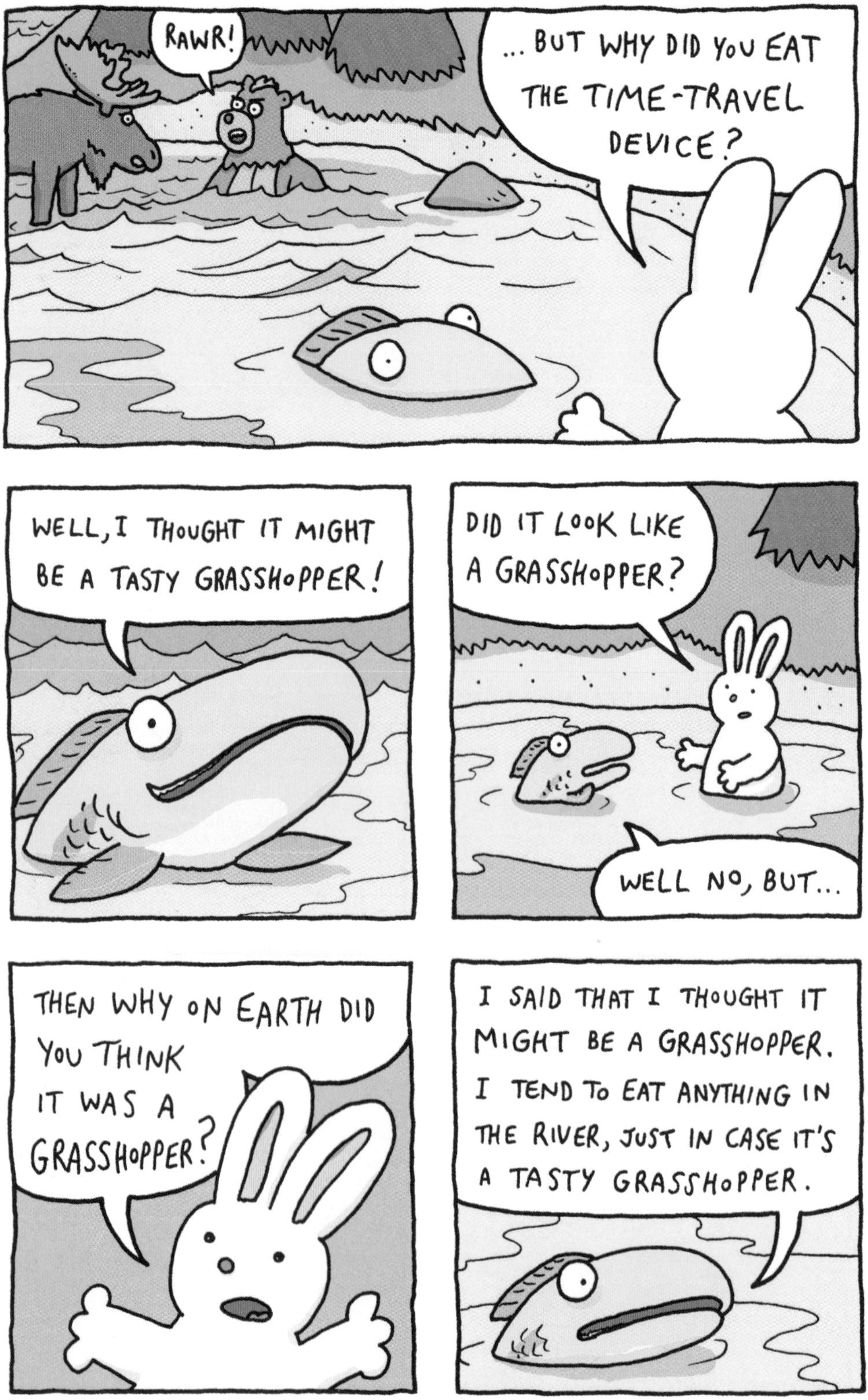
RAWR!
...BUT WHY DID YOU EAT THE TIME-TRAVEL DEVICE?
WELL, I THOUGHT IT MIGHT BE A TASTY GRASSHOPPER!
DID IT LOOK LIKE A GRASSHOPPER?
WELL NO, BUT...
THEN WHY ON EARTH DID YOU THINK IT WAS A GRASSHOPPER?
I SAID THAT I THOUGHT IT MIGHT BE A GRASSHOPPER. I TEND TO EAT ANYTHING IN THE RIVER, JUST IN CASE IT'S A TASTY GRASSHOPPER.

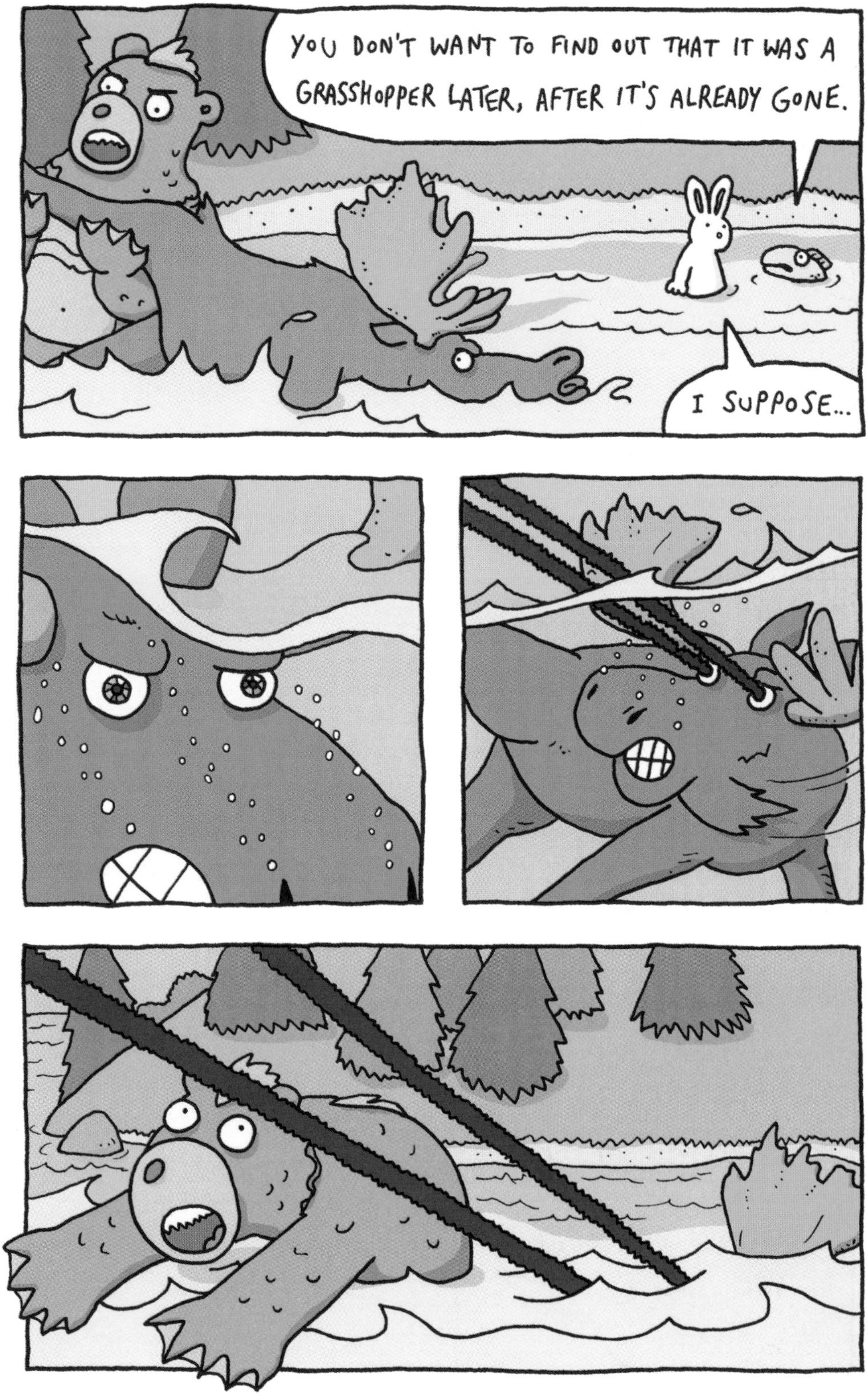
YOU DON'T WANT TO FIND OUT THAT IT WAS A GRASSHOPPER LATER, AFTER IT'S ALREADY GONE.
I SUPPOSE...

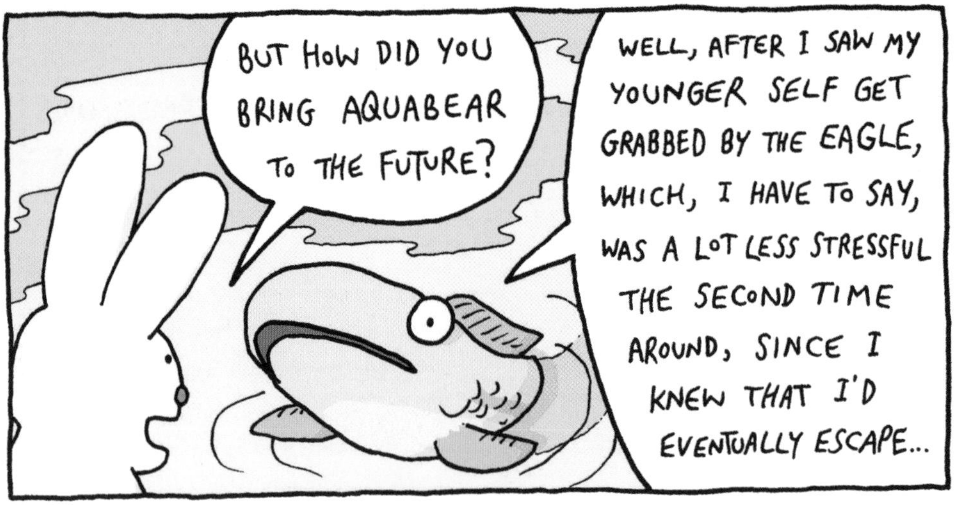
BUT HOW DID YOU BRING AQUABEAR TO THE FUTURE?
WELL, AFTER I SAW MY YOUNGER SELF GET GRABBED BY THE EAGLE, WHICH, I HAVE TO SAY, WAS A LOT LESS STRESSFUL THE SECOND TIME AROUND, SINCE I KNEW THAT I'D EVENTUALLY ESCAPE...

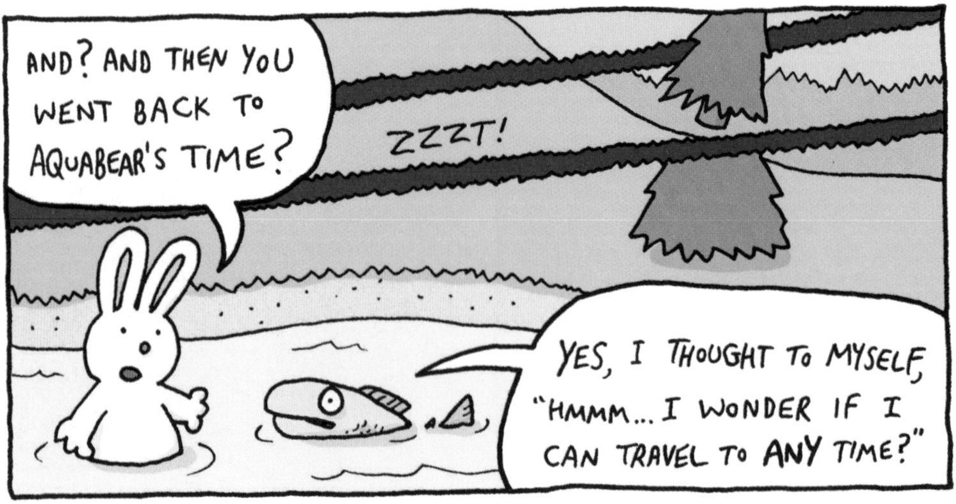
AND? AND THEN YOU WENT BACK TO AQUABEAR'S TIME?
ZZZT!
YES, I THOUGHT TO MYSELF, "HMMM... I WONDER IF I CAN TRAVEL TO ANY TIME?"

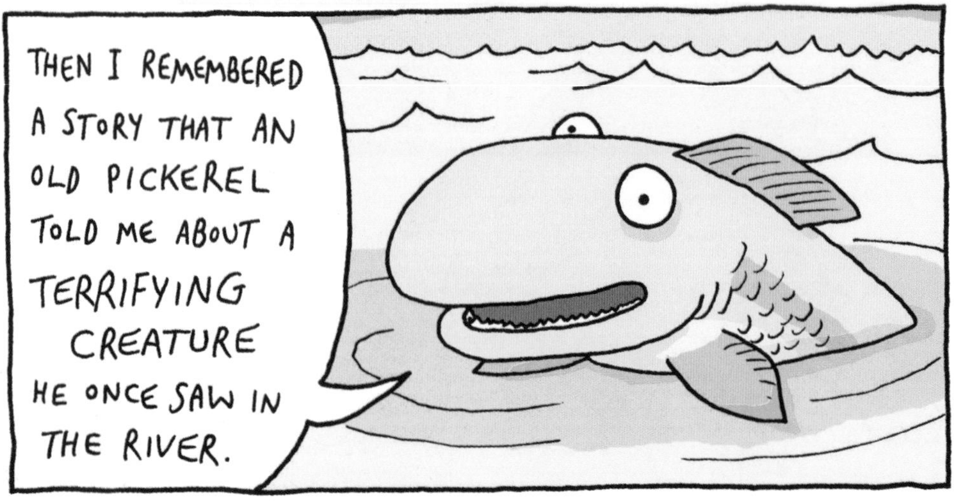
THEN I REMEMBERED A STORY THAT AN OLD PICKEREL TOLD ME ABOUT A TERRIFYING CREATURE HE ONCE SAW IN THE RIVER.

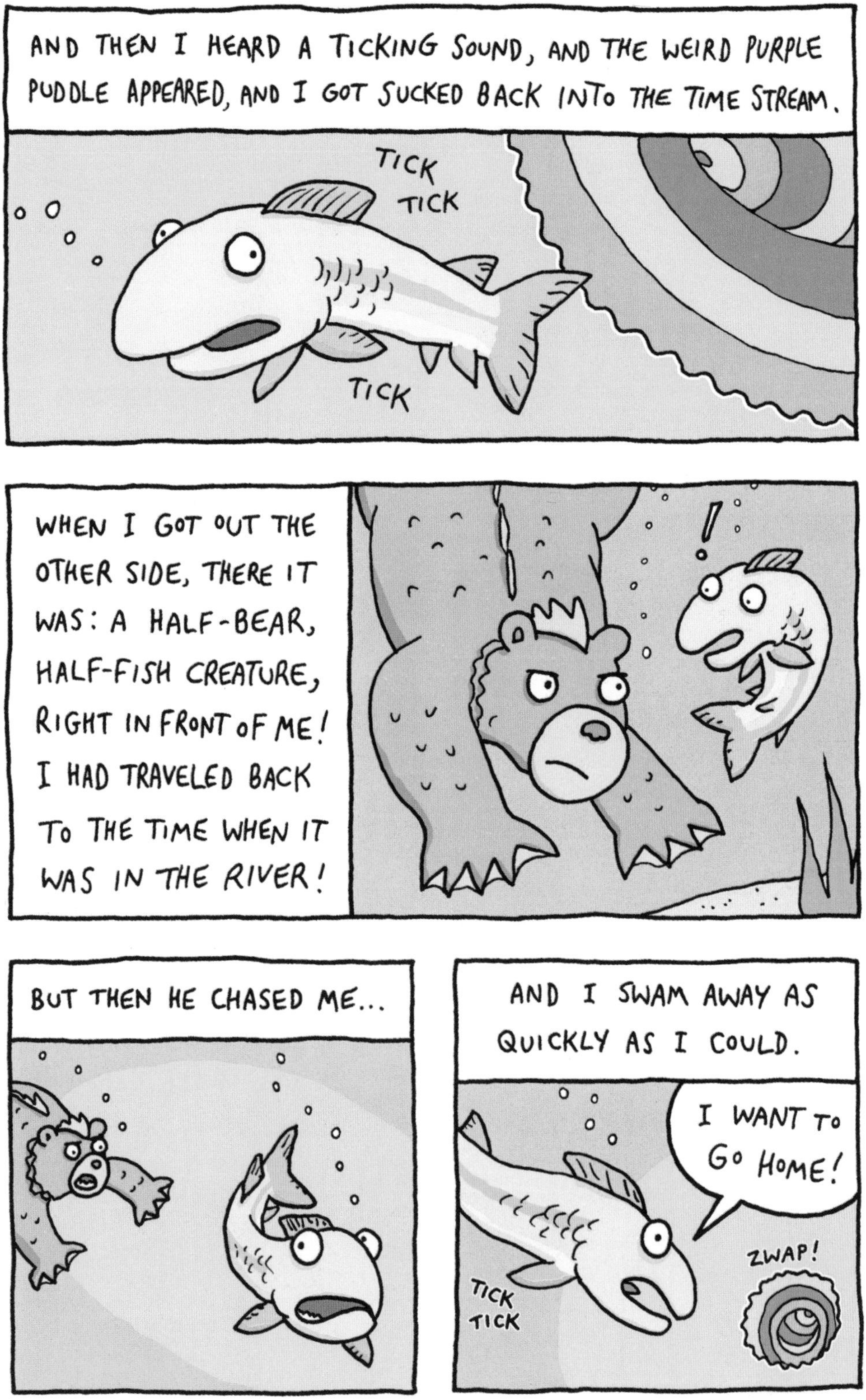
AND THEN I HEARD A TICKING SOUND, AND THE WEIRD PURPLE PUDDLE APPEARED, AND I GOT SUCKED BACK INTO THE TIME STREAM.
TICK
TICK
TICK
WHEN I GOT OUT THE OTHER SIDE, THERE IT WAS: A HALF-BEAR, HALF-FISH CREATURE, RIGHT IN FRONT OF ME! I HAD TRAVELED BACK TO THE TIME WHEN IT WAS IN THE RIVER!
!
BUT THEN HE CHASED ME...
AND I SWAM AWAY AS QUICKLY AS I COULD.
I WANT TO GO HOME!
ZWAP!
TICK
TICK

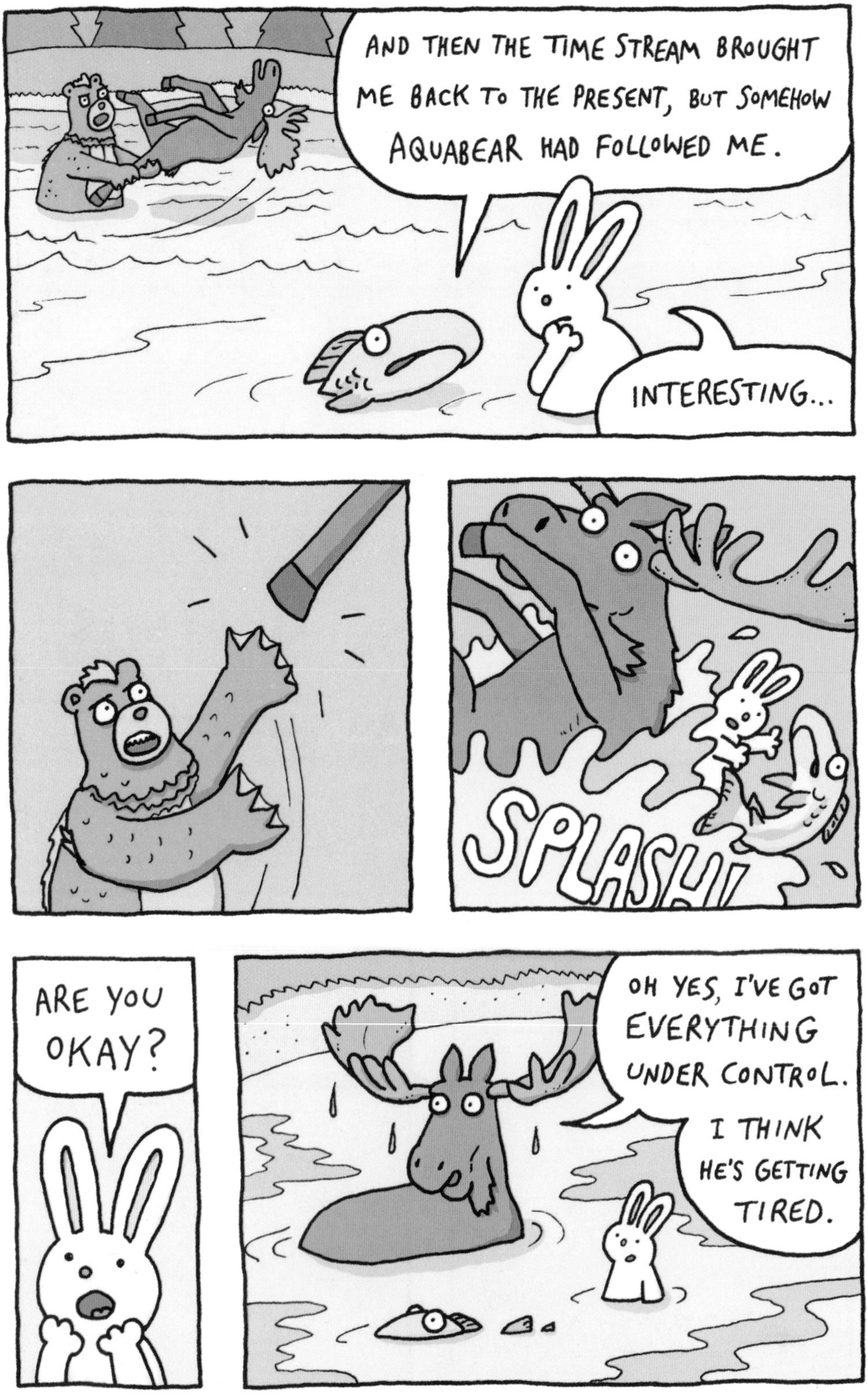
AND THEN THE TIME STREAM BROUGHT ME BACK TO THE PRESENT, BUT SOMEHOW AQUABEAR HAD FOLLOWED ME.
INTERESTING...
SPLASH!
ARE YOU OKAY?
OH YES, I'VE GOT EVERYTHING UNDER CONTROL.
I THINK HE'S GETTING TIRED.

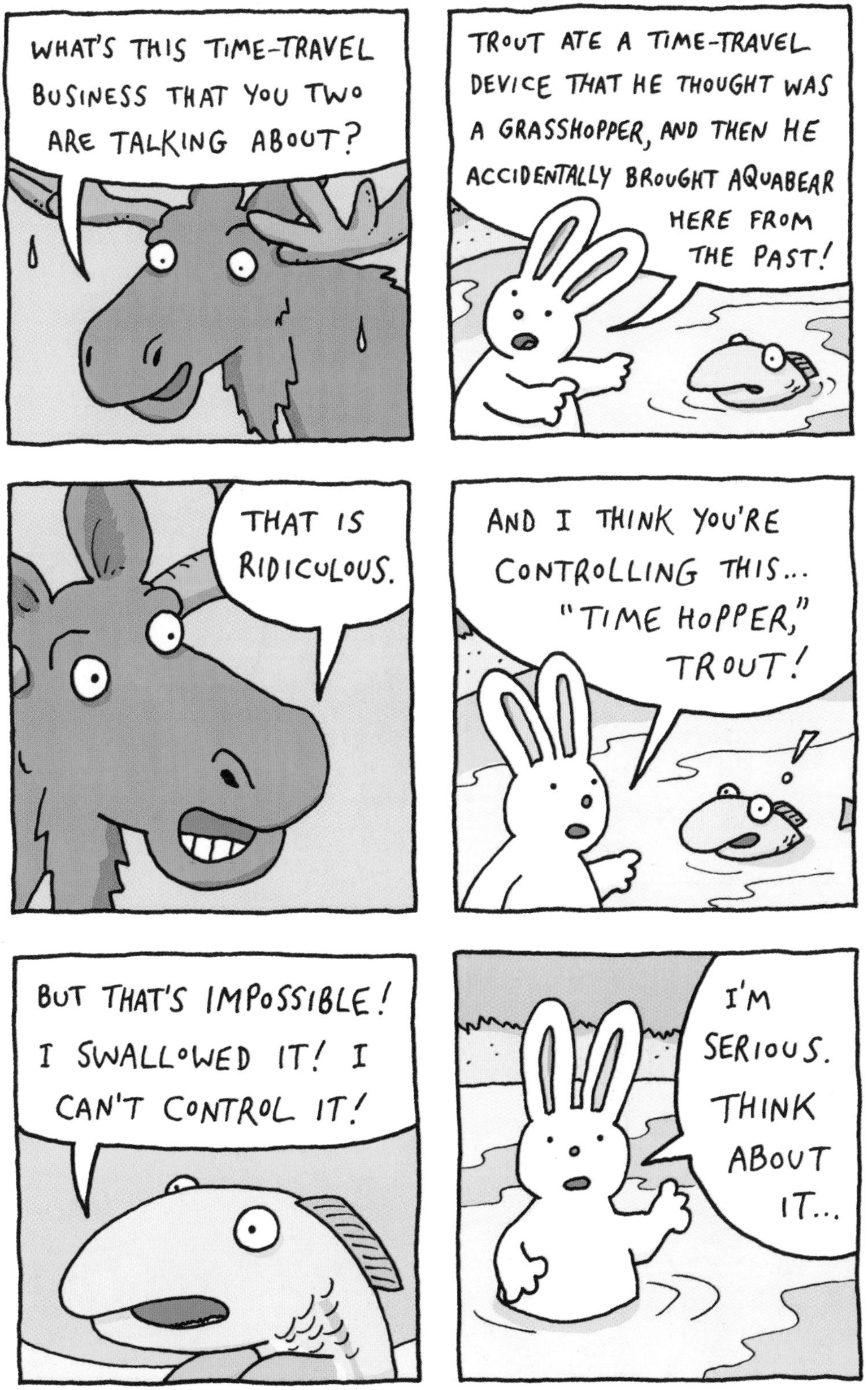
WHAT'S THIS TIME-TRAVEL BUSINESS THAT YOU TWO ARE TALKING ABOUT?
TROUT ATE A TIME-TRAVEL DEVICE THAT HE THOUGHT WAS A GRASSHOPPER, AND THEN HE ACCIDENTALLY BROUGHT AQUABEAR HERE FROM THE PAST!
THAT IS RIDICULOUS.
AND I THINK YOU'RE CONTROLLING THIS... "TIME HOPPER," TROUT!
!
BUT THAT'S IMPOSSIBLE! I SWALLOWED IT! I CAN'T CONTROL IT!
I'M SERIOUS. THINK ABOUT IT...

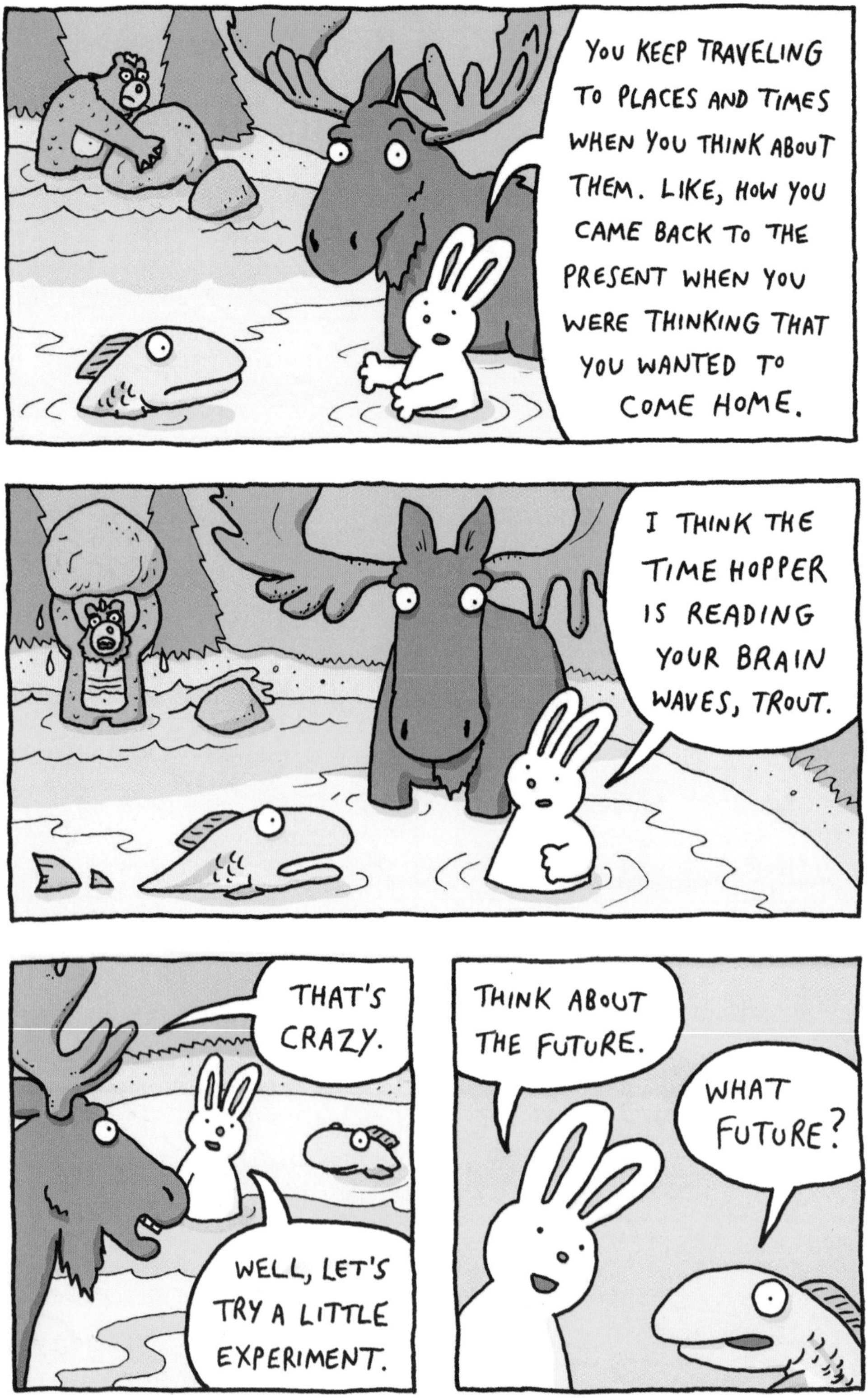
YOU KEEP TRAVELING TO PLACES AND TIMES WHEN YOU THINK ABOUT THEM. LIKE, HOW YOU CAME BACK TO THE PRESENT WHEN YOU WERE THINKING THAT YOU WANTED TO COME HOME.
I THINK THE TIME HOPPER IS READING YOUR BRAIN WAVES, TROUT.
THAT'S CRAZY.
WELL, LET'S TRY A LITTLE EXPERIMENT.
THINK ABOUT THE FUTURE.
WHAT FUTURE?

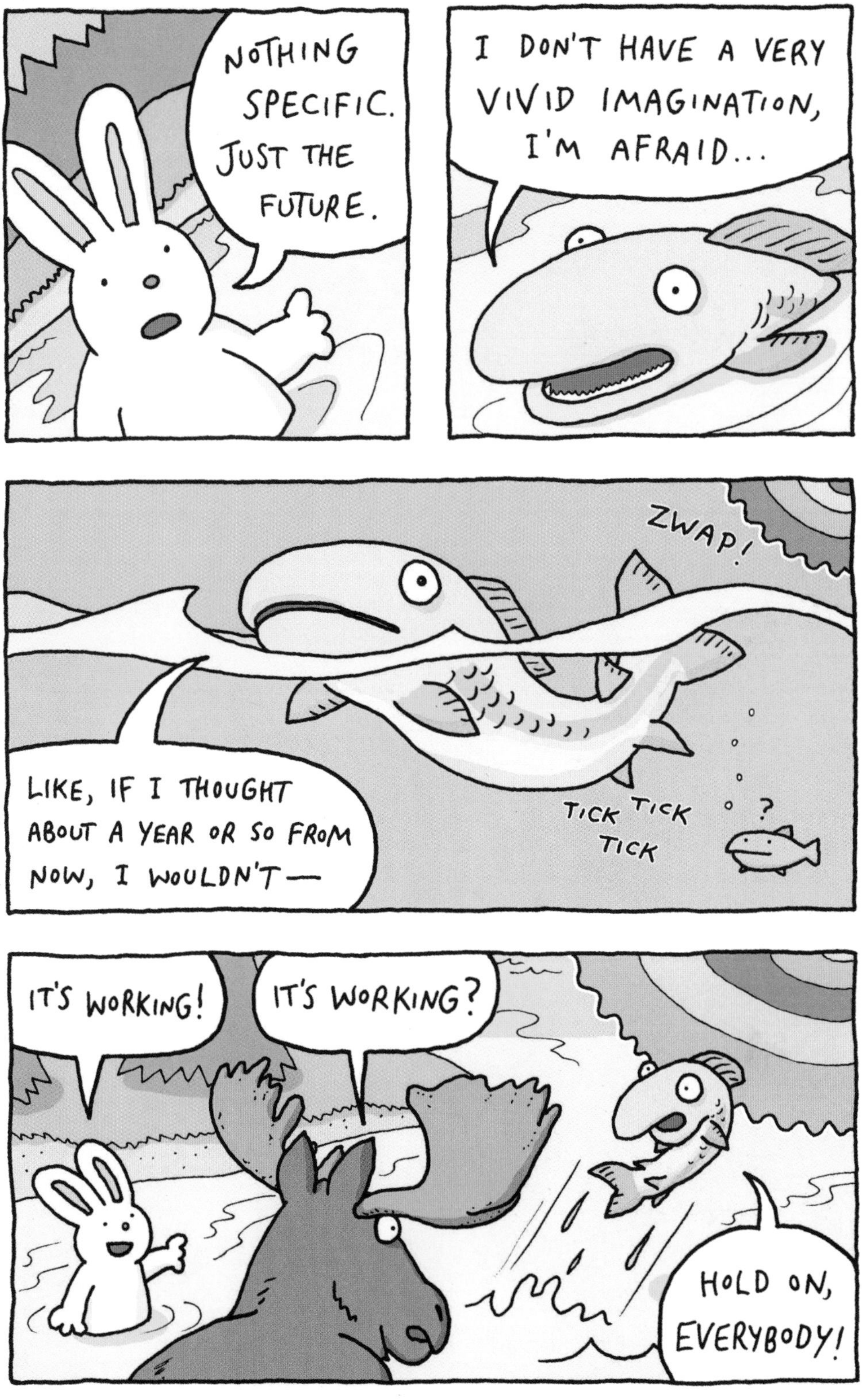
NOTHING SPECIFIC. JUST THE FUTURE.
I DON'T HAVE A VERY VIVID IMAGINATION, I'M AFRAID...
ZWAP!
LIKE, IF I THOUGHT ABOUT A YEAR OR SO FROM NOW, I WOULDN'T—
TICK TICK TICK
?
IT'S WORKING!
IT'S WORKING?
HOLD ON, EVERYBODY!

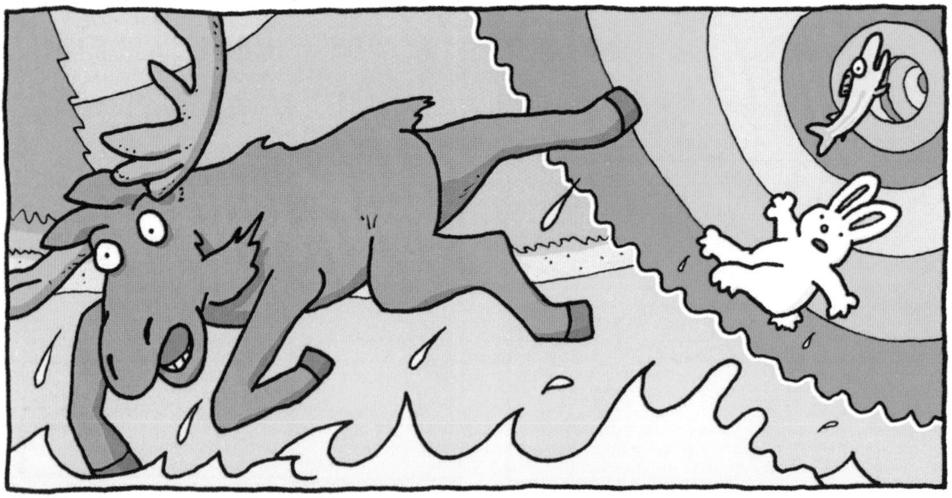

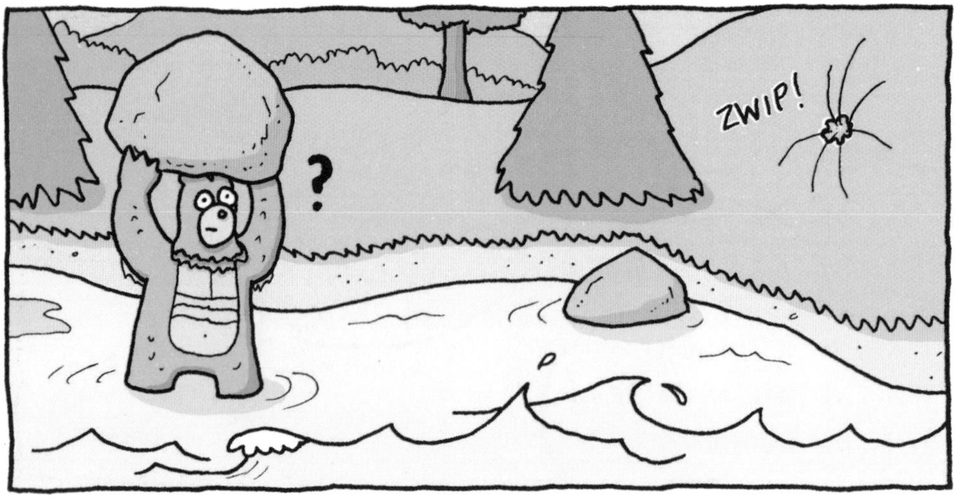
?
ZWIP!

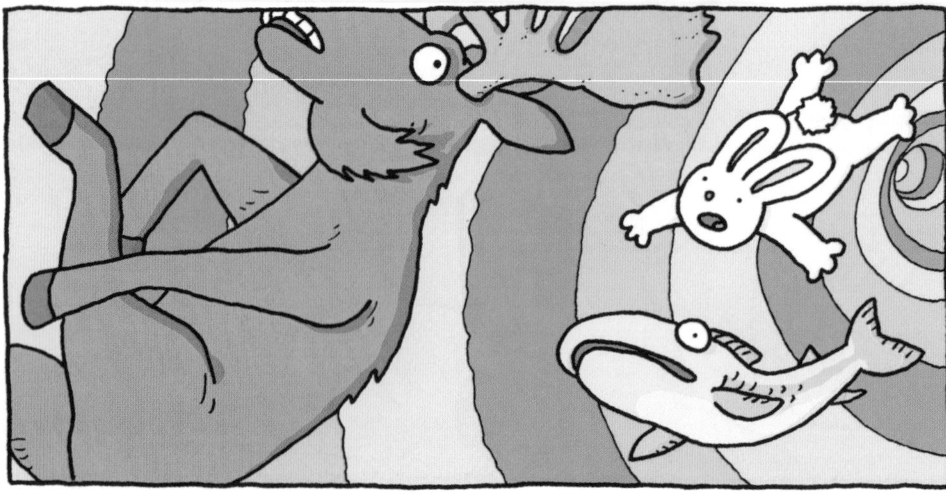

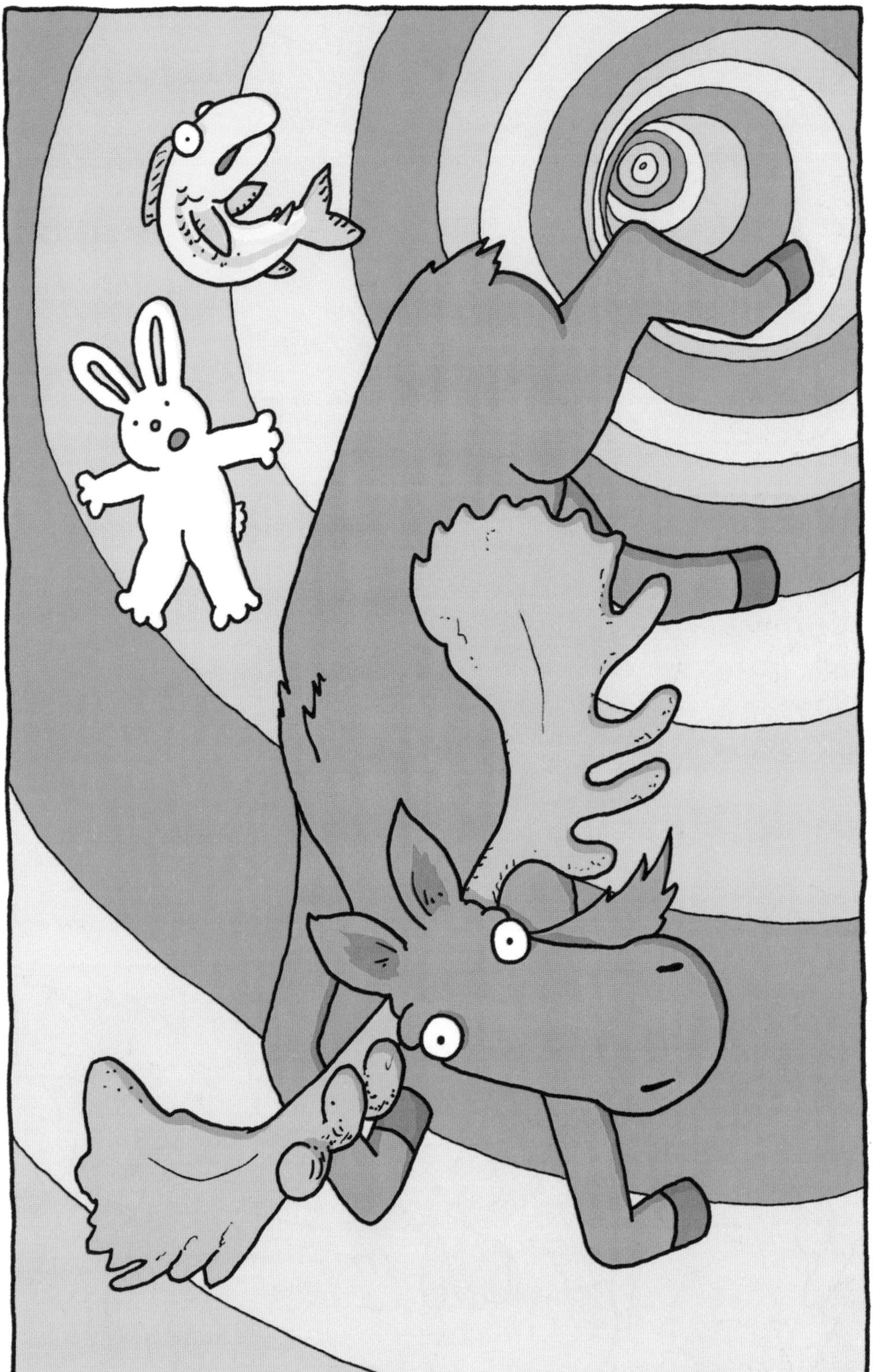

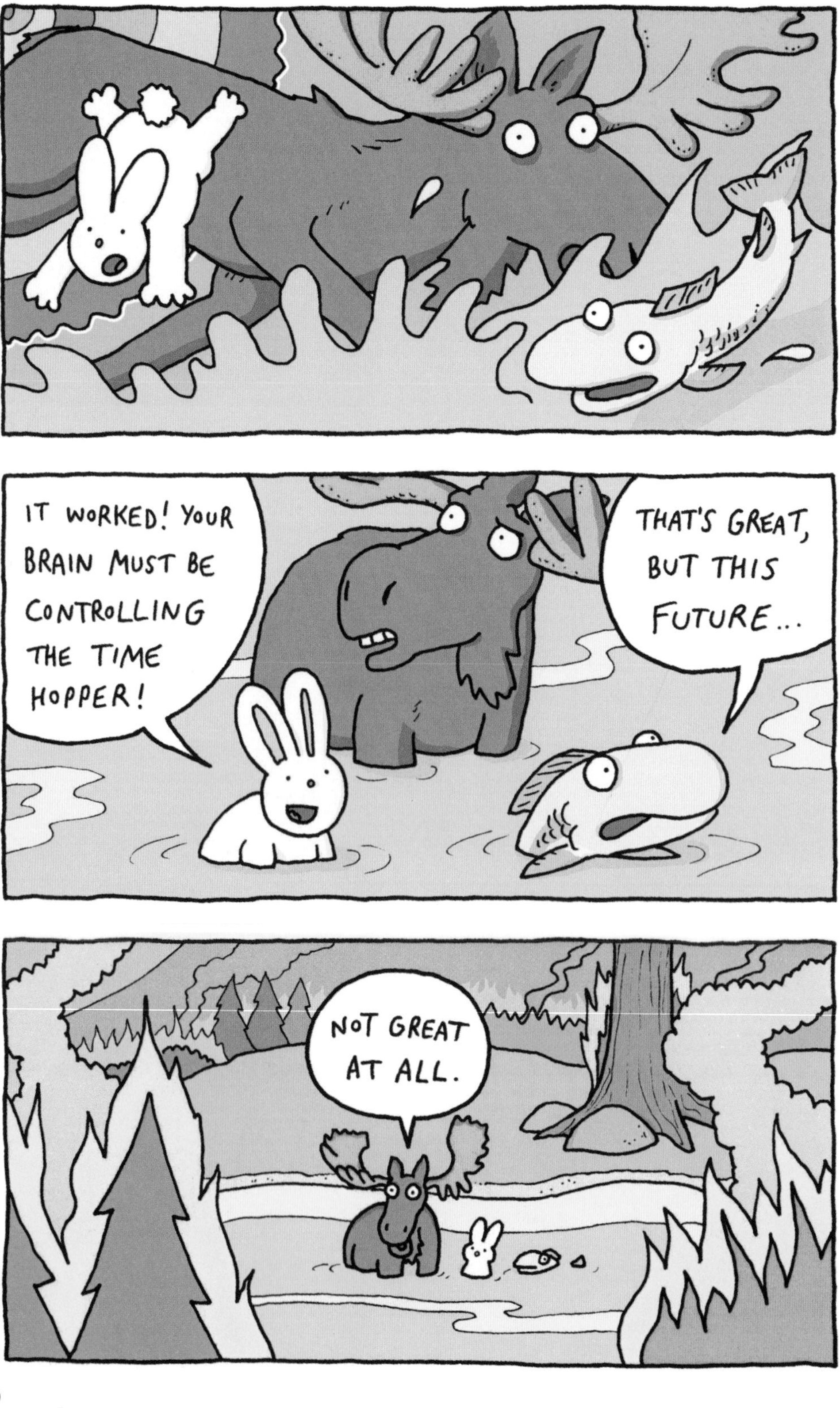
IT WORKED! YOUR BRAIN MUST BE CONTROLLING THE TIME HOPPER!
THAT'S GREAT, BUT THIS FUTURE...
NOT GREAT AT ALL.

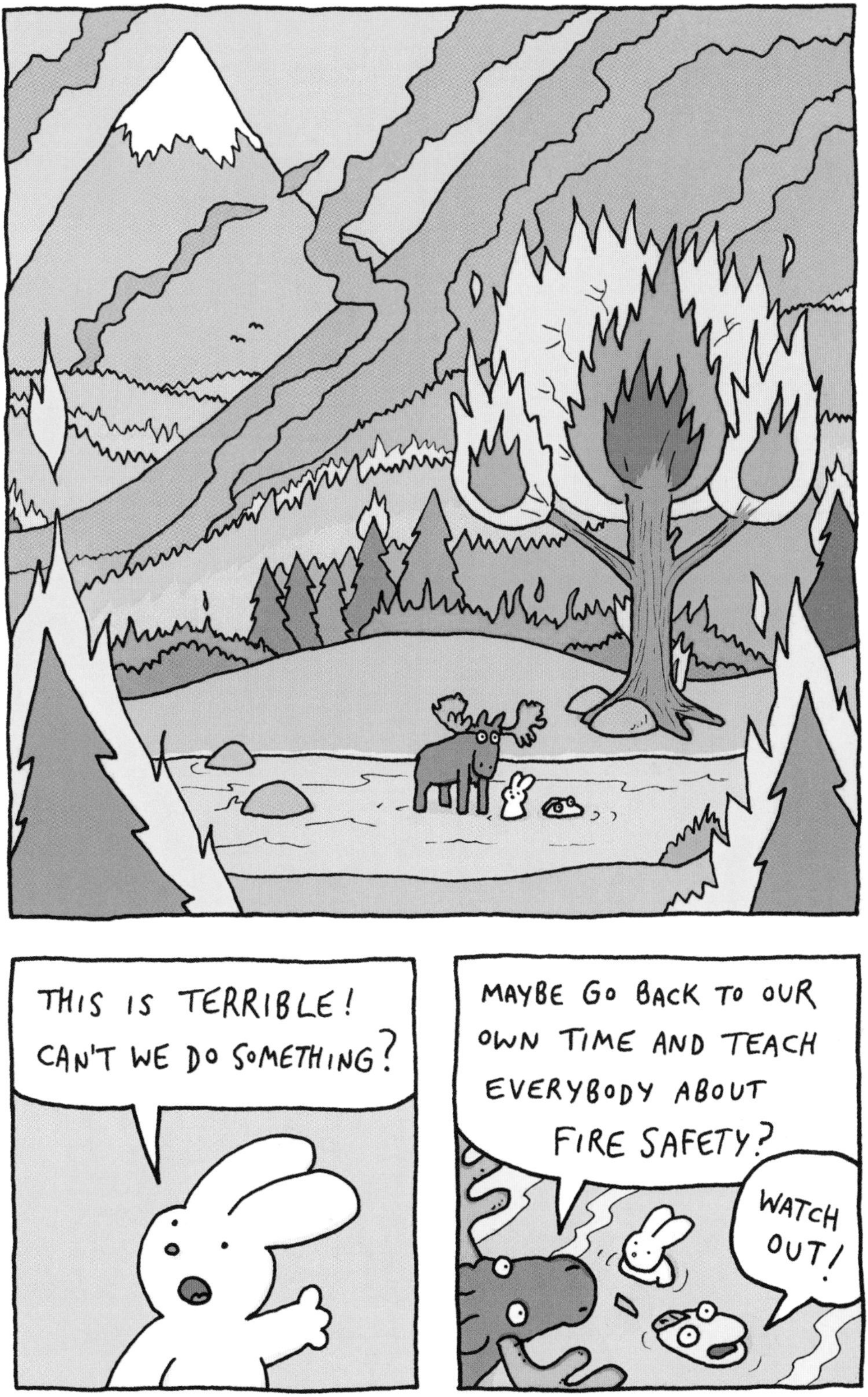
THIS IS TERRIBLE! CAN'T WE DO SOMETHING?
MAYBE GO BACK TO OUR OWN TIME AND TEACH EVERYBODY ABOUT FIRE SAFETY?
WATCH OUT!

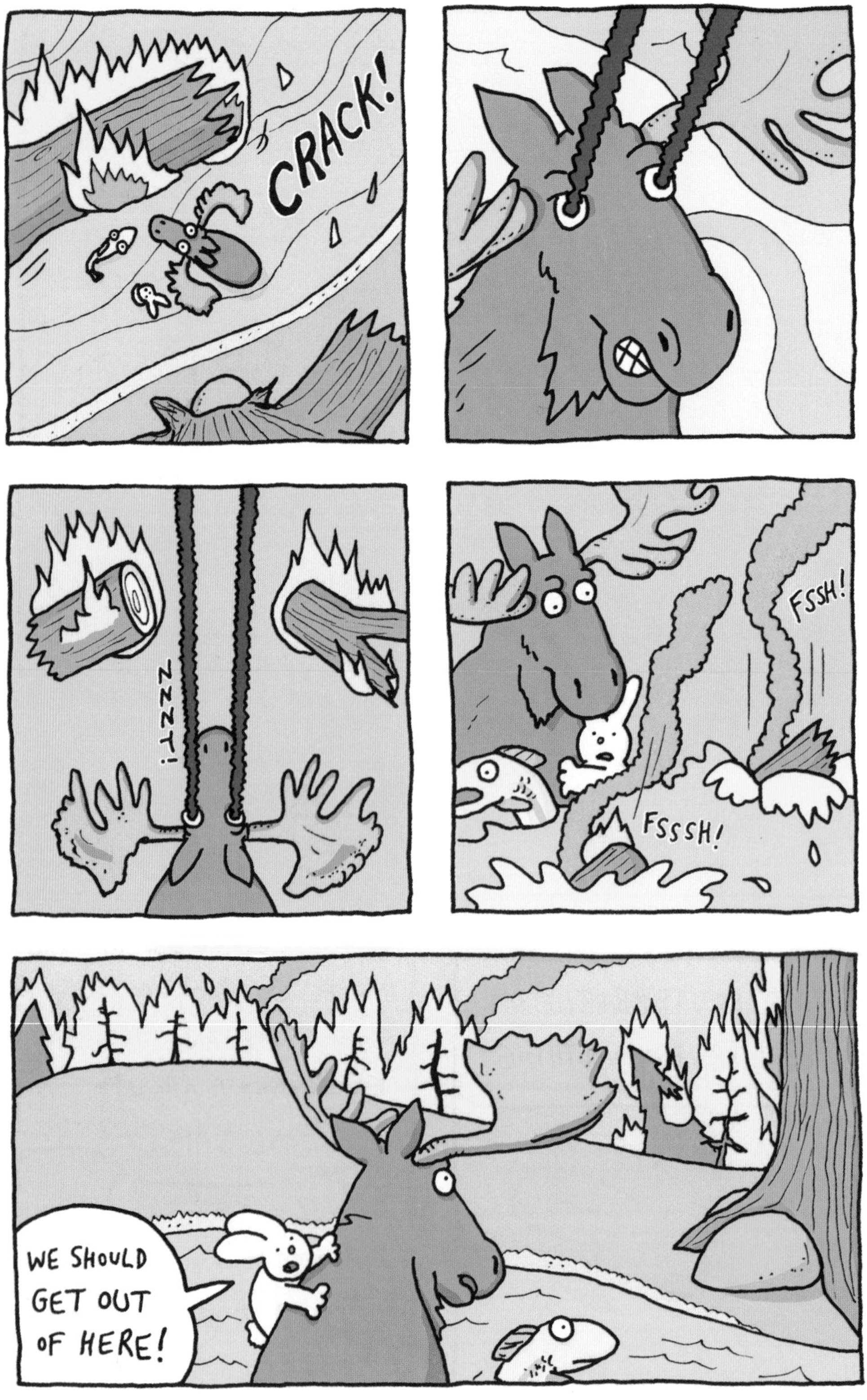
CRACK!
ZNNT!
FSSH!
FSSSH!
WE SHOULD GET OUT OF HERE!

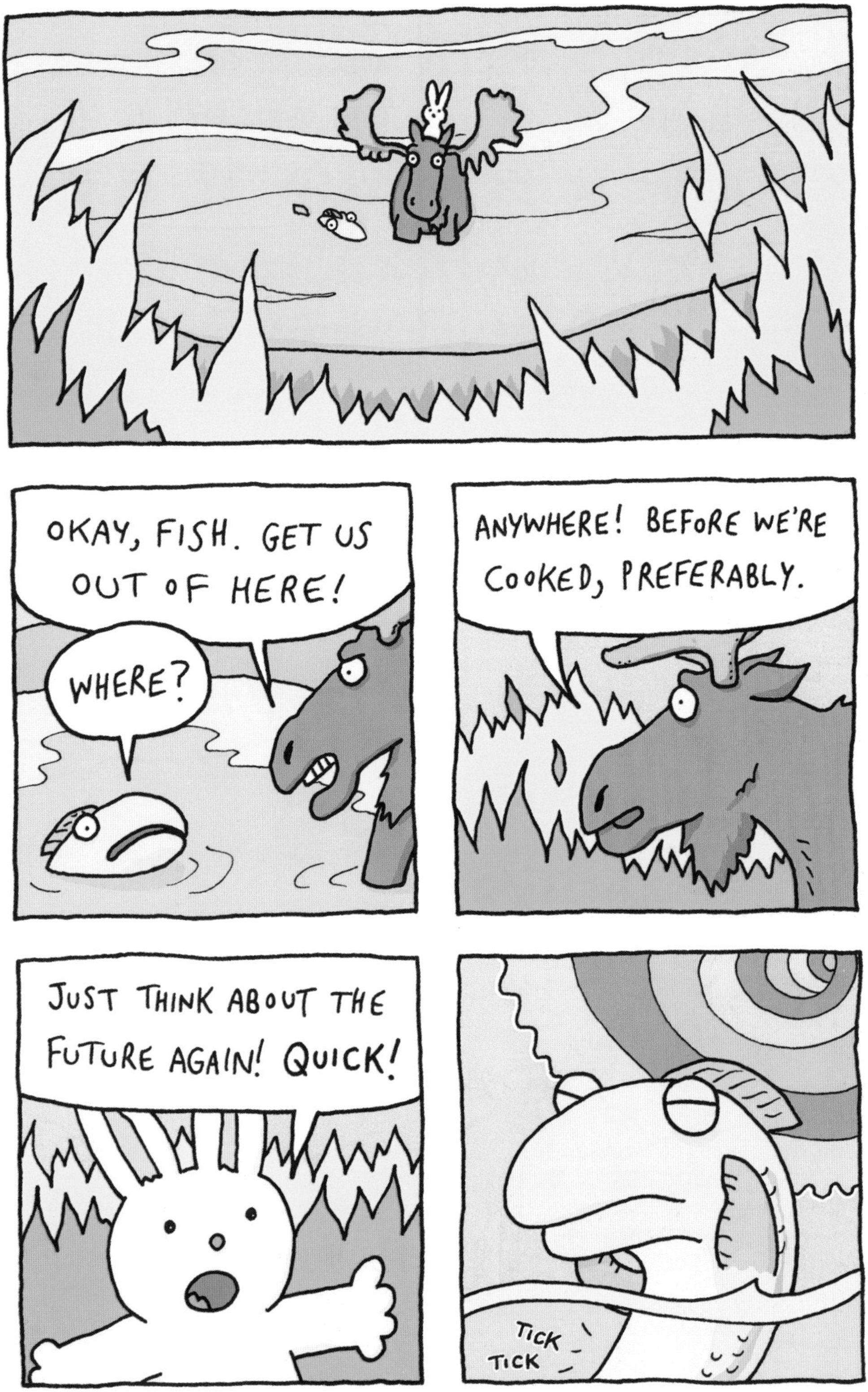
OKAY, FISH. GET US OUT OF HERE!
WHERE?
ANYWHERE! BEFORE WE'RE COOKED, PREFERABLY.
JUST THINK ABOUT THE FUTURE AGAIN! QUICK!
TICK
TICK

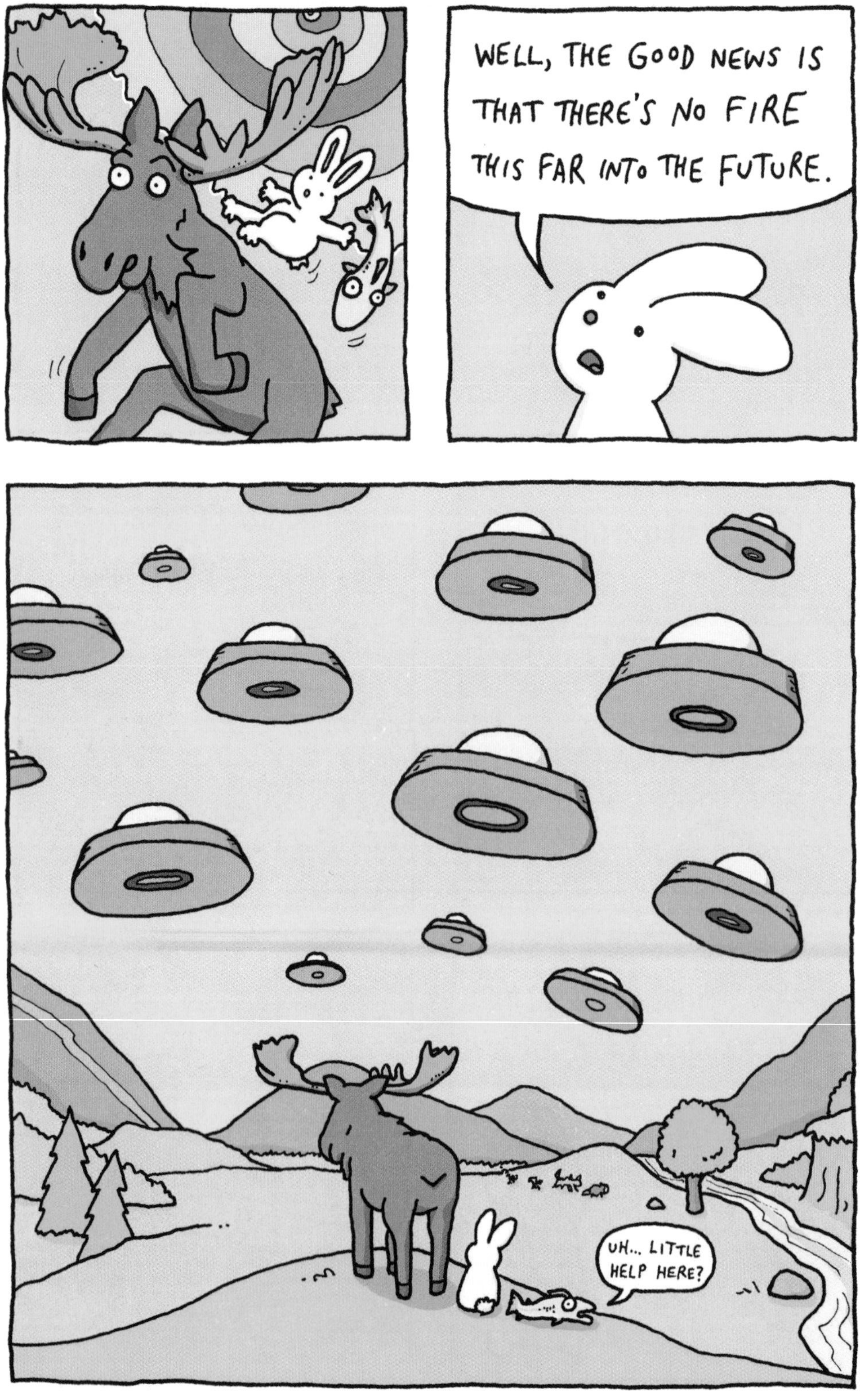
WELL, THE GOOD NEWS IS THAT THERE'S NO FIRE THIS FAR INTO THE FUTURE.
UH... LITTLE HELP HERE?

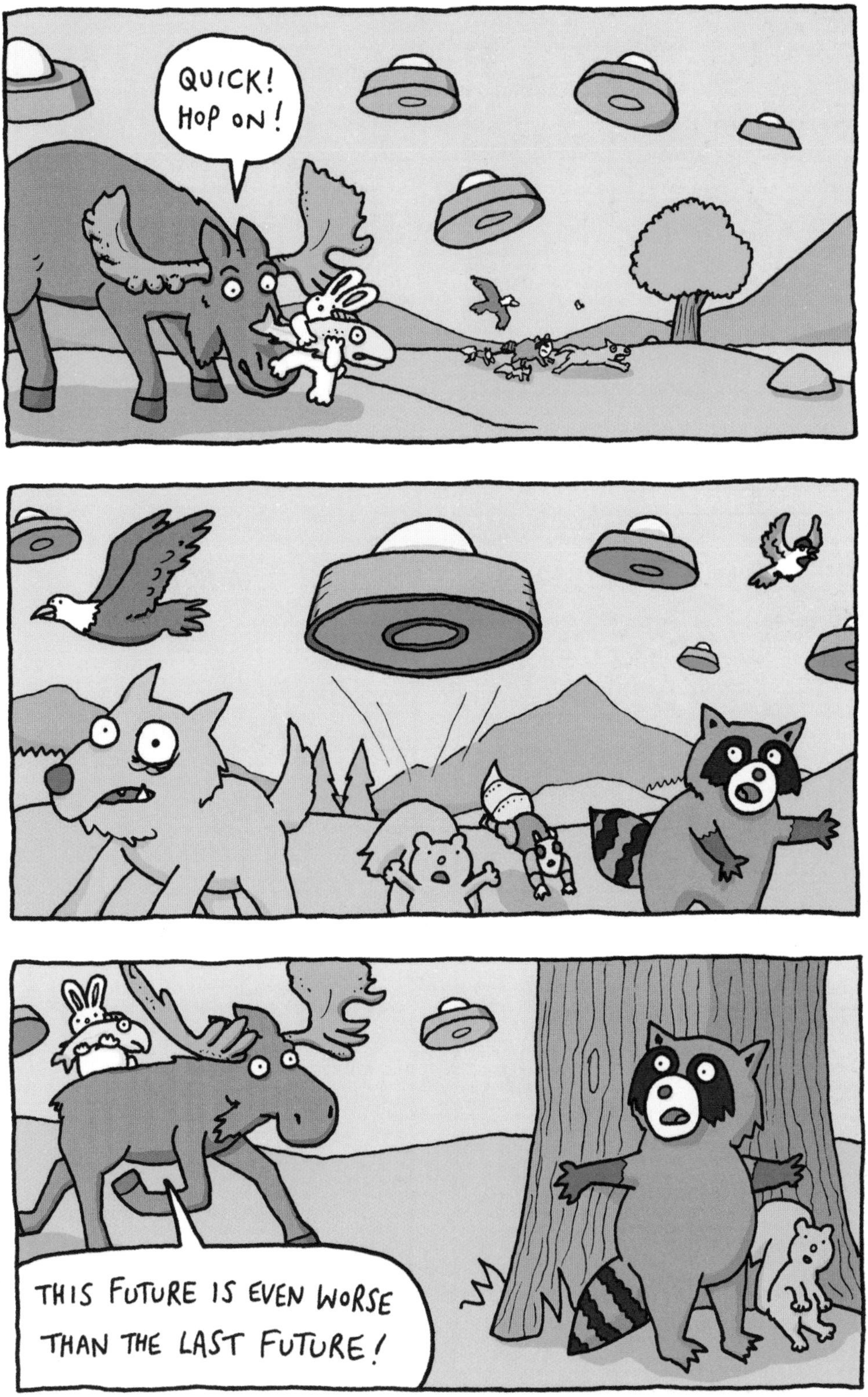
QUICK! HOP ON!
THIS FUTURE IS EVEN WORSE THAN THE LAST FUTURE!

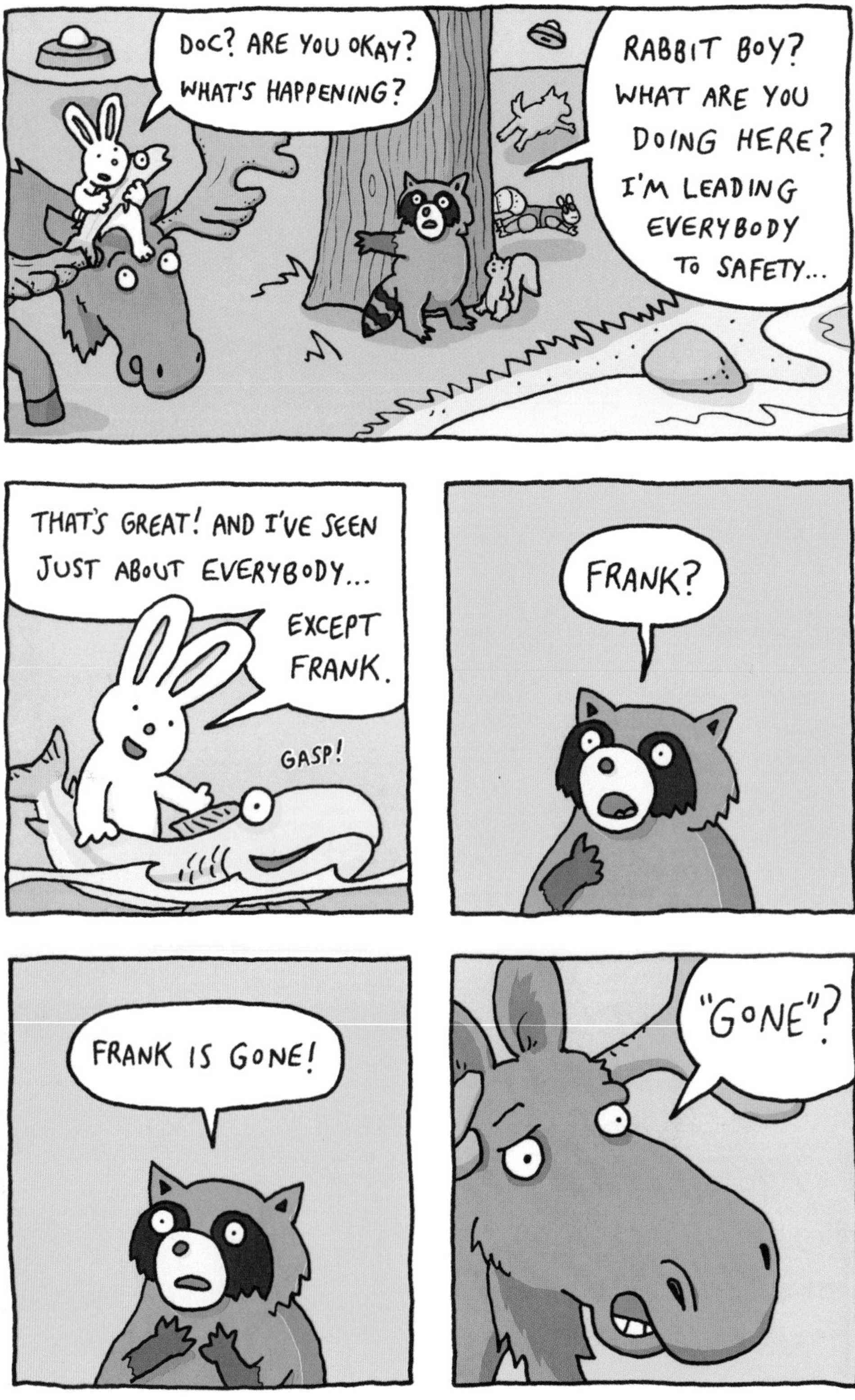
DOC? ARE YOU OKAY? WHAT'S HAPPENING?
RABBIT BOY? WHAT ARE YOU DOING HERE? I'M LEADING EVERYBODY TO SAFETY...
THAT'S GREAT! AND I'VE SEEN JUST ABOUT EVERYBODY...
EXCEPT FRANK.
GASP!
FRANK?
FRANK IS GONE!
"GONE"?

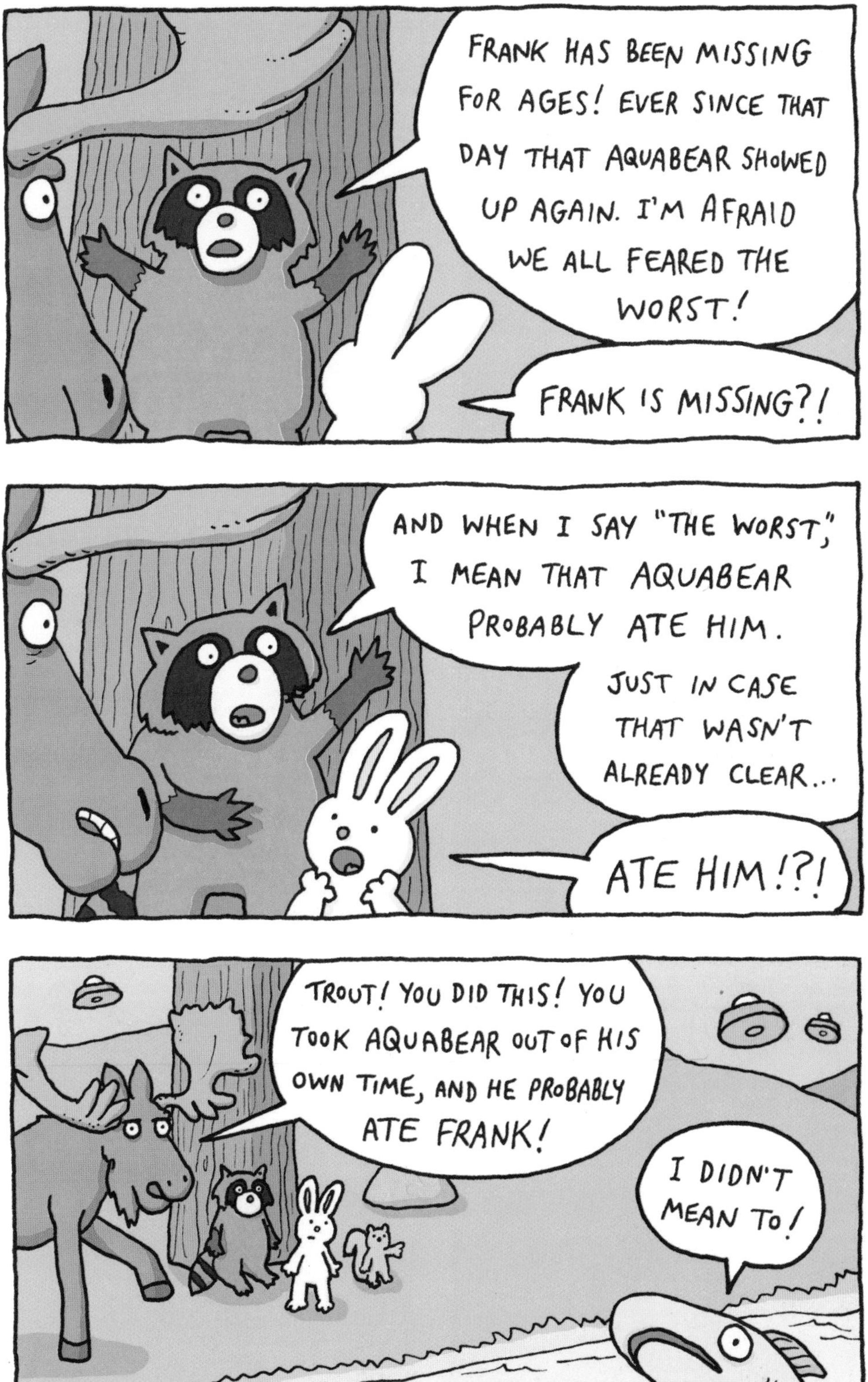
FRANK HAS BEEN MISSING FOR AGES! EVER SINCE THAT DAY THAT AQUABEAR SHOWED UP AGAIN. I'M AFRAID WE ALL FEARED THE WORST!
FRANK IS MISSING?!
AND WHEN I SAY "THE WORST," I MEAN THAT AQUABEAR PROBABLY ATE HIM.
JUST IN CASE THAT WASN'T ALREADY CLEAR...
ATE HIM!?!
TROUT! YOU DID THIS! YOU TOOK AQUABEAR OUT OF HIS OWN TIME, AND HE PROBABLY ATE FRANK!
I DIDN'T MEAN TO!

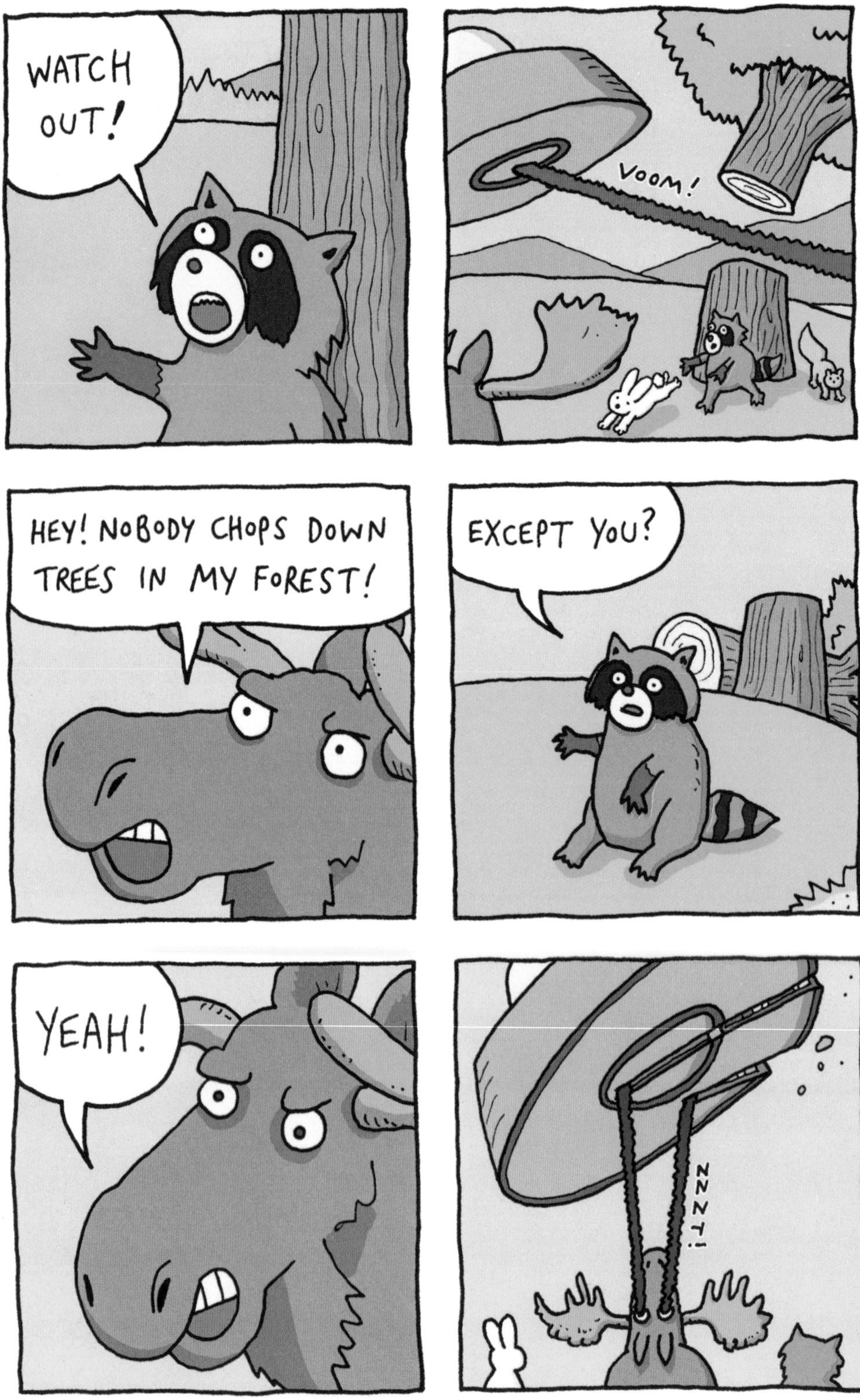
WATCH OUT!
VOOM!
HEY! NOBODY CHOPS DOWN TREES IN MY FOREST!
EXCEPT YOU?
YEAH!
ZZZT!

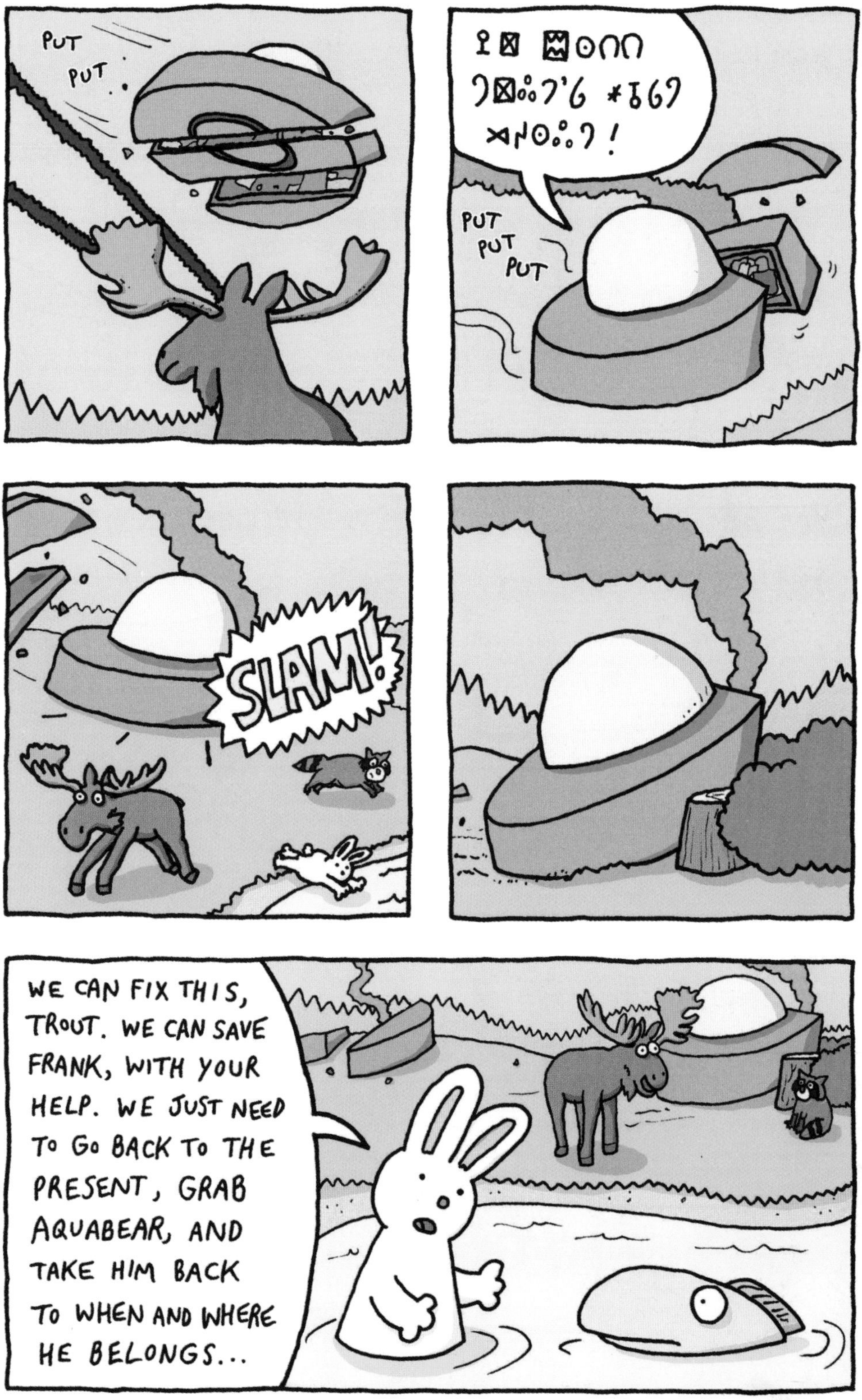
PUT PUT
PUT PUT PUT
SLAM!
WE CAN FIX THIS, TROUT. WE CAN SAVE FRANK, WITH YOUR HELP. WE JUST NEED TO GO BACK TO THE PRESENT, GRAB AQUABEAR, AND TAKE HIM BACK TO WHEN AND WHERE HE BELONGS...

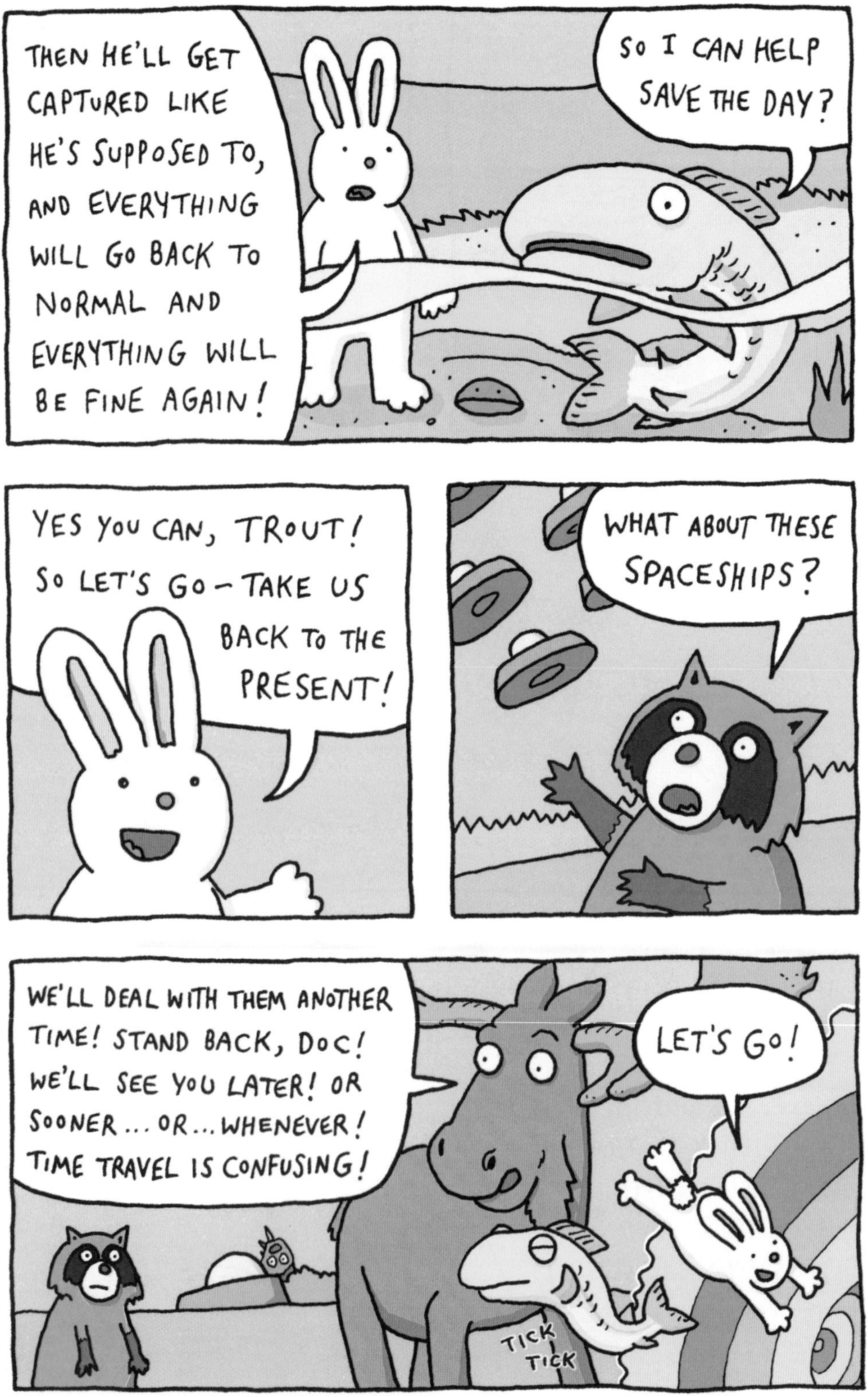
THEN HE'LL GET CAPTURED LIKE HE'S SUPPOSED TO, AND EVERYTHING WILL GO BACK TO NORMAL AND EVERYTHING WILL BE FINE AGAIN!
SO I CAN HELP SAVE THE DAY?
YES YOU CAN, TROUT! SO LET'S GO—TAKE US BACK TO THE PRESENT!
WHAT ABOUT THESE SPACESHIPS?
WE'LL DEAL WITH THEM ANOTHER TIME! STAND BACK, DOC! WE'LL SEE YOU LATER! OR SOONER... OR... WHENEVER! TIME TRAVEL IS CONFUSING!
LET'S GO!
TICK TICK

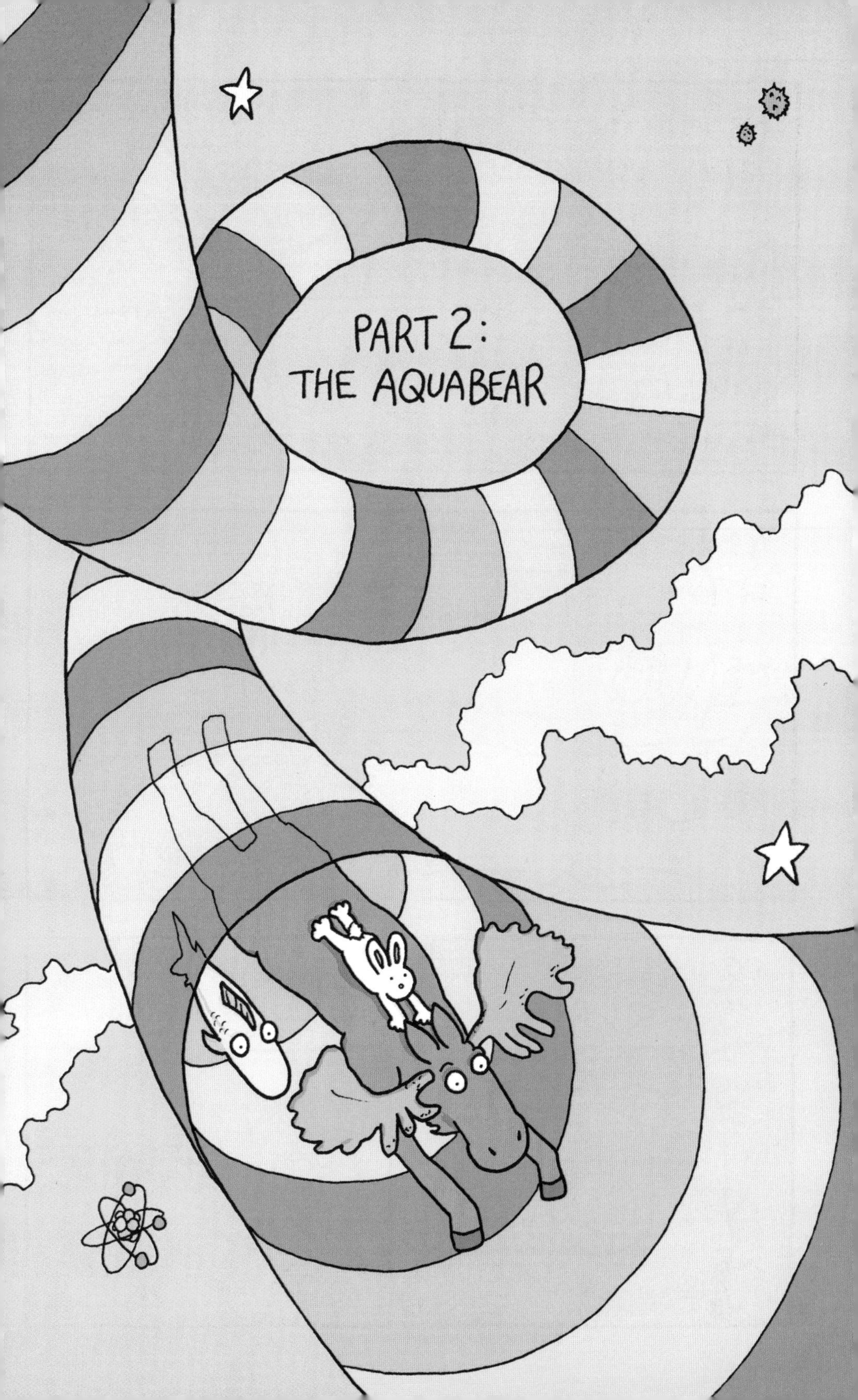
PART 2:
THE AQUABEAR

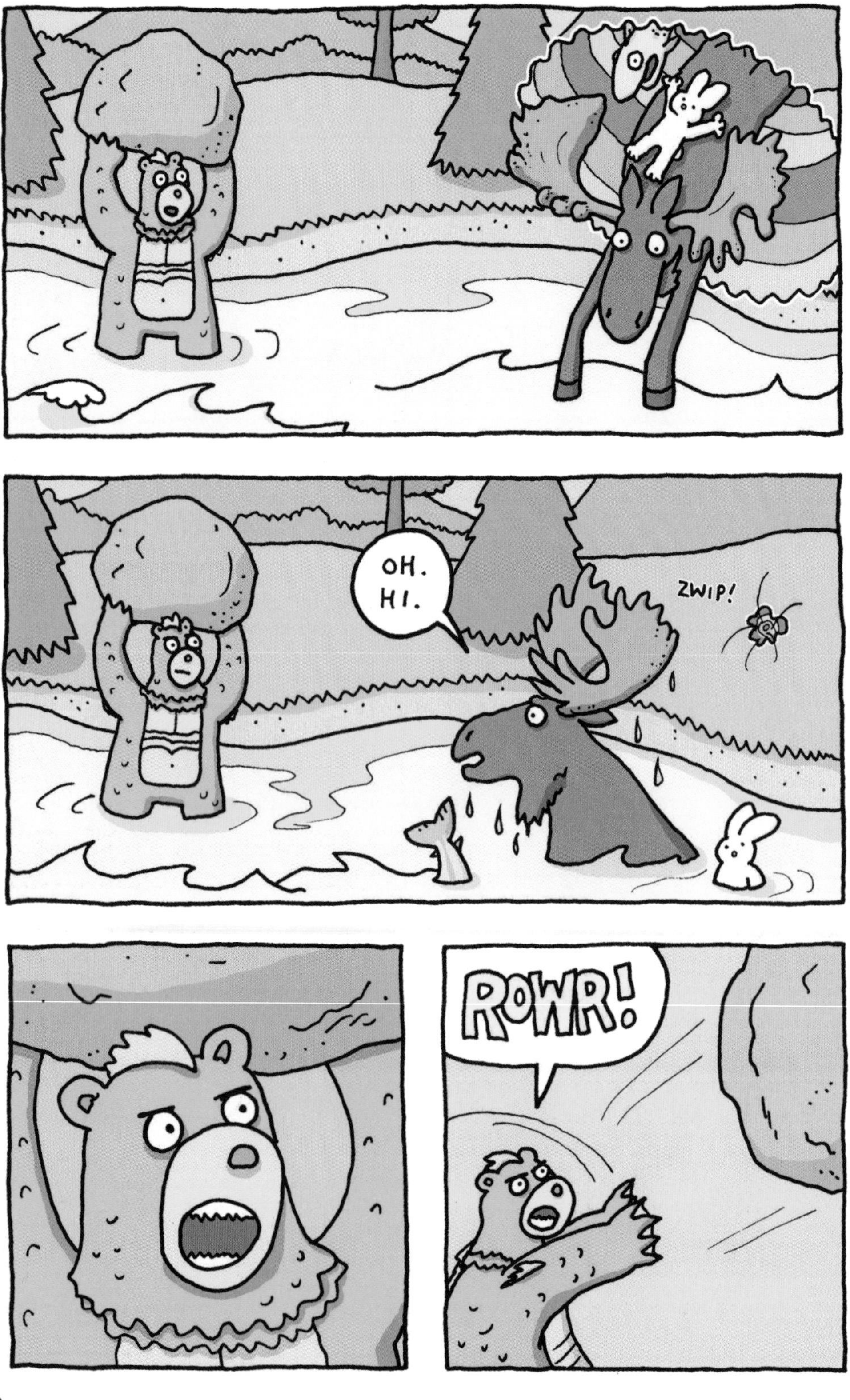
OH.
HI.
ZWIP!
ROWR!

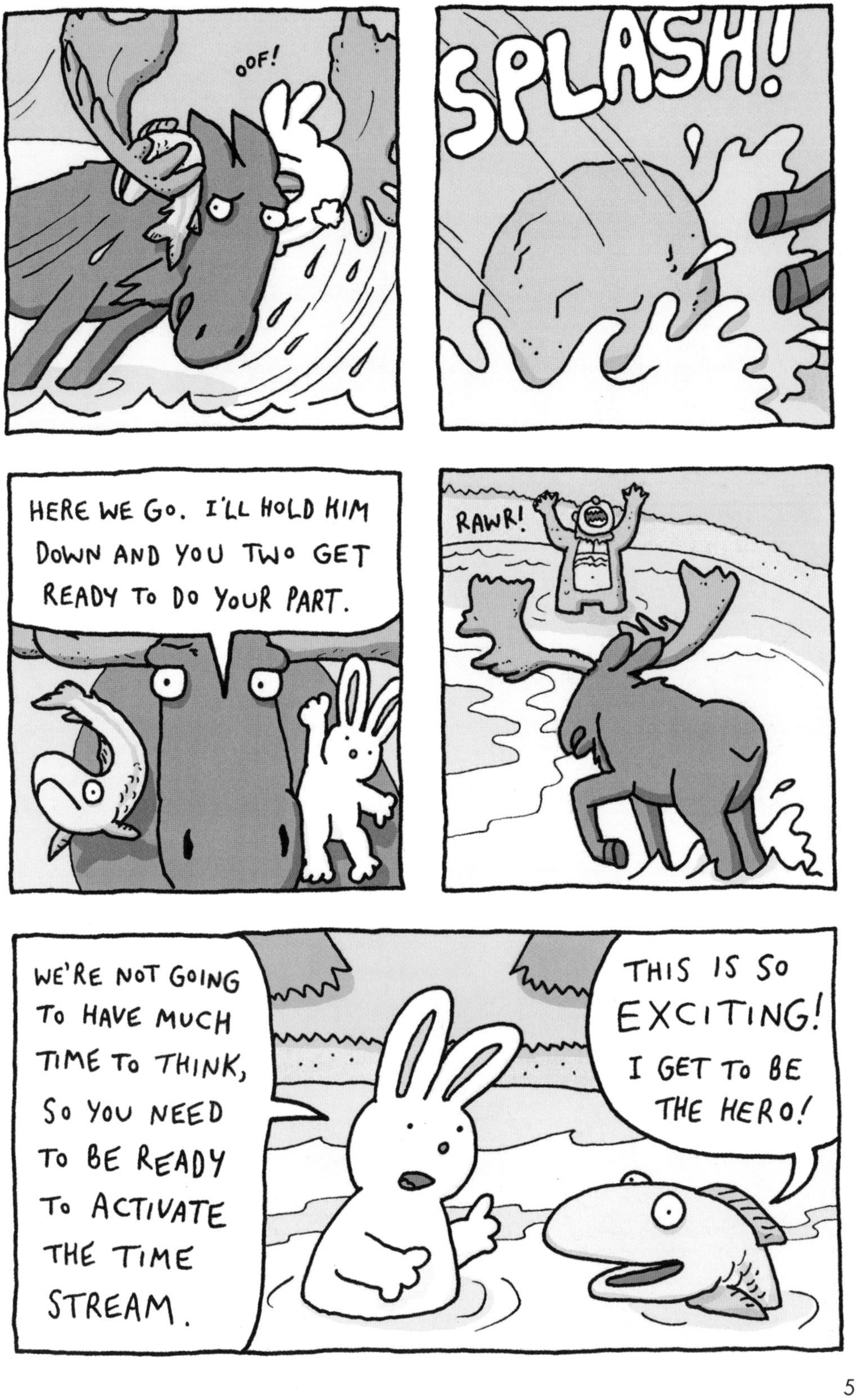
OOF!
SPLASH!
HERE WE GO. I'LL HOLD HIM DOWN AND YOU TWO GET READY TO DO YOUR PART.
RAWR!
WE'RE NOT GOING TO HAVE MUCH TIME TO THINK, SO YOU NEED TO BE READY TO ACTIVATE THE TIME STREAM.
THIS IS SO EXCITING! I GET TO BE THE HERO!

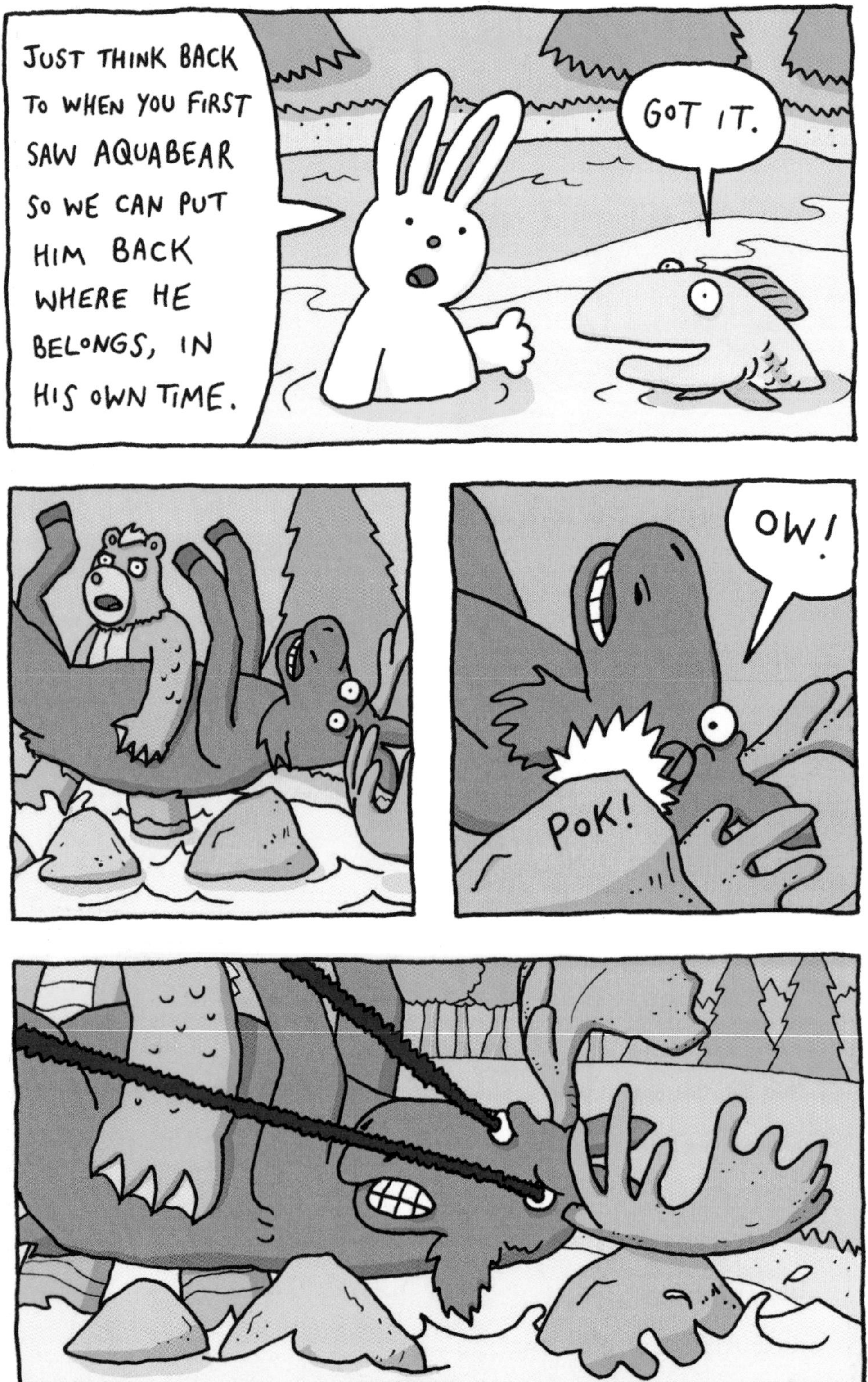
JUST THINK BACK TO WHEN YOU FIRST SAW AQUABEAR SO WE CAN PUT HIM BACK WHERE HE BELONGS, IN HIS OWN TIME.
GOT IT.
OW!
POK!

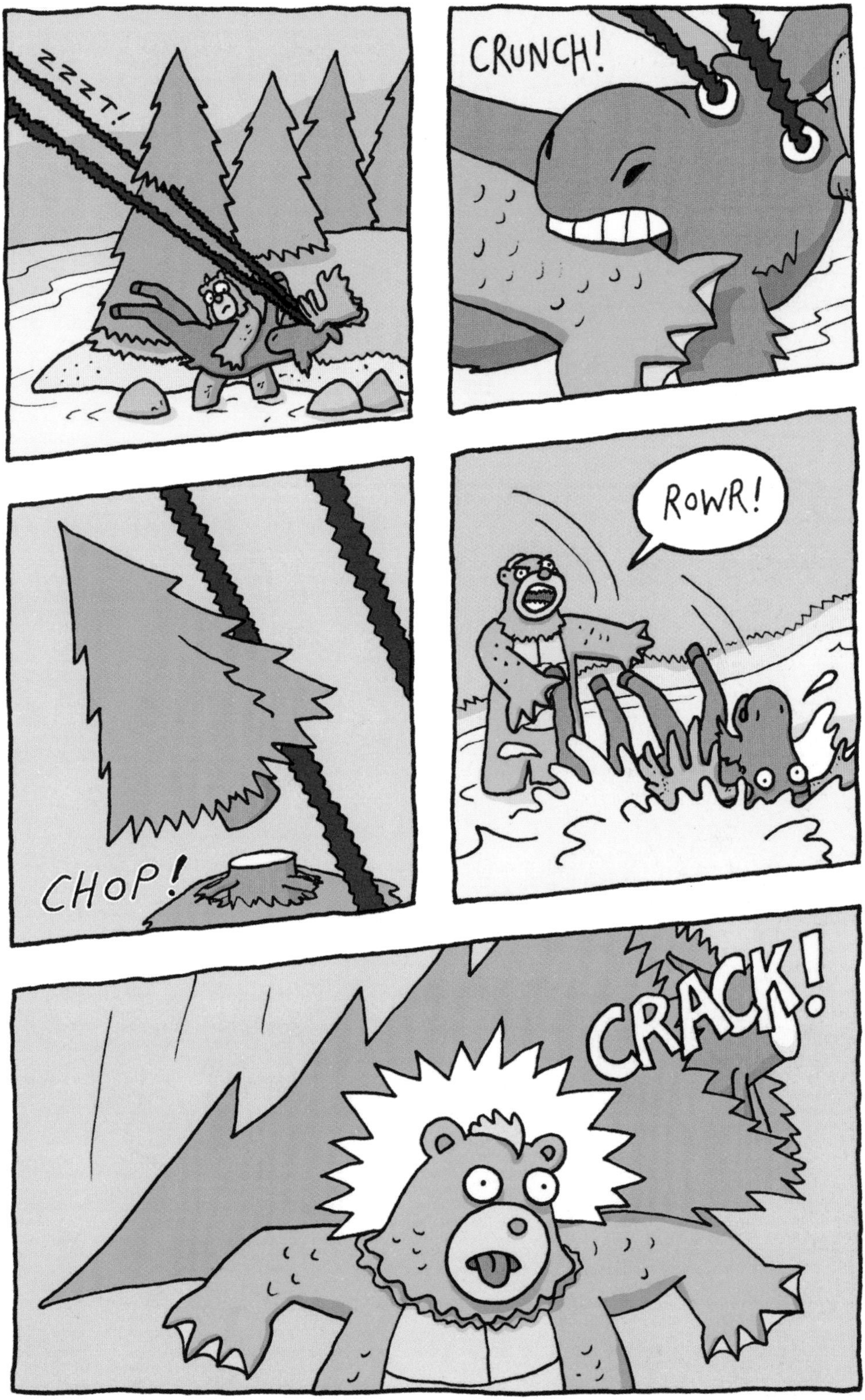
ZZZZT!
CRUNCH!
CHOP!
ROWR!
CRACK!

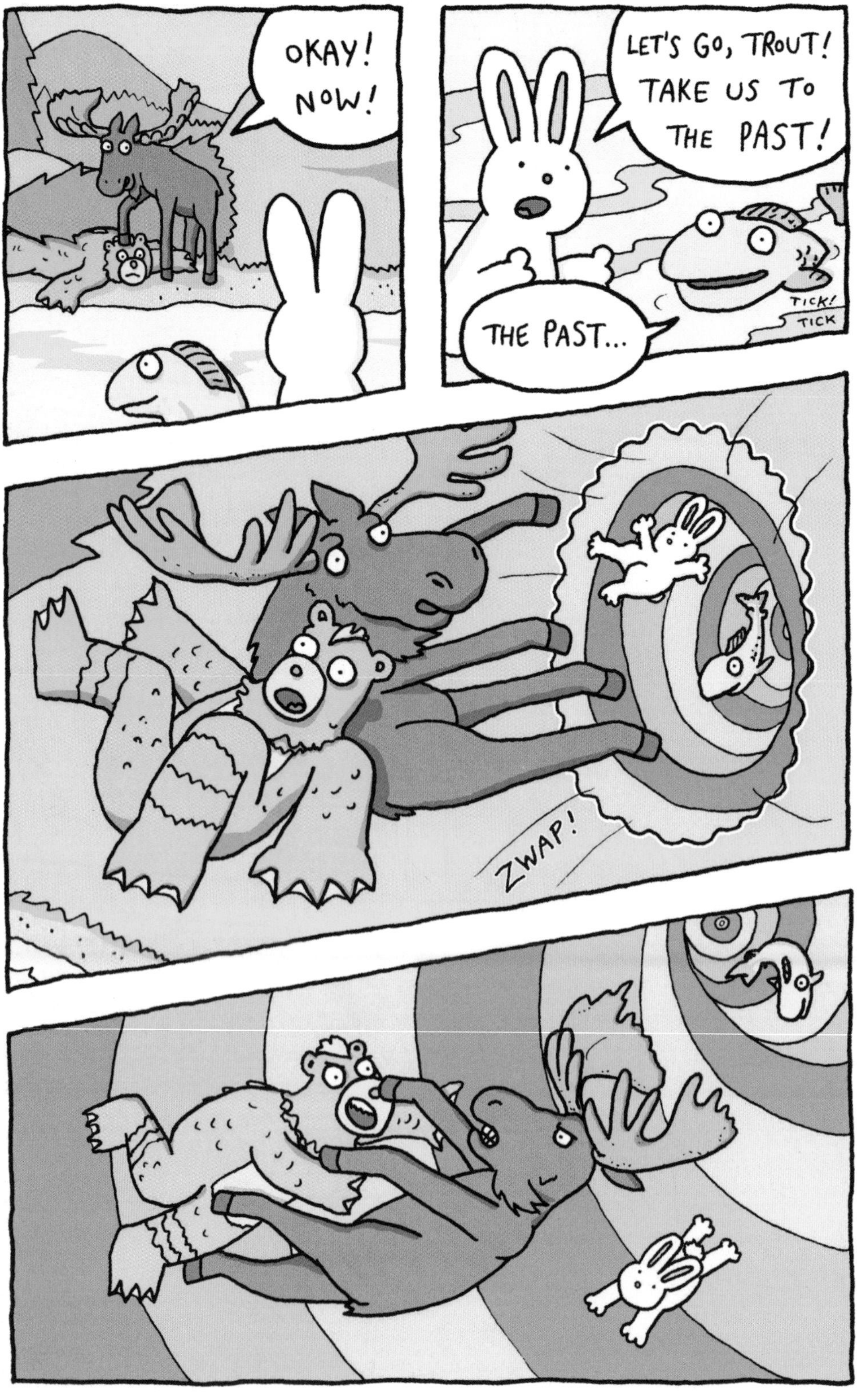
OKAY! NOW!
LET'S GO, TROUT! TAKE US TO THE PAST!
THE PAST...
TICK! TICK
ZWAP!

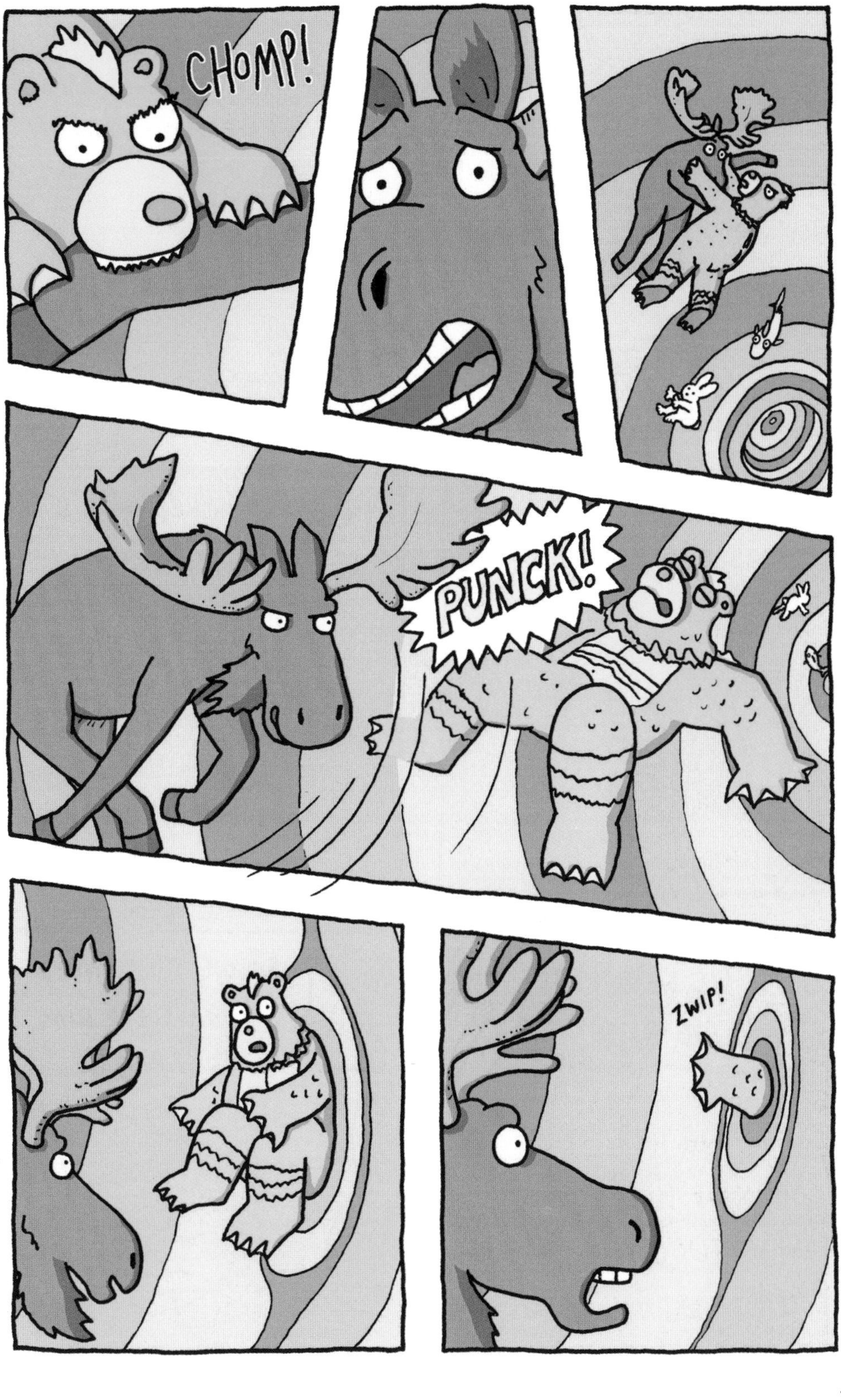
CHOMP!
PUNCK!
ZWIP!

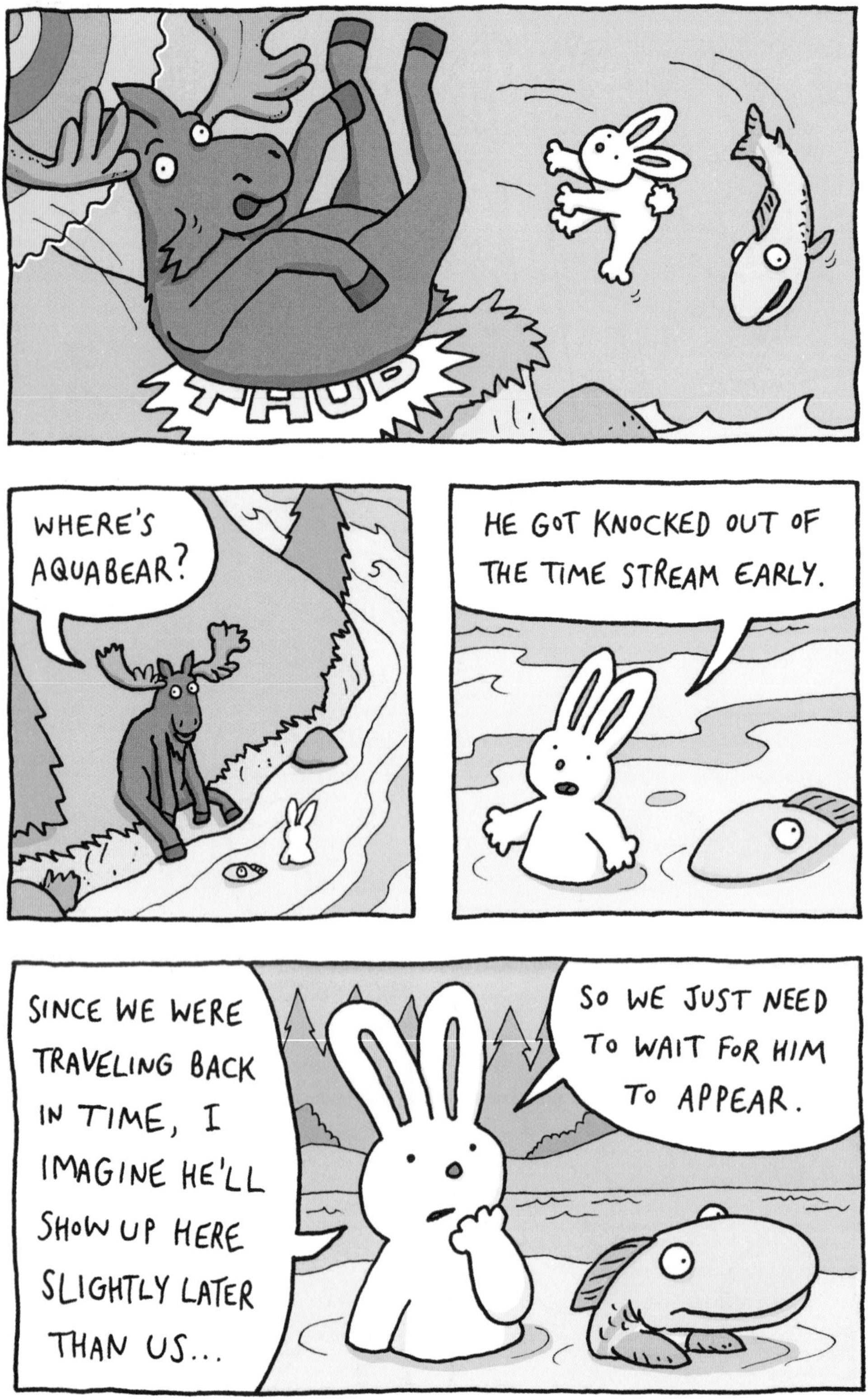
THUD
WHERE'S AQUABEAR?
HE GOT KNOCKED OUT OF THE TIME STREAM EARLY.
SINCE WE WERE TRAVELING BACK IN TIME, I IMAGINE HE'LL SHOW UP HERE SLIGHTLY LATER THAN US...
SO WE JUST NEED TO WAIT FOR HIM TO APPEAR.

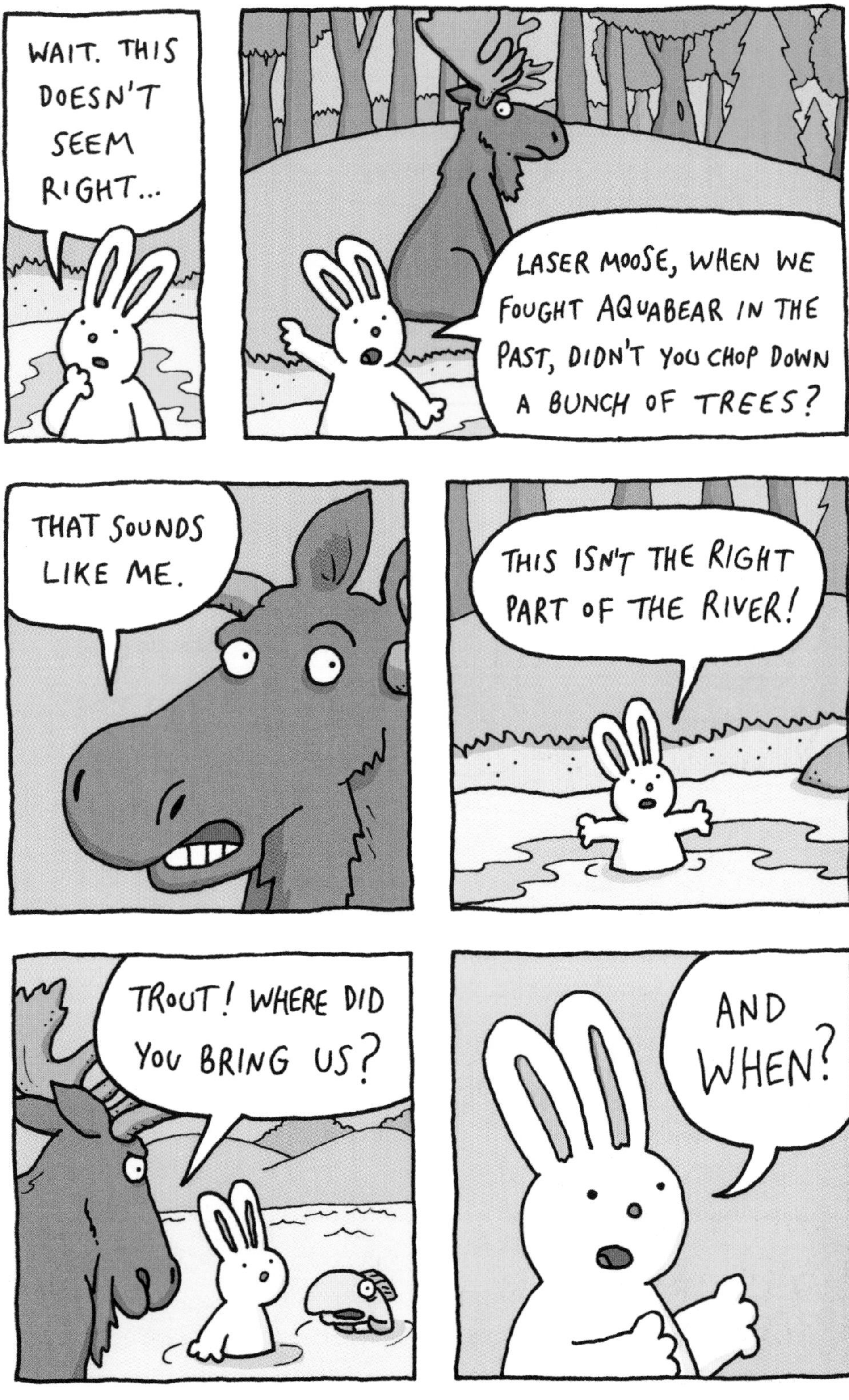
WAIT. THIS DOESN'T SEEM RIGHT...
LASER MOOSE, WHEN WE FOUGHT AQUABEAR IN THE PAST, DIDN'T YOU CHOP DOWN A BUNCH OF TREES?
THAT SOUNDS LIKE ME.
THIS ISN'T THE RIGHT PART OF THE RIVER!
TROUT! WHERE DID YOU BRING US?
AND WHEN?

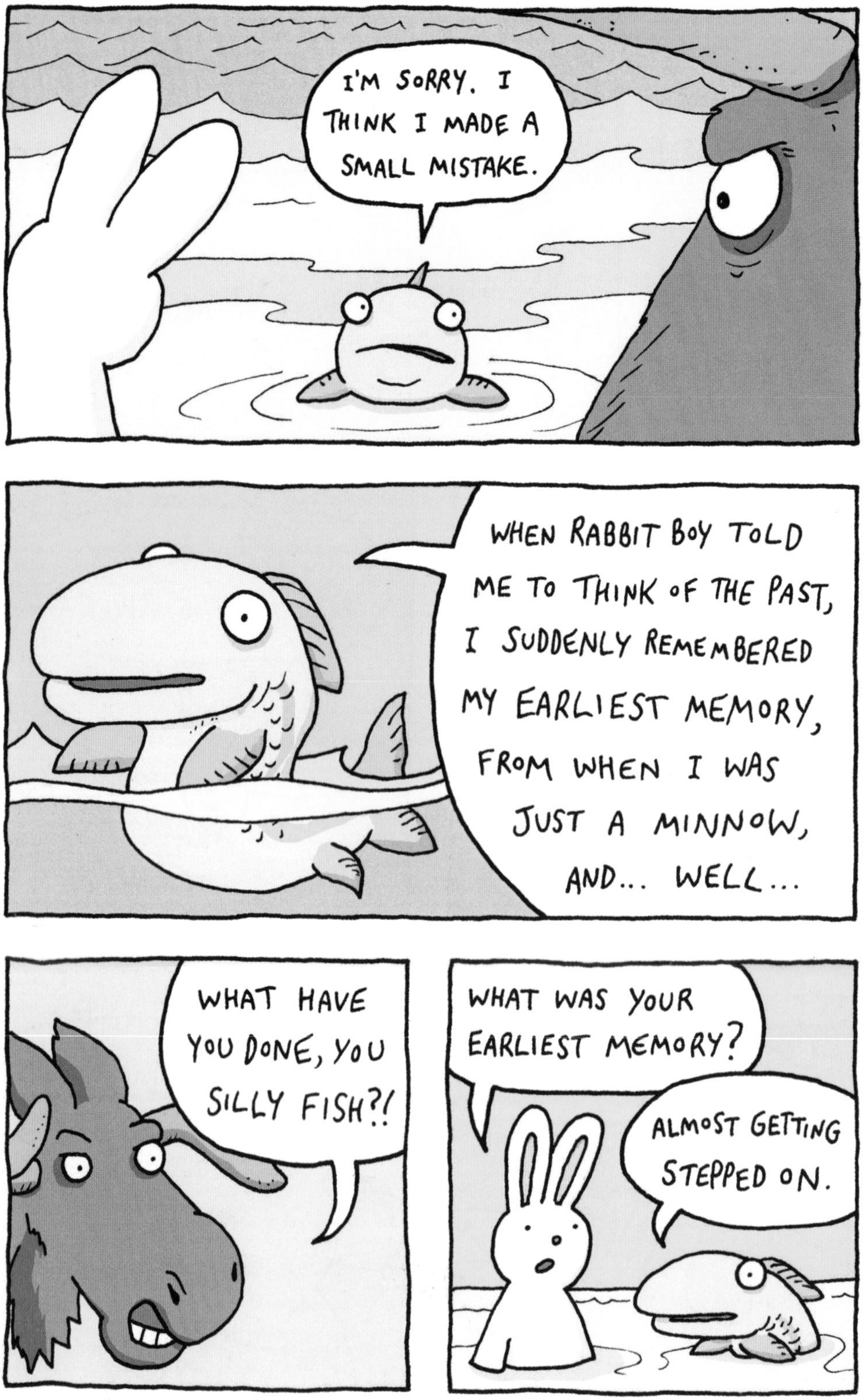

I'M SORRY. I THINK I MADE A SMALL MISTAKE.
WHEN RABBIT BOY TOLD ME TO THINK OF THE PAST, I SUDDENLY REMEMBERED MY EARLIEST MEMORY, FROM WHEN I WAS JUST A MINNOW, AND... WELL...
WHAT HAVE YOU DONE, YOU SILLY FISH?!
WHAT WAS YOUR EARLIEST MEMORY?
ALMOST GETTING STEPPED ON.

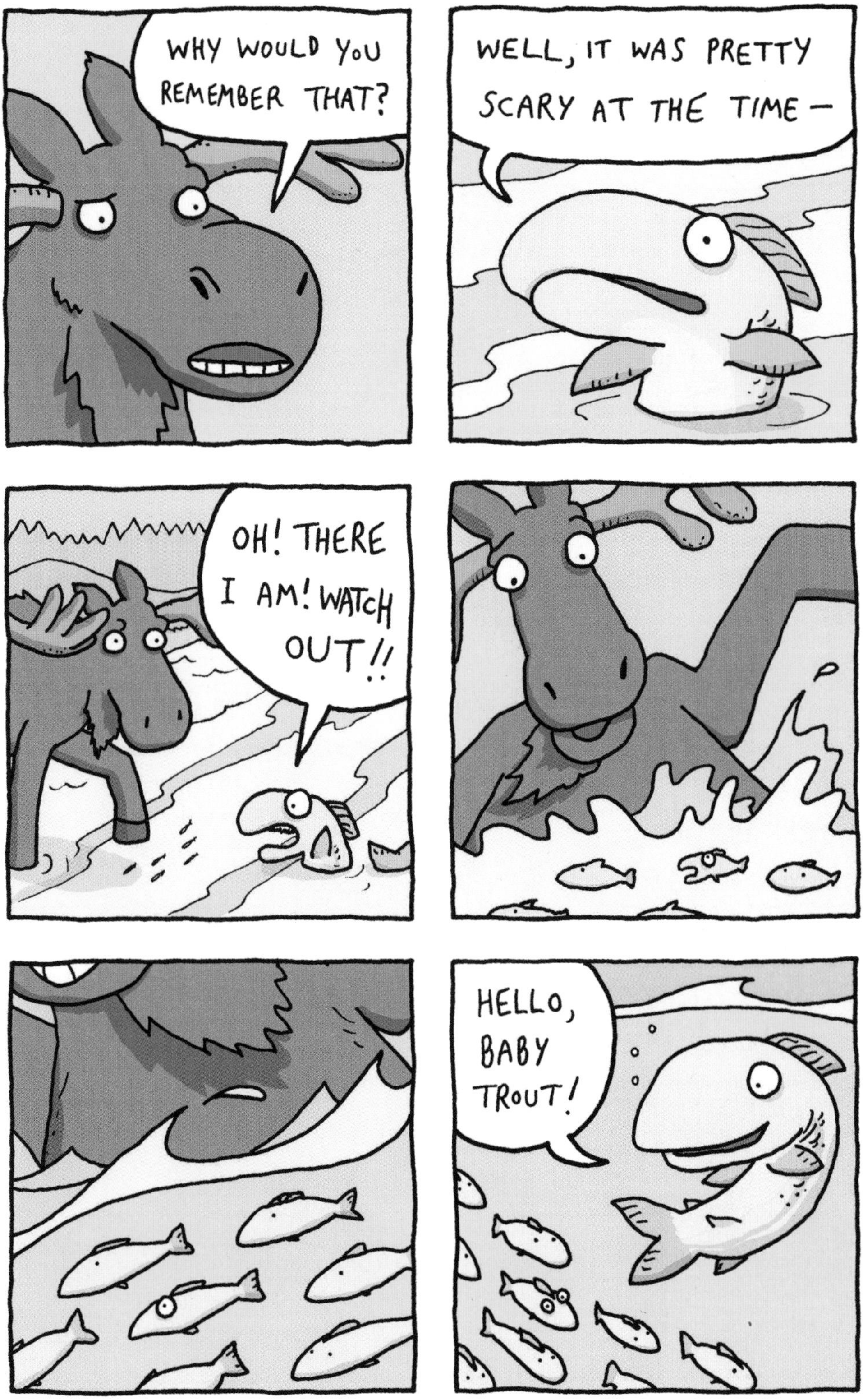
WHY WOULD YOU REMEMBER THAT?
WELL, IT WAS PRETTY SCARY AT THE TIME –
OH! THERE I AM! WATCH OUT!!
HELLO, BABY TROUT!

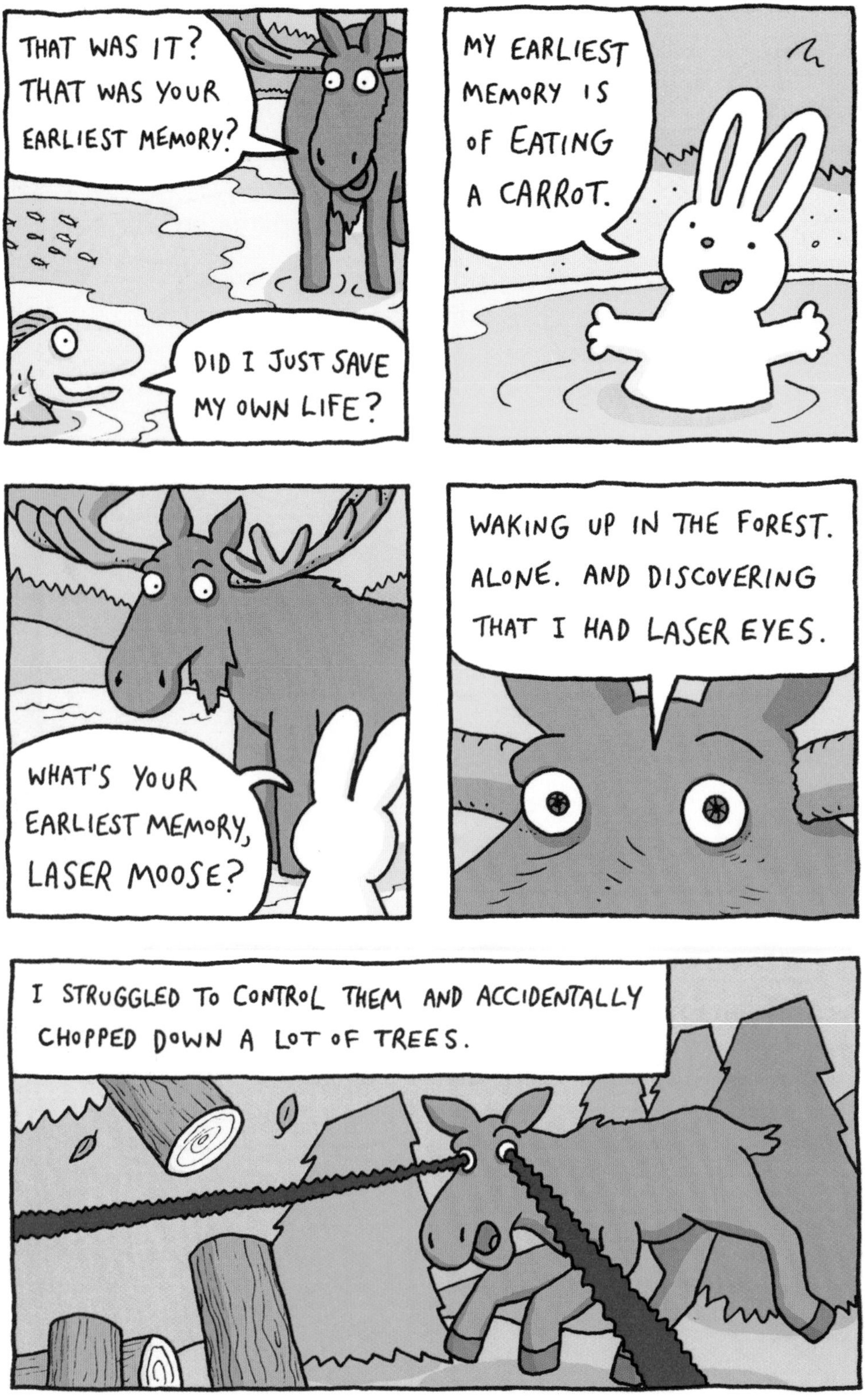
THAT WAS IT? THAT WAS YOUR EARLIEST MEMORY?
DID I JUST SAVE MY OWN LIFE?
MY EARLIEST MEMORY IS OF EATING A CARROT.
WHAT'S YOUR EARLIEST MEMORY, LASER MOOSE?
WAKING UP IN THE FOREST. ALONE. AND DISCOVERING THAT I HAD LASER EYES.
I STRUGGLED TO CONTROL THEM AND ACCIDENTALLY CHOPPED DOWN A LOT OF TREES.

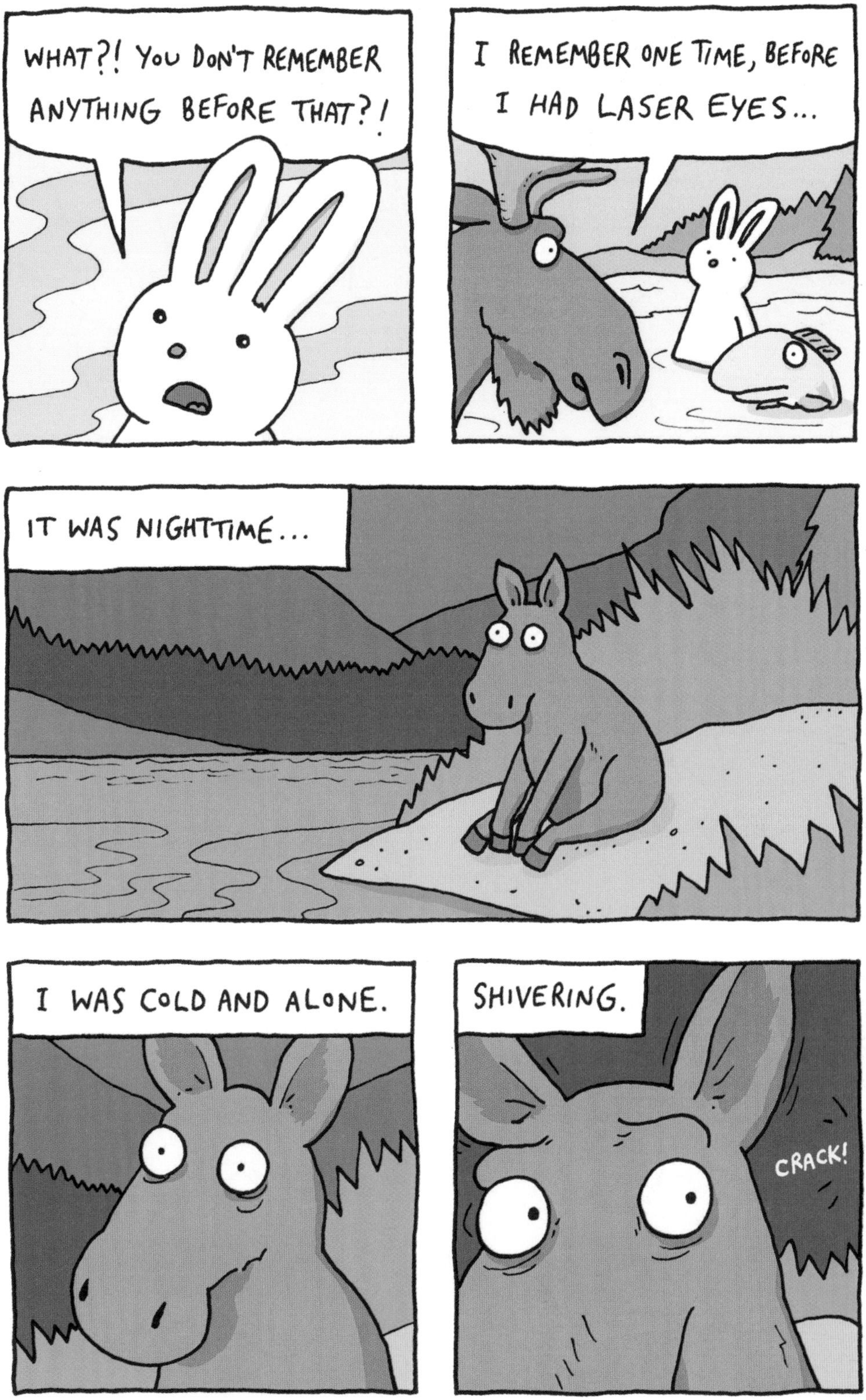
WHAT?! YOU DON'T REMEMBER ANYTHING BEFORE THAT?!
I REMEMBER ONE TIME, BEFORE I HAD LASER EYES...
IT WAS NIGHTTIME...
I WAS COLD AND ALONE.
SHIVERING.
CRACK!

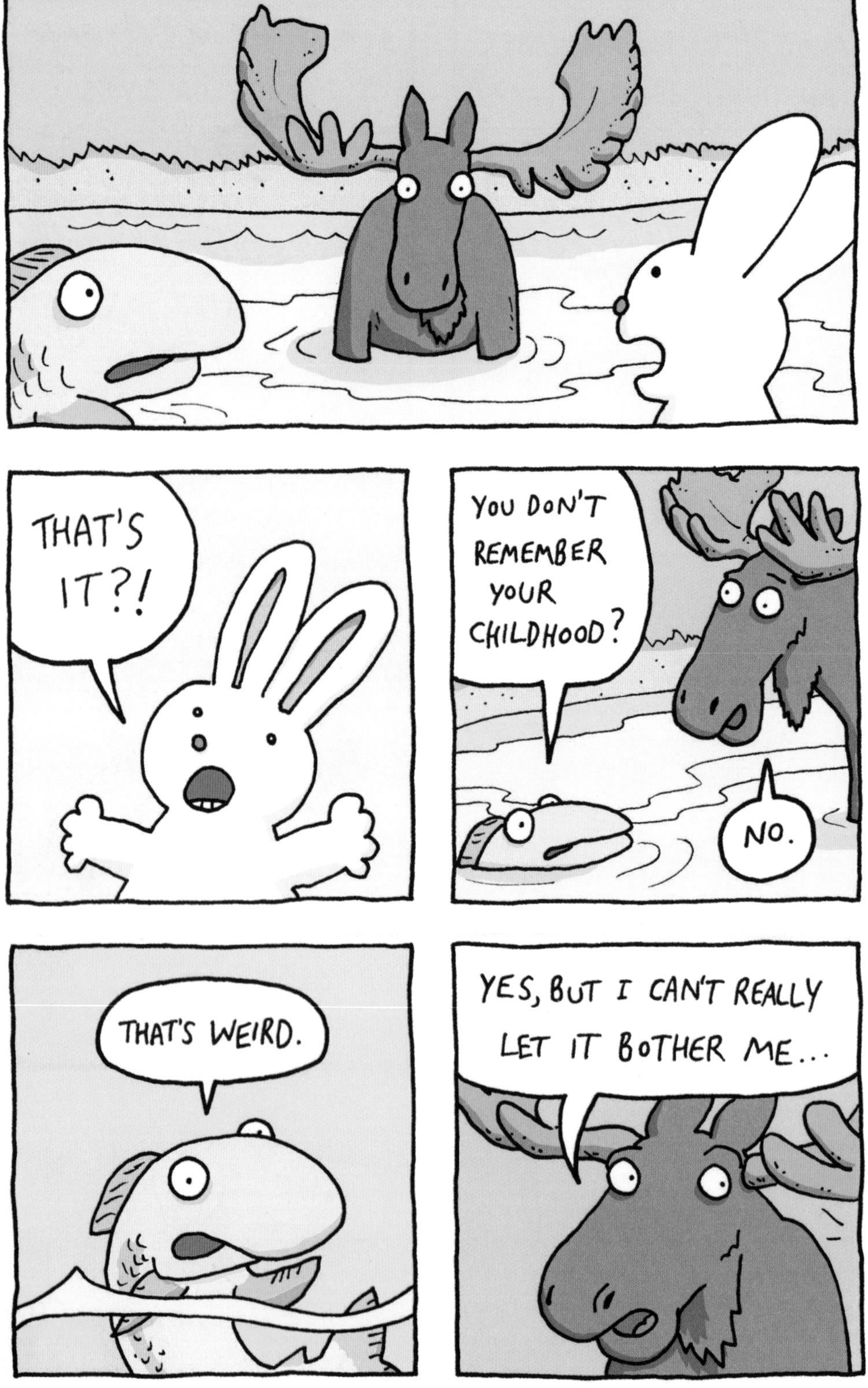
THAT'S IT?!
YOU DON'T REMEMBER YOUR CHILDHOOD?
NO.
THAT'S WEIRD.
YES, BUT I CAN'T REALLY LET IT BOTHER ME...

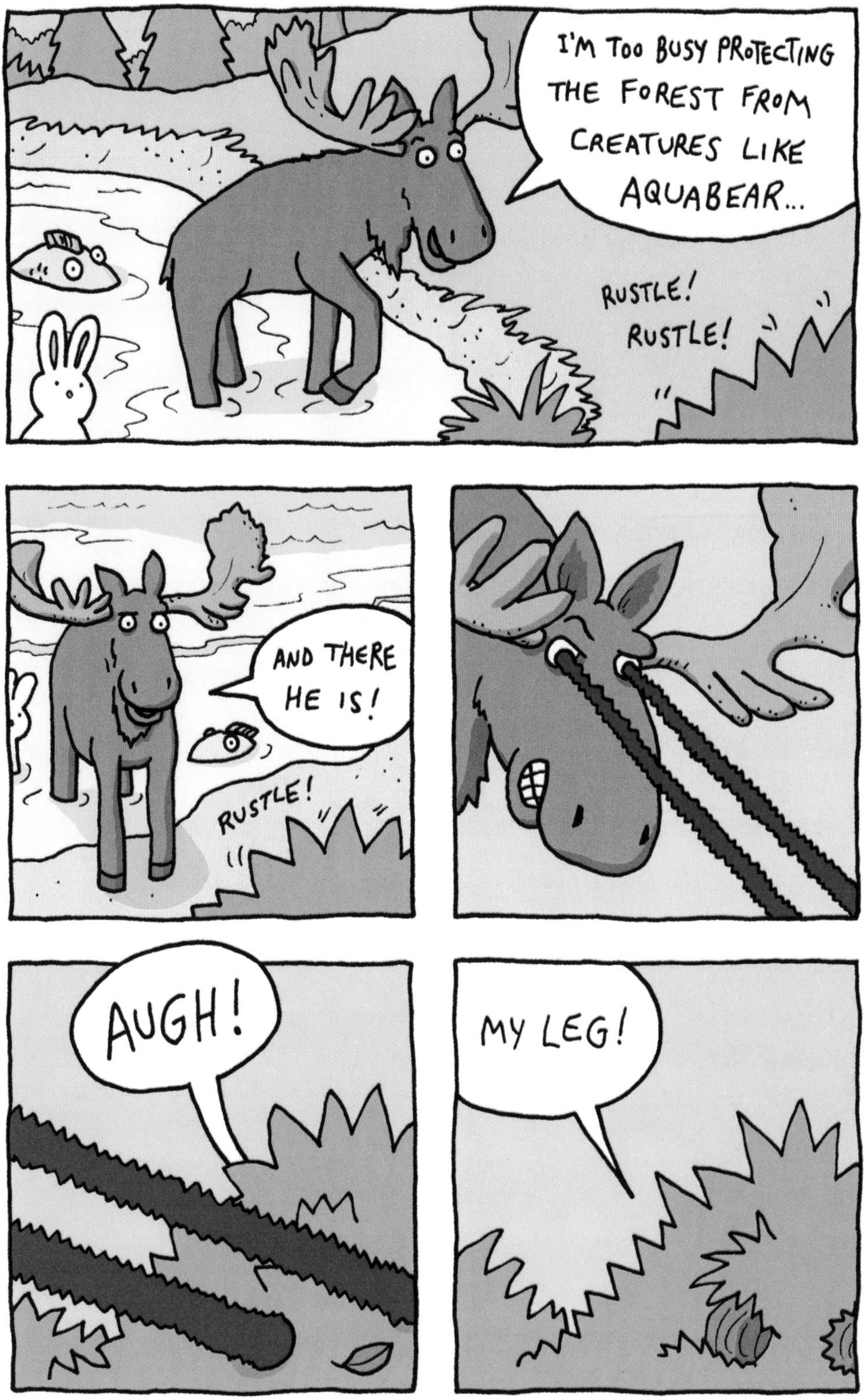
I'M TOO BUSY PROTECTING THE FOREST FROM CREATURES LIKE AQUABEAR...
RUSTLE! RUSTLE!
AND THERE HE IS!
RUSTLE!
AUGH!
MY LEG!

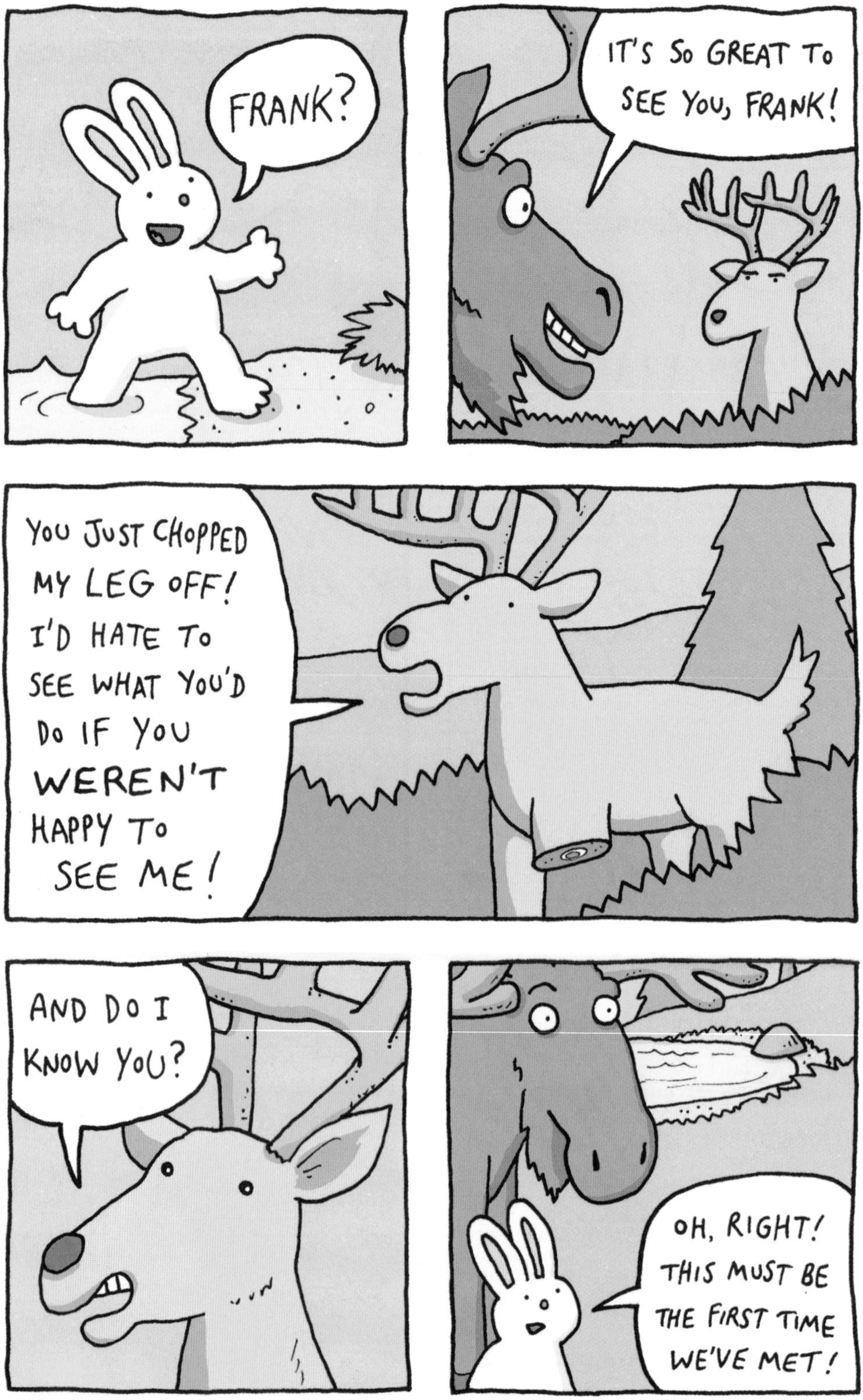
FRANK?
IT'S SO GREAT TO SEE YOU, FRANK!
YOU JUST CHOPPED MY LEG OFF! I'D HATE TO SEE WHAT YOU'D DO IF YOU WEREN'T HAPPY TO SEE ME!
AND DO I KNOW YOU?
OH, RIGHT! THIS MUST BE THE FIRST TIME WE'VE MET!

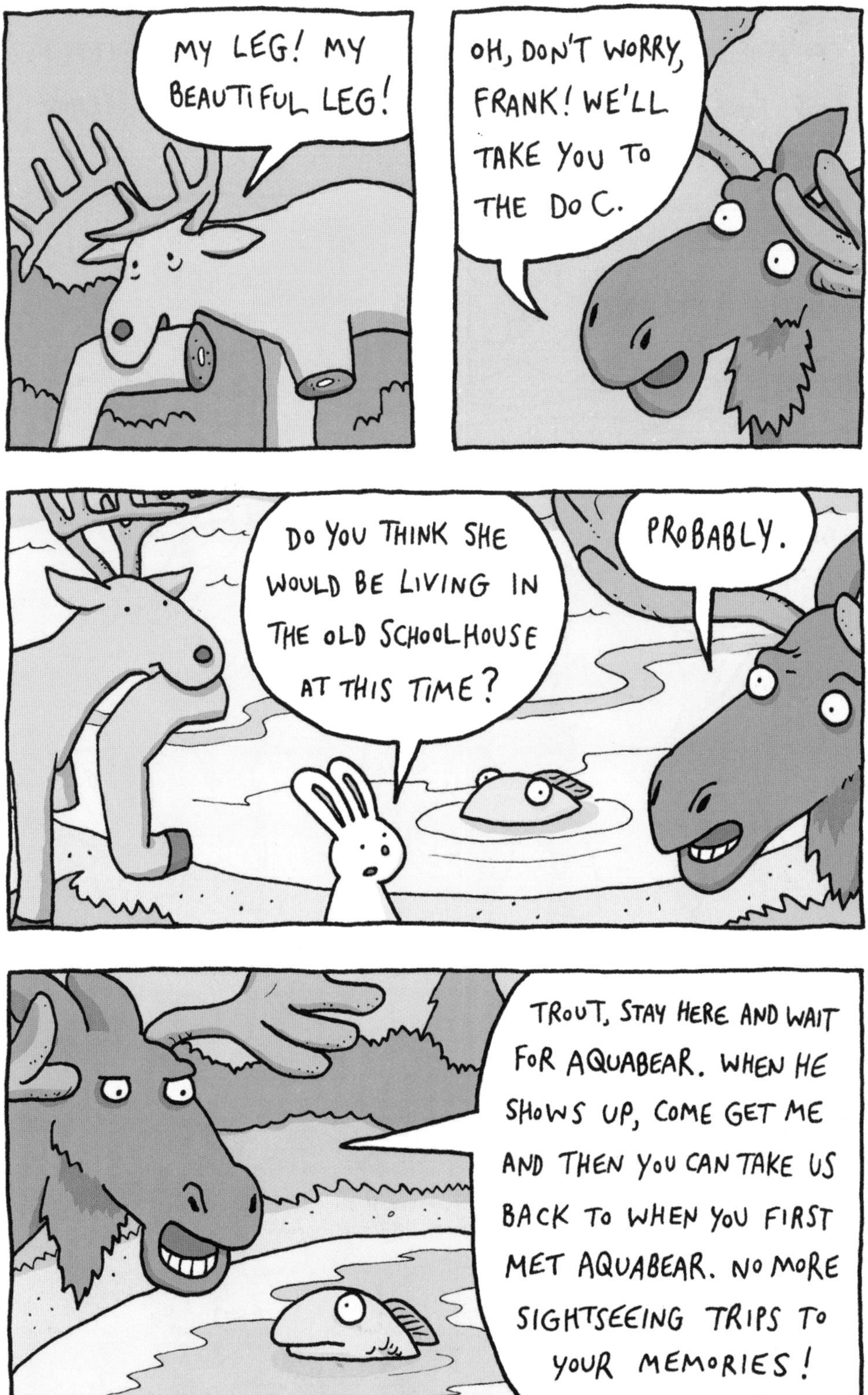
MY LEG! MY BEAUTIFUL LEG!
OH, DON'T WORRY, FRANK! WE'LL TAKE YOU TO THE DOC.
DO YOU THINK SHE WOULD BE LIVING IN THE OLD SCHOOLHOUSE AT THIS TIME?
PROBABLY.
TROUT, STAY HERE AND WAIT FOR AQUABEAR. WHEN HE SHOWS UP, COME GET ME AND THEN YOU CAN TAKE US BACK TO WHEN YOU FIRST MET AQUABEAR. NO MORE SIGHTSEEING TRIPS TO YOUR MEMORIES!

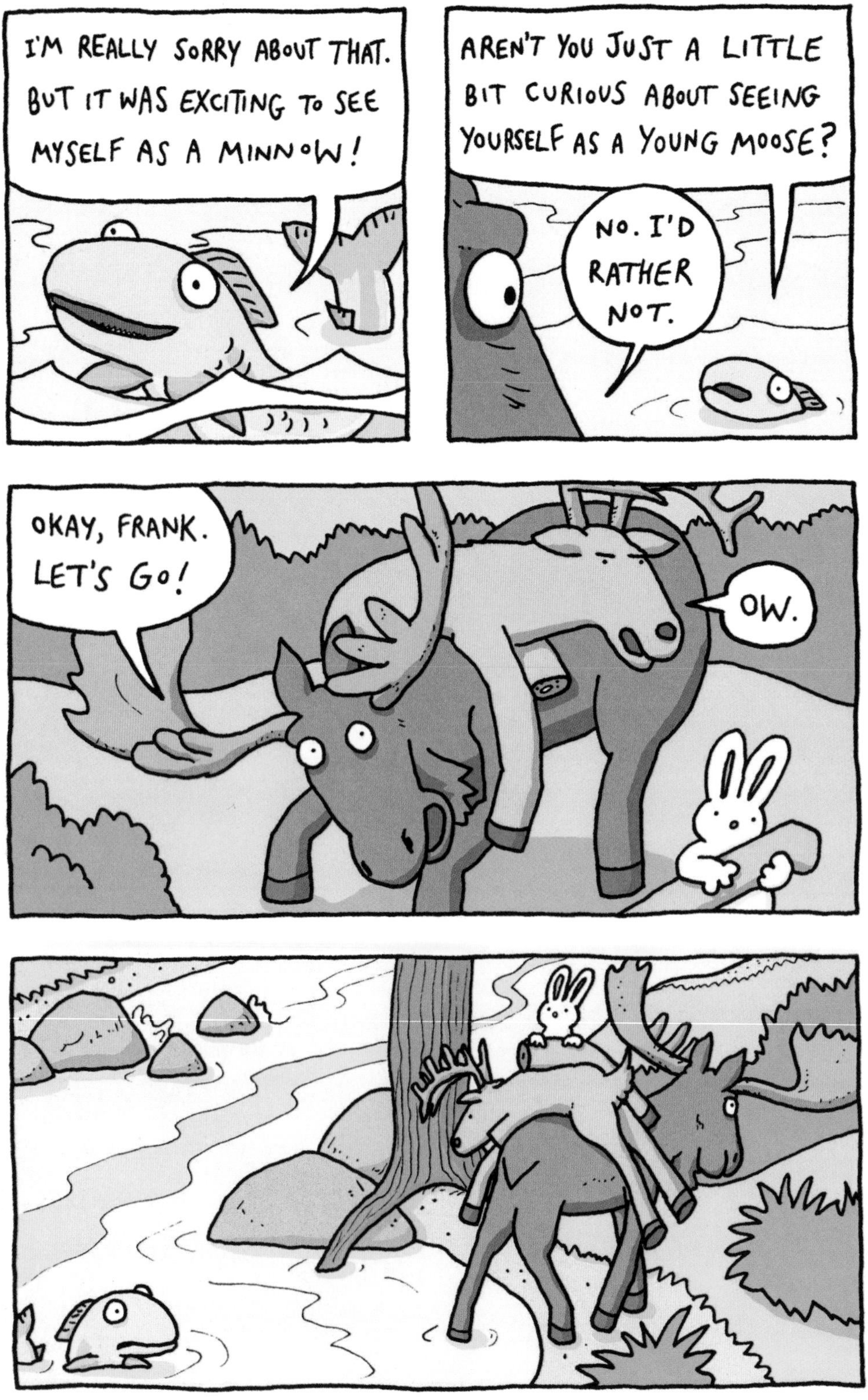
I'M REALLY SORRY ABOUT THAT. BUT IT WAS EXCITING TO SEE MYSELF AS A MINNOW!
AREN'T YOU JUST A LITTLE BIT CURIOUS ABOUT SEEING YOURSELF AS A YOUNG MOOSE?
NO. I'D RATHER NOT.
OKAY, FRANK. LET'S GO!
OW.

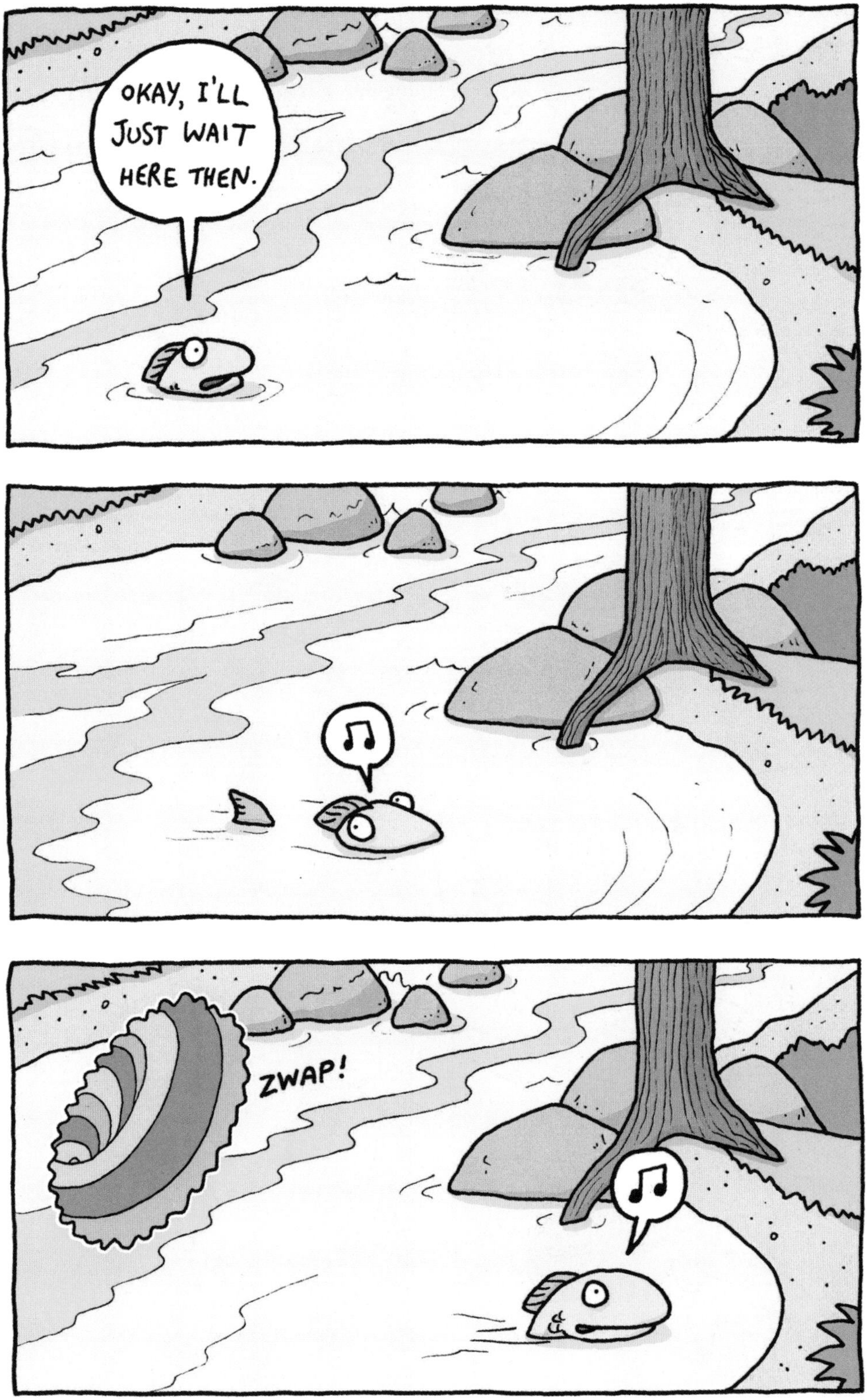
OKAY, I'LL JUST WAIT HERE THEN.
ZWAP!

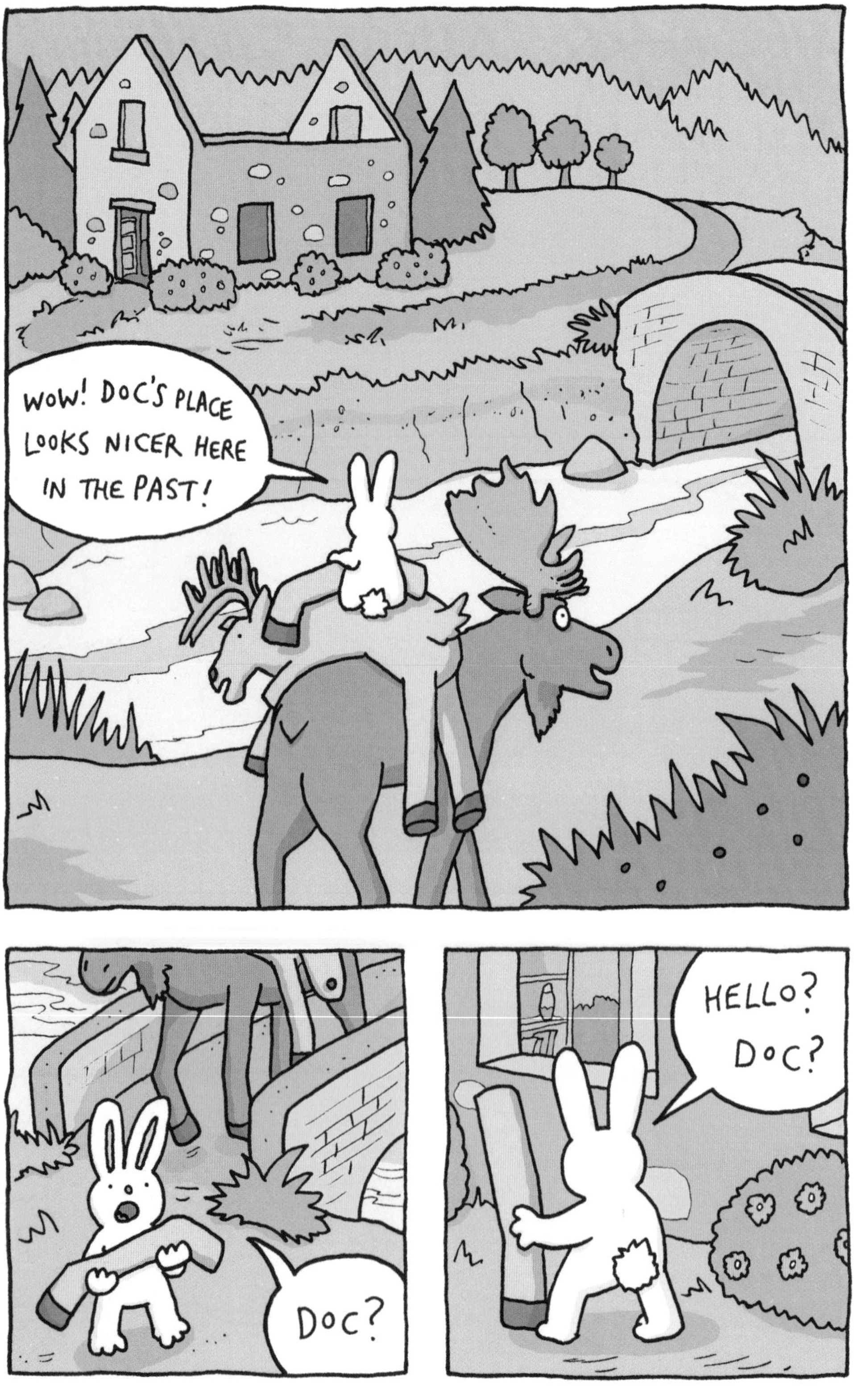
WOW! DOC'S PLACE LOOKS NICER HERE IN THE PAST!
DOC?
HELLO? DOC?

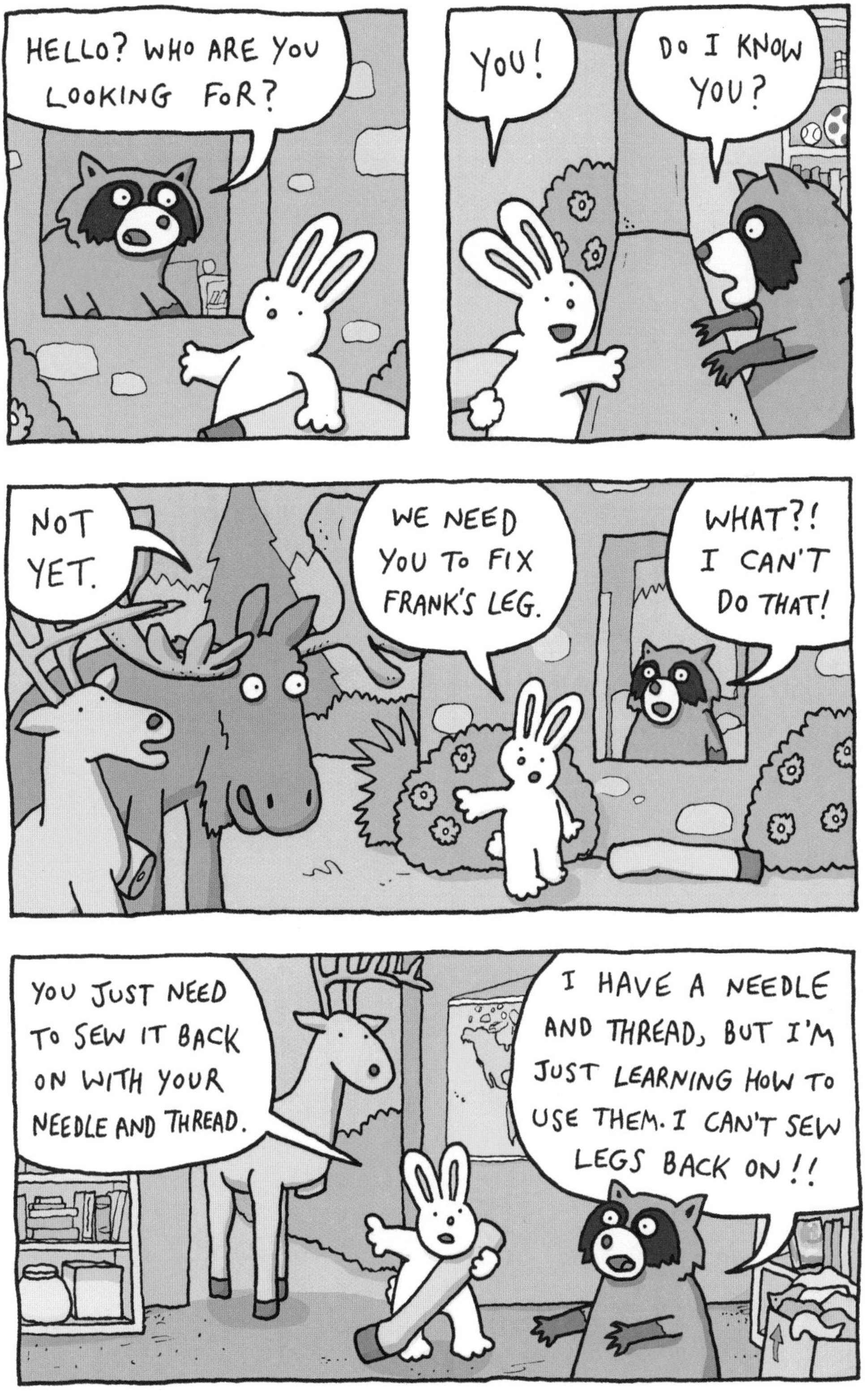
HELLO? WHO ARE YOU LOOKING FOR?
YOU!
DO I KNOW YOU?
NOT YET.
WE NEED YOU TO FIX FRANK'S LEG.
WHAT?! I CAN'T DO THAT!
YOU JUST NEED TO SEW IT BACK ON WITH YOUR NEEDLE AND THREAD.
I HAVE A NEEDLE AND THREAD, BUT I'M JUST LEARNING HOW TO USE THEM. I CAN'T SEW LEGS BACK ON!!

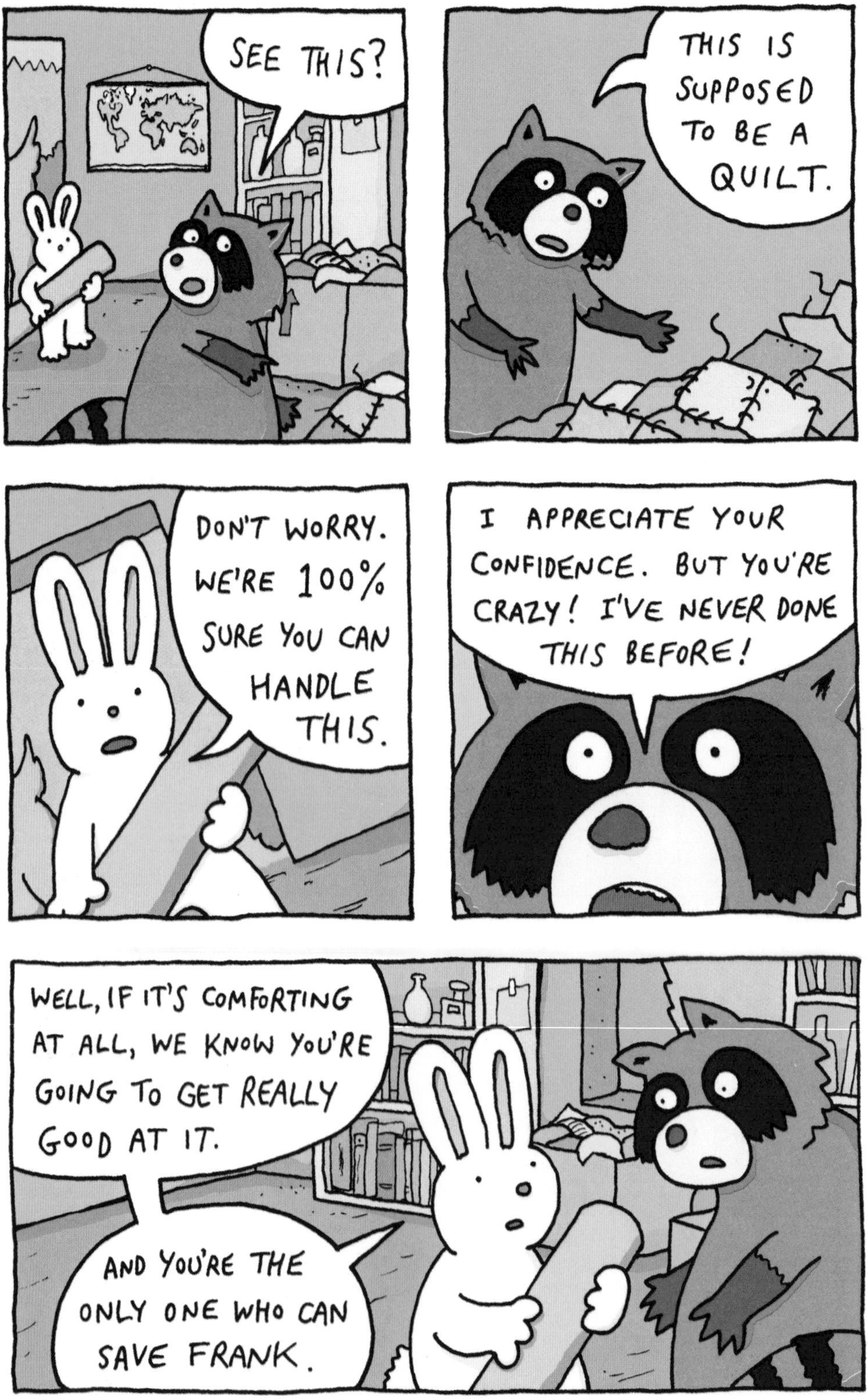
SEE THIS?
THIS IS SUPPOSED TO BE A QUILT.
DON'T WORRY. WE'RE 100% SURE YOU CAN HANDLE THIS.
I APPRECIATE YOUR CONFIDENCE. BUT YOU'RE CRAZY! I'VE NEVER DONE THIS BEFORE!
WELL, IF IT'S COMFORTING AT ALL, WE KNOW YOU'RE GOING TO GET REALLY GOOD AT IT.
AND YOU'RE THE ONLY ONE WHO CAN SAVE FRANK.

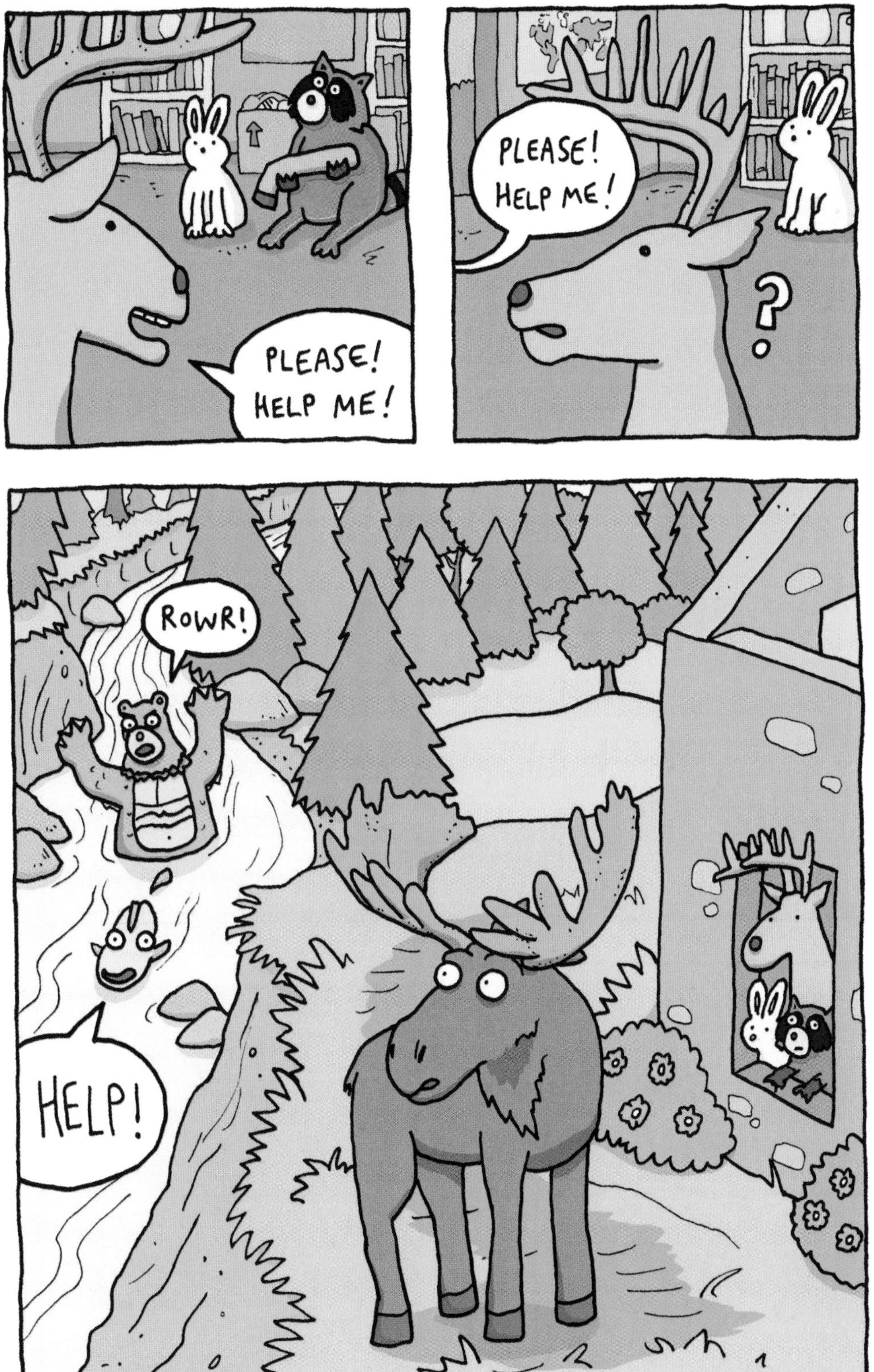
PLEASE! HELP ME!
PLEASE! HELP ME!
?
ROWR!
HELP!

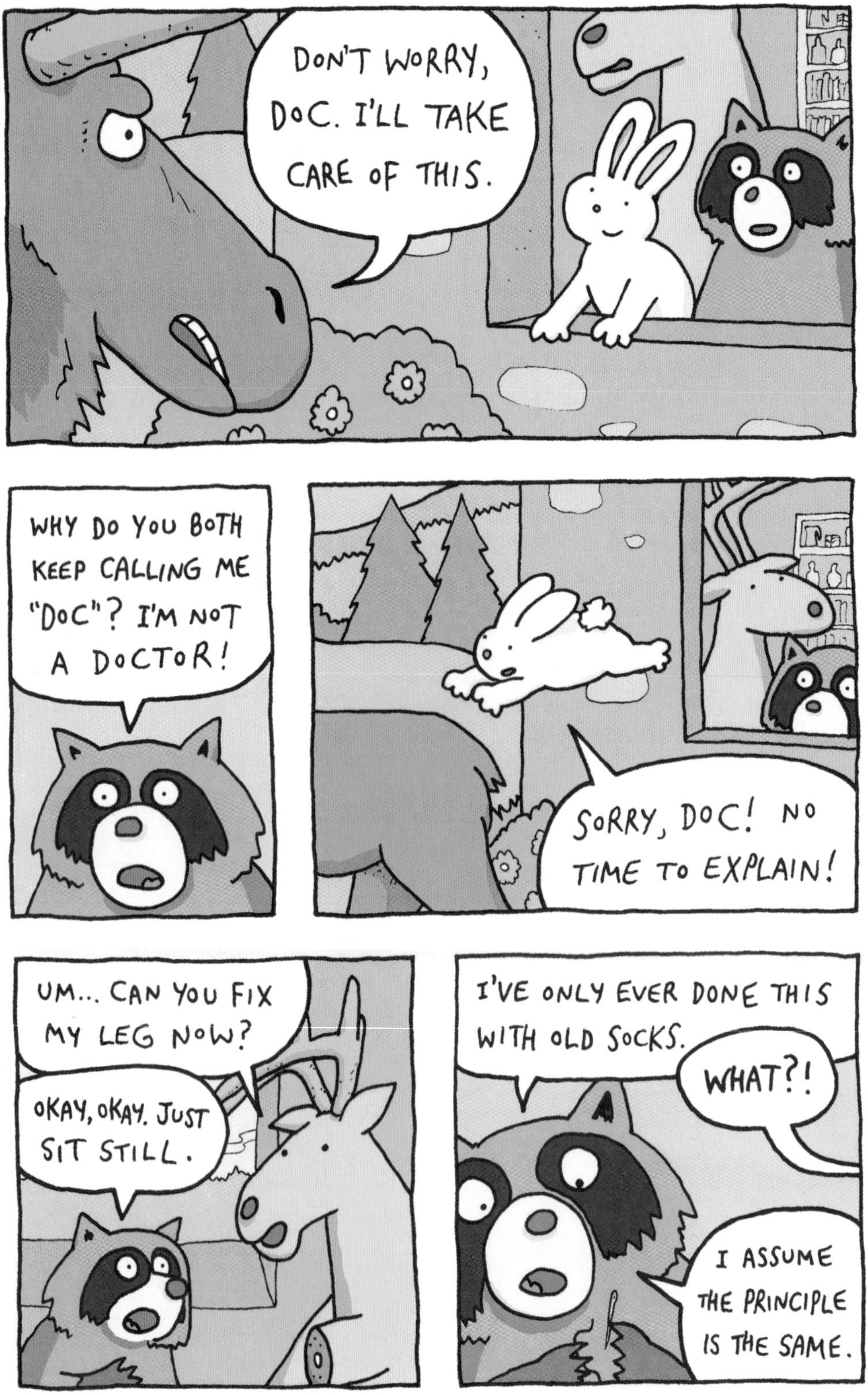
DON'T WORRY, DOC. I'LL TAKE CARE OF THIS.
WHY DO YOU BOTH KEEP CALLING ME "DOC"? I'M NOT A DOCTOR!
SORRY, DOC! NO TIME TO EXPLAIN!
UM... CAN YOU FIX MY LEG NOW?
OKAY, OKAY. JUST SIT STILL.
I'VE ONLY EVER DONE THIS WITH OLD SOCKS.
WHAT?!
I ASSUME THE PRINCIPLE IS THE SAME.

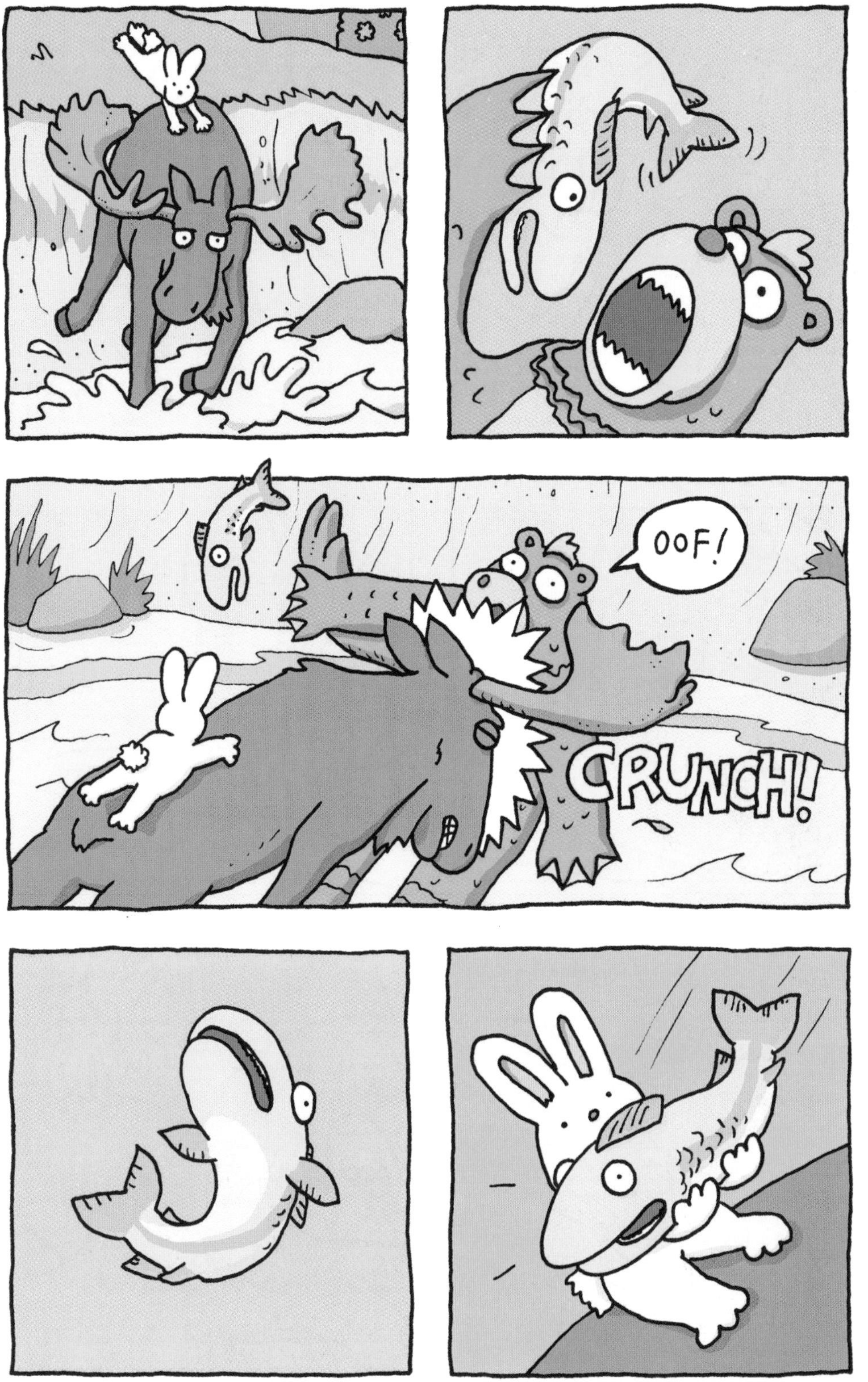
OOF!
CRUNCH!

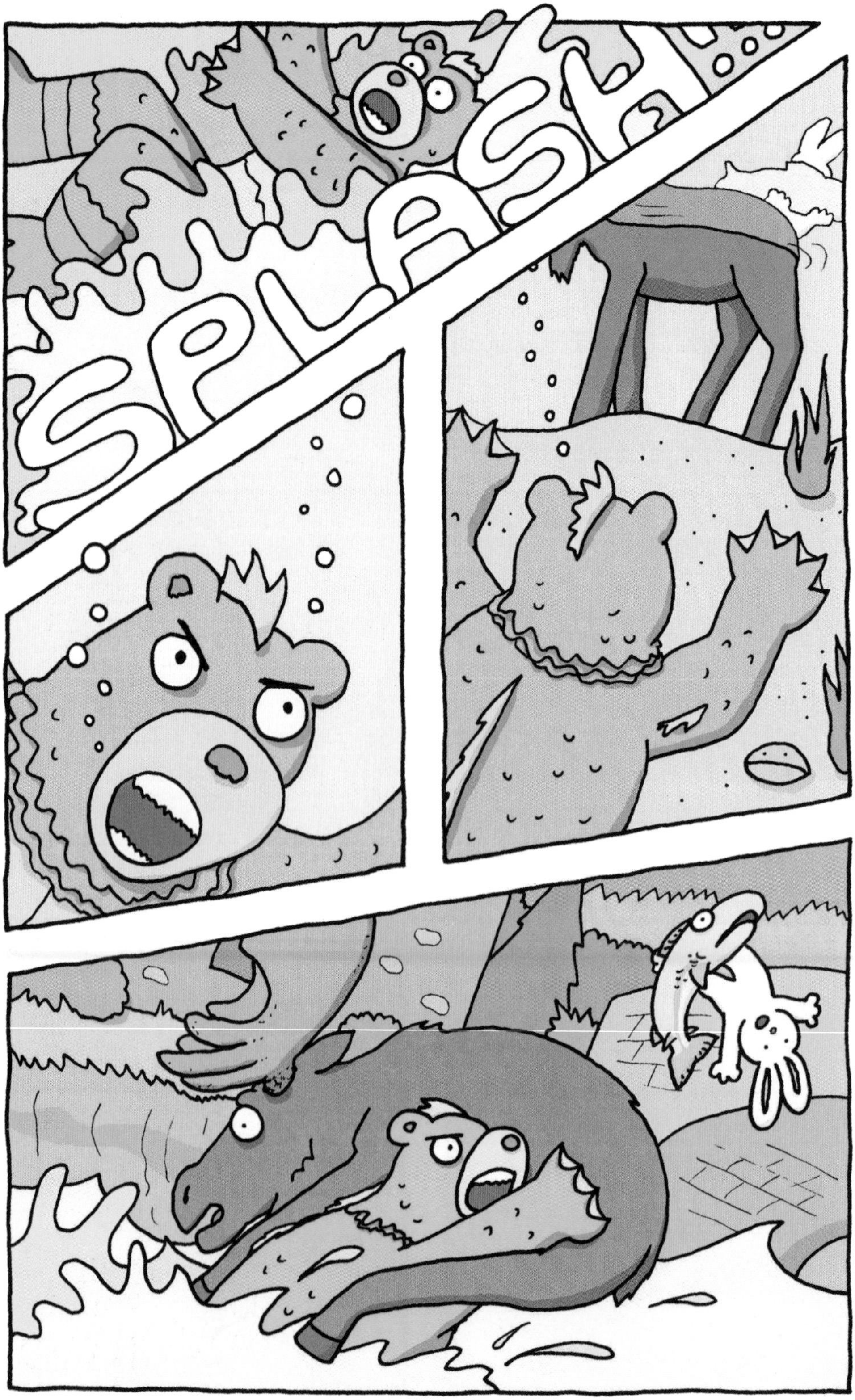
SPLASH

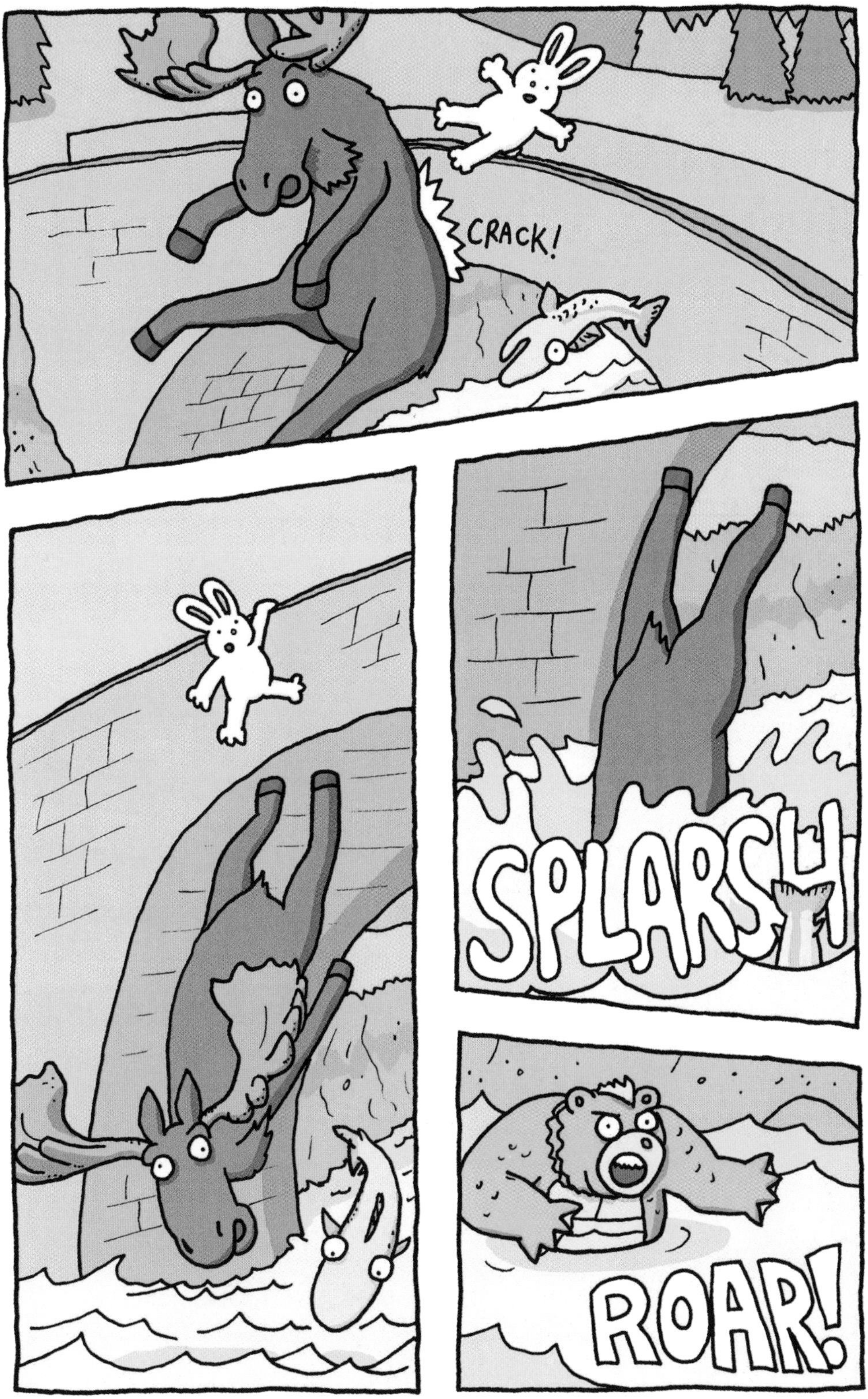
CRACK!
SPLARSH
ROAR!

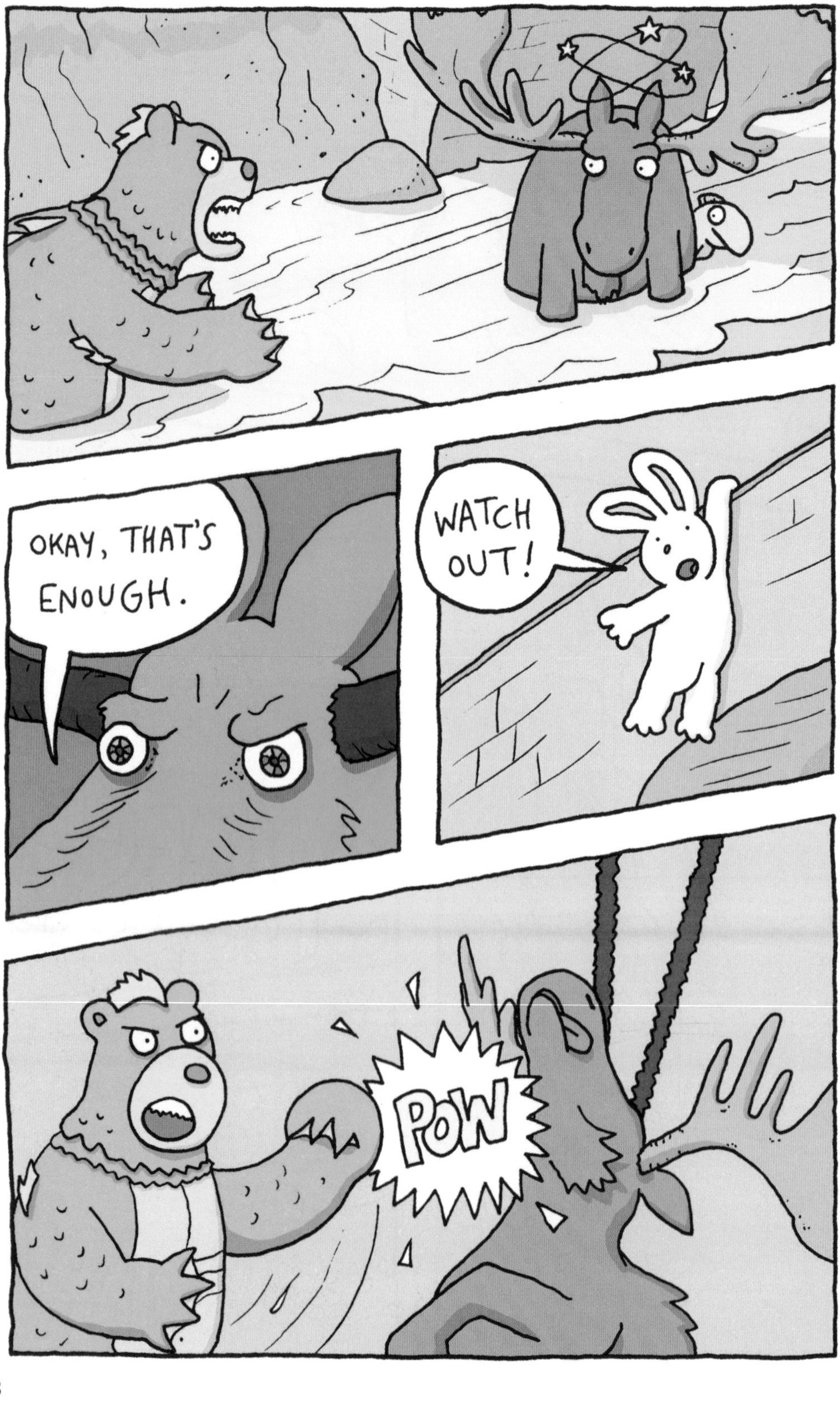
OKAY, THAT'S ENOUGH.
WATCH OUT!
POW

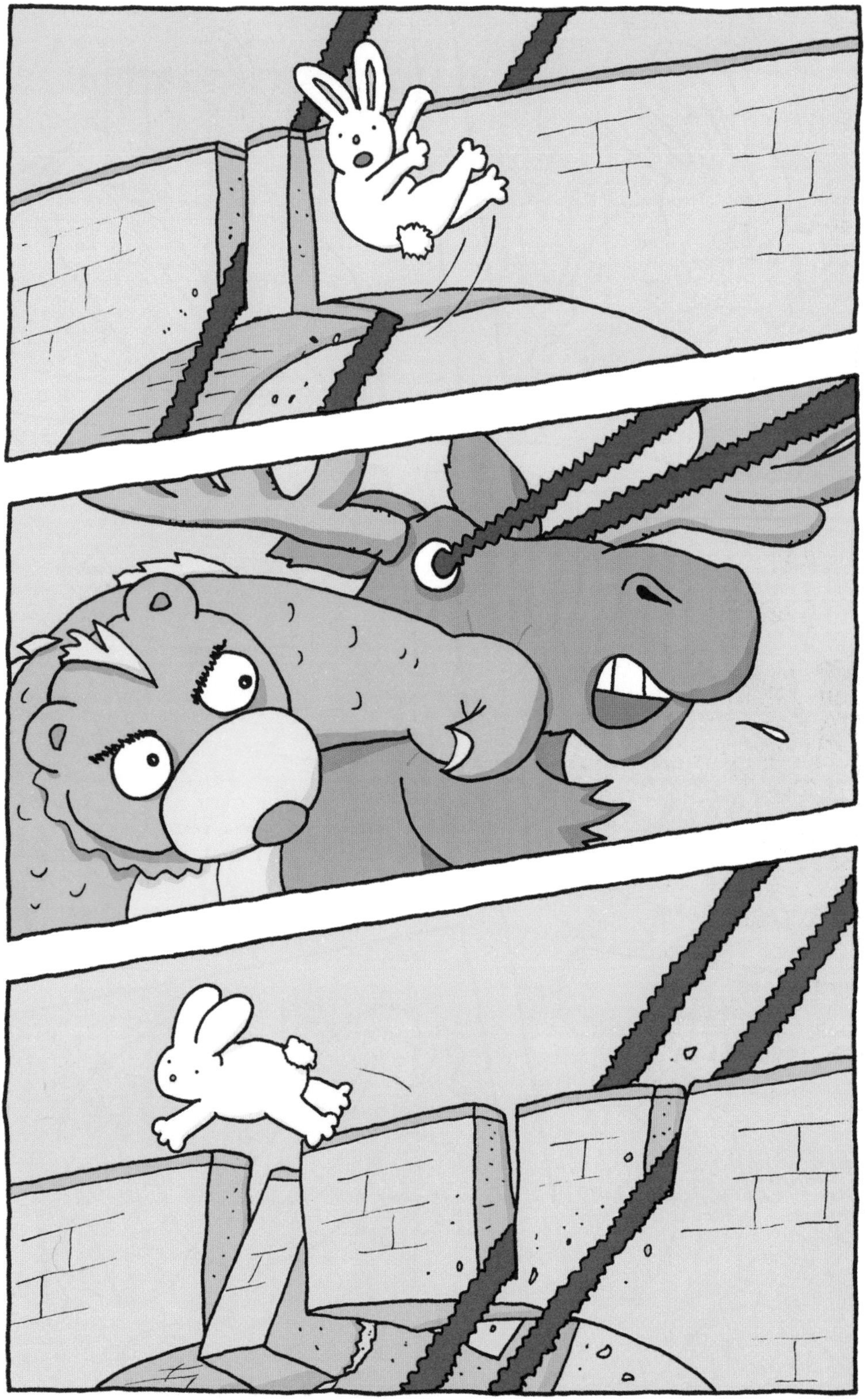

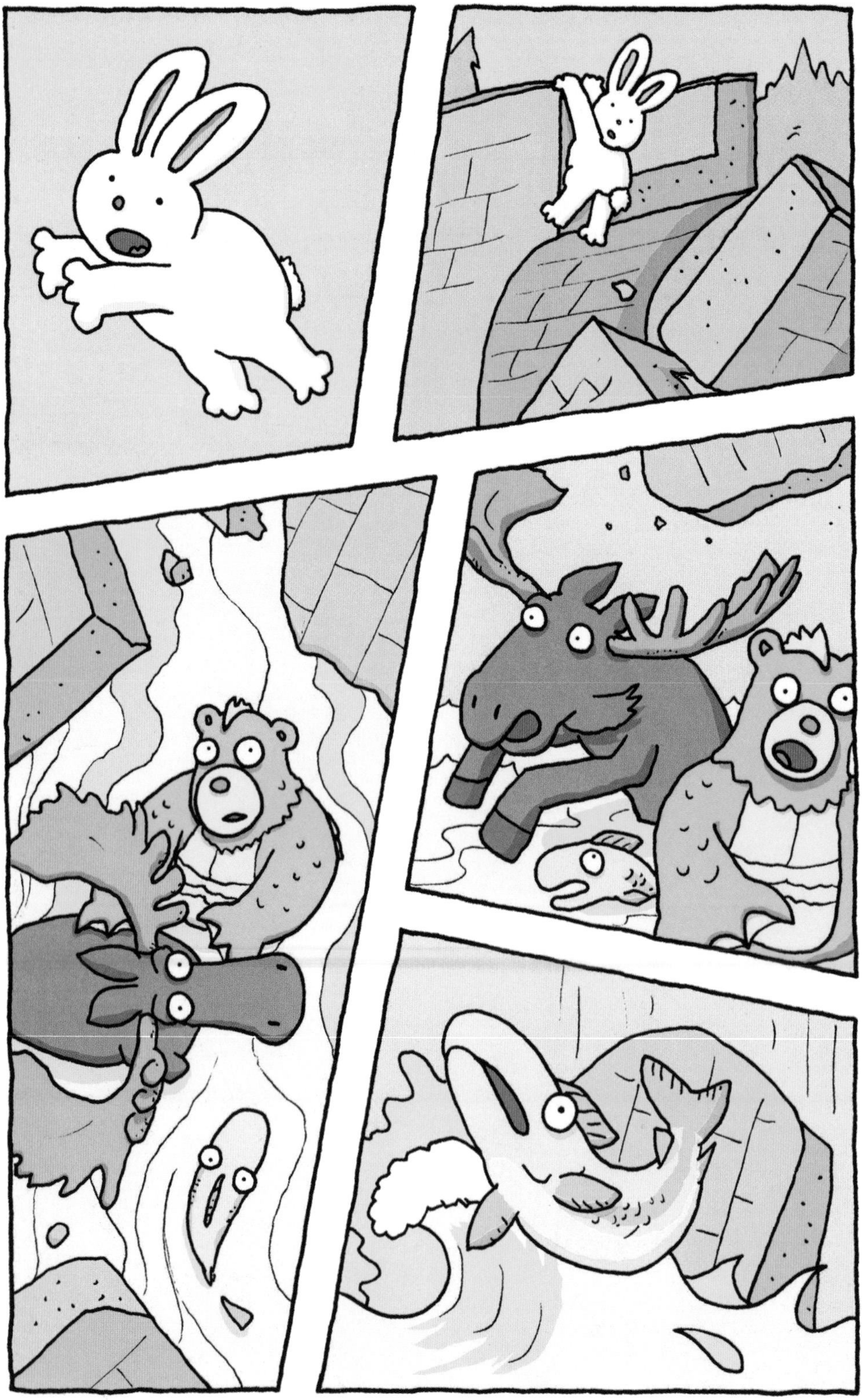

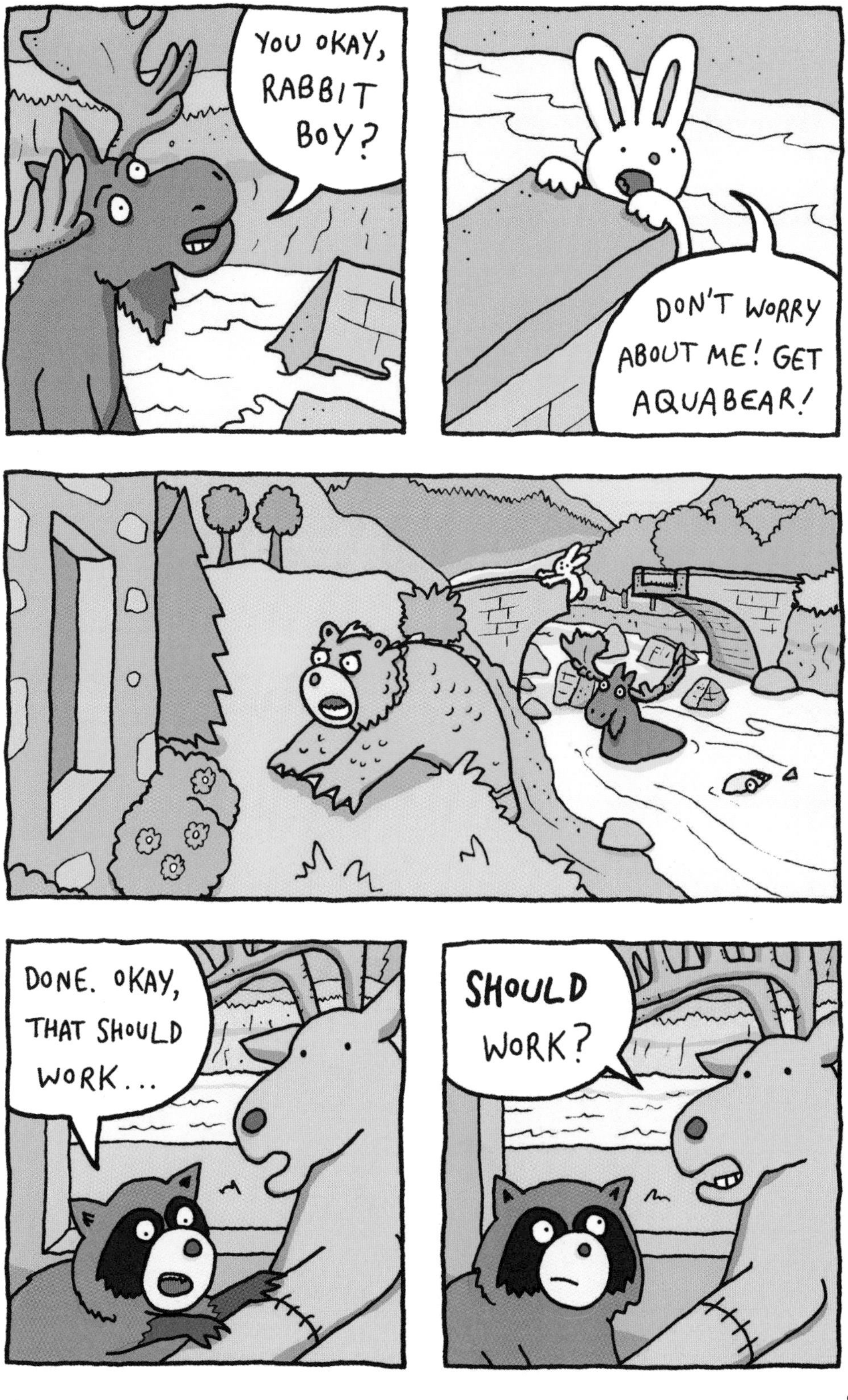
YOU OKAY, RABBIT BOY?
DON'T WORRY ABOUT ME! GET AQUABEAR!
DONE. OKAY, THAT SHOULD WORK...
SHOULD WORK?

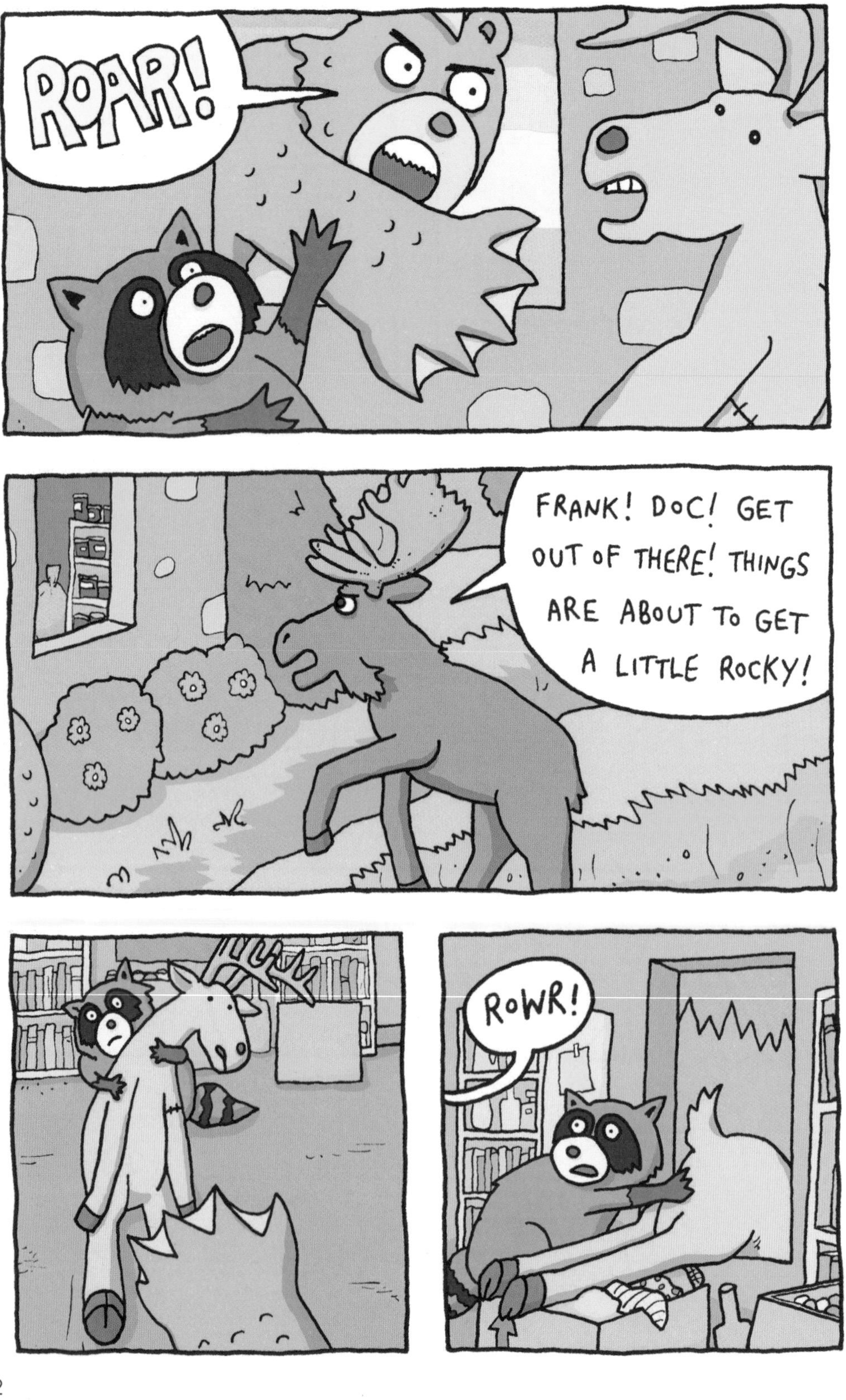
ROAR!
FRANK! DOC! GET OUT OF THERE! THINGS ARE ABOUT TO GET A LITTLE ROCKY!
ROWR!

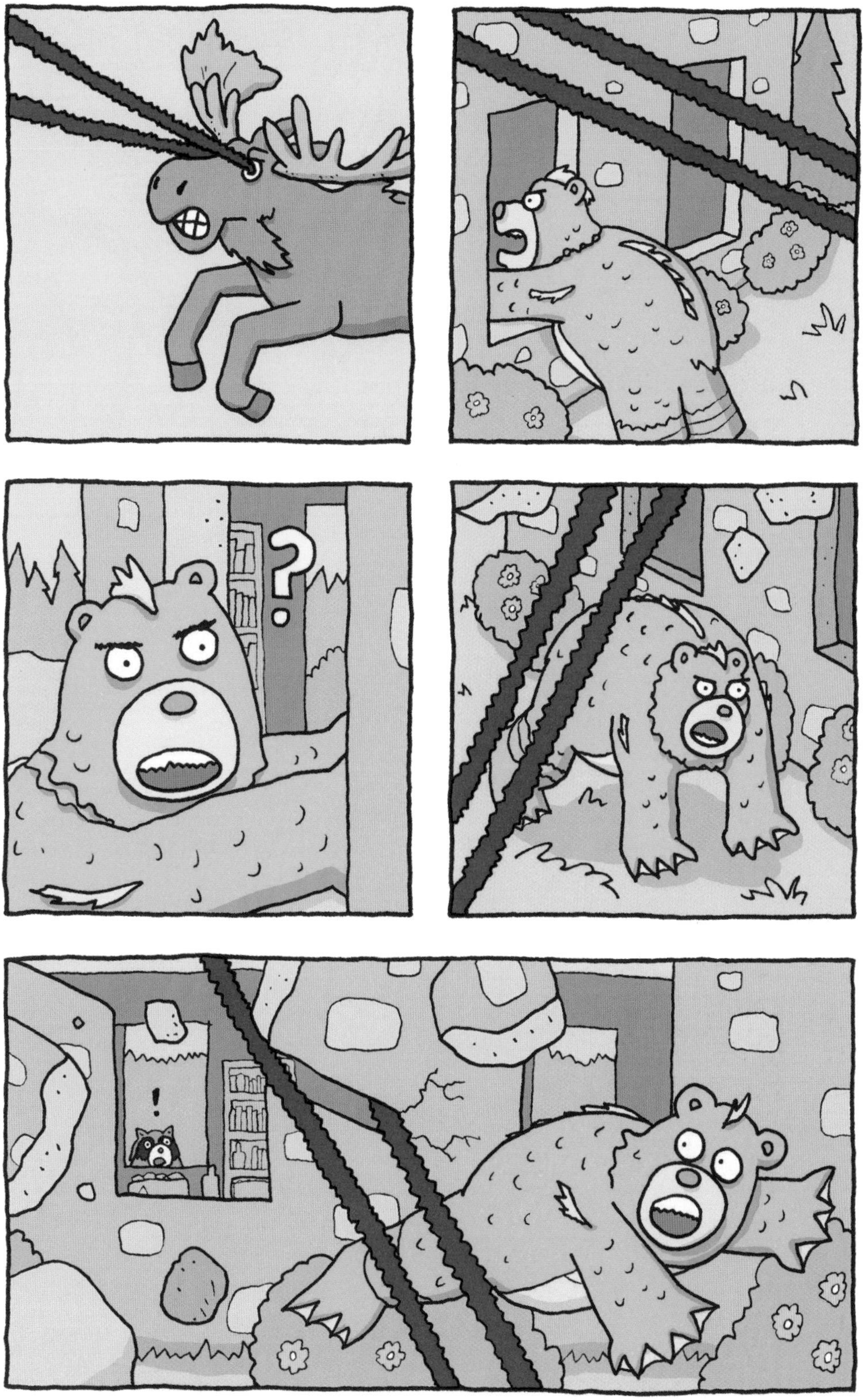
?
!

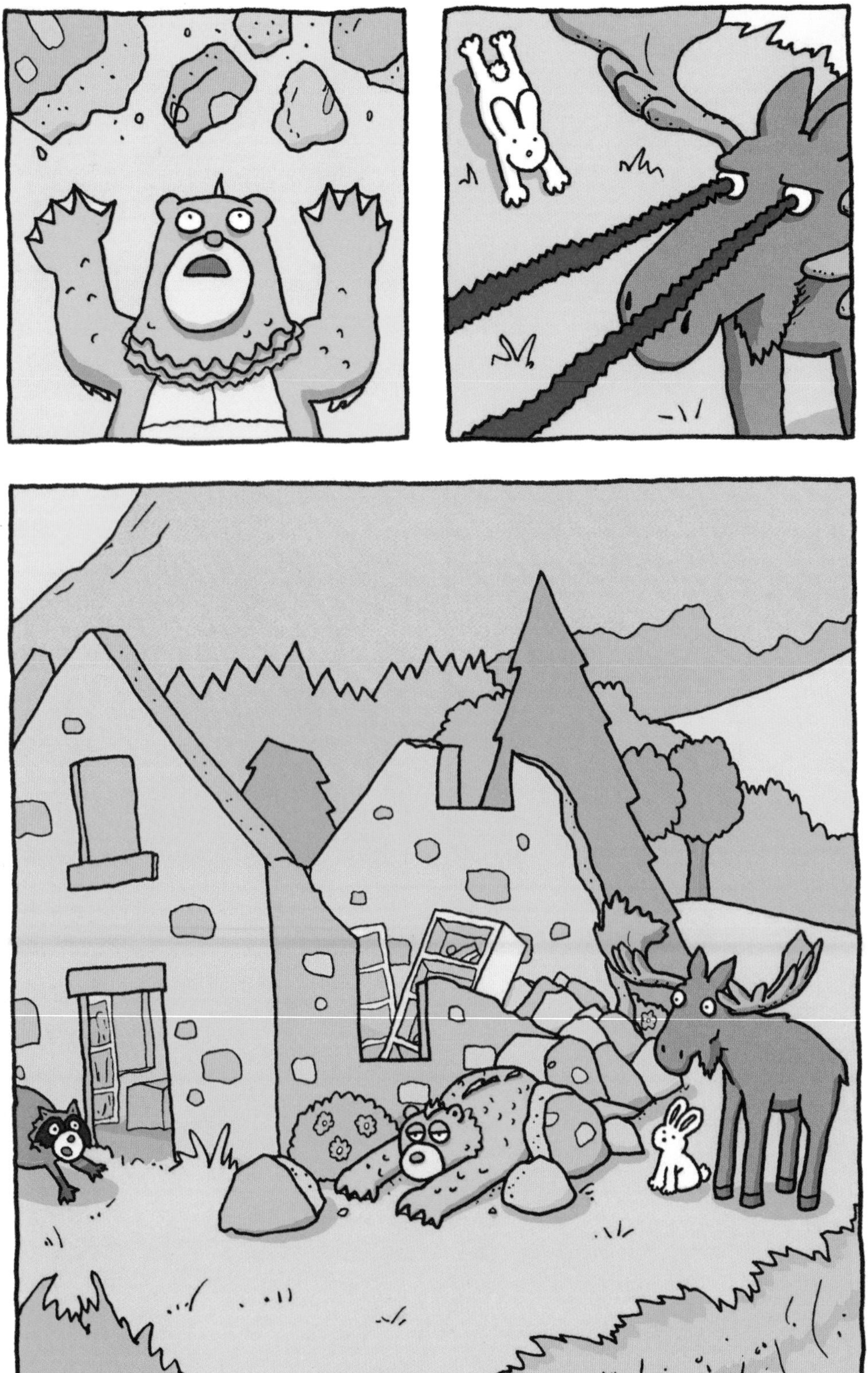

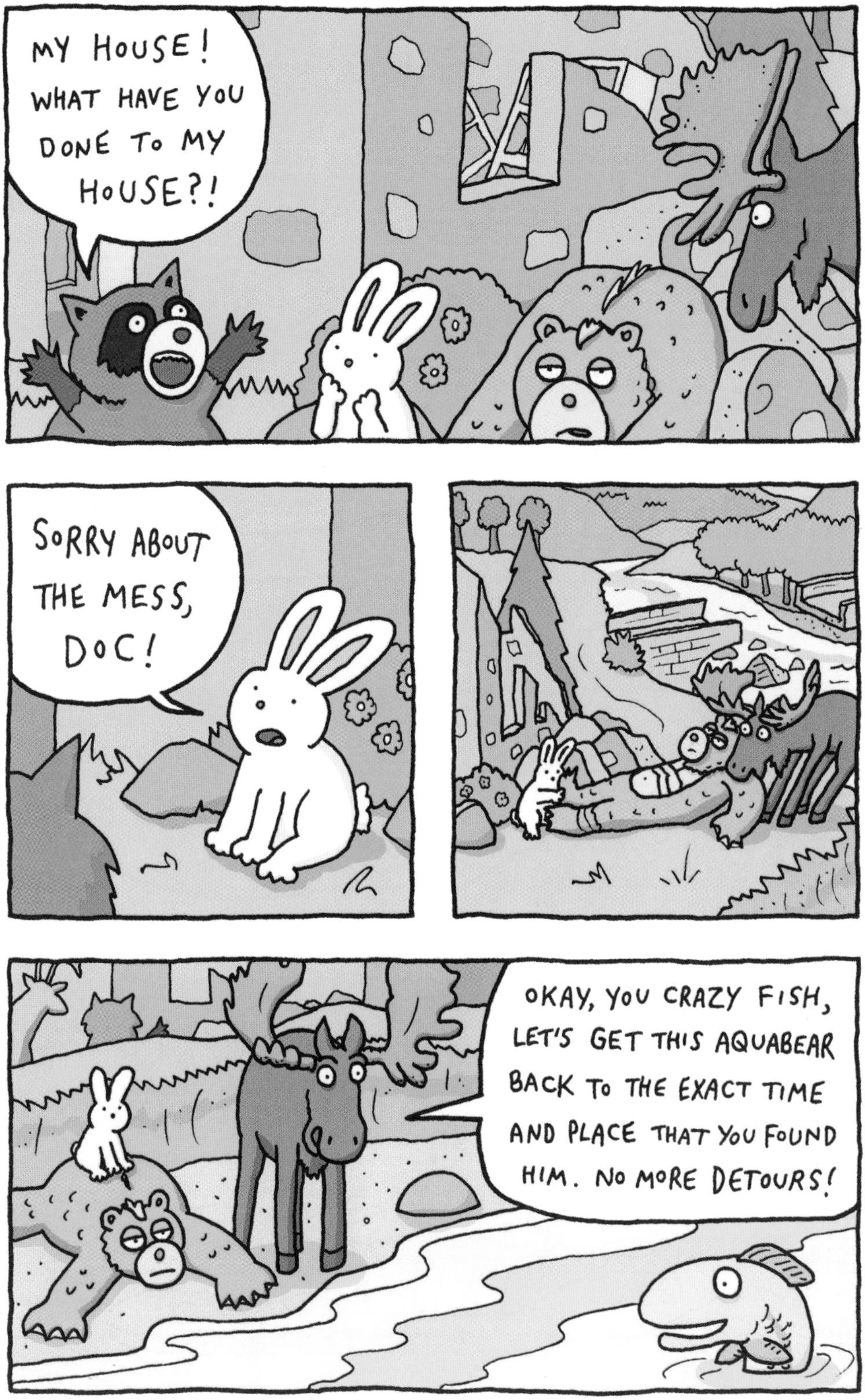
MY HOUSE! WHAT HAVE YOU DONE TO MY HOUSE?!
SORRY ABOUT THE MESS, DOC!
OKAY, YOU CRAZY FISH, LET'S GET THIS AQUABEAR BACK TO THE EXACT TIME AND PLACE THAT YOU FOUND HIM. NO MORE DETOURS!

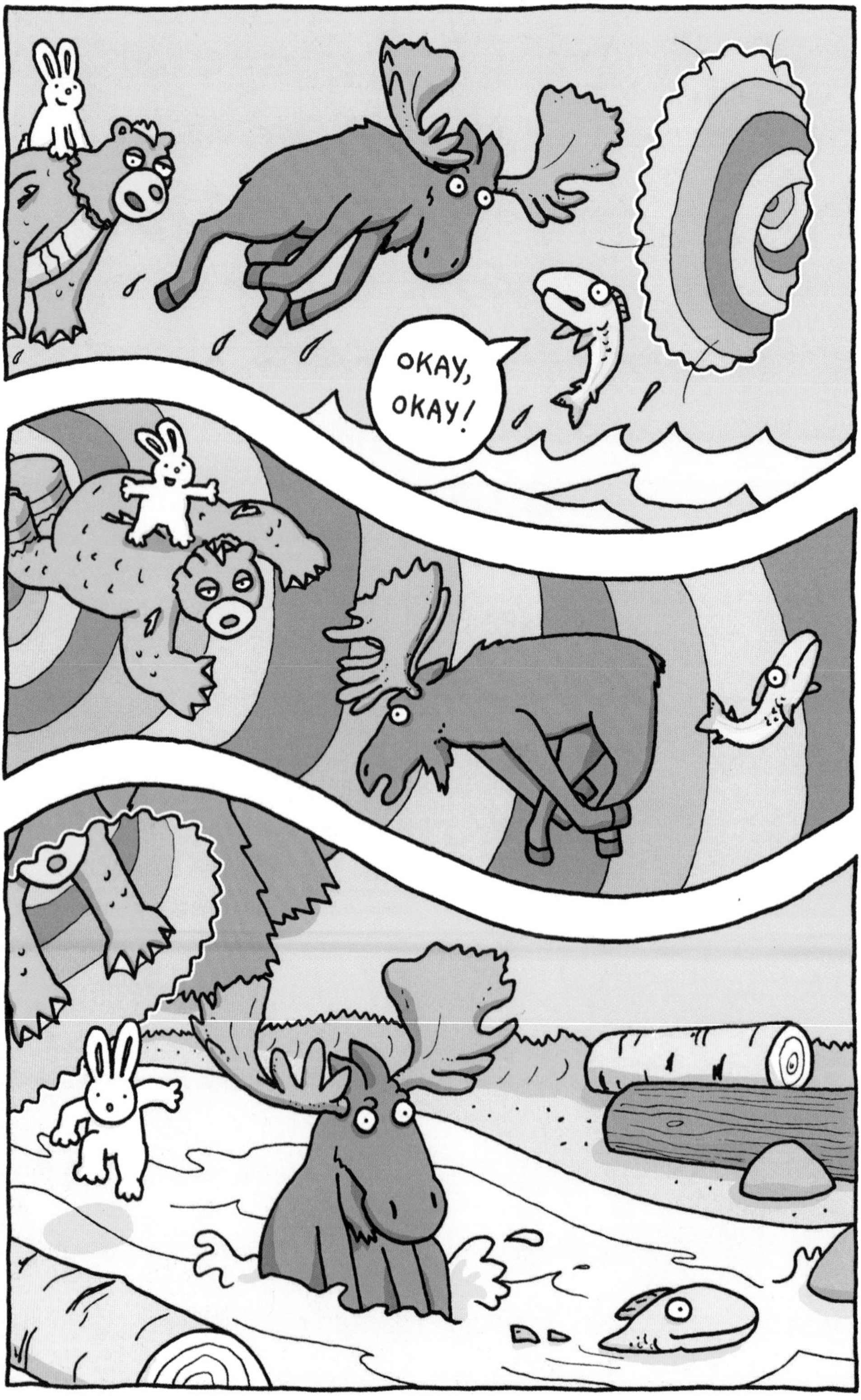
OKAY,
OKAY!

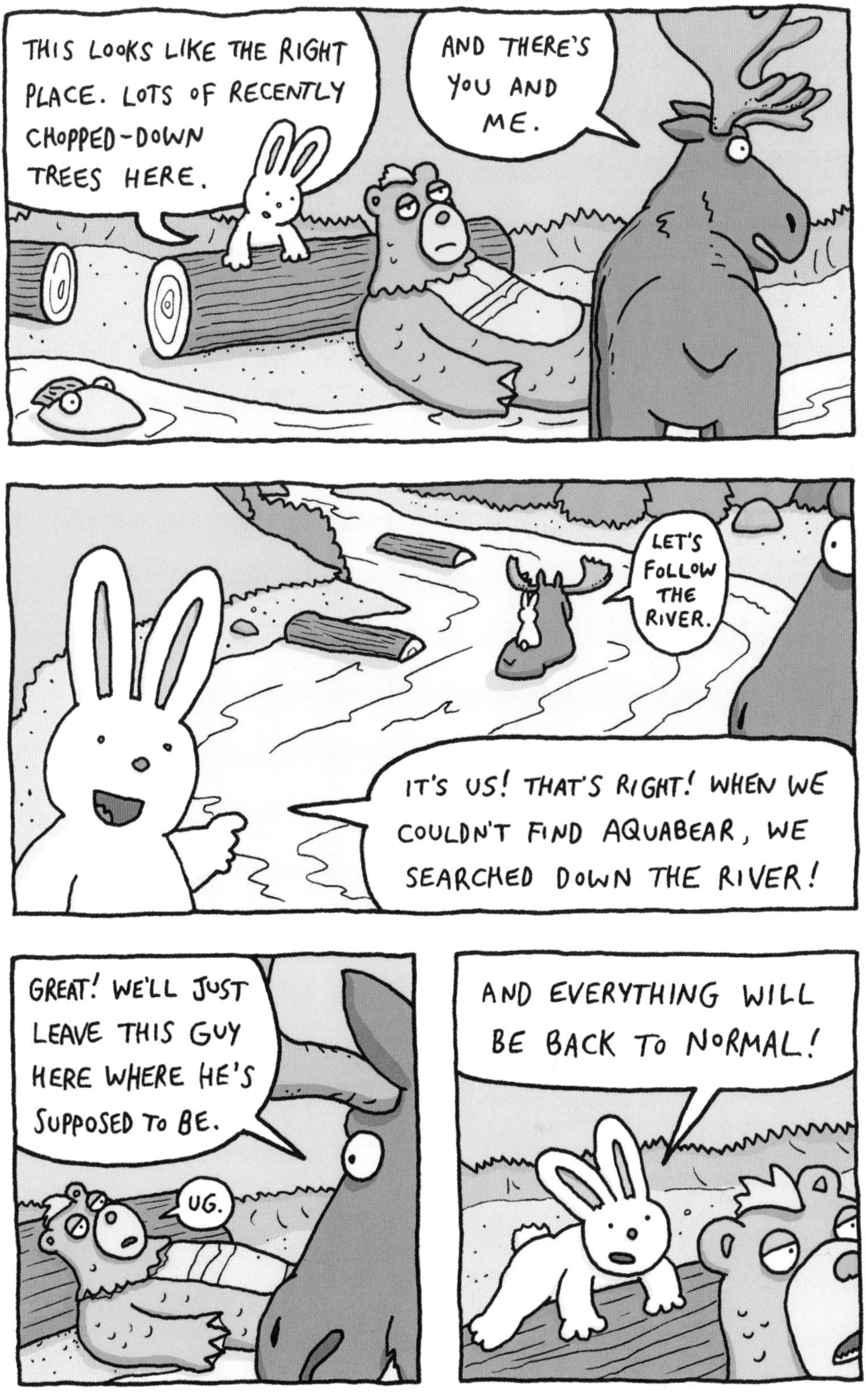
THIS LOOKS LIKE THE RIGHT PLACE. LOTS OF RECENTLY CHOPPED-DOWN TREES HERE.
AND THERE'S YOU AND ME.
LET'S FOLLOW THE RIVER.
IT'S US! THAT'S RIGHT! WHEN WE COULDN'T FIND AQUABEAR, WE SEARCHED DOWN THE RIVER!
GREAT! WE'LL JUST LEAVE THIS GUY HERE WHERE HE'S SUPPOSED TO BE.
UG.
AND EVERYTHING WILL BE BACK TO NORMAL!

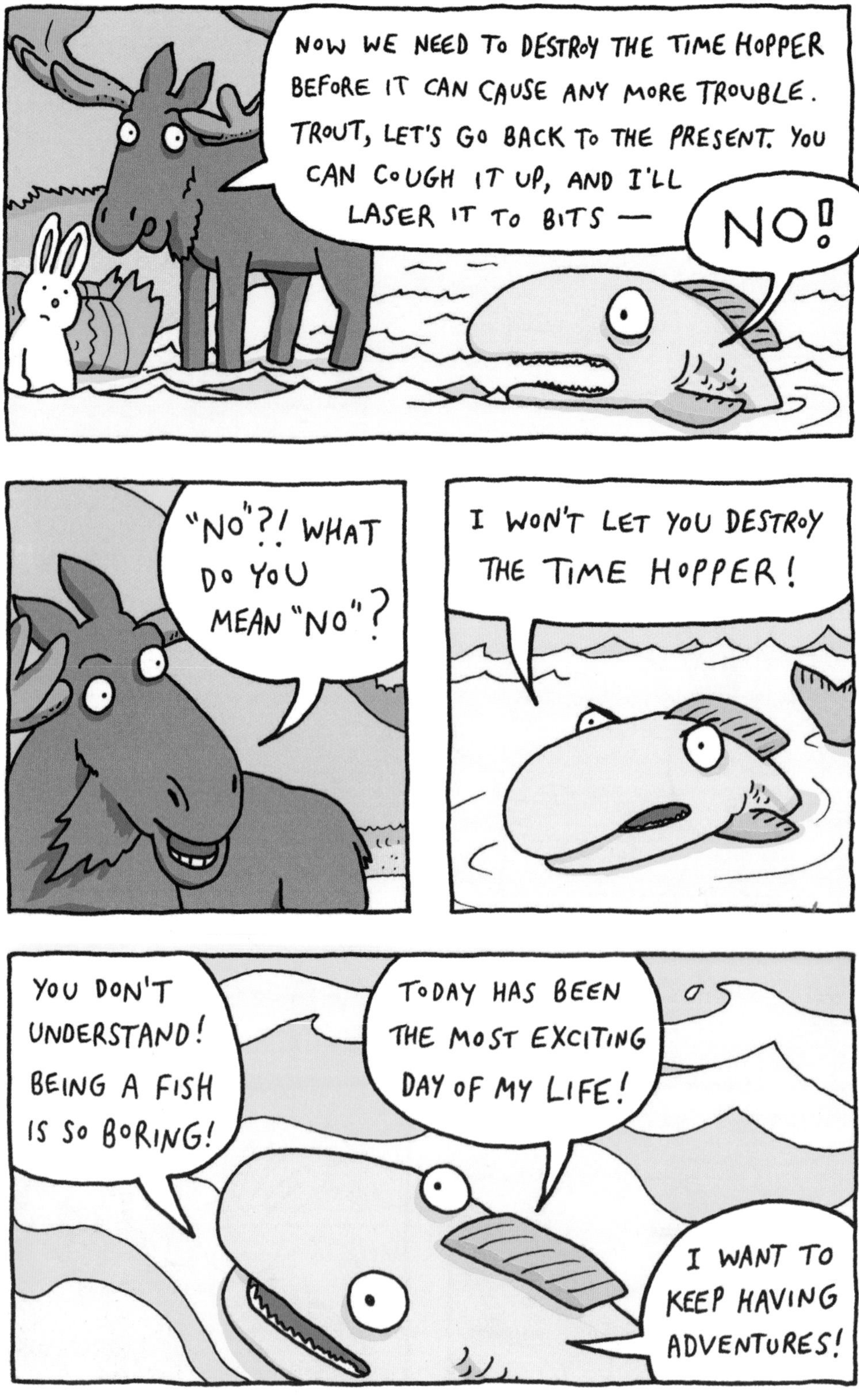
NOW WE NEED TO DESTROY THE TIME HOPPER BEFORE IT CAN CAUSE ANY MORE TROUBLE. TROUT, LET'S GO BACK TO THE PRESENT. YOU CAN COUGH IT UP, AND I'LL LASER IT TO BITS —
NO!
"NO"?! WHAT DO YOU MEAN "NO"?
I WON'T LET YOU DESTROY THE TIME HOPPER!
YOU DON'T UNDERSTAND! BEING A FISH IS SO BORING!
TODAY HAS BEEN THE MOST EXCITING DAY OF MY LIFE!
I WANT TO KEEP HAVING ADVENTURES!

IT'S TOO DANGEROUS, TROUT! WE HAVE TO DESTROY THE TIME HOPPER.
NO! I FINALLY FEEL LIKE I'M TRULY LIVING MY LIFE!
I'VE SPENT YEARS JUST SWIMMING AROUND, NOT DOING MUCH OF ANYTHING...
AND NOW I HAVE THIS CHANCE TO SEE THE WORLD.
ALL IT WAS...
ALL IT IS...
AND ALL IT WILL BE!
TICK
TICK
TICK

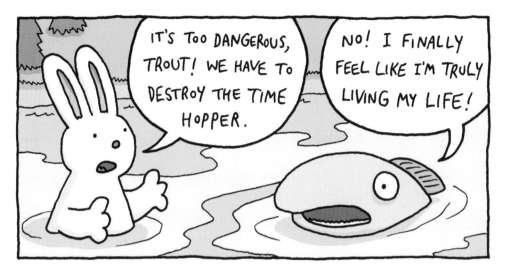

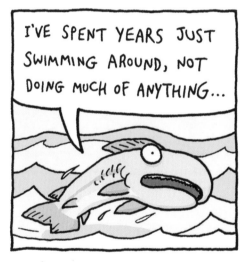

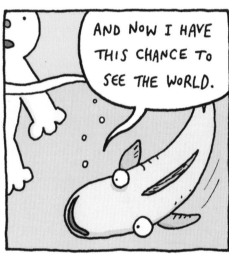

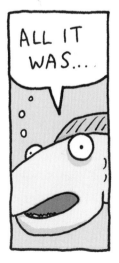

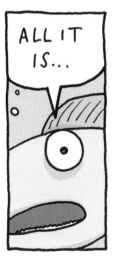

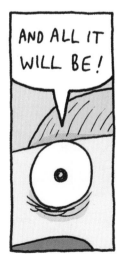

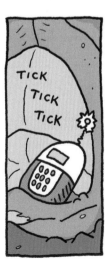

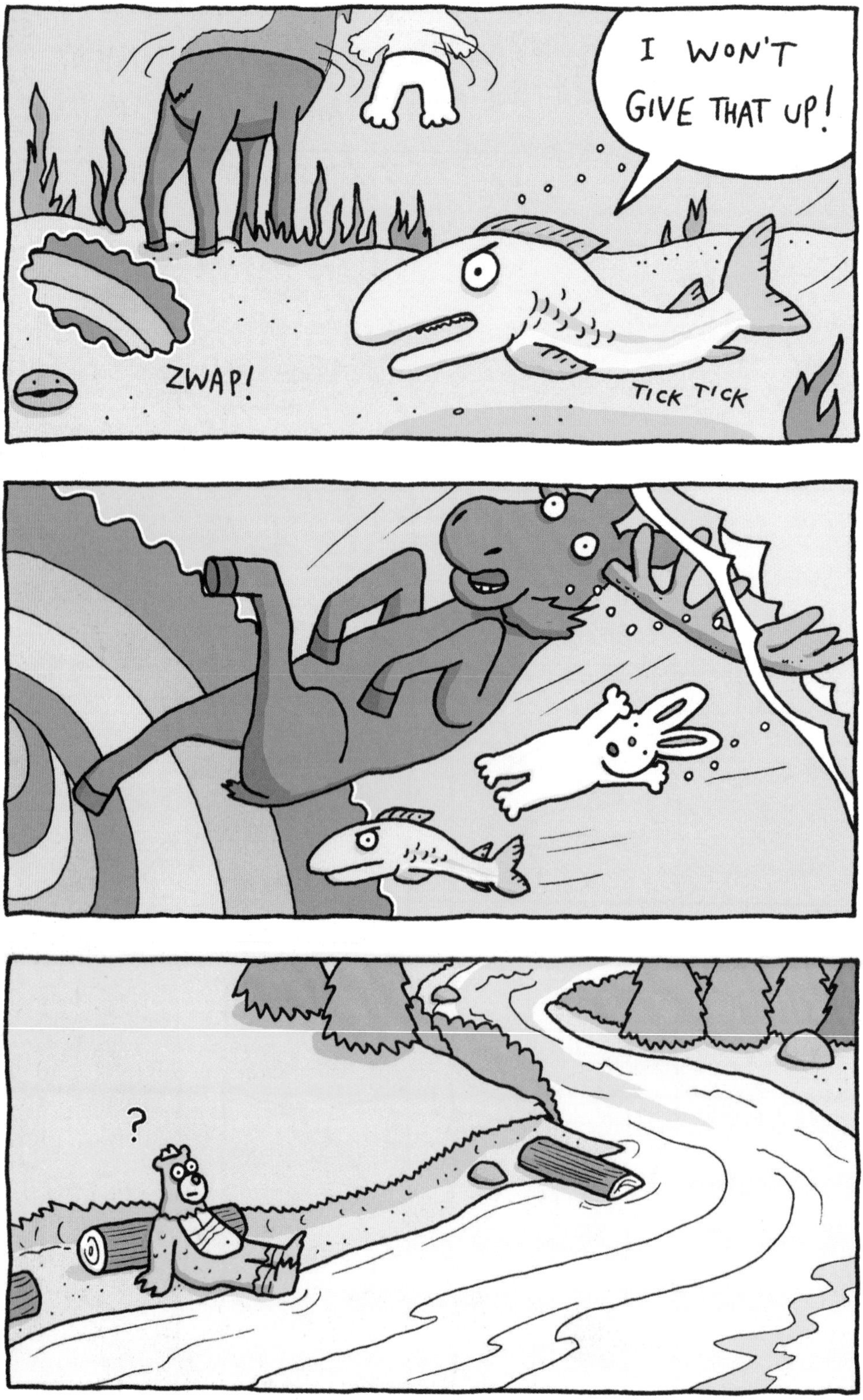
I WON'T GIVE THAT UP!
ZWAP!
TICK TICK
?

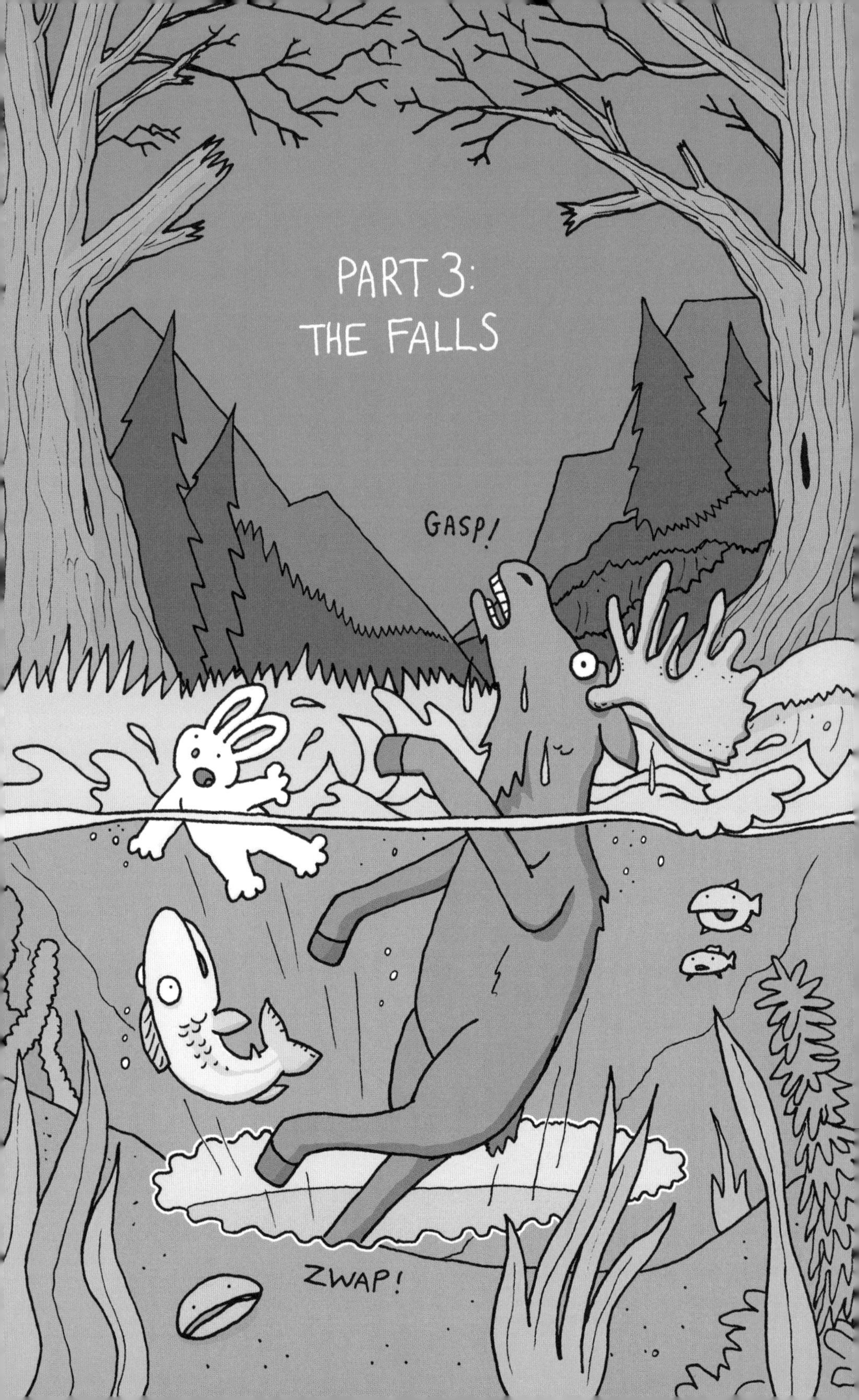
PART 3:
THE FALLS
GASP!
ZWAP!

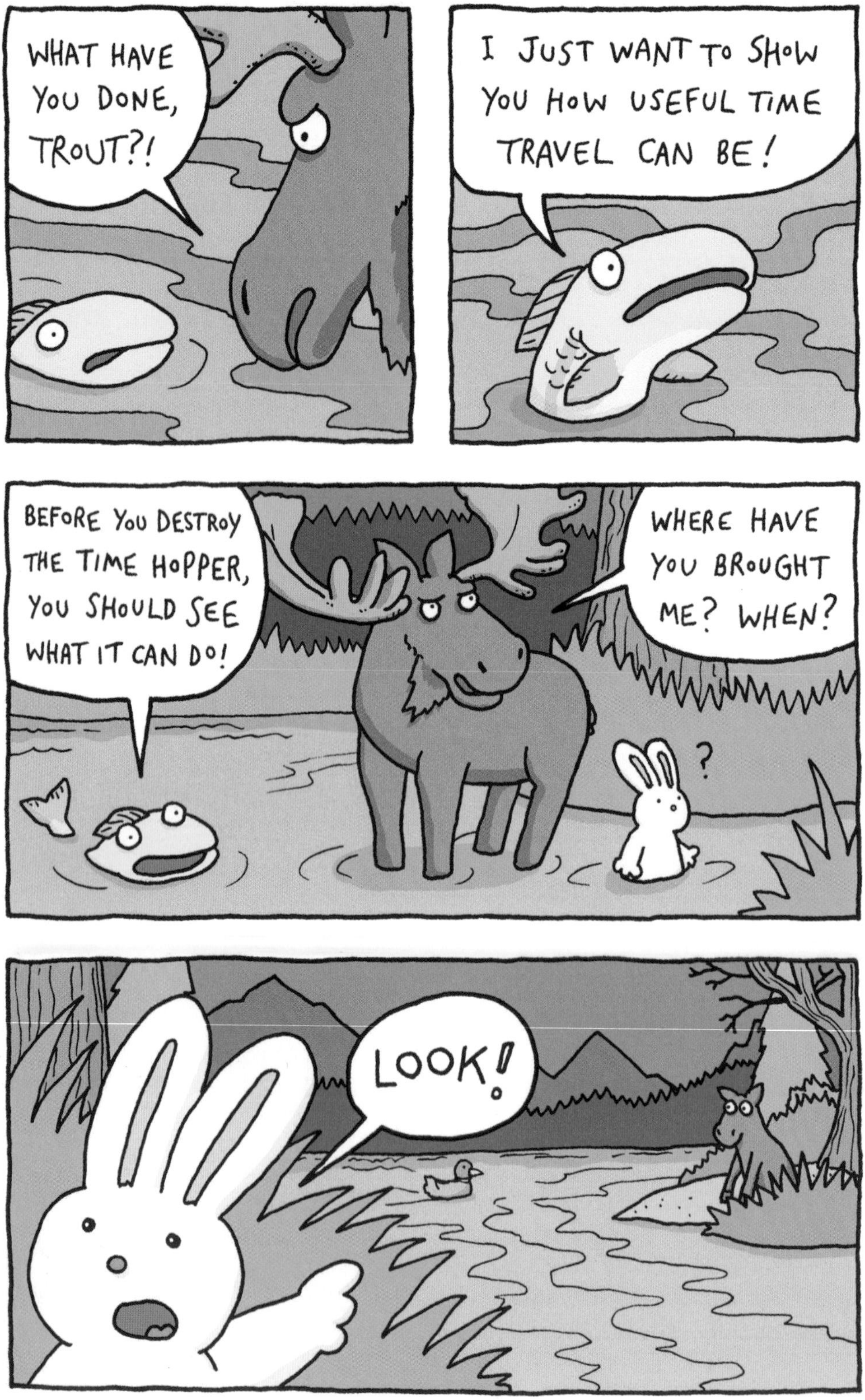
WHAT HAVE YOU DONE, TROUT?!
I JUST WANT TO SHOW YOU HOW USEFUL TIME TRAVEL CAN BE!
BEFORE YOU DESTROY THE TIME HOPPER, YOU SHOULD SEE WHAT IT CAN DO!
WHERE HAVE YOU BROUGHT ME? WHEN?
?
LOOK!

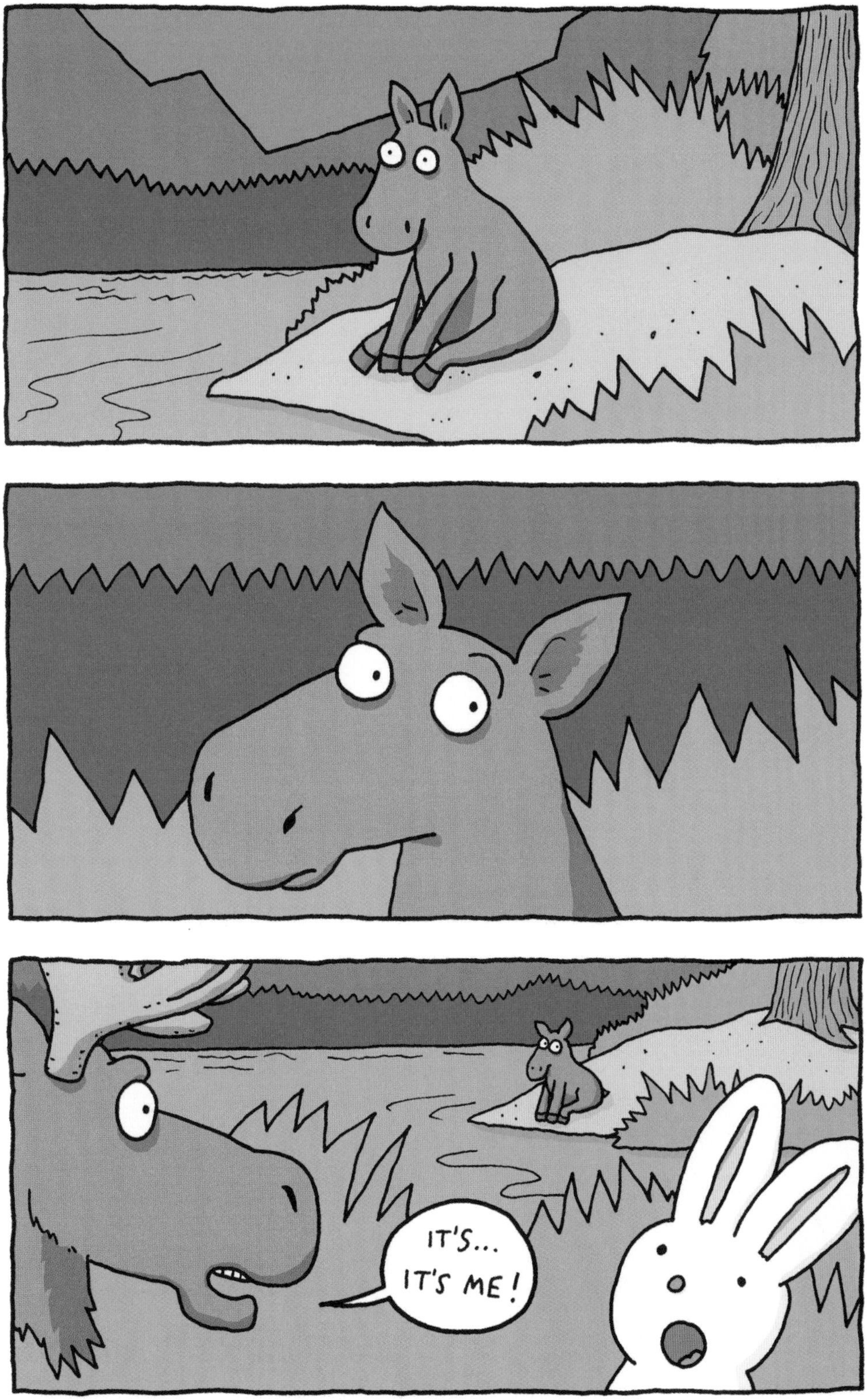
IT'S...
IT'S ME!

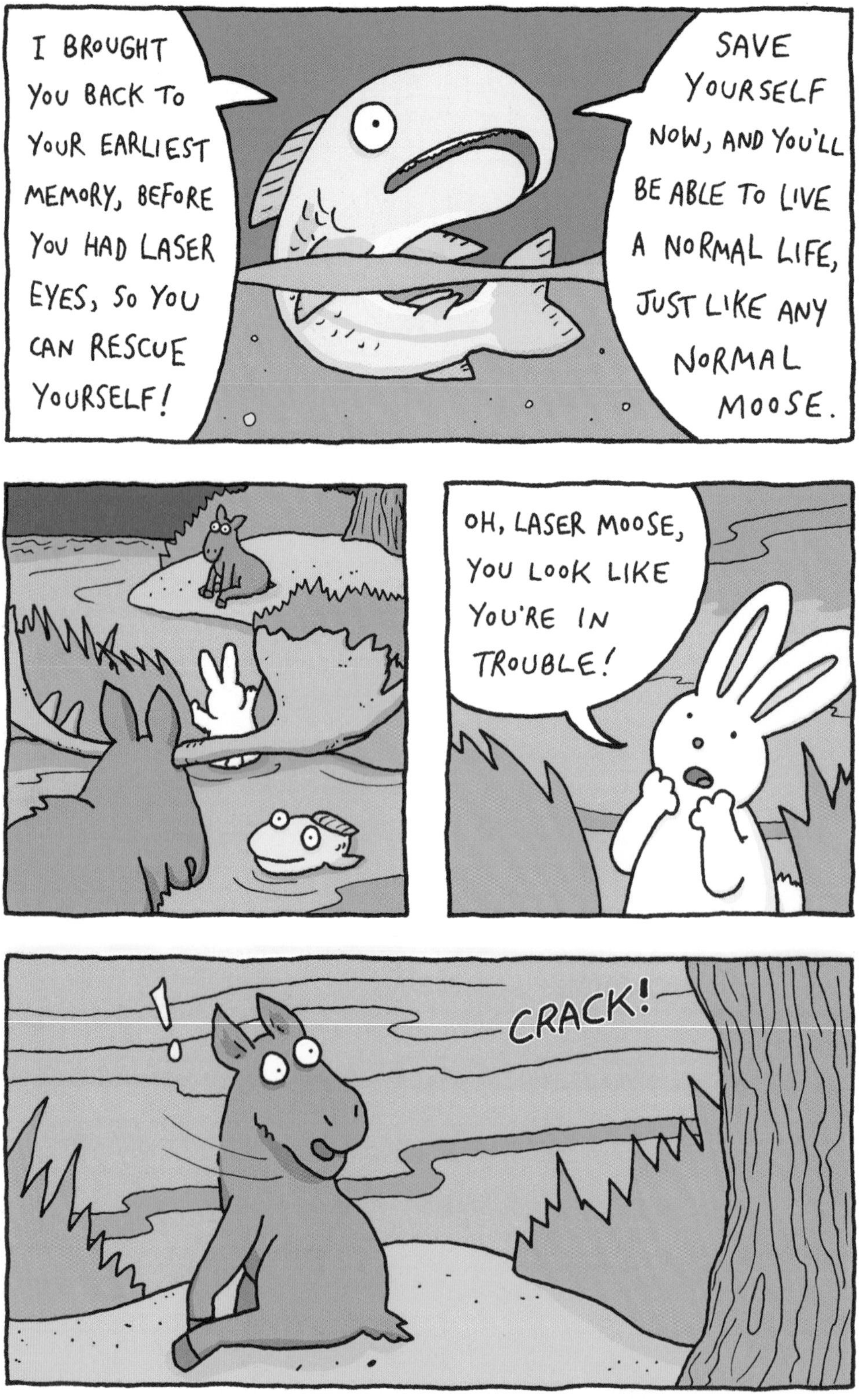
I BROUGHT YOU BACK TO YOUR EARLIEST MEMORY, BEFORE YOU HAD LASER EYES, SO YOU CAN RESCUE YOURSELF!
SAVE YOURSELF NOW, AND YOU'LL BE ABLE TO LIVE A NORMAL LIFE, JUST LIKE ANY NORMAL MOOSE.
OH, LASER MOOSE, YOU LOOK LIKE YOU'RE IN TROUBLE!
!
CRACK!

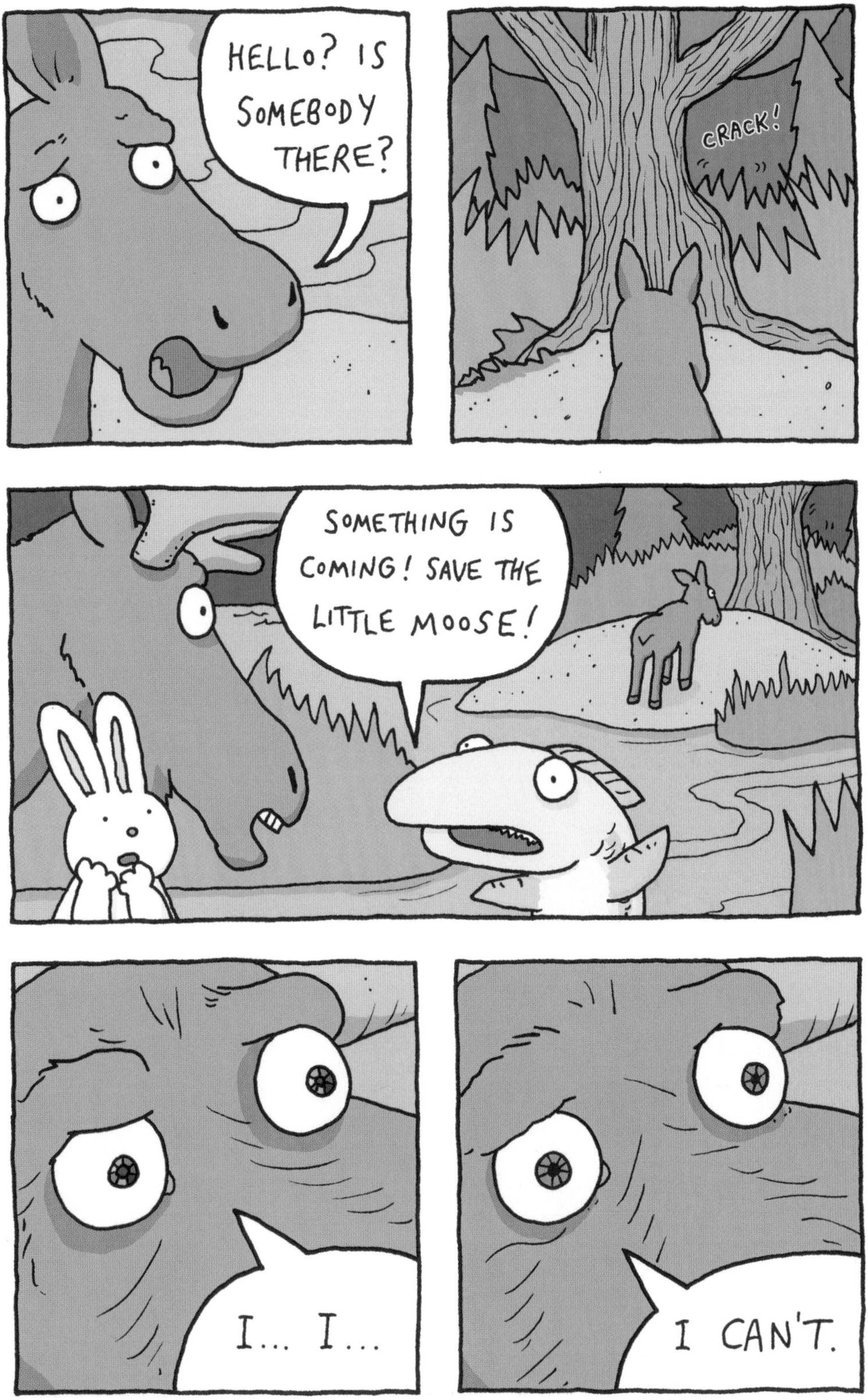
HELLO? IS SOMEBODY THERE?
CRACK!
SOMETHING IS COMING! SAVE THE LITTLE MOOSE!
I... I...
I CAN'T.

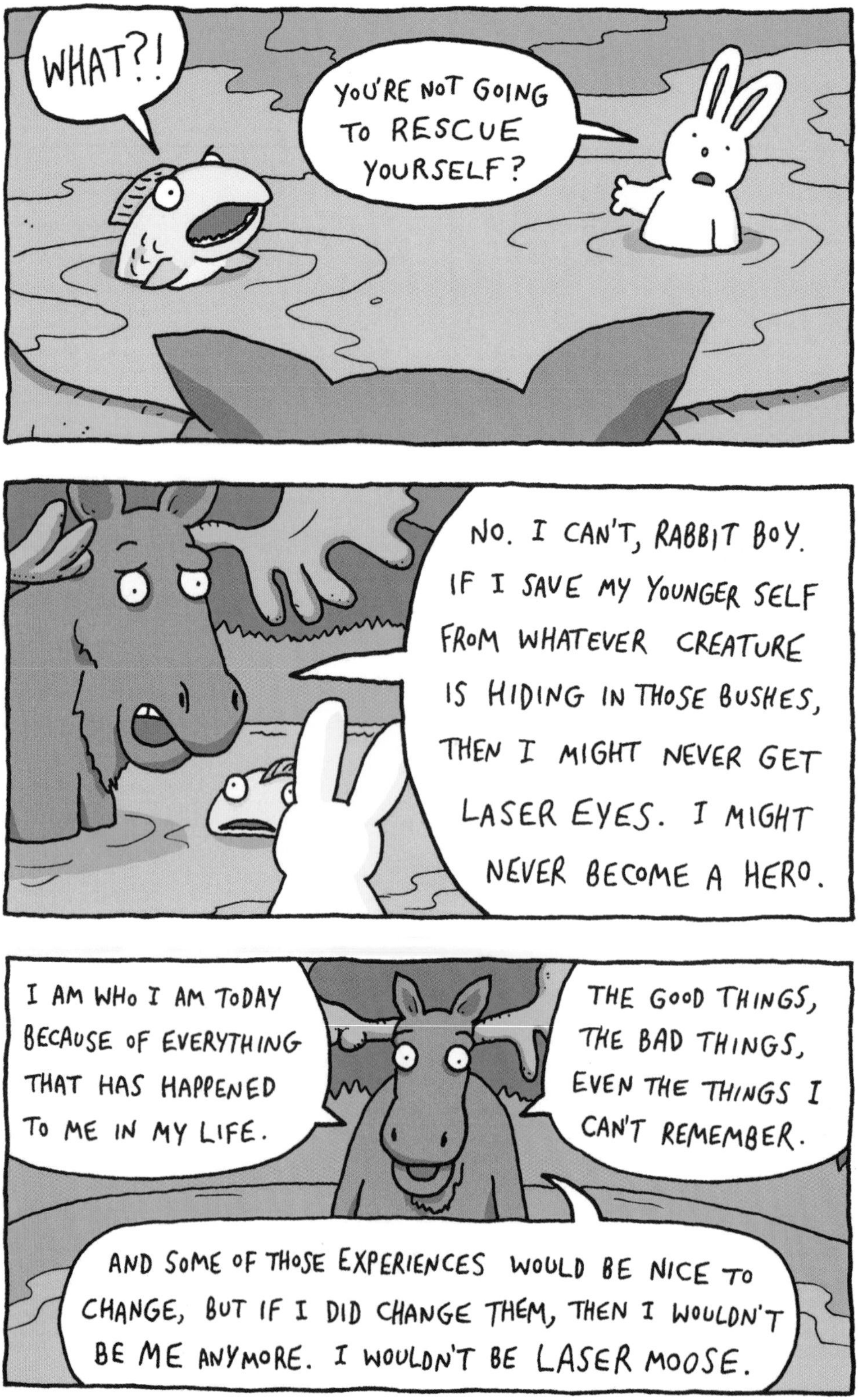
WHAT?!
YOU'RE NOT GOING TO RESCUE YOURSELF?
NO. I CAN'T, RABBIT BOY. IF I SAVE MY YOUNGER SELF FROM WHATEVER CREATURE IS HIDING IN THOSE BUSHES, THEN I MIGHT NEVER GET LASER EYES. I MIGHT NEVER BECOME A HERO.
I AM WHO I AM TODAY BECAUSE OF EVERYTHING THAT HAS HAPPENED TO ME IN MY LIFE.
THE GOOD THINGS, THE BAD THINGS, EVEN THE THINGS I CAN'T REMEMBER.
AND SOME OF THOSE EXPERIENCES WOULD BE NICE TO CHANGE, BUT IF I DID CHANGE THEM, THEN I WOULDN'T BE ME ANYMORE. I WOULDN'T BE LASER MOOSE.

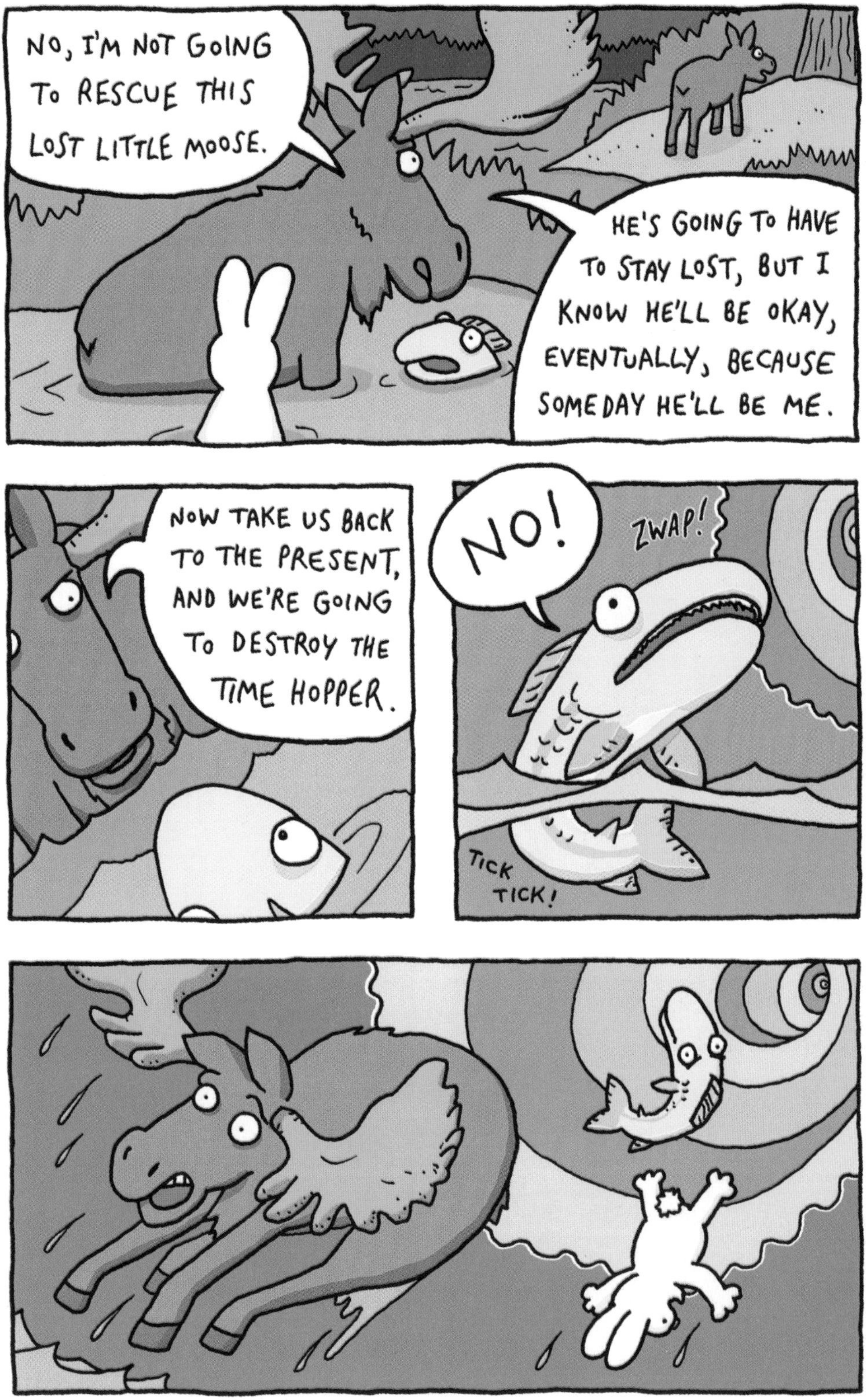

NO, I'M NOT GOING TO RESCUE THIS LOST LITTLE MOOSE.
HE'S GOING TO HAVE TO STAY LOST, BUT I KNOW HE'LL BE OKAY, EVENTUALLY, BECAUSE SOMEDAY HE'LL BE ME.
NOW TAKE US BACK TO THE PRESENT, AND WE'RE GOING TO DESTROY THE TIME HOPPER.
NO!
ZWAP!
TICK TICK!

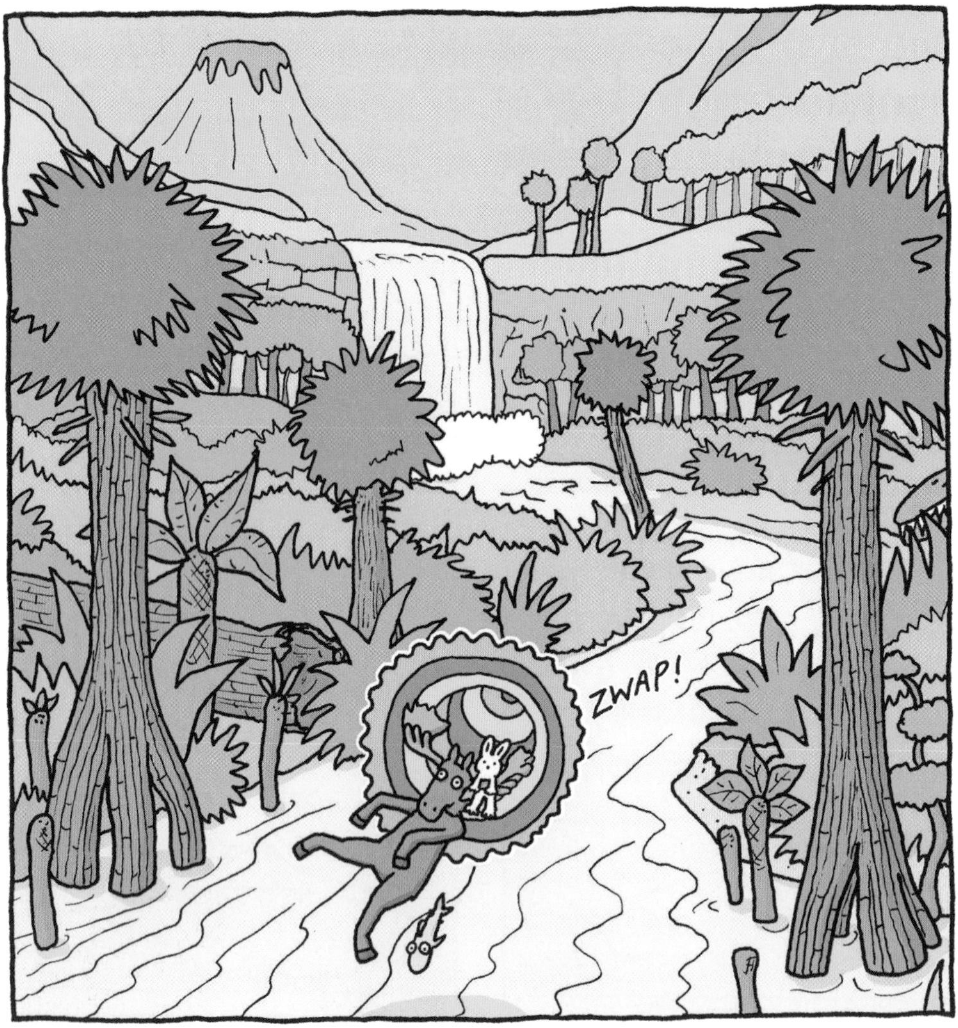
ZWAP!

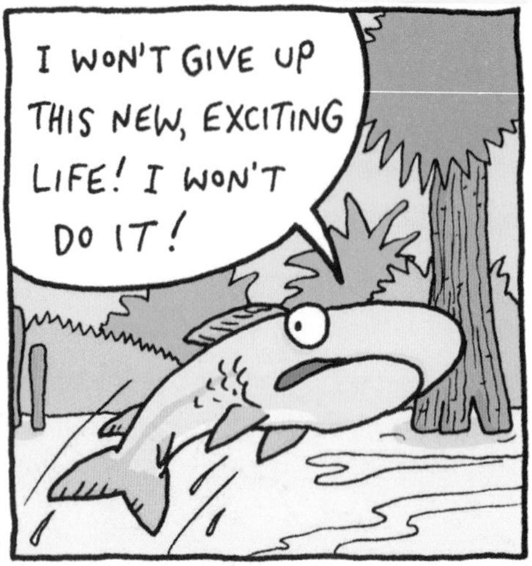
I WON'T GIVE UP THIS NEW, EXCITING LIFE! I WON'T DO IT!

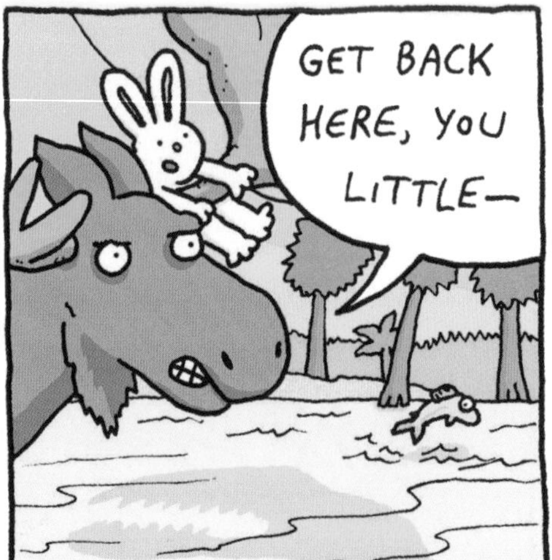
GET BACK HERE, YOU LITTLE—

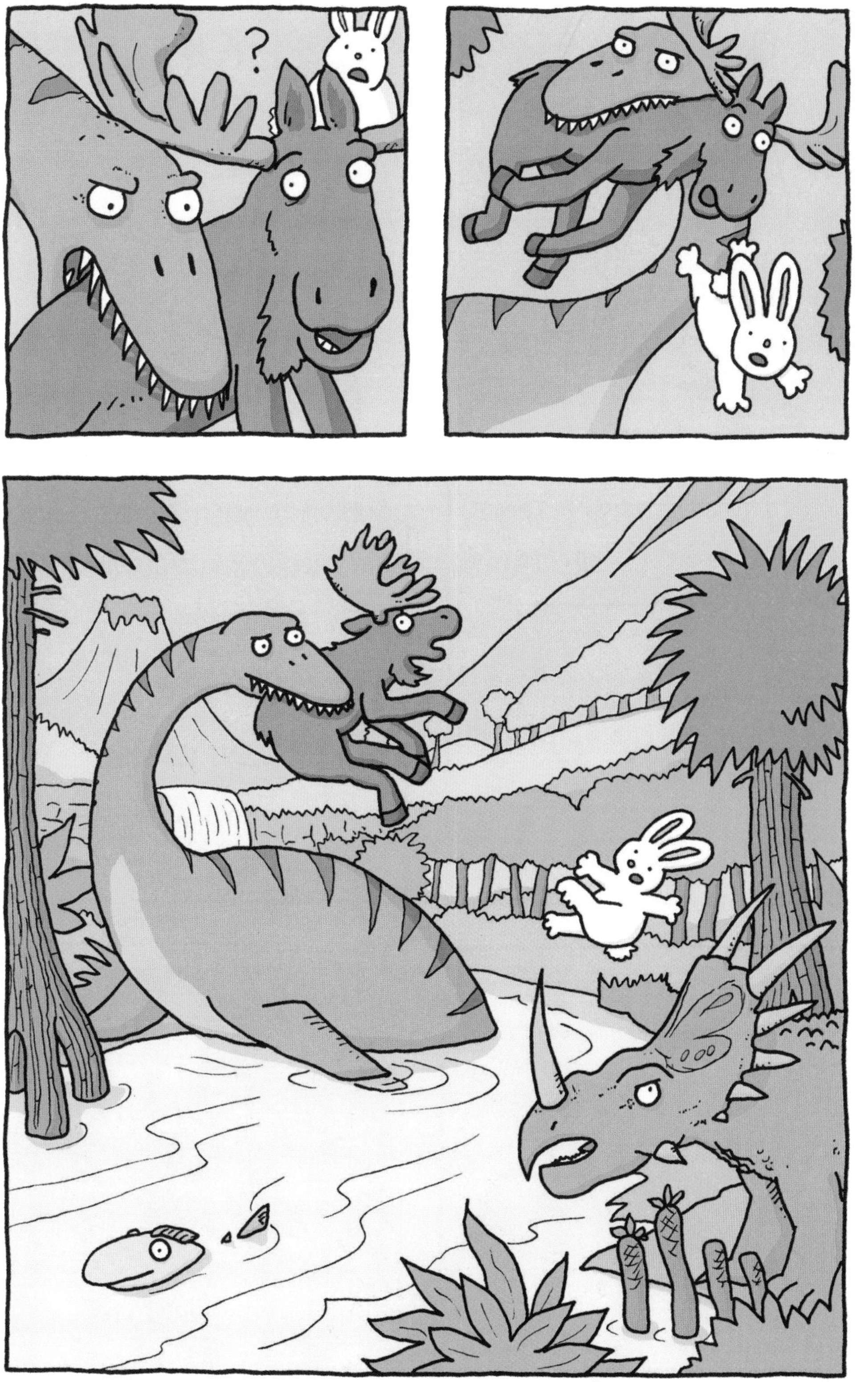

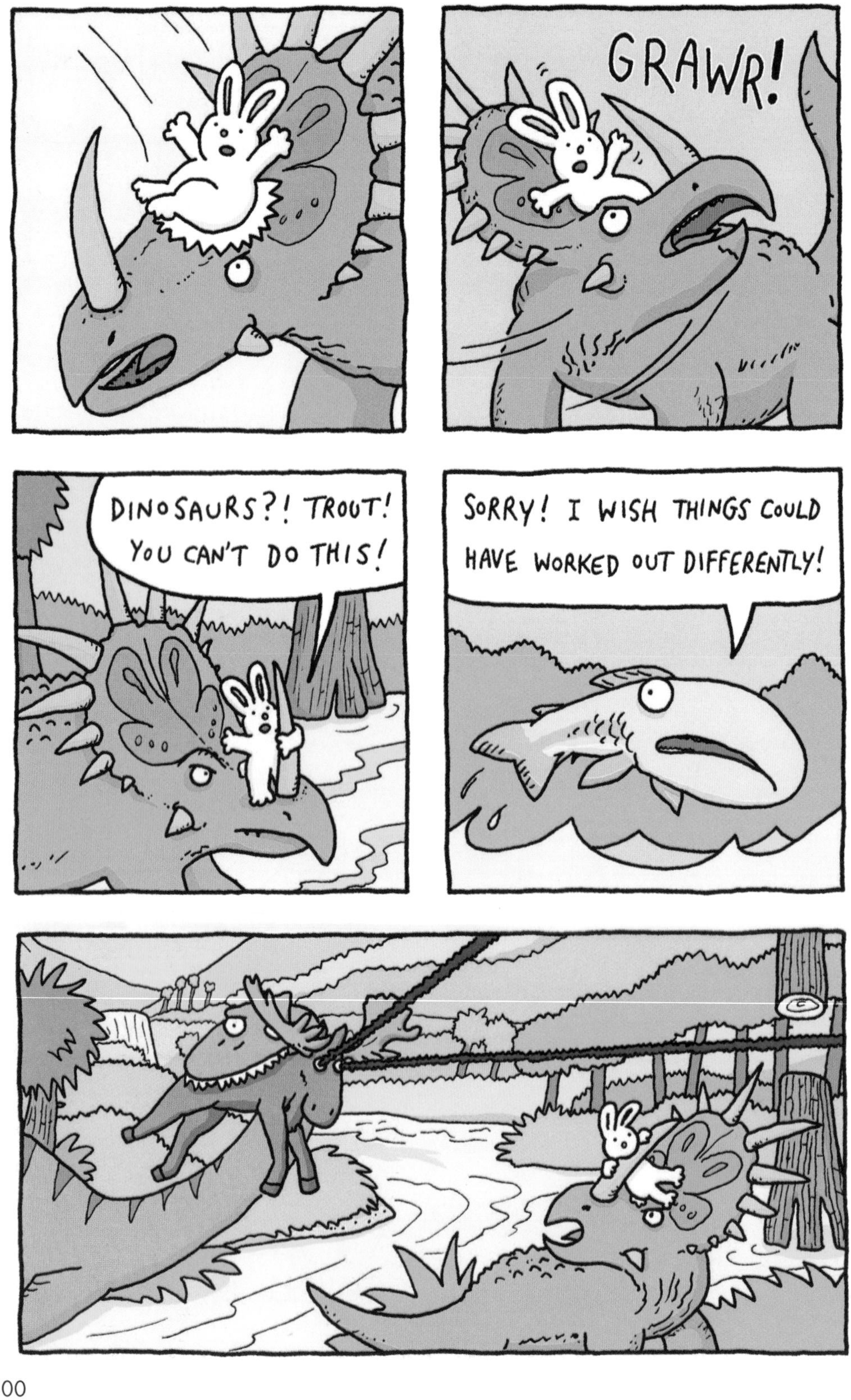
GRAWR!
DINOSAURS?! TROUT! YOU CAN'T DO THIS!
SORRY! I WISH THINGS COULD HAVE WORKED OUT DIFFERENTLY!

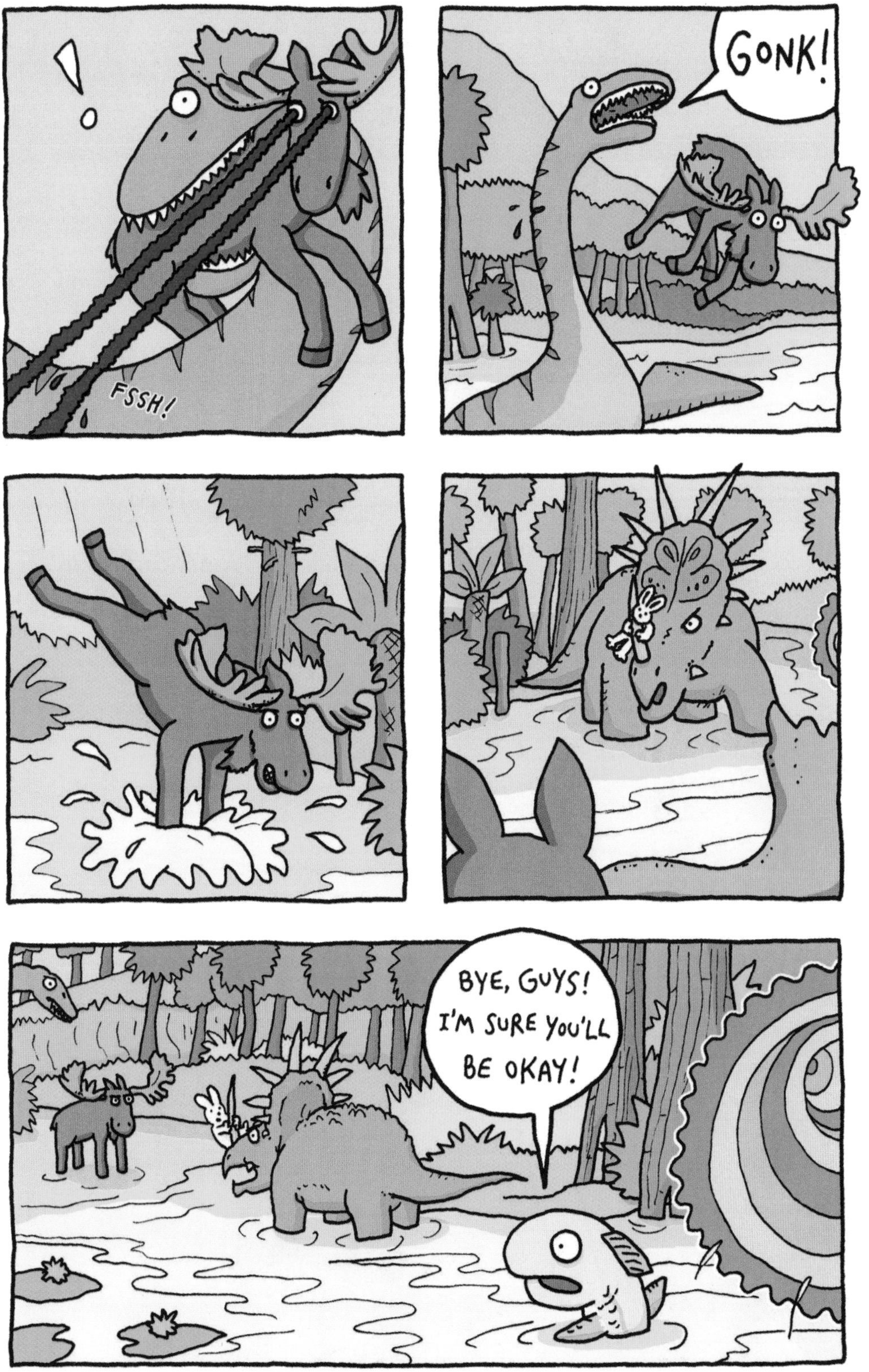
!
FSSH!
GONK!
BYE, GUYS! I'M SURE YOU'LL BE OKAY!

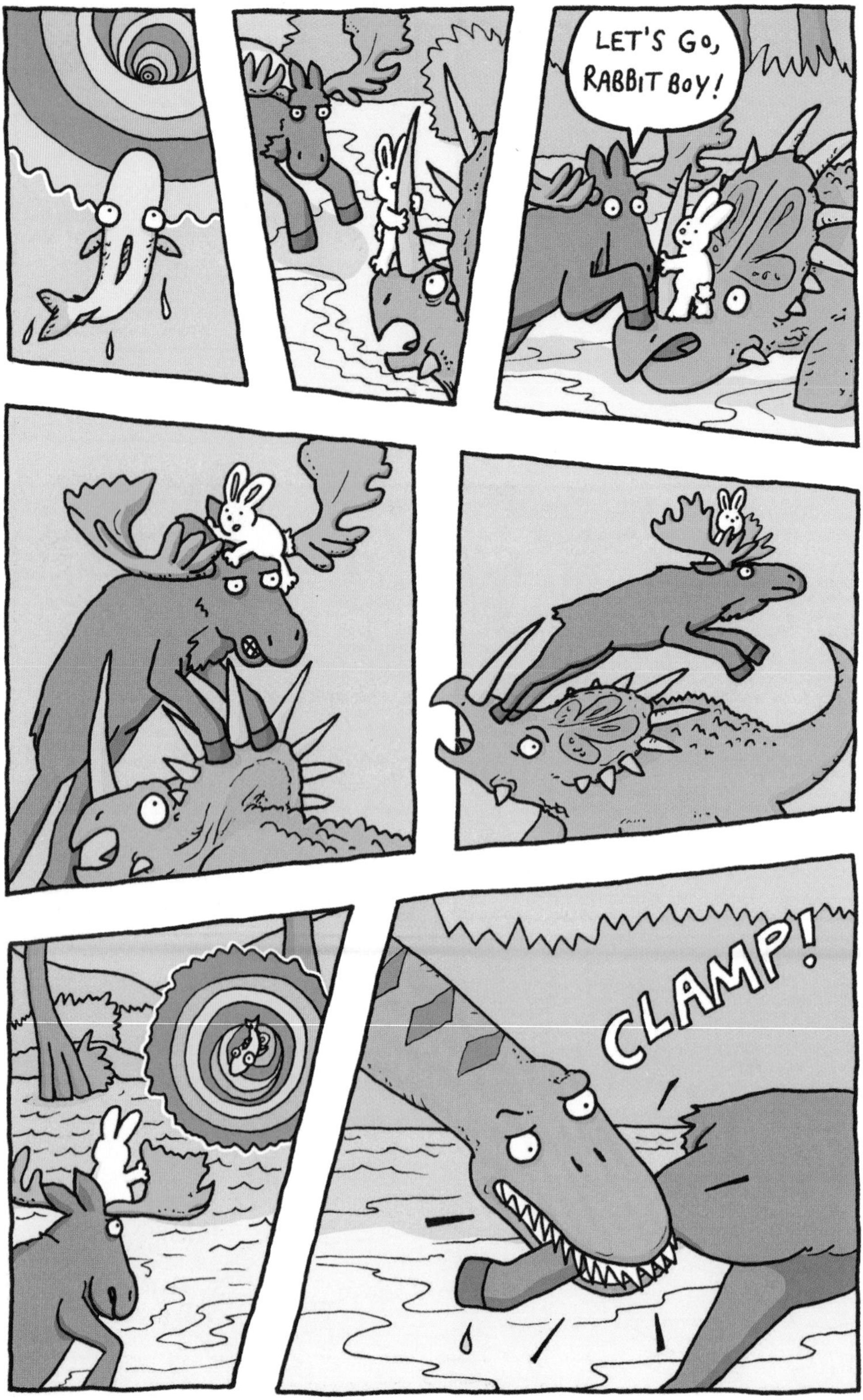
LET'S GO, RABBIT BOY!
CLAMP!

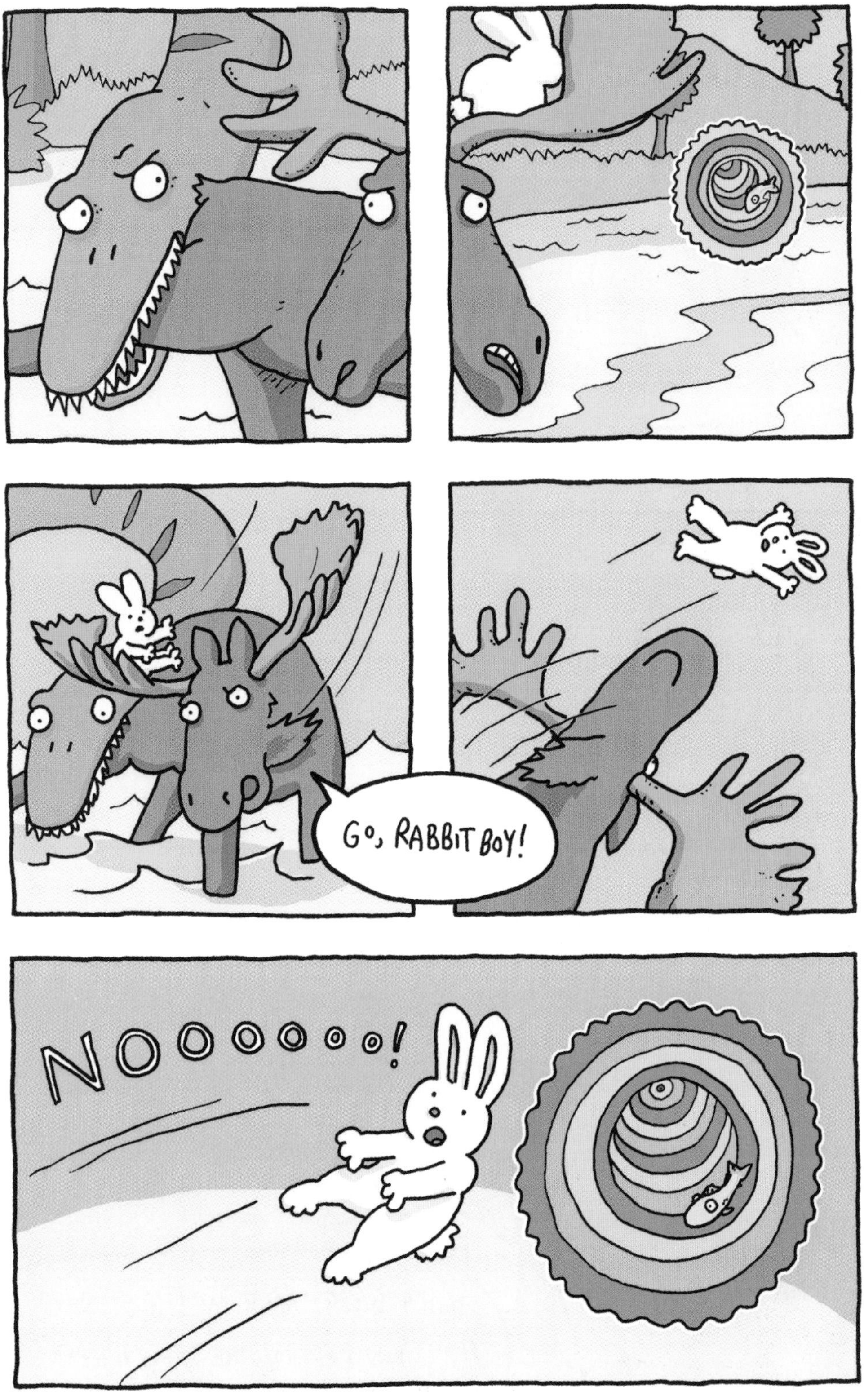
GO, RABBIT BOY!
NOOOOOO!

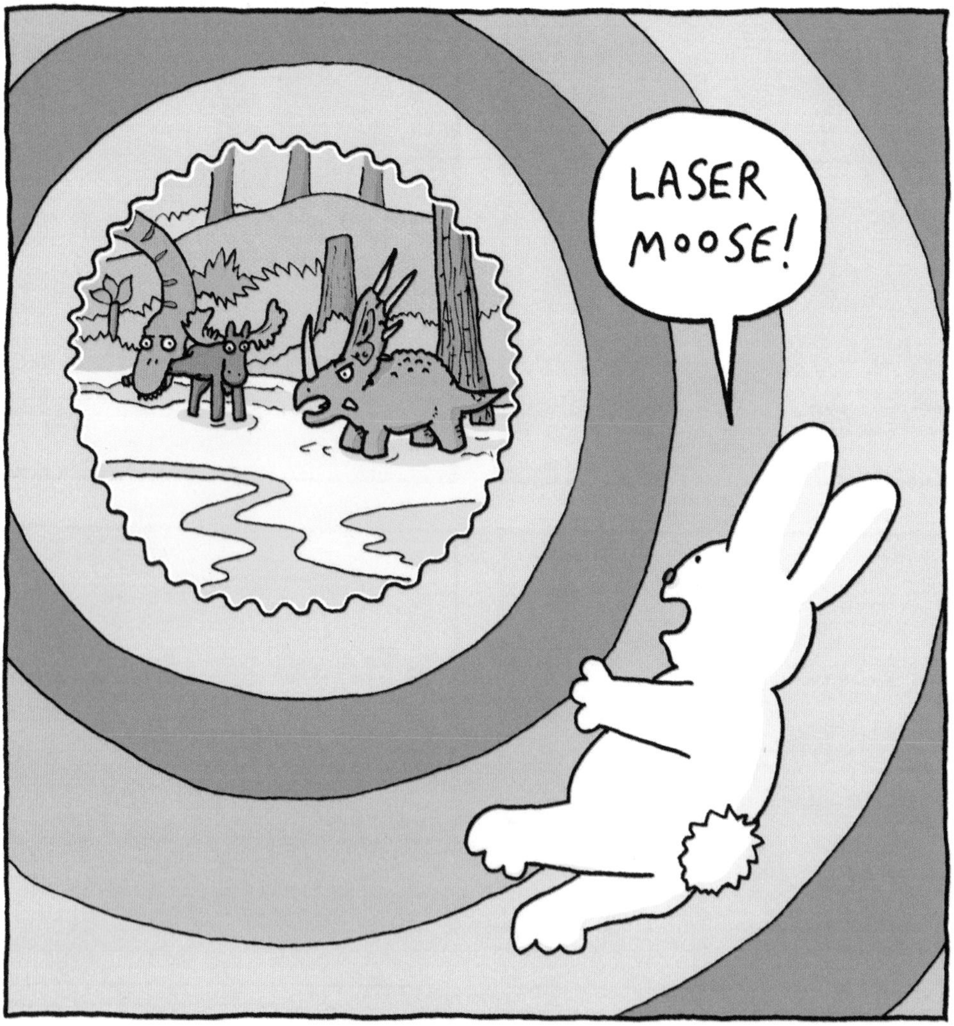
LASER MOOSE!

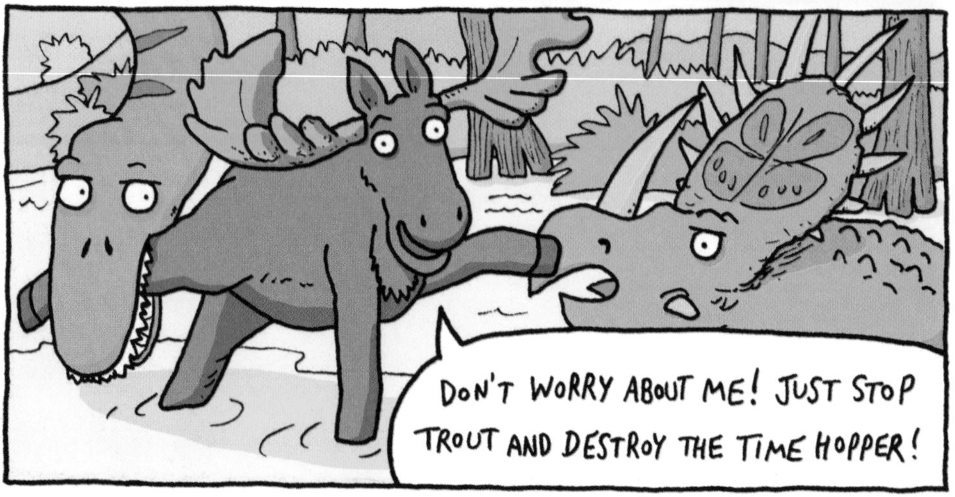
DON'T WORRY ABOUT ME! JUST STOP TROUT AND DESTROY THE TIME HOPPER!

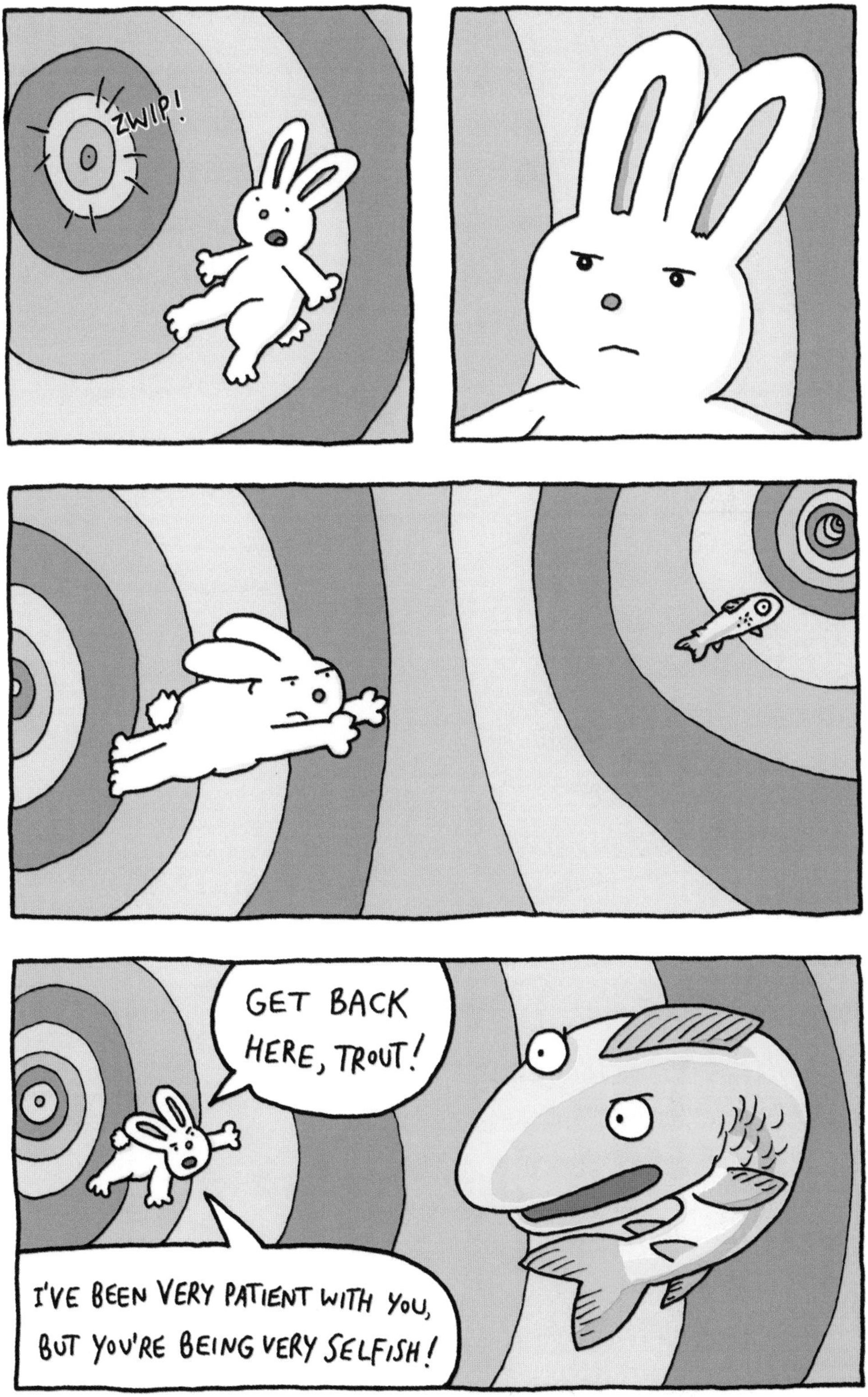
ZWIP!
GET BACK HERE, TROUT!
I'VE BEEN VERY PATIENT WITH YOU, BUT YOU'RE BEING VERY SELFISH!

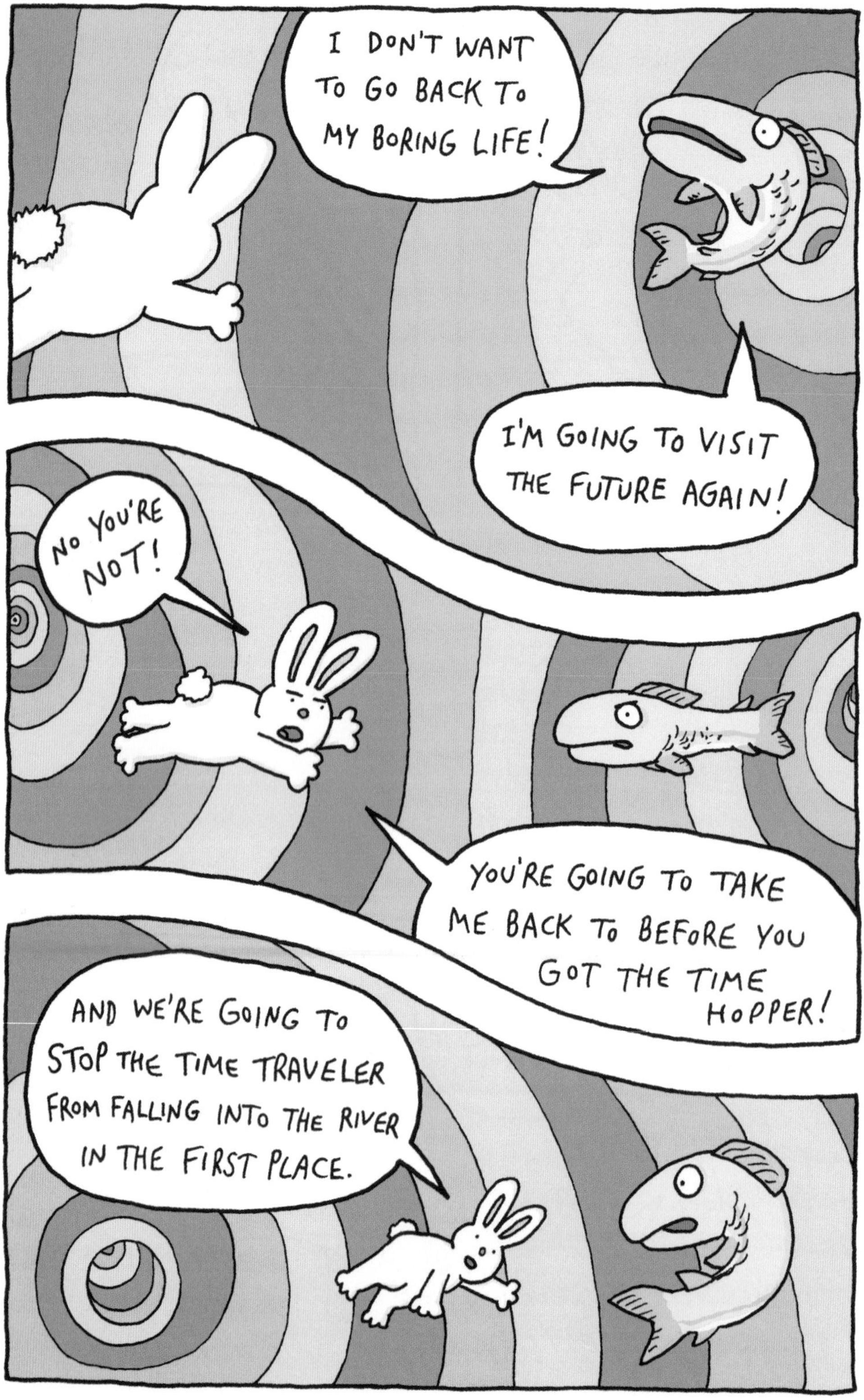
I DON'T WANT TO GO BACK TO MY BORING LIFE!
I'M GOING TO VISIT THE FUTURE AGAIN!
NO YOU'RE NOT!
YOU'RE GOING TO TAKE ME BACK TO BEFORE YOU GOT THE TIME HOPPER!
AND WE'RE GOING TO STOP THE TIME TRAVELER FROM FALLING INTO THE RIVER IN THE FIRST PLACE.

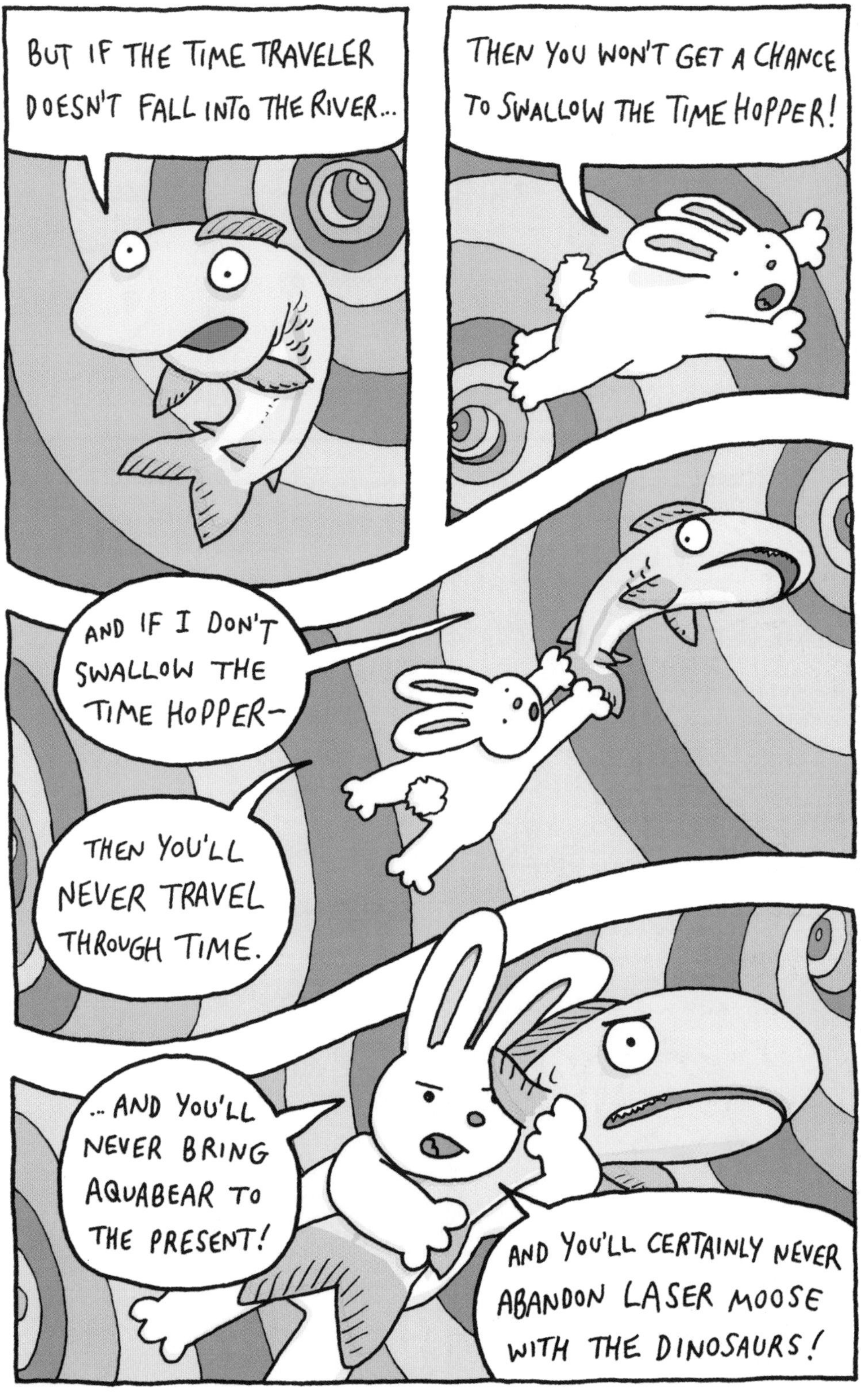
BUT IF THE TIME TRAVELER DOESN'T FALL INTO THE RIVER...
THEN YOU WON'T GET A CHANCE TO SWALLOW THE TIME HOPPER!
AND IF I DON'T SWALLOW THE TIME HOPPER–
THEN YOU'LL NEVER TRAVEL THROUGH TIME.
...AND YOU'LL NEVER BRING AQUABEAR TO THE PRESENT!
AND YOU'LL CERTAINLY NEVER ABANDON LASER MOOSE WITH THE DINOSAURS!

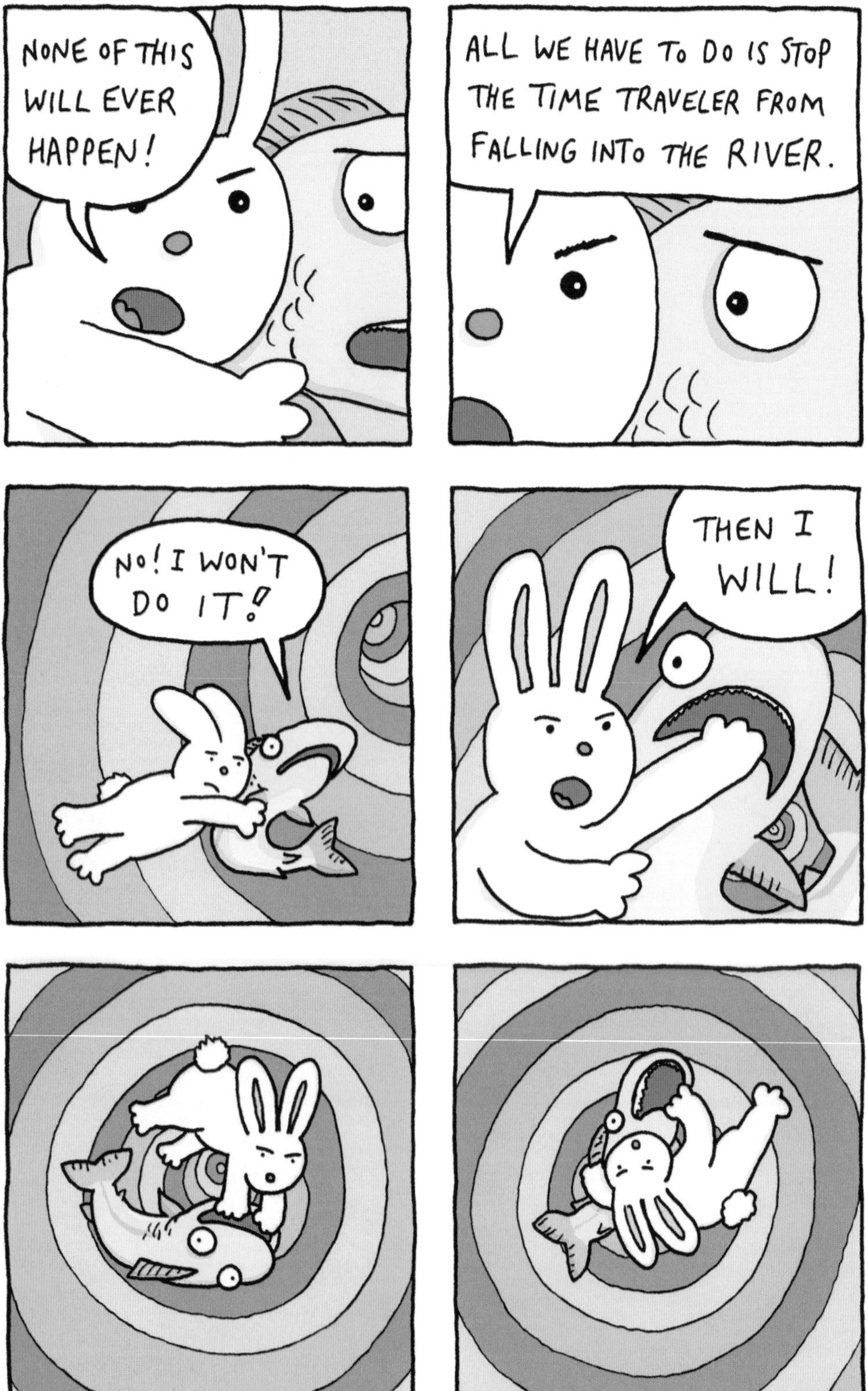
NONE OF THIS WILL EVER HAPPEN!
ALL WE HAVE TO DO IS STOP THE TIME TRAVELER FROM FALLING INTO THE RIVER.
NO! I WON'T DO IT!
THEN I WILL!

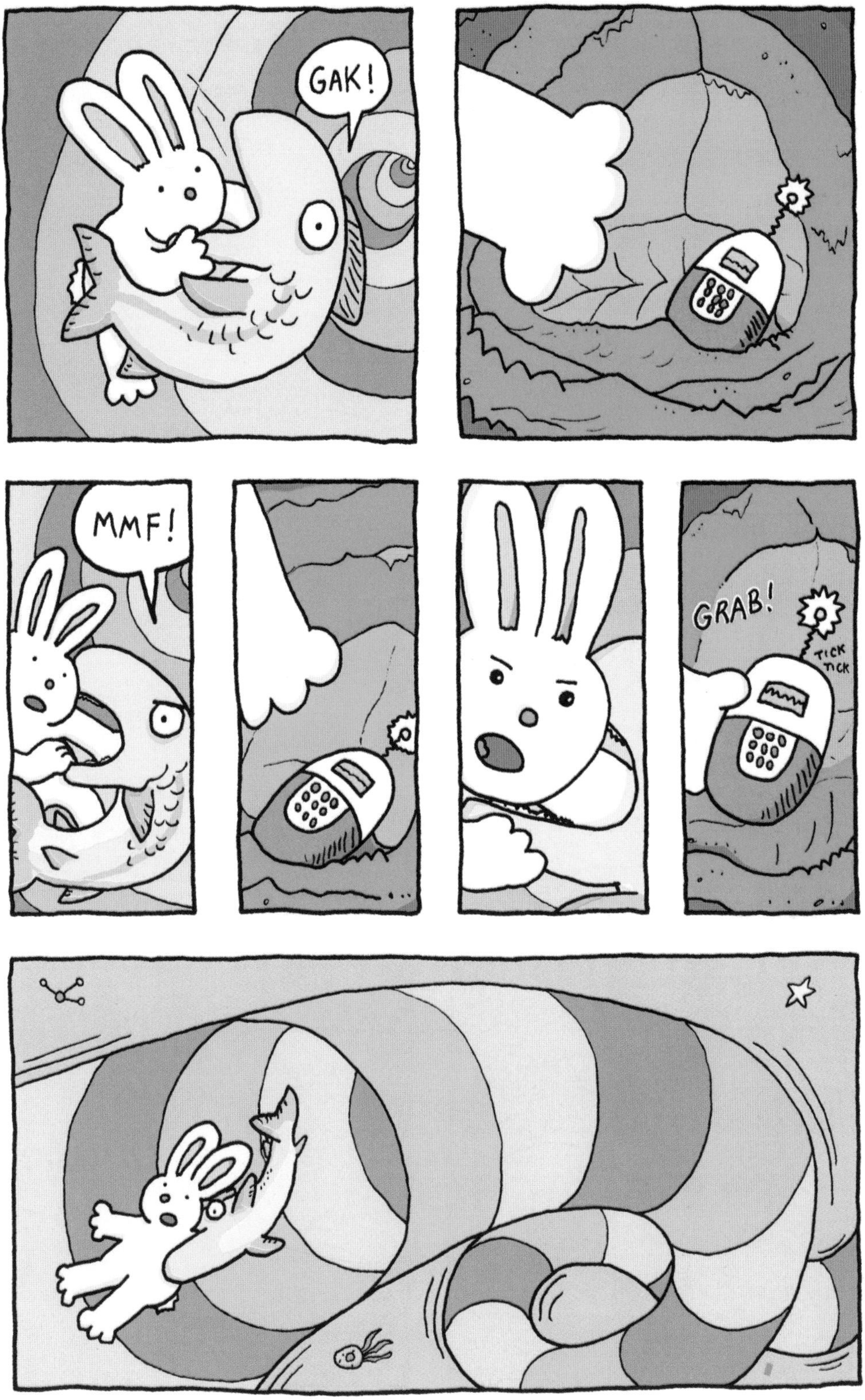
GAK!
MMF!
GRAB!
TICK
TICK

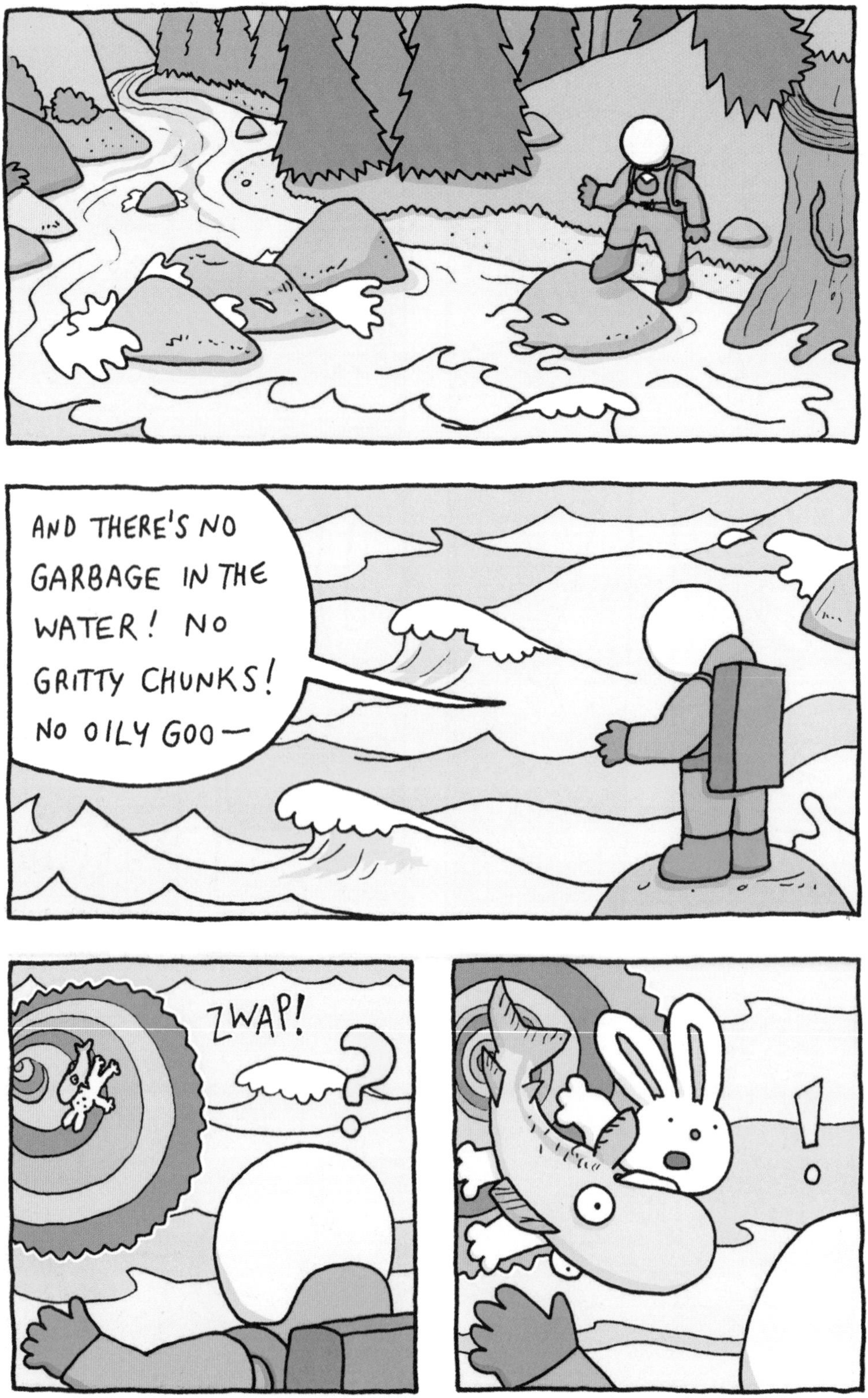
AND THERE'S NO GARBAGE IN THE WATER! NO GRITTY CHUNKS! NO OILY GOO—
ZWAP!
?
!

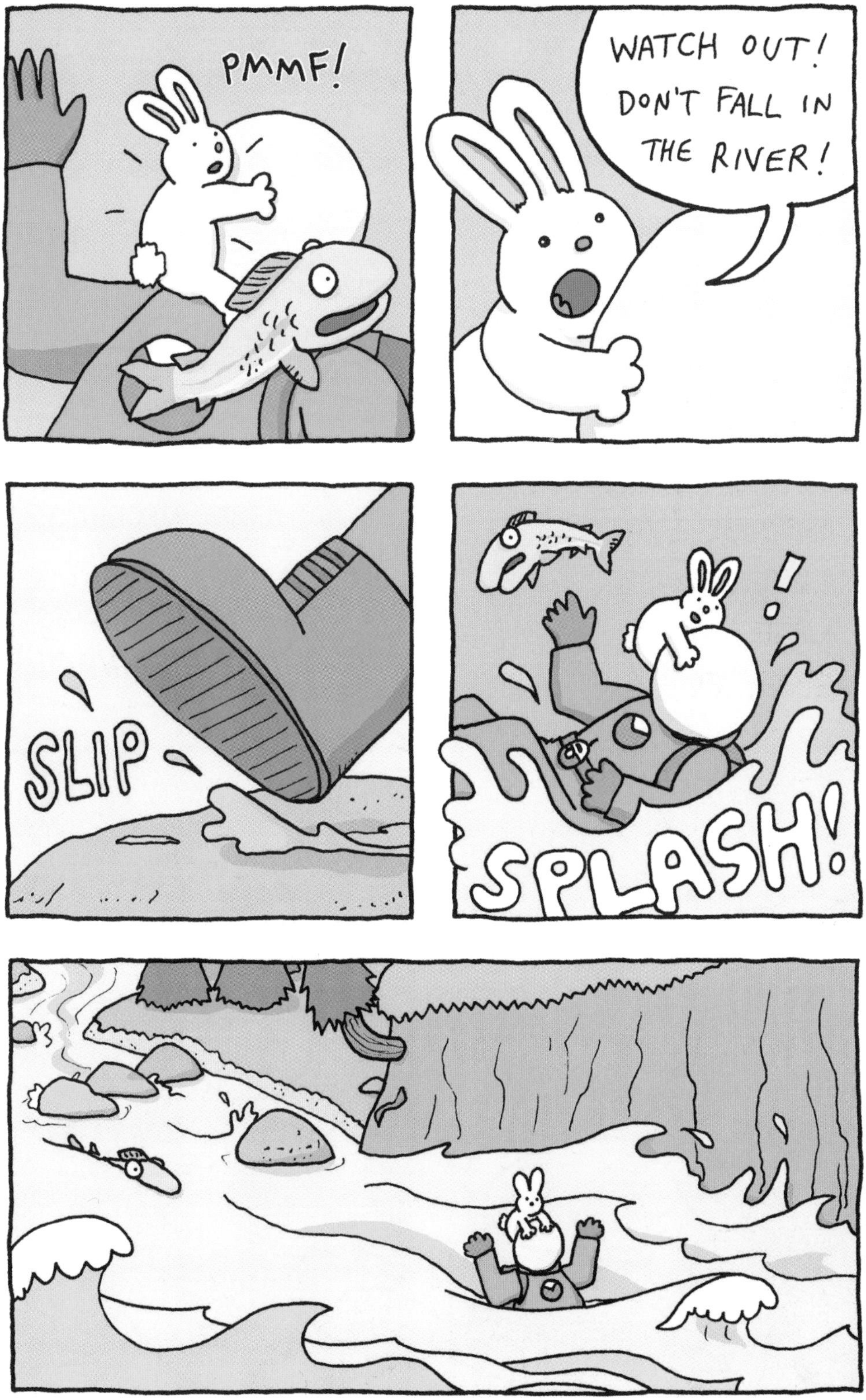
PMMF!
WATCH OUT! DON'T FALL IN THE RIVER!
SLIP
!
SPLASH!

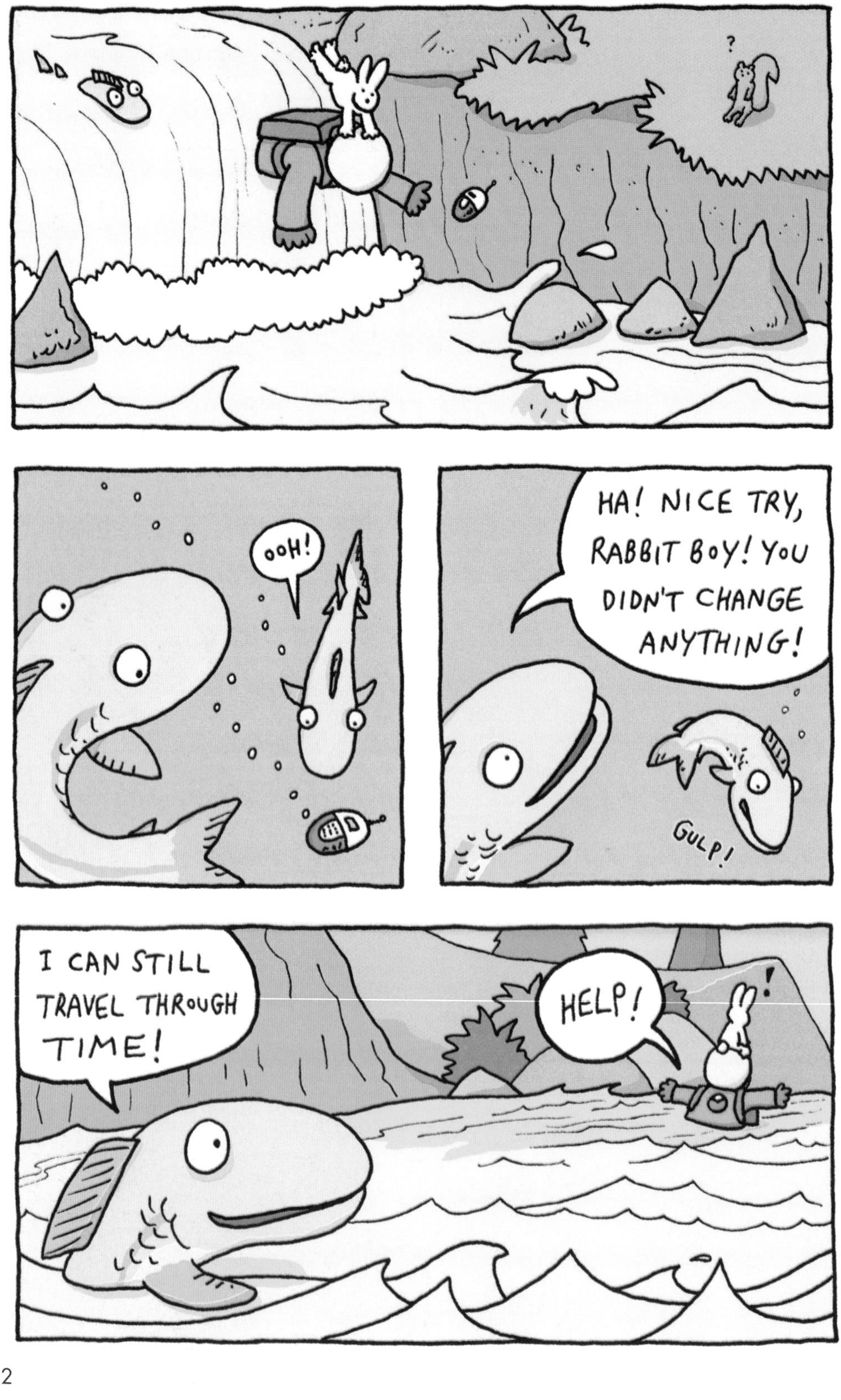
OOH!
HA! NICE TRY, RABBIT BOY! YOU DIDN'T CHANGE ANYTHING!
GULP!
I CAN STILL TRAVEL THROUGH TIME!
HELP!

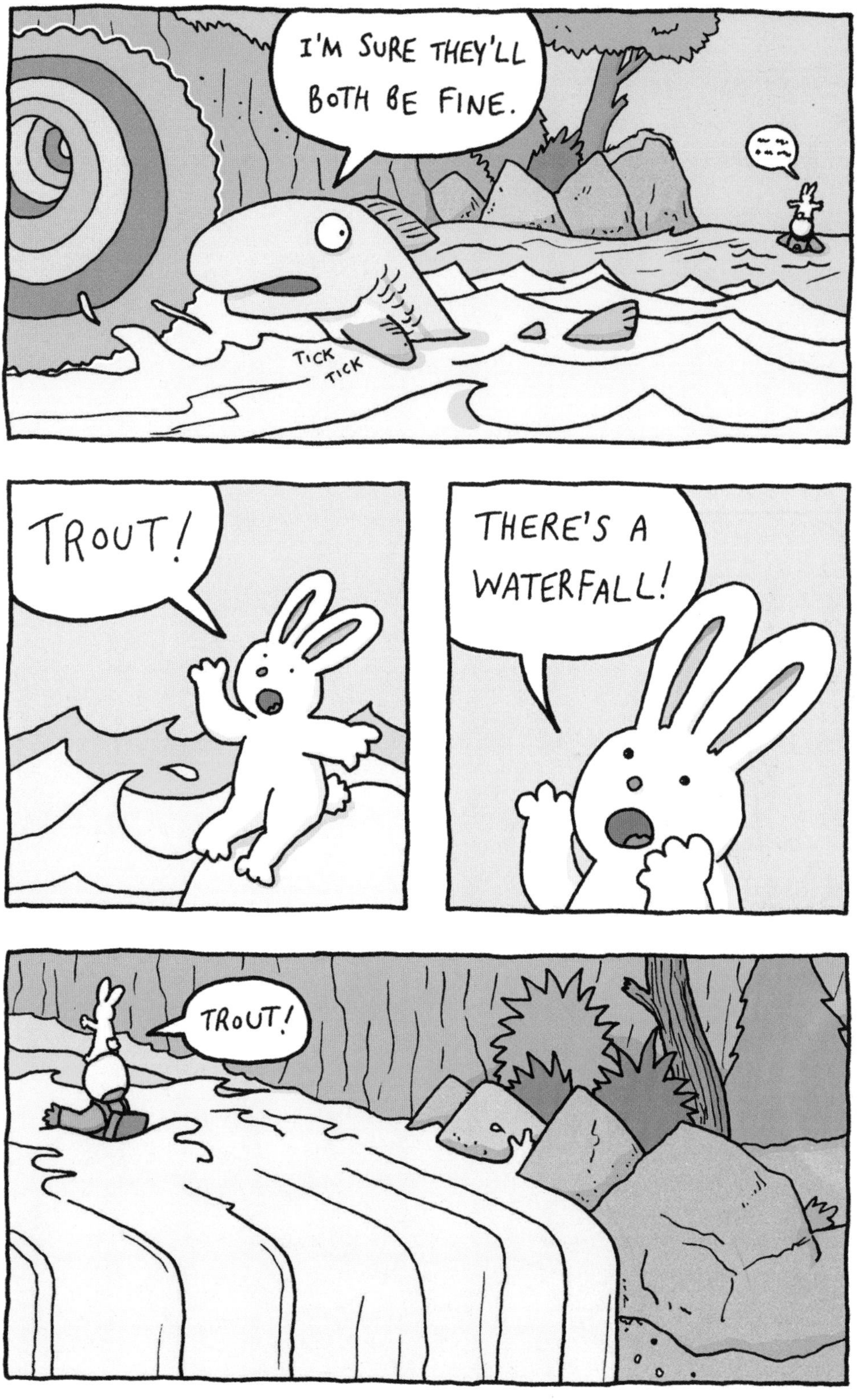
I'M SURE THEY'LL BOTH BE FINE.
TICK TICK
TROUT!
THERE'S A WATERFALL!
TROUT!

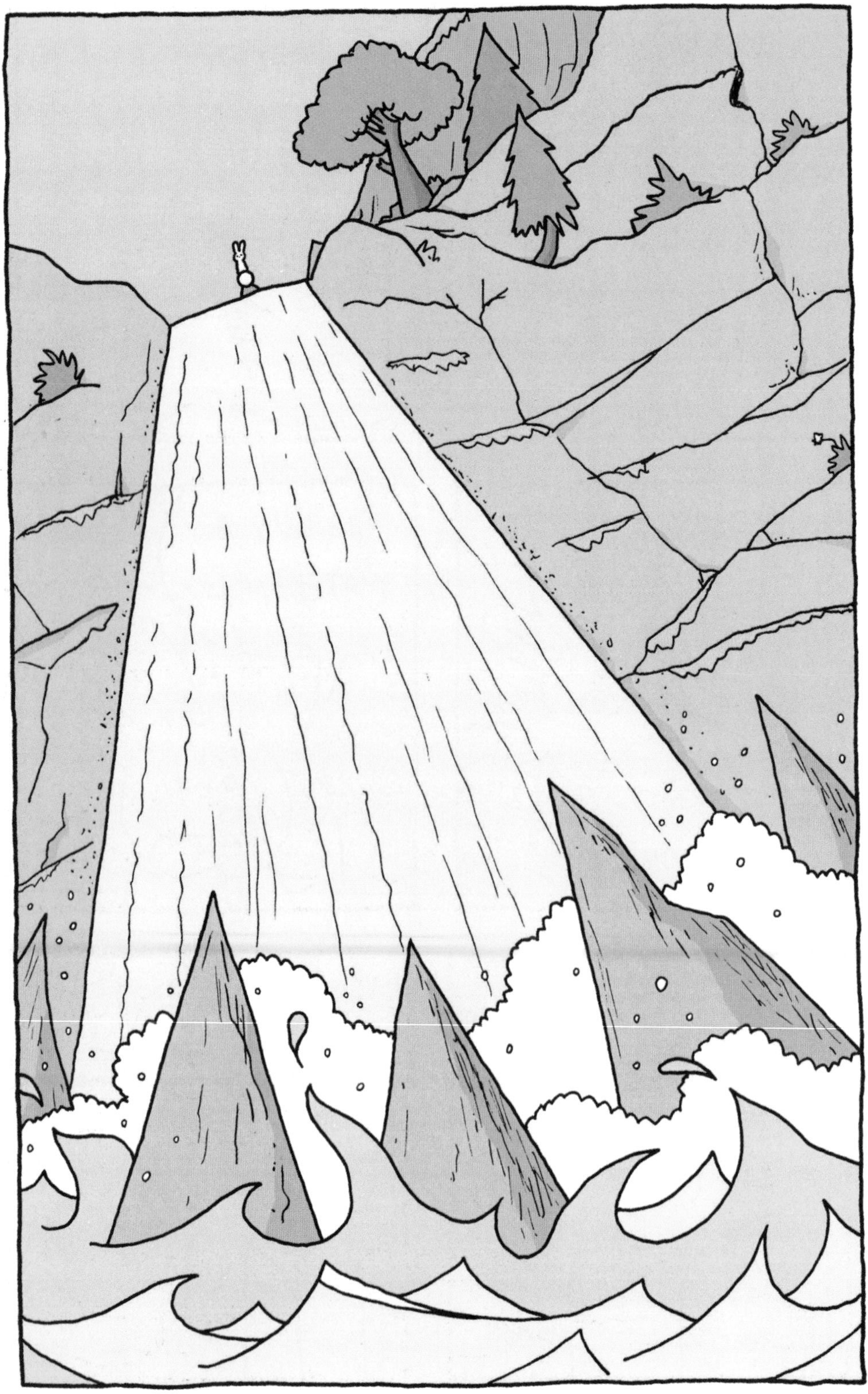

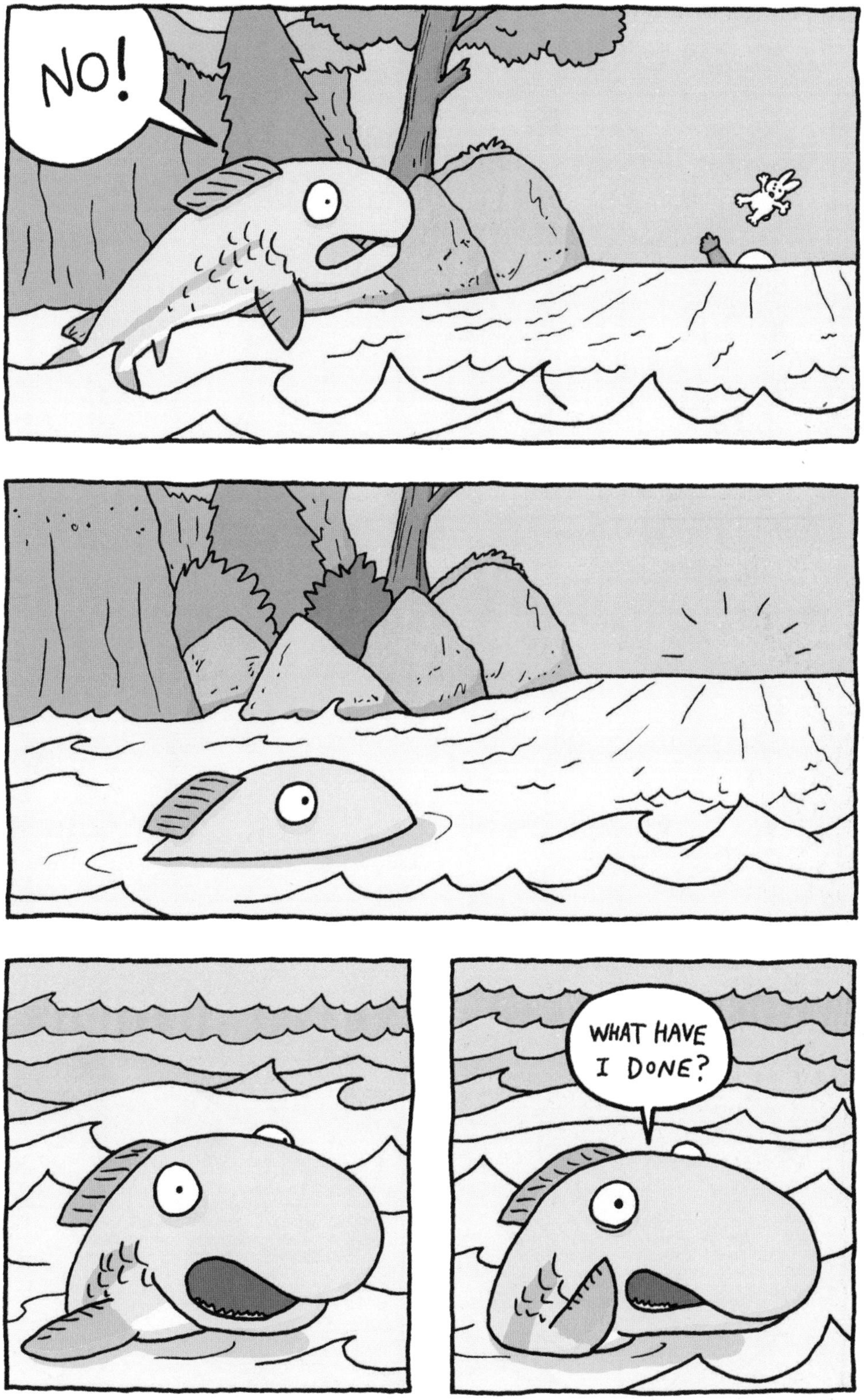
NO!
WHAT HAVE I DONE?

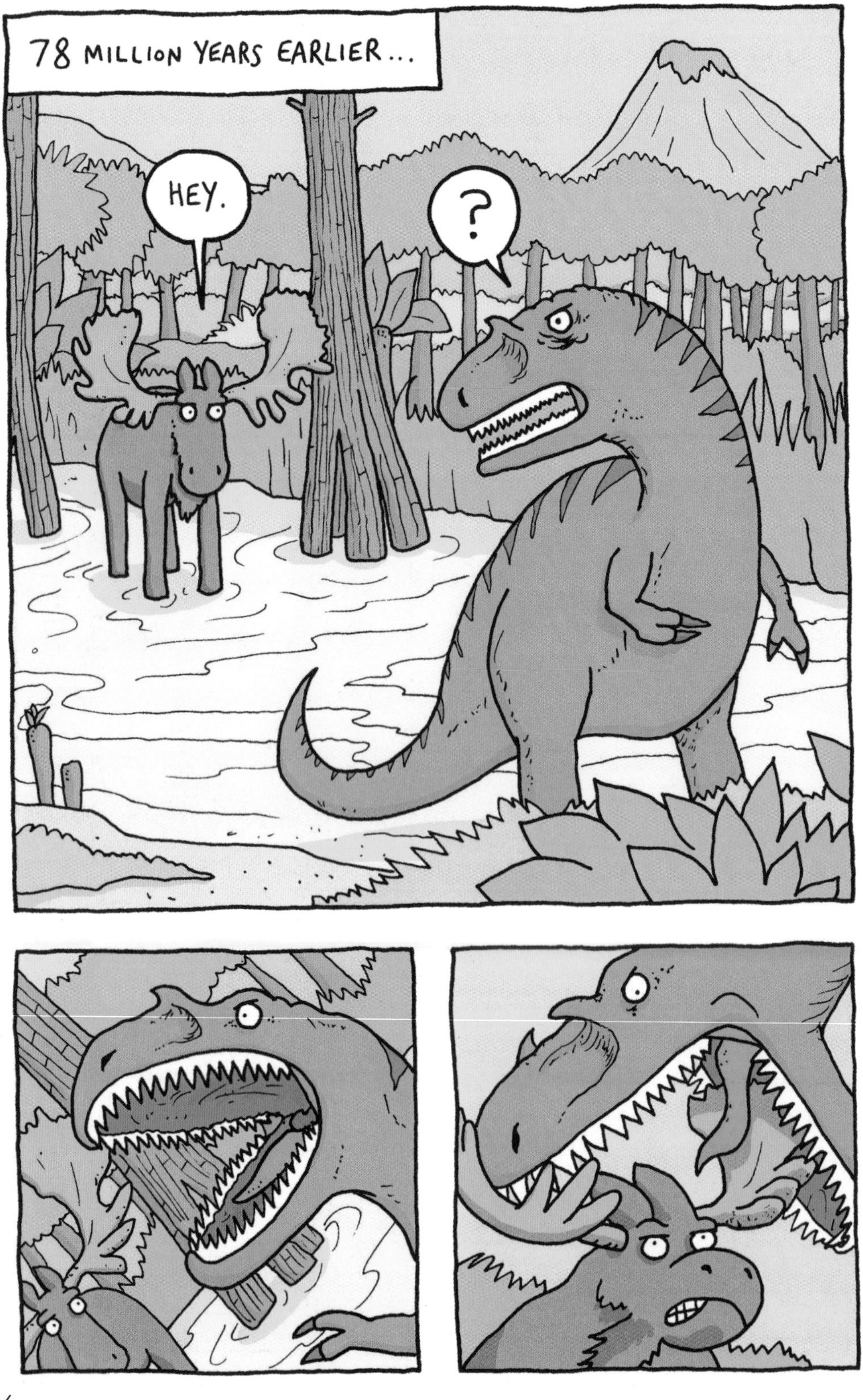
78 MILLION YEARS EARLIER...
HEY.
?

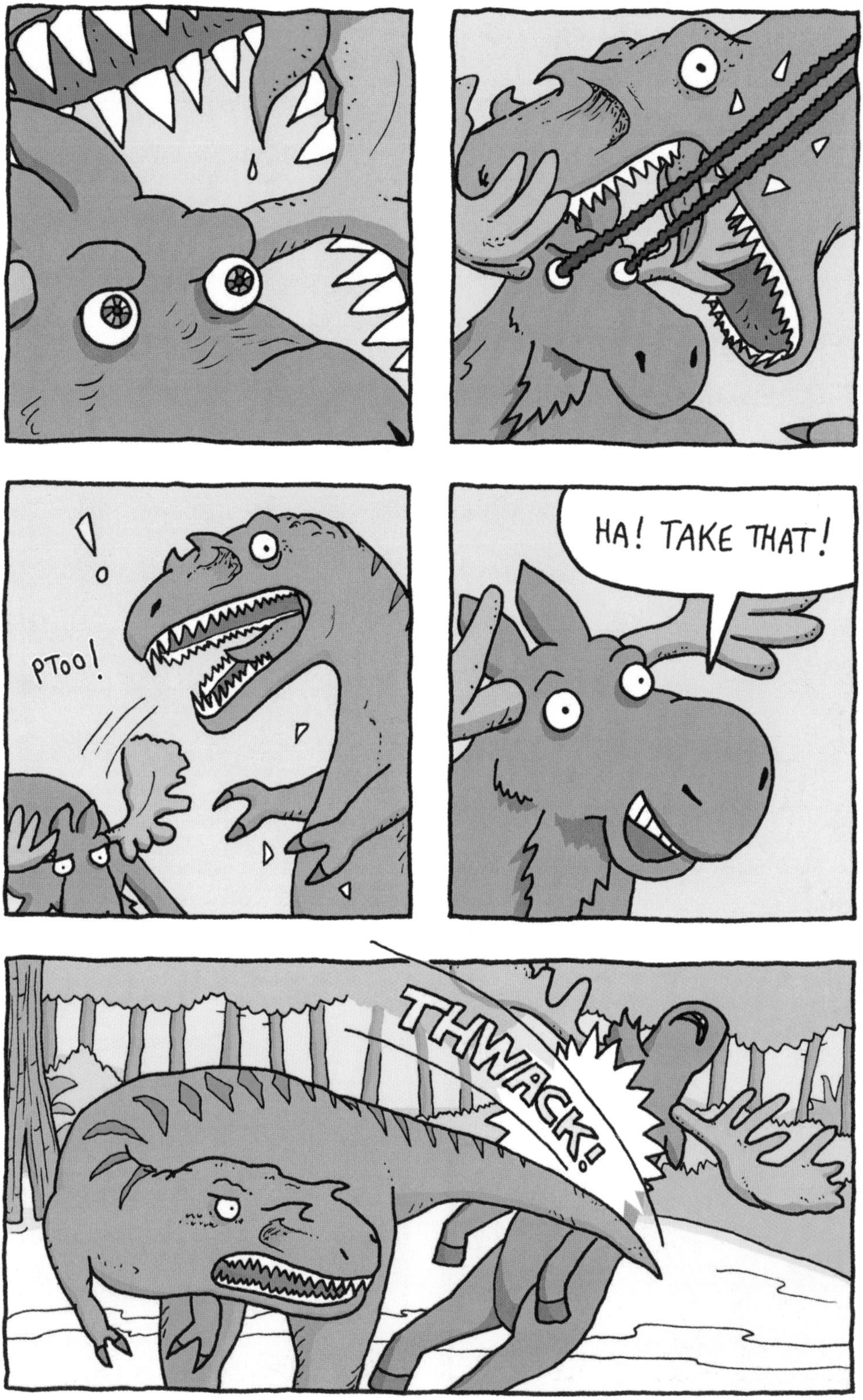
PTOO!
HA! TAKE THAT!
THWACK!

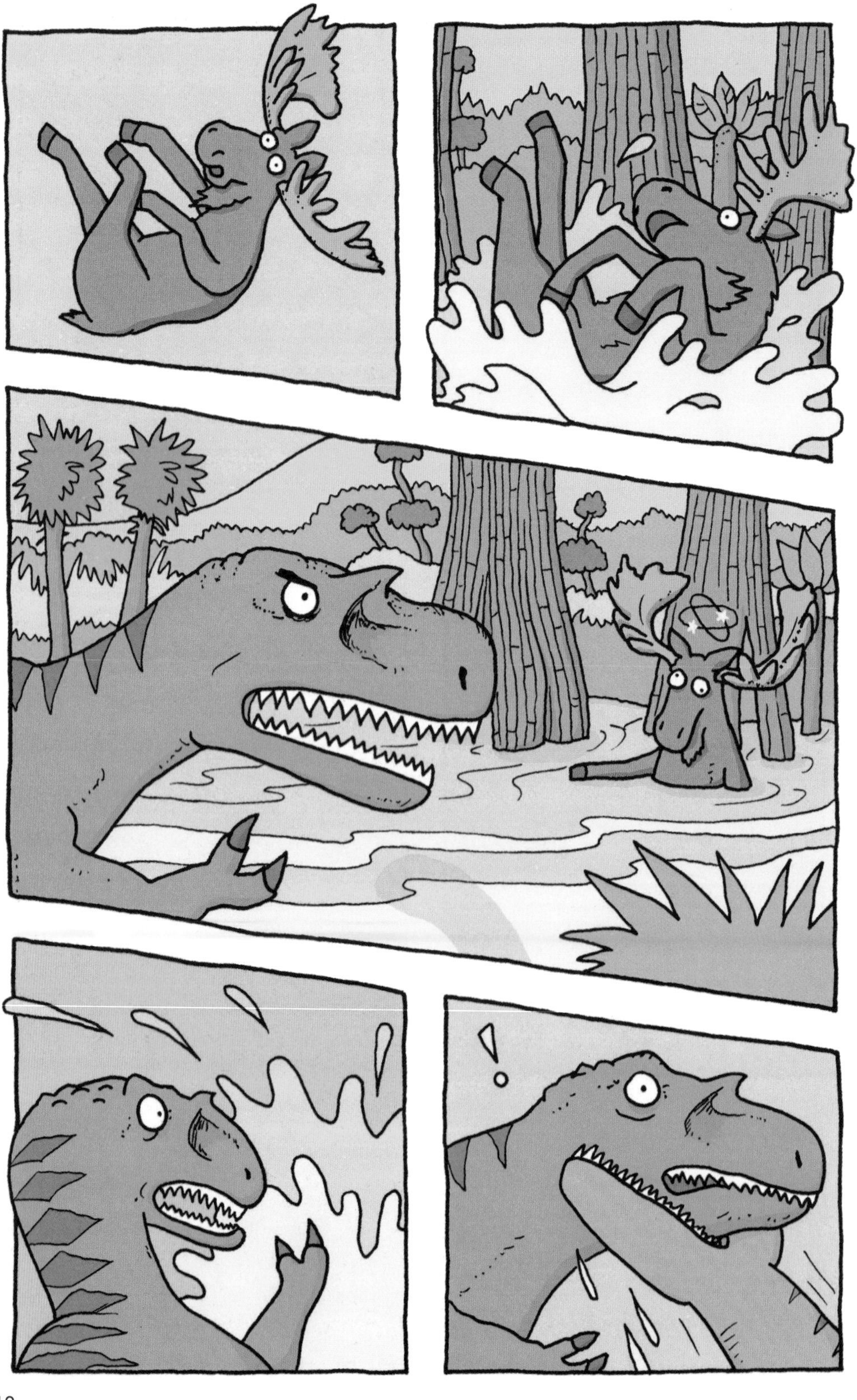
!

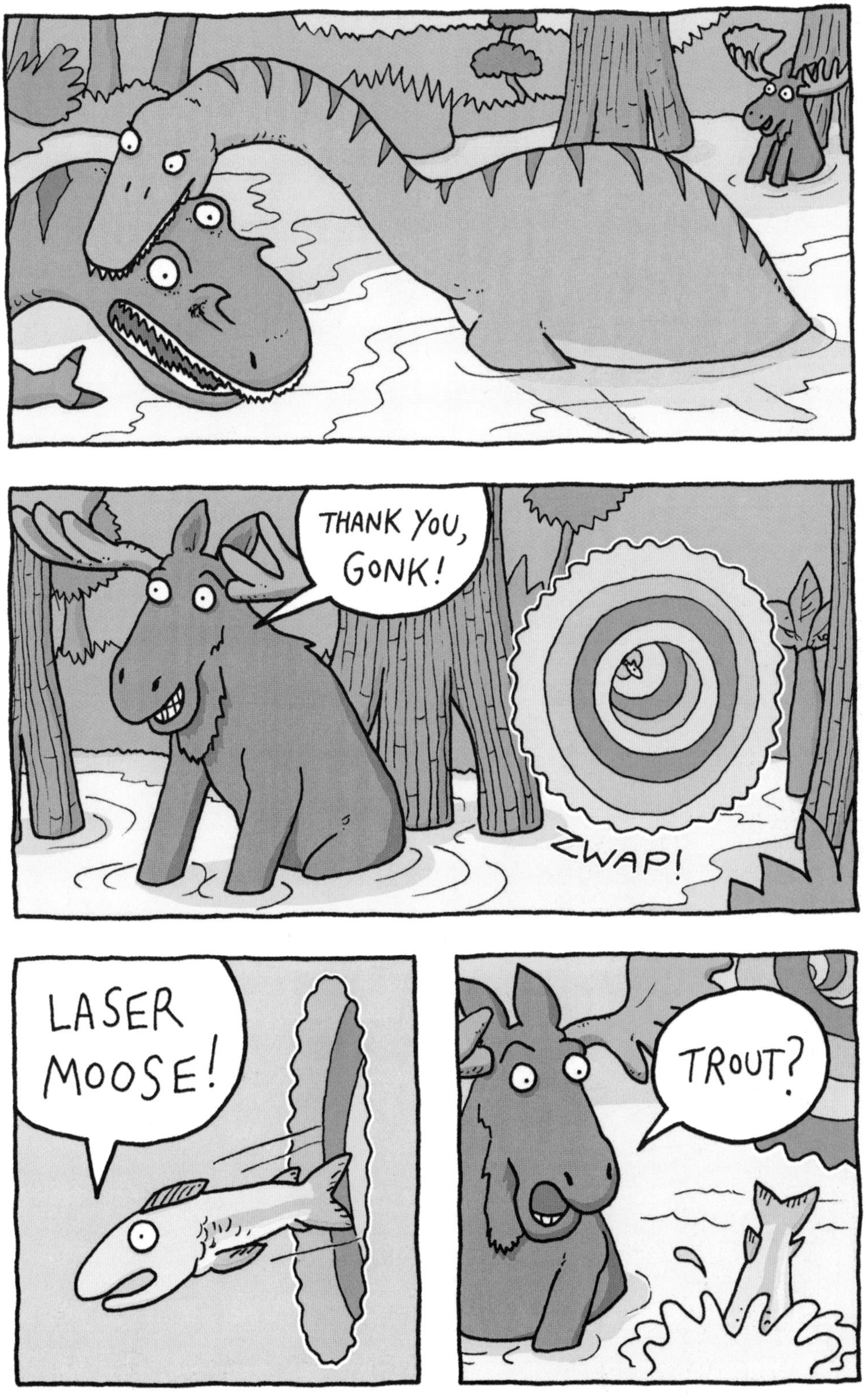
THANK YOU, GONK!
ZWAP!
LASER MOOSE!
TROUT?

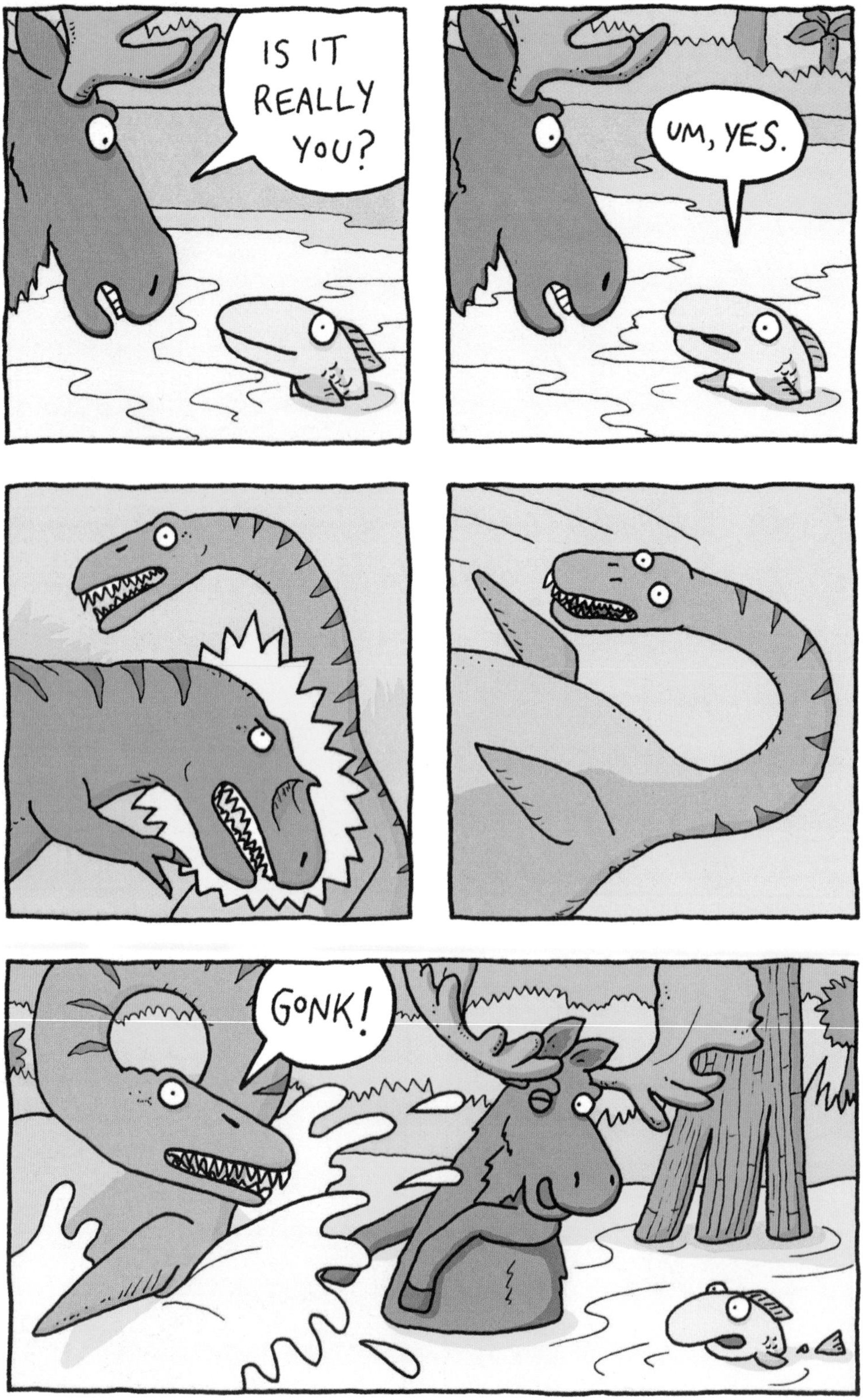
IS IT REALLY YOU?
UM, YES.
GONK!

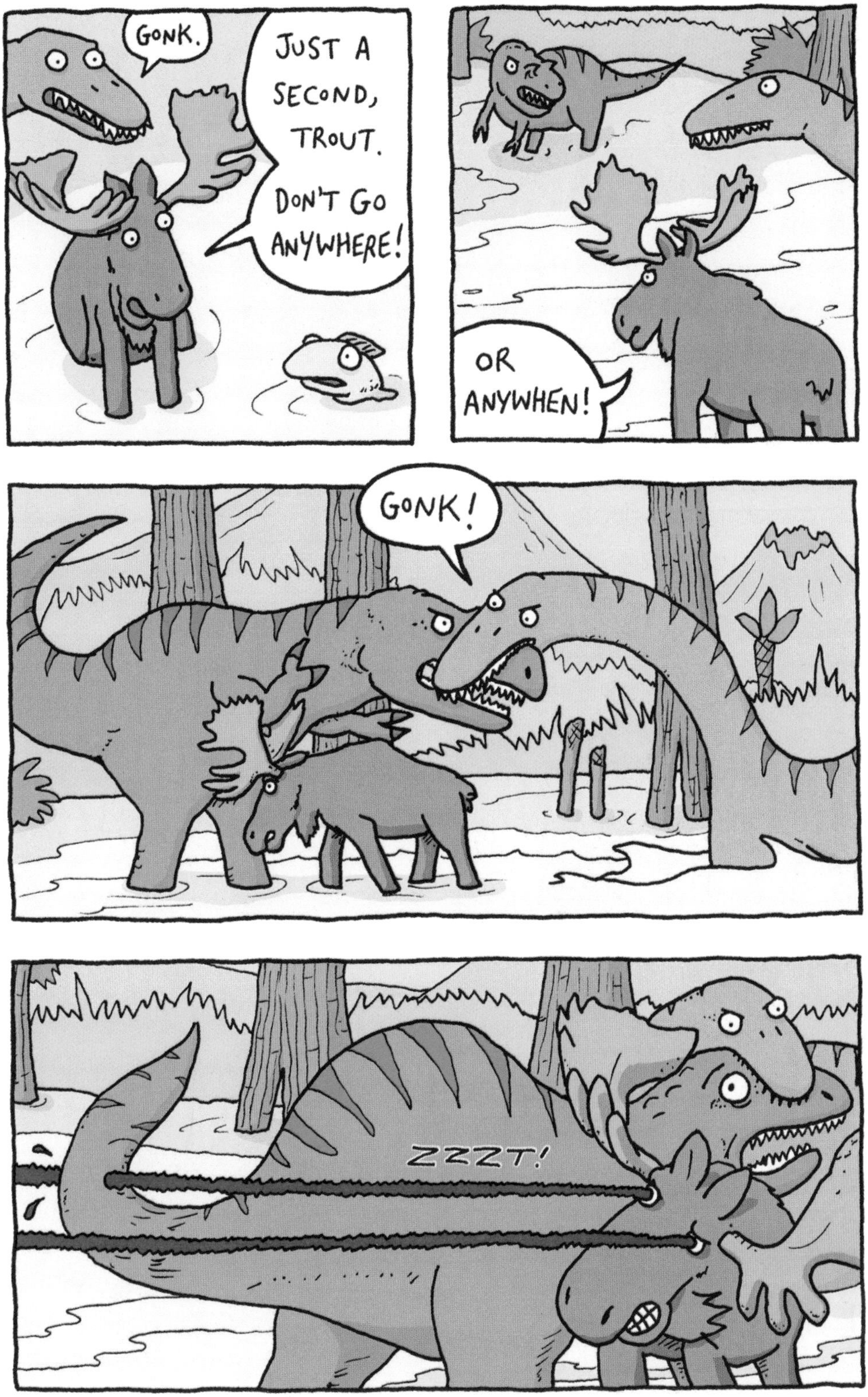
GONK.
JUST A SECOND, TROUT. DON'T GO ANYWHERE!
OR ANYWHEN!
GONK!
ZZZT!

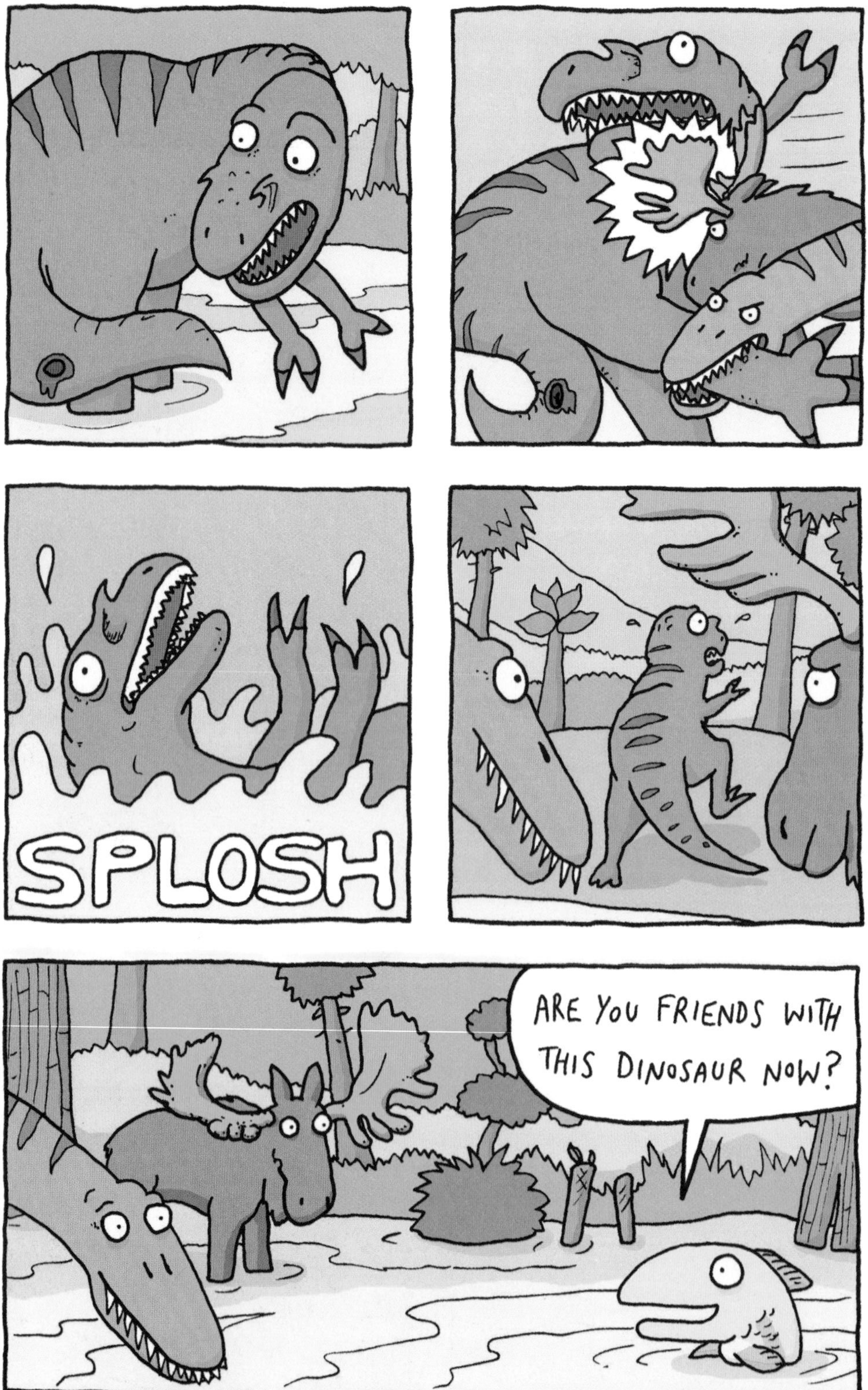
SPLOSH
ARE YOU FRIENDS WITH THIS DINOSAUR NOW?

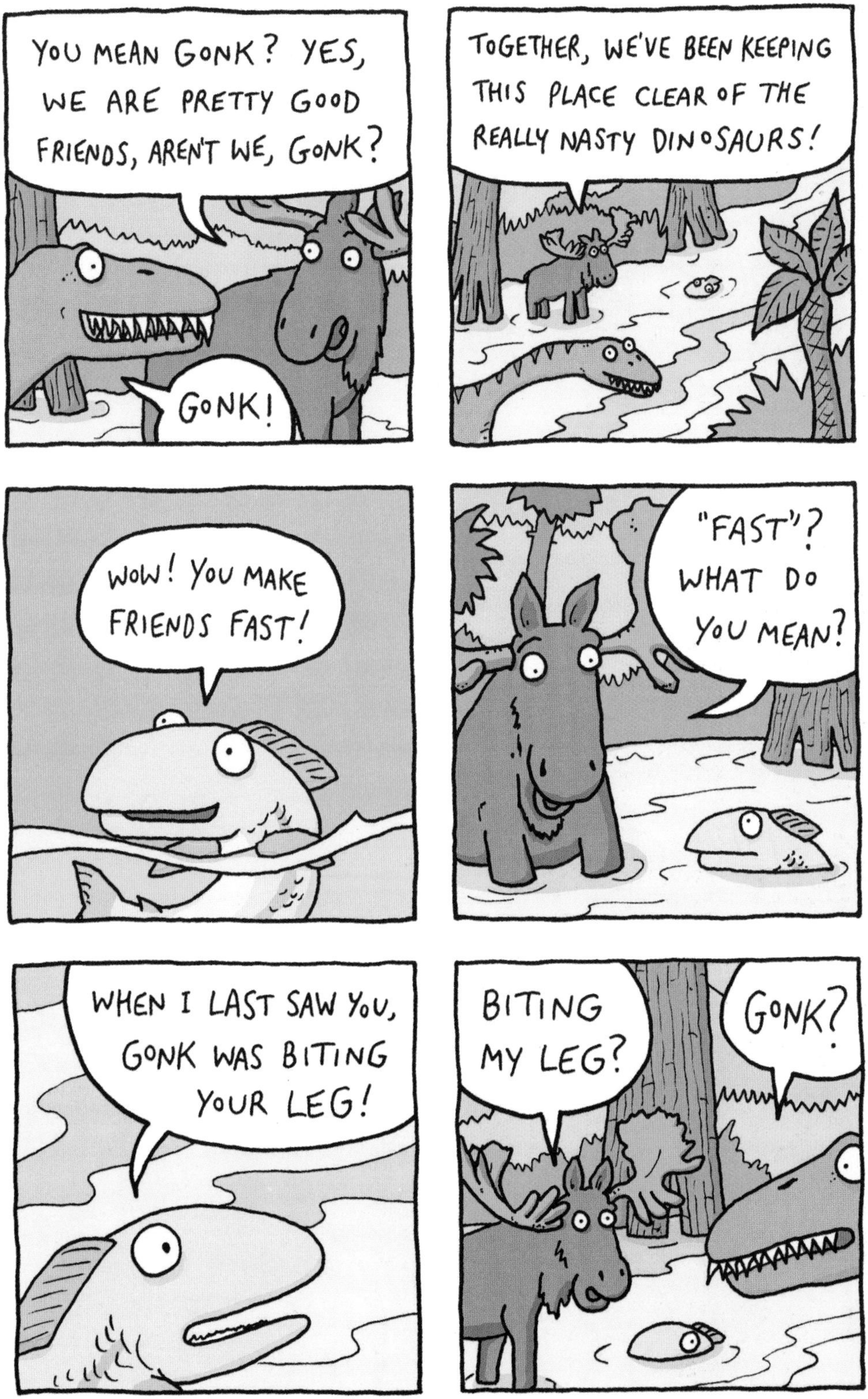
YOU MEAN GONK? YES, WE ARE PRETTY GOOD FRIENDS, AREN'T WE, GONK?
GONK!
TOGETHER, WE'VE BEEN KEEPING THIS PLACE CLEAR OF THE REALLY NASTY DINOSAURS!
WOW! YOU MAKE FRIENDS FAST!
"FAST"? WHAT DO YOU MEAN?
WHEN I LAST SAW YOU, GONK WAS BITING YOUR LEG!
BITING MY LEG?
GONK?

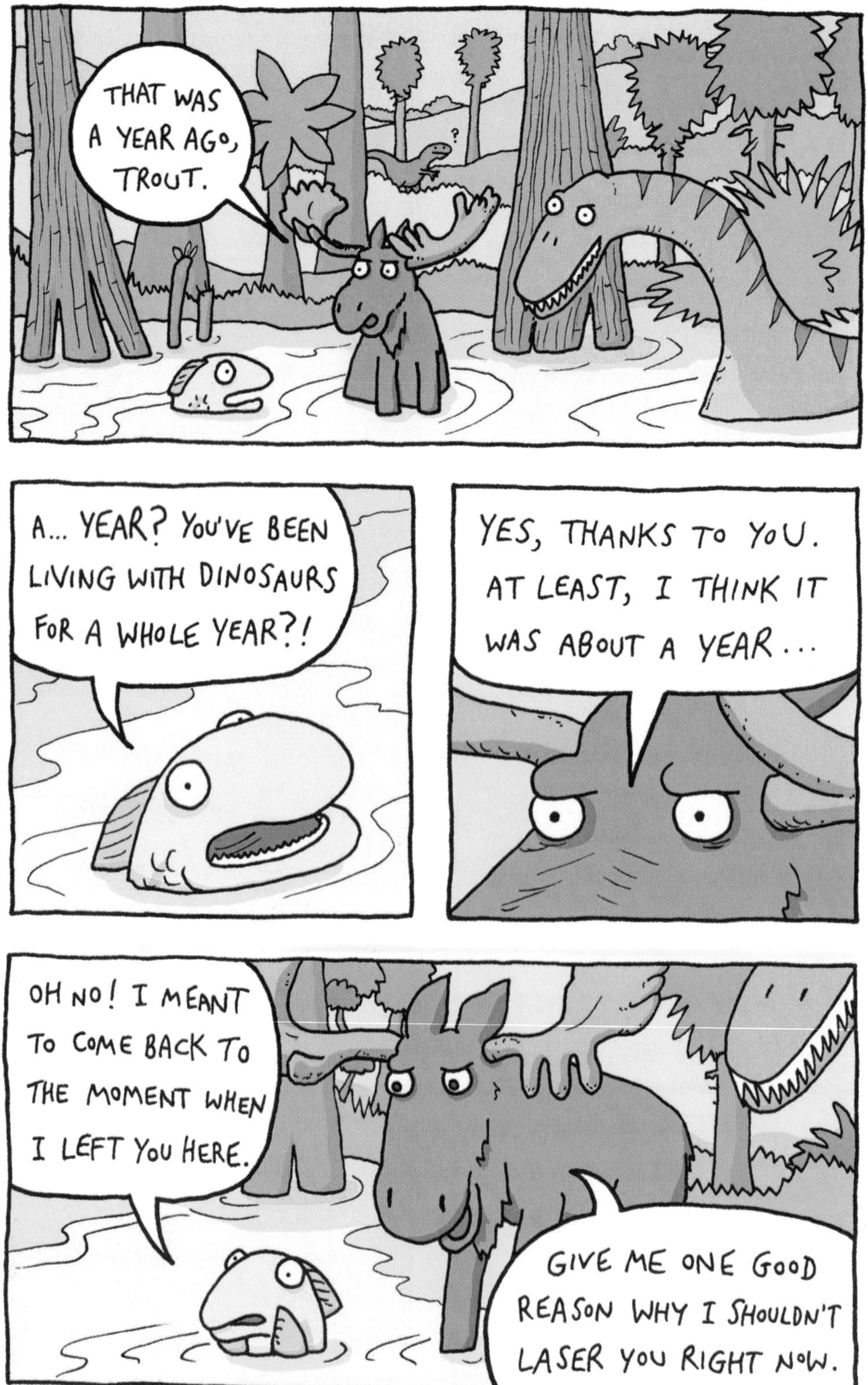
THAT WAS A YEAR AGO, TROUT.
A... YEAR? YOU'VE BEEN LIVING WITH DINOSAURS FOR A WHOLE YEAR?!
YES, THANKS TO YOU. AT LEAST, I THINK IT WAS ABOUT A YEAR...
OH NO! I MEANT TO COME BACK TO THE MOMENT WHEN I LEFT YOU HERE.
GIVE ME ONE GOOD REASON WHY I SHOULDN'T LASER YOU RIGHT NOW.

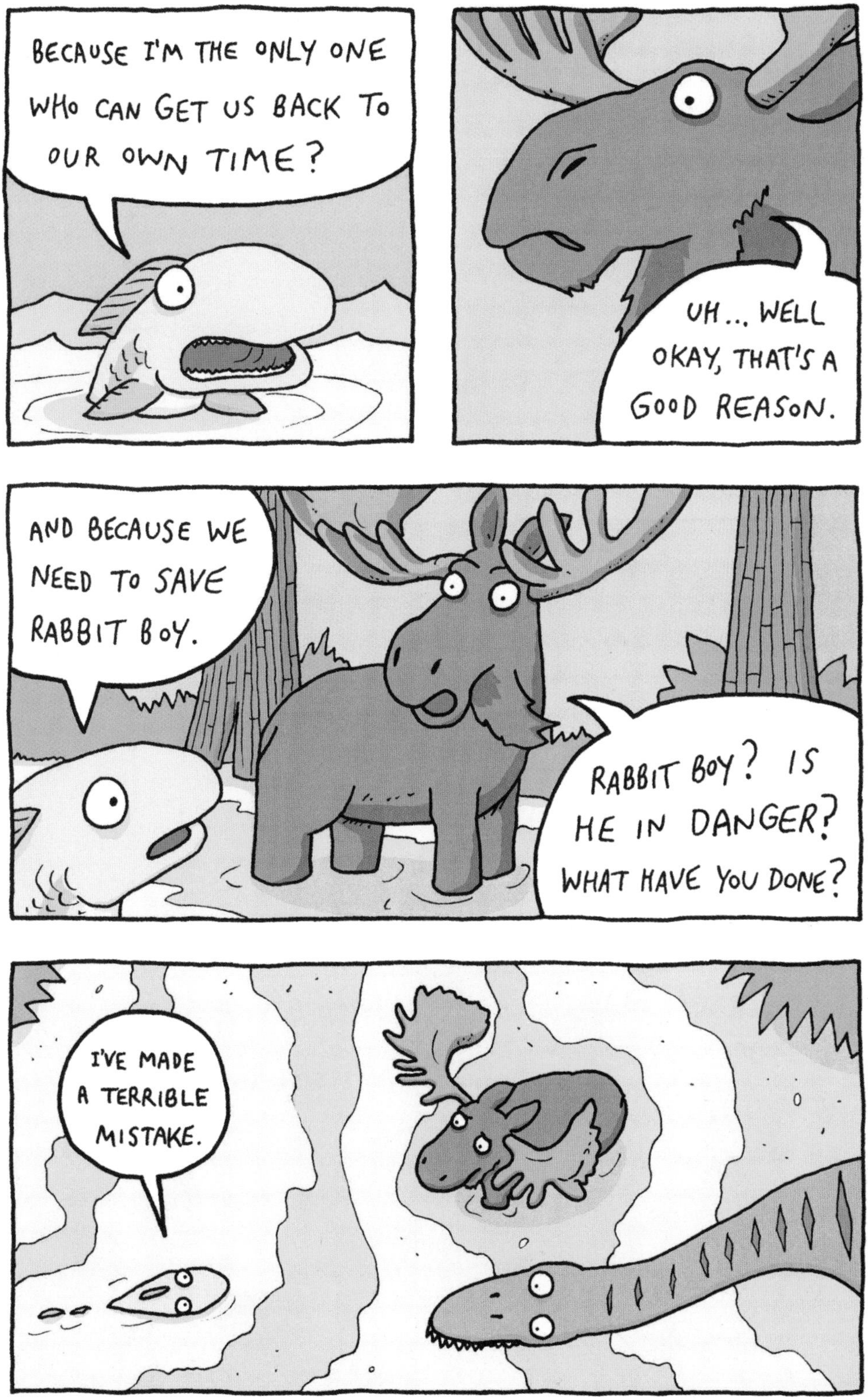
BECAUSE I'M THE ONLY ONE WHO CAN GET US BACK TO OUR OWN TIME?
UH... WELL OKAY, THAT'S A GOOD REASON.
AND BECAUSE WE NEED TO SAVE RABBIT BOY.
RABBIT BOY? IS HE IN DANGER? WHAT HAVE YOU DONE?
I'VE MADE A TERRIBLE MISTAKE.

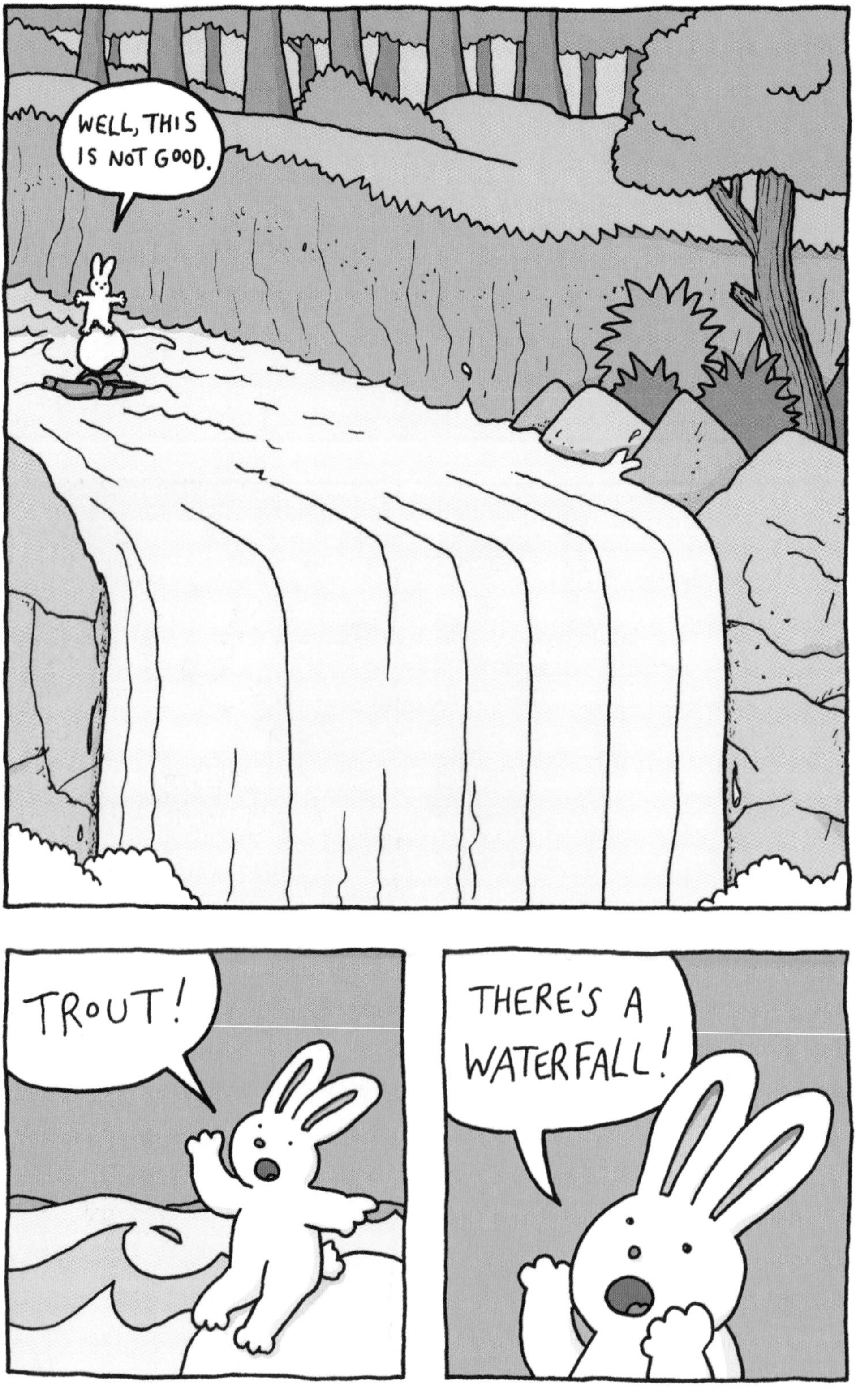
WELL, THIS IS NOT GOOD.
TROUT!
THERE'S A WATERFALL!

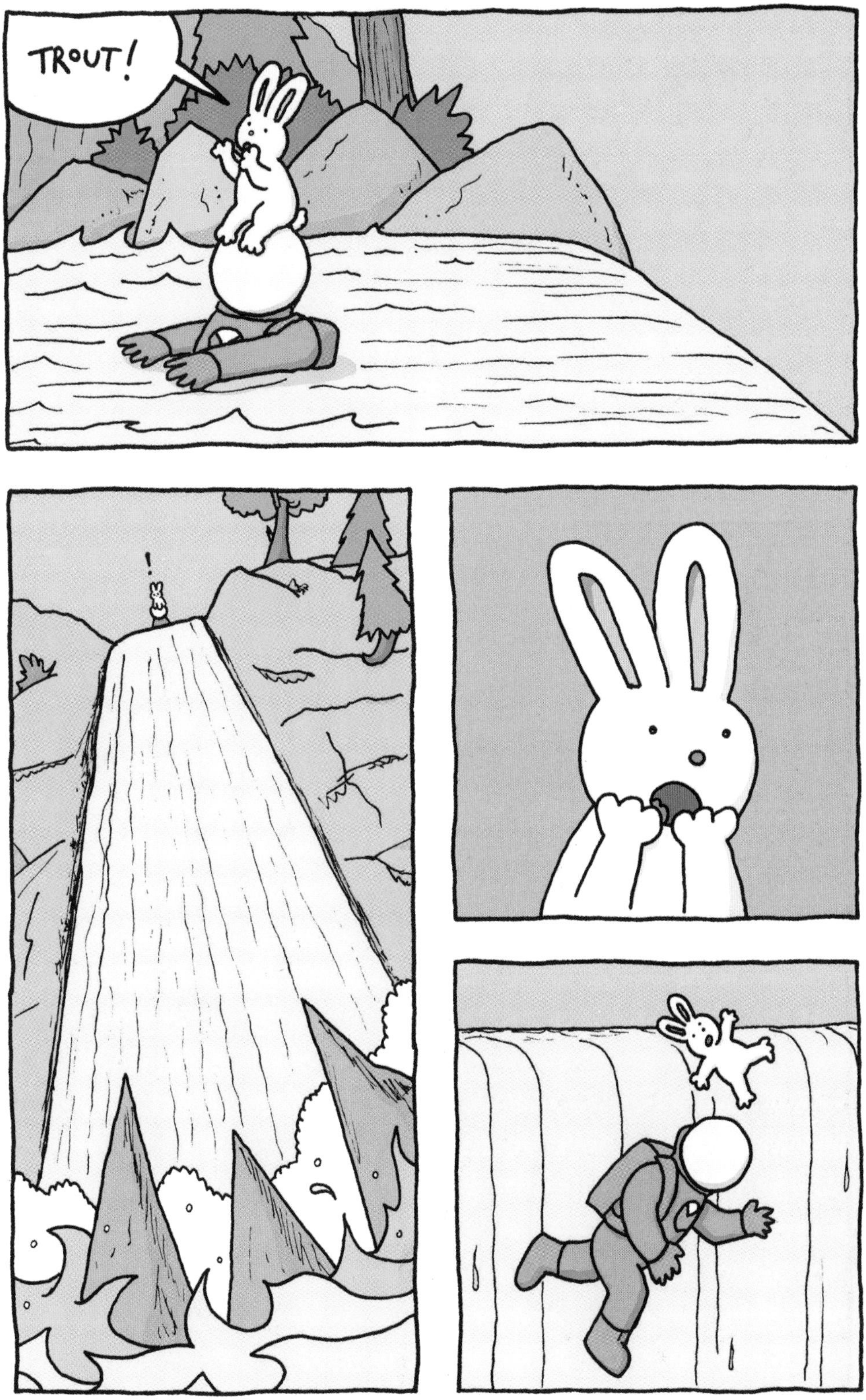
TROUT!
!

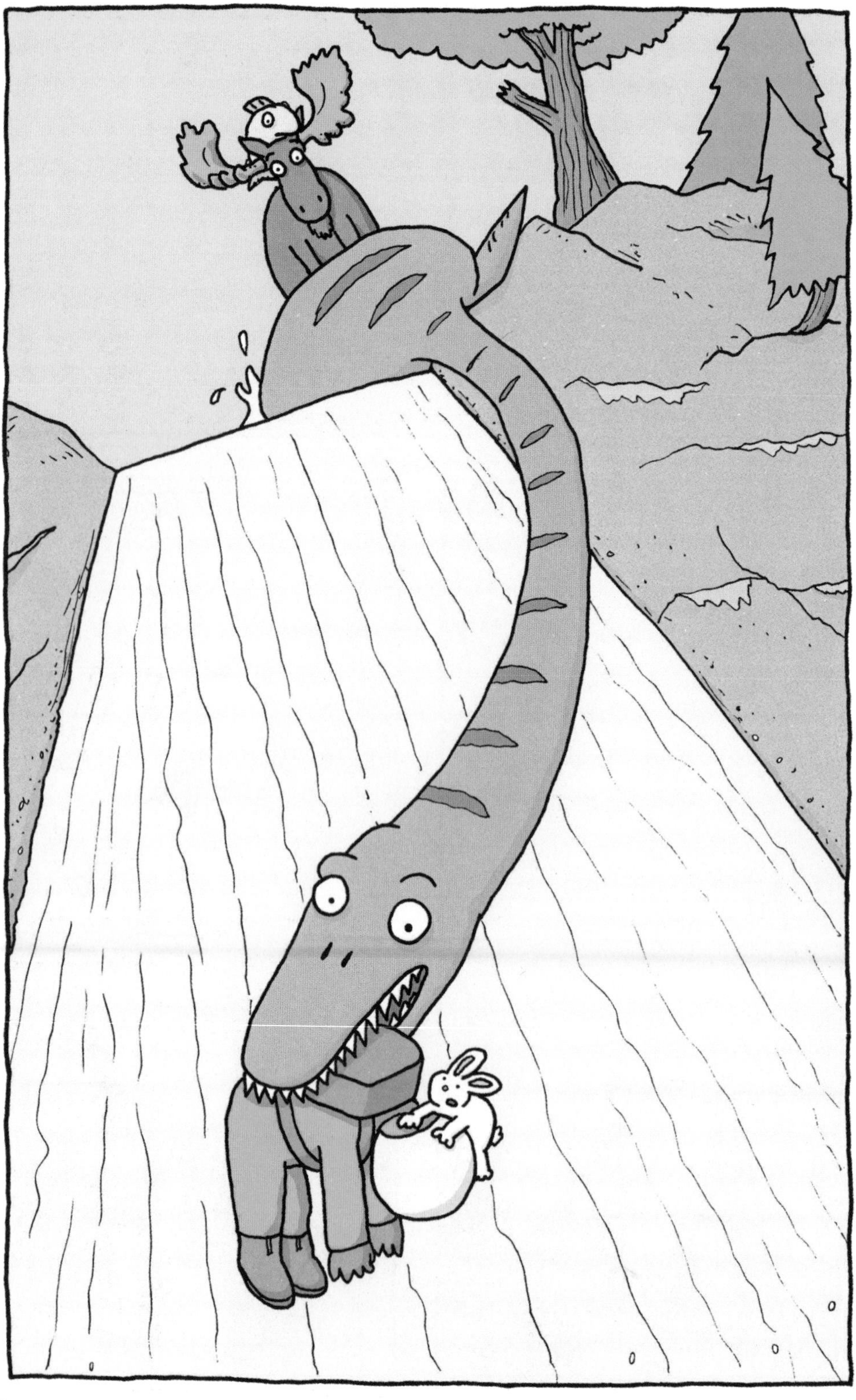

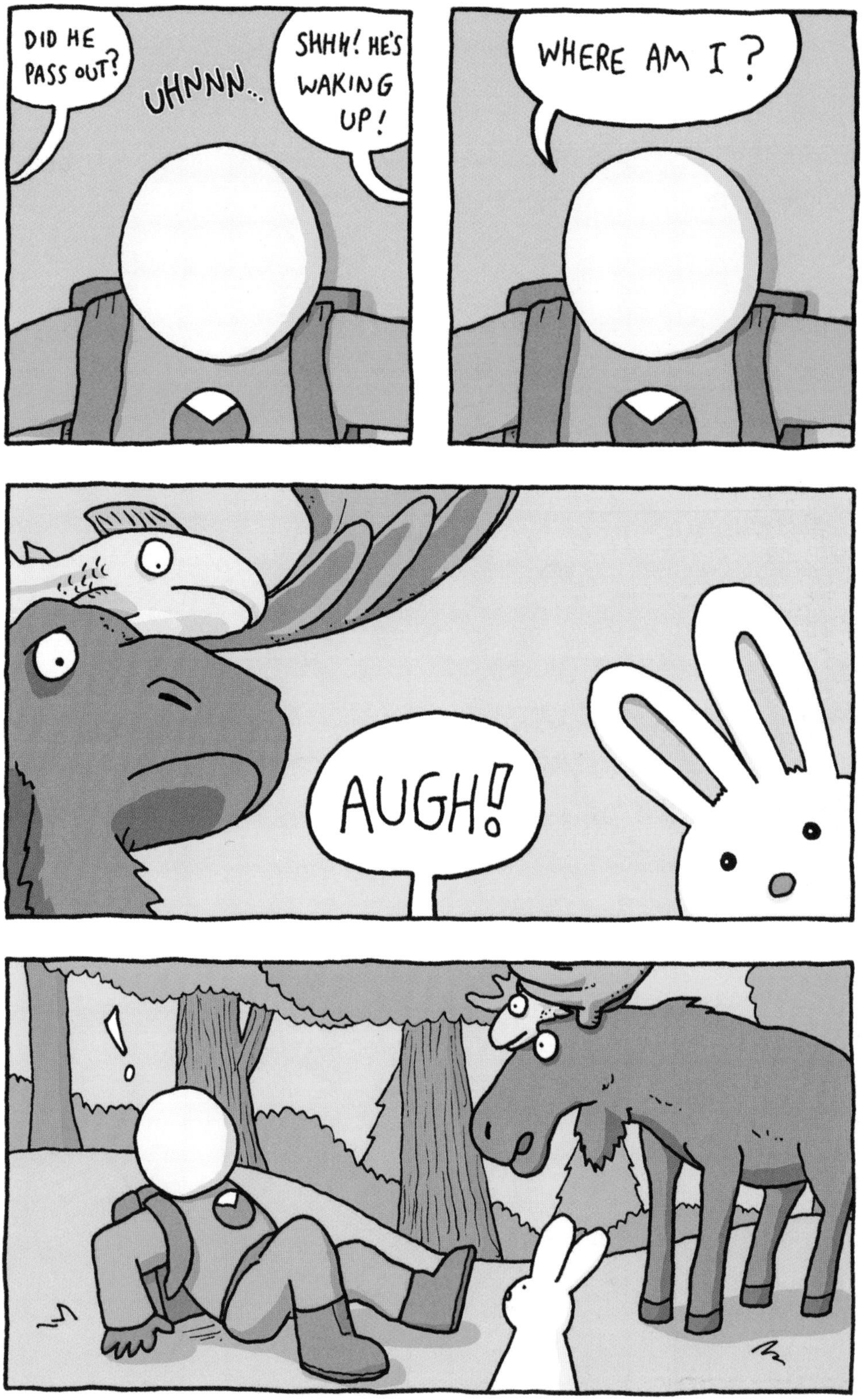
DID HE PASS OUT?
UHNNN...
SHHH! HE'S WAKING UP!
WHERE AM I?
AUGH!!

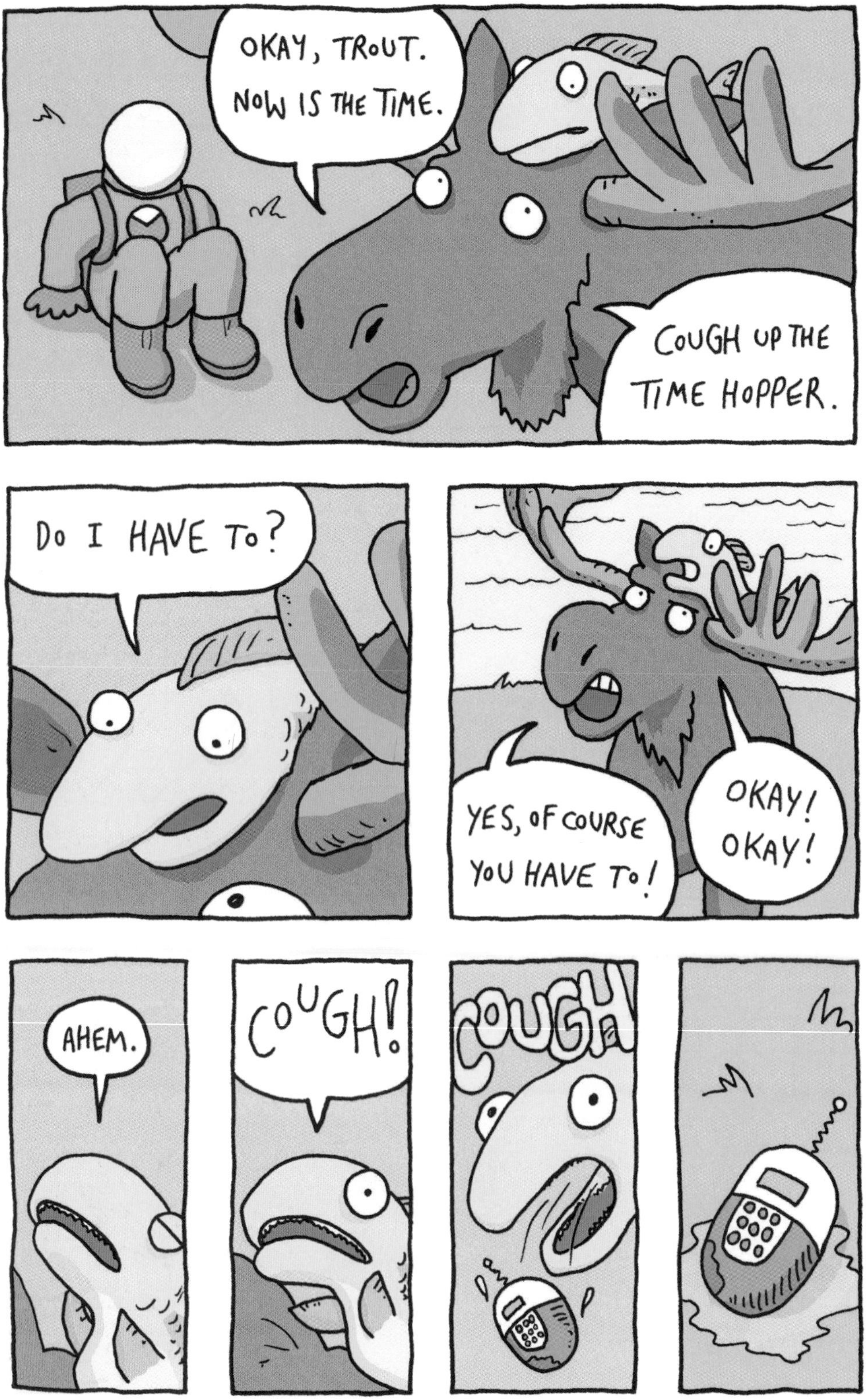
OKAY, TROUT. NOW IS THE TIME.
COUGH UP THE TIME HOPPER.
DO I HAVE TO?
YES, OF COURSE YOU HAVE TO!
OKAY! OKAY!
AHEM.
COUGH!
COUGH

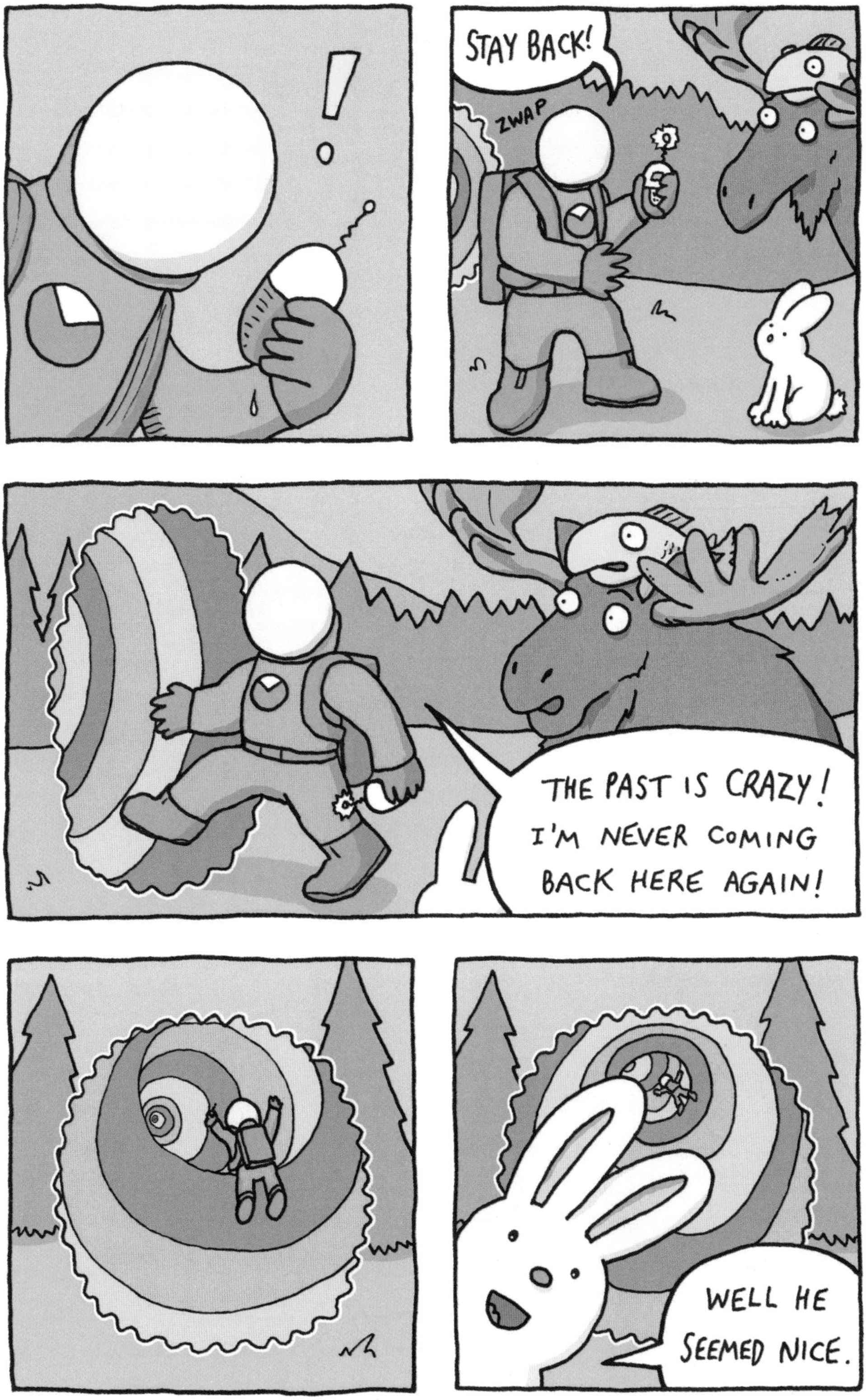
STAY BACK!
ZWAP
THE PAST IS CRAZY! I'M NEVER COMING BACK HERE AGAIN!
WELL HE SEEMED NICE.

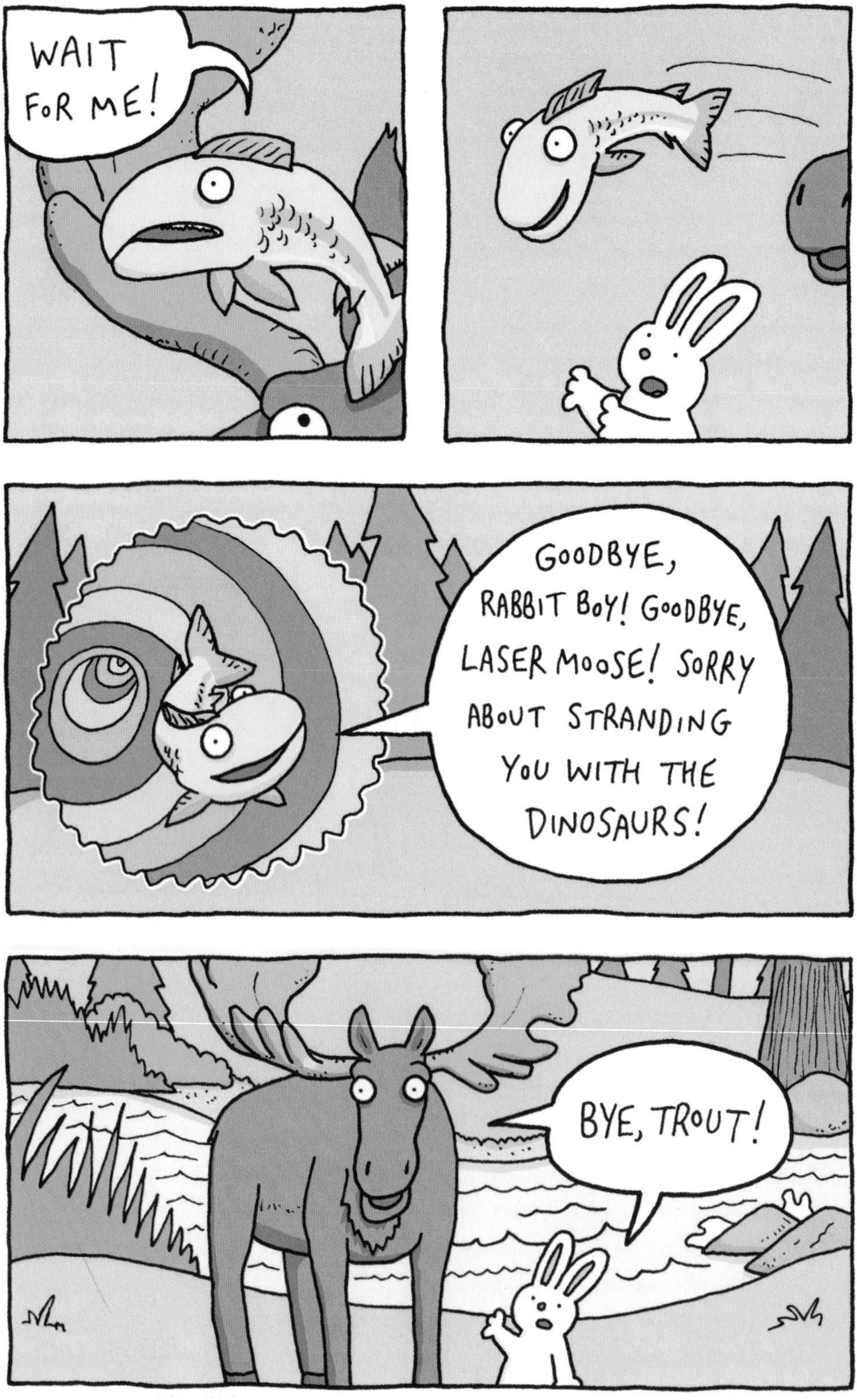
WAIT FOR ME!
GOODBYE, RABBIT BOY! GOODBYE, LASER MOOSE! SORRY ABOUT STRANDING YOU WITH THE DINOSAURS!
BYE, TROUT!

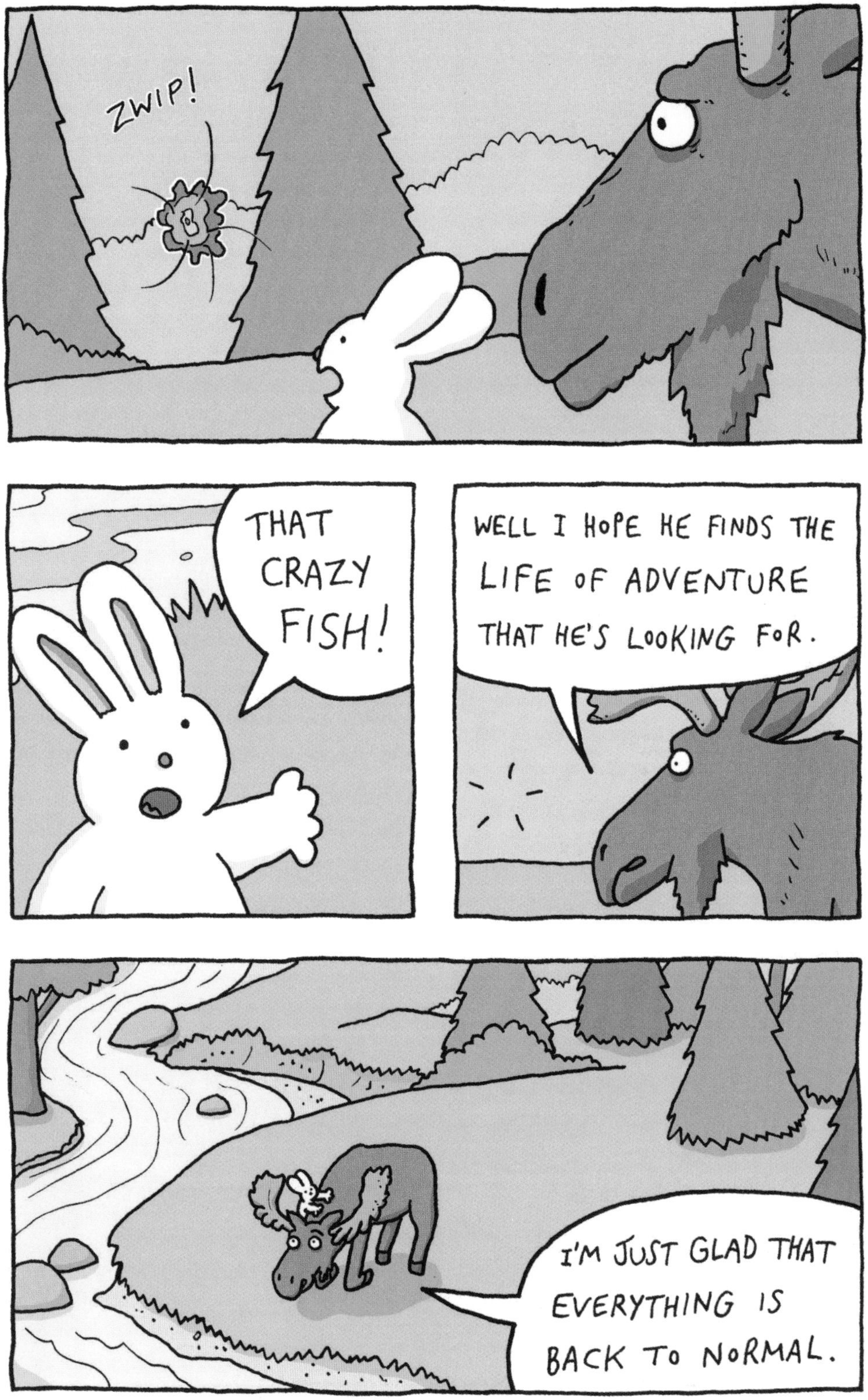
ZWIP!
THAT CRAZY FISH!
WELL I HOPE HE FINDS THE LIFE OF ADVENTURE THAT HE'S LOOKING FOR.
I'M JUST GLAD THAT EVERYTHING IS BACK TO NORMAL.

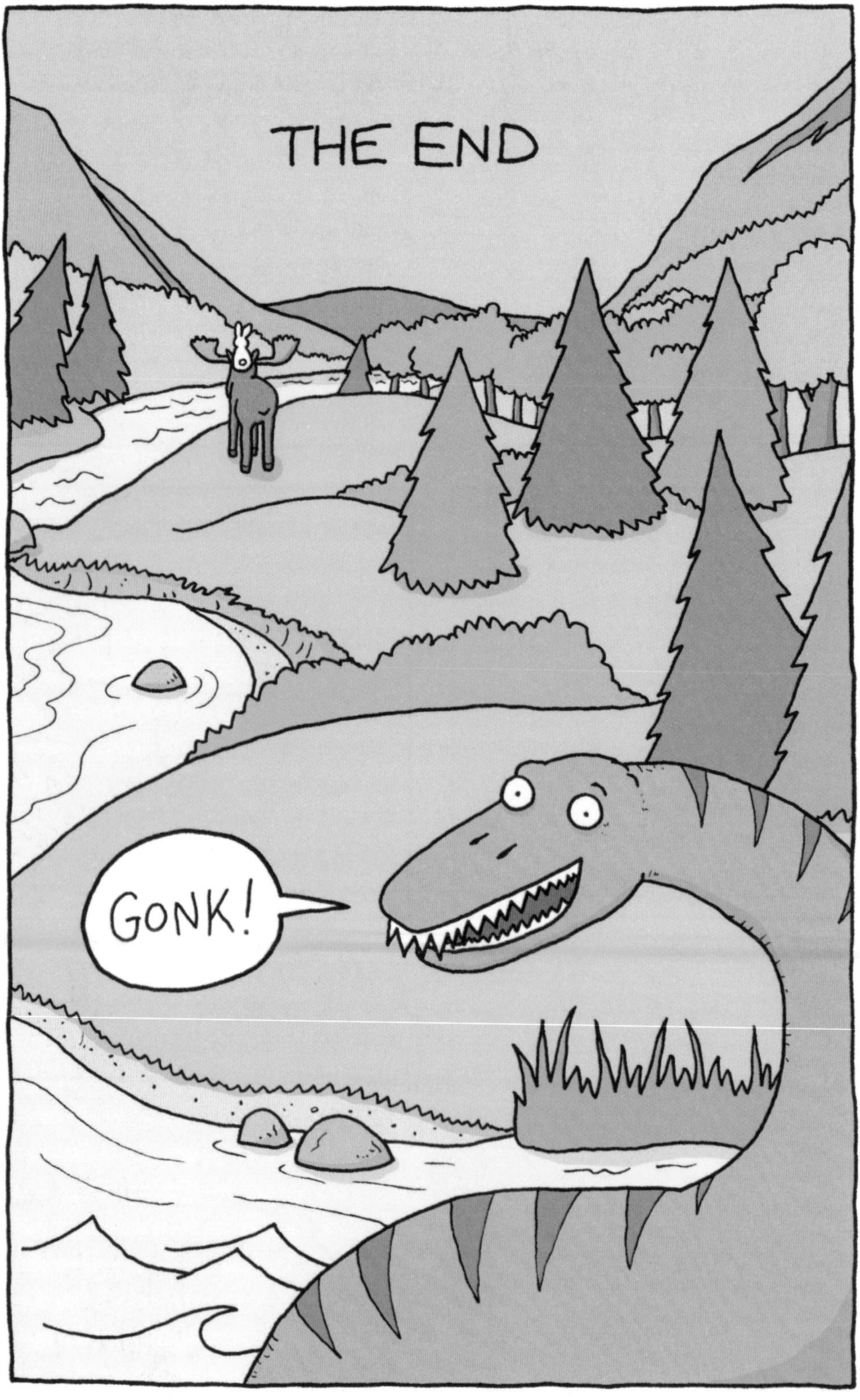
THE END
GONK!

MORE TO EXPLORE!

Learn About TIME TRAVEL!

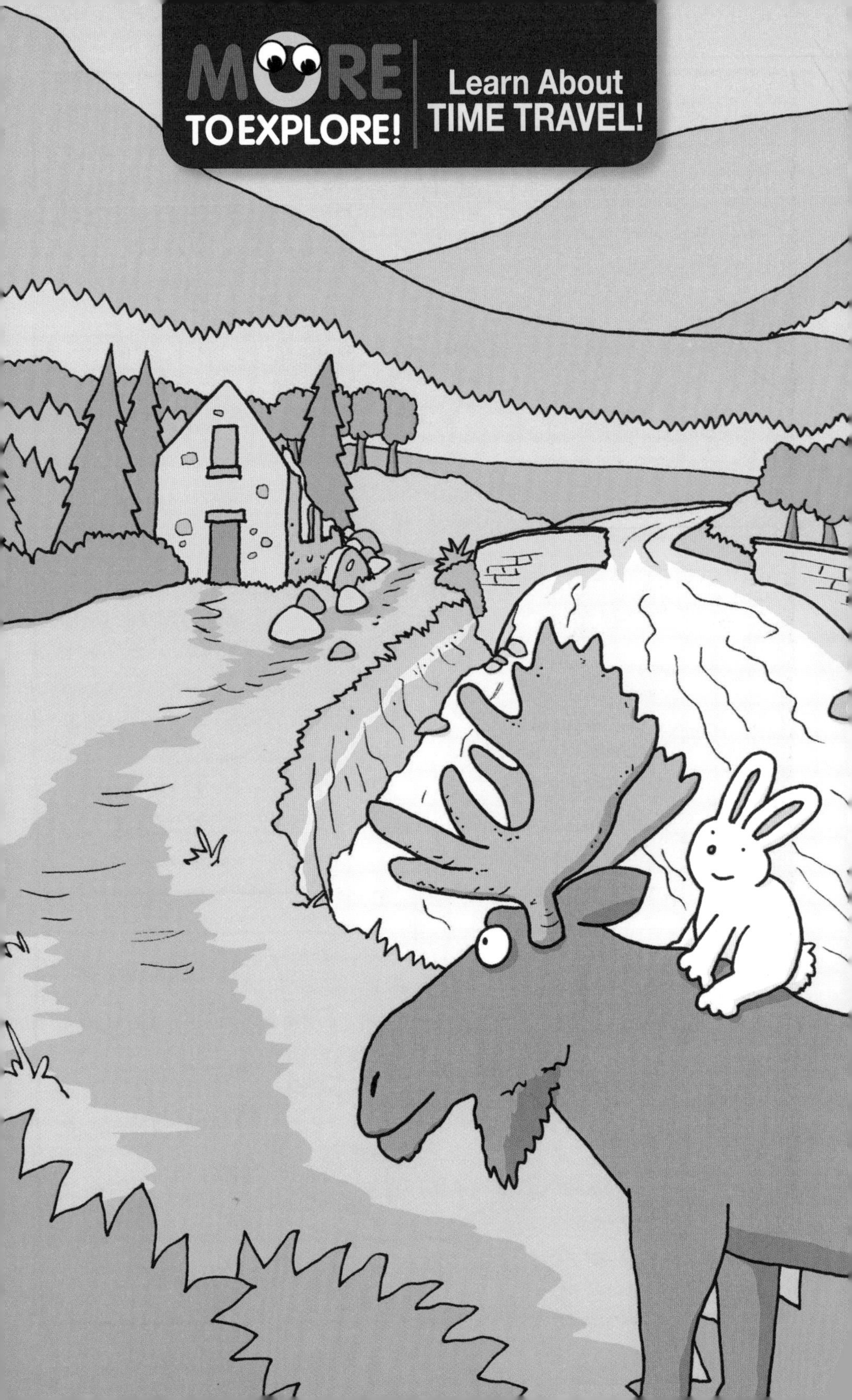

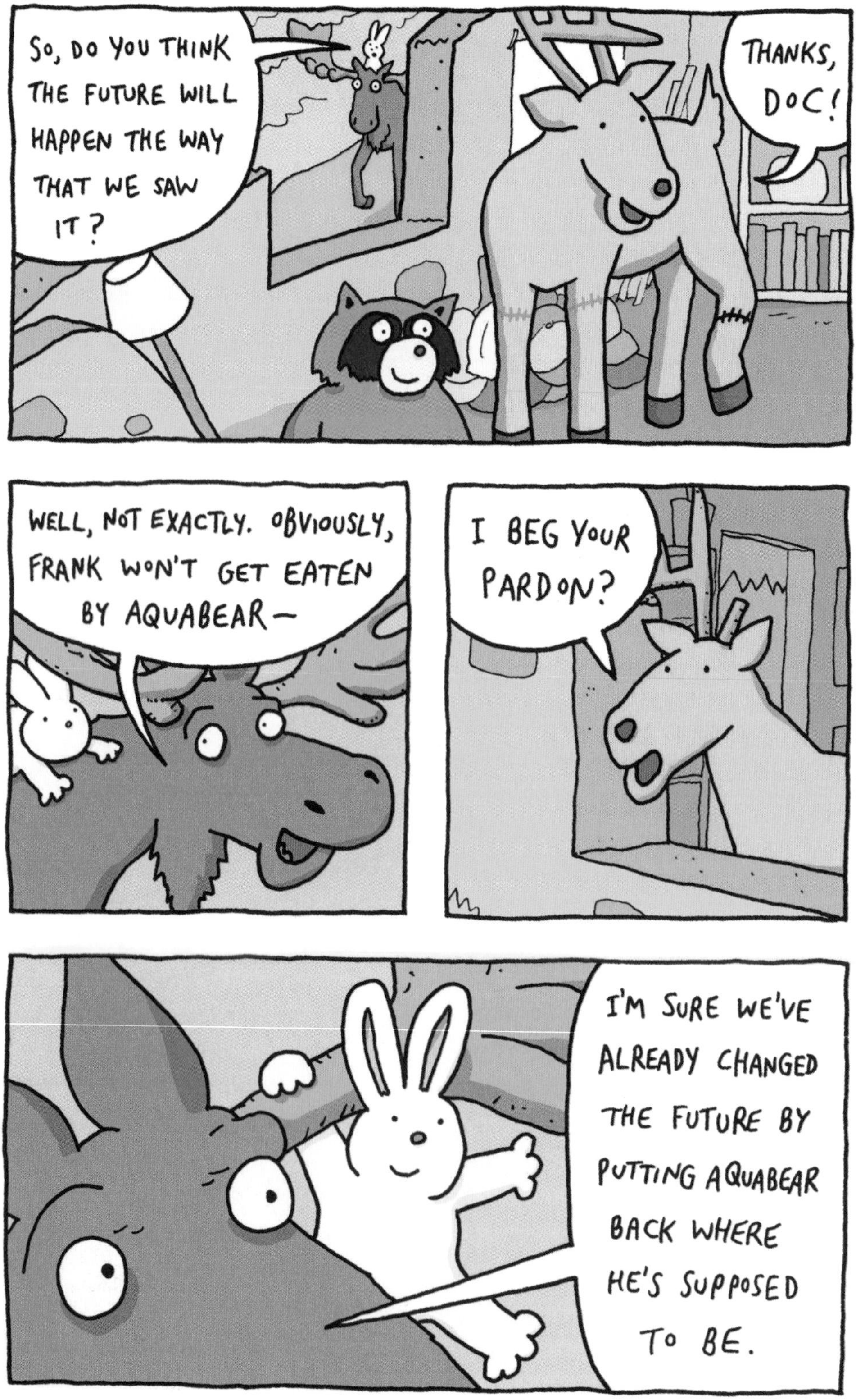
SO, DO YOU THINK THE FUTURE WILL HAPPEN THE WAY THAT WE SAW IT?
THANKS, DOC!
WELL, NOT EXACTLY. OBVIOUSLY, FRANK WON'T GET EATEN BY AQUABEAR—
I BEG YOUR PARDON?
I'M SURE WE'VE ALREADY CHANGED THE FUTURE BY PUTTING AQUABEAR BACK WHERE HE'S SUPPOSED TO BE.

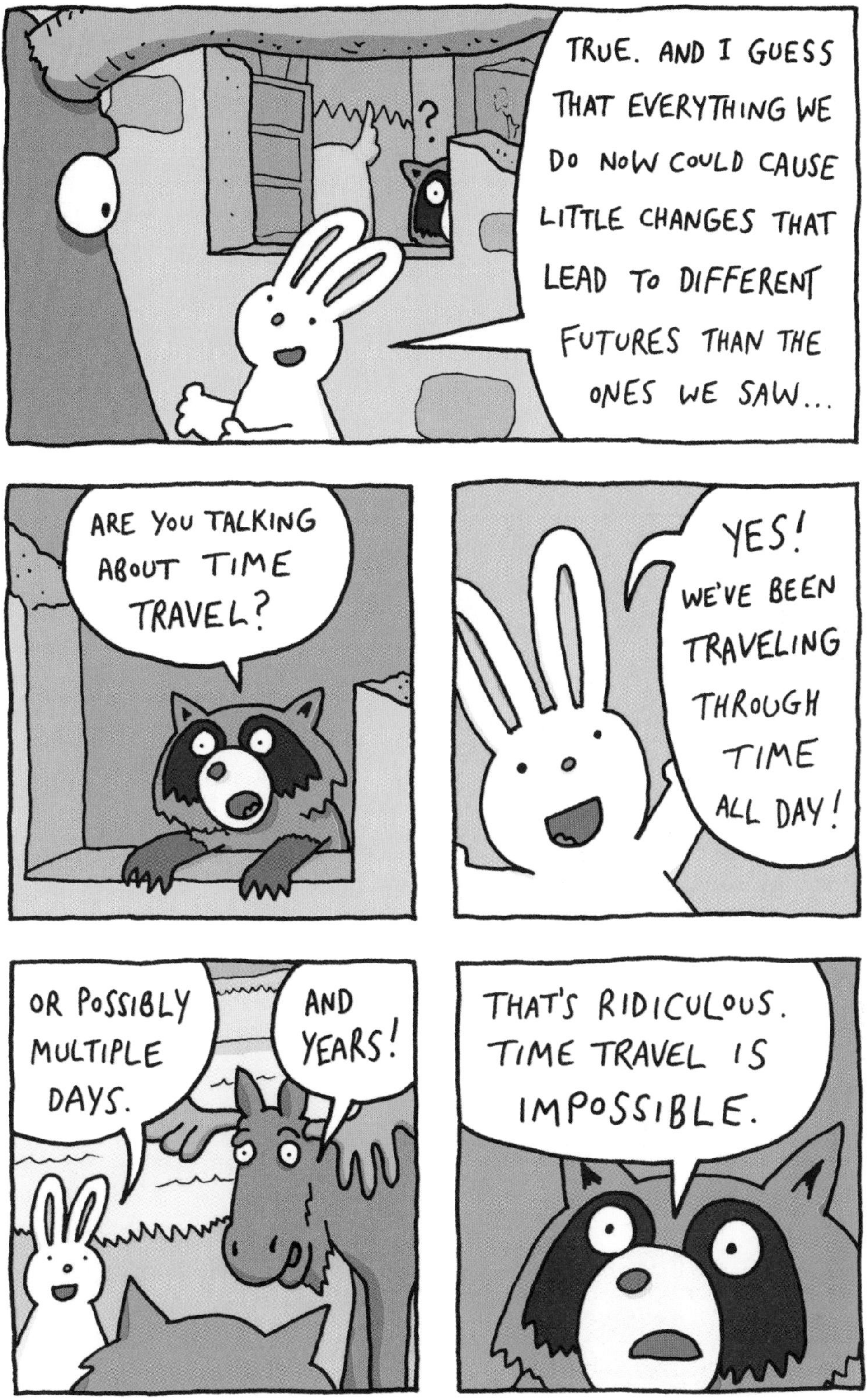
TRUE. AND I GUESS THAT EVERYTHING WE DO NOW COULD CAUSE LITTLE CHANGES THAT LEAD TO DIFFERENT FUTURES THAN THE ONES WE SAW...
ARE YOU TALKING ABOUT TIME TRAVEL?
YES! WE'VE BEEN TRAVELING THROUGH TIME ALL DAY!
OR POSSIBLY MULTIPLE DAYS.
AND YEARS!
THAT'S RIDICULOUS. TIME TRAVEL IS IMPOSSIBLE.

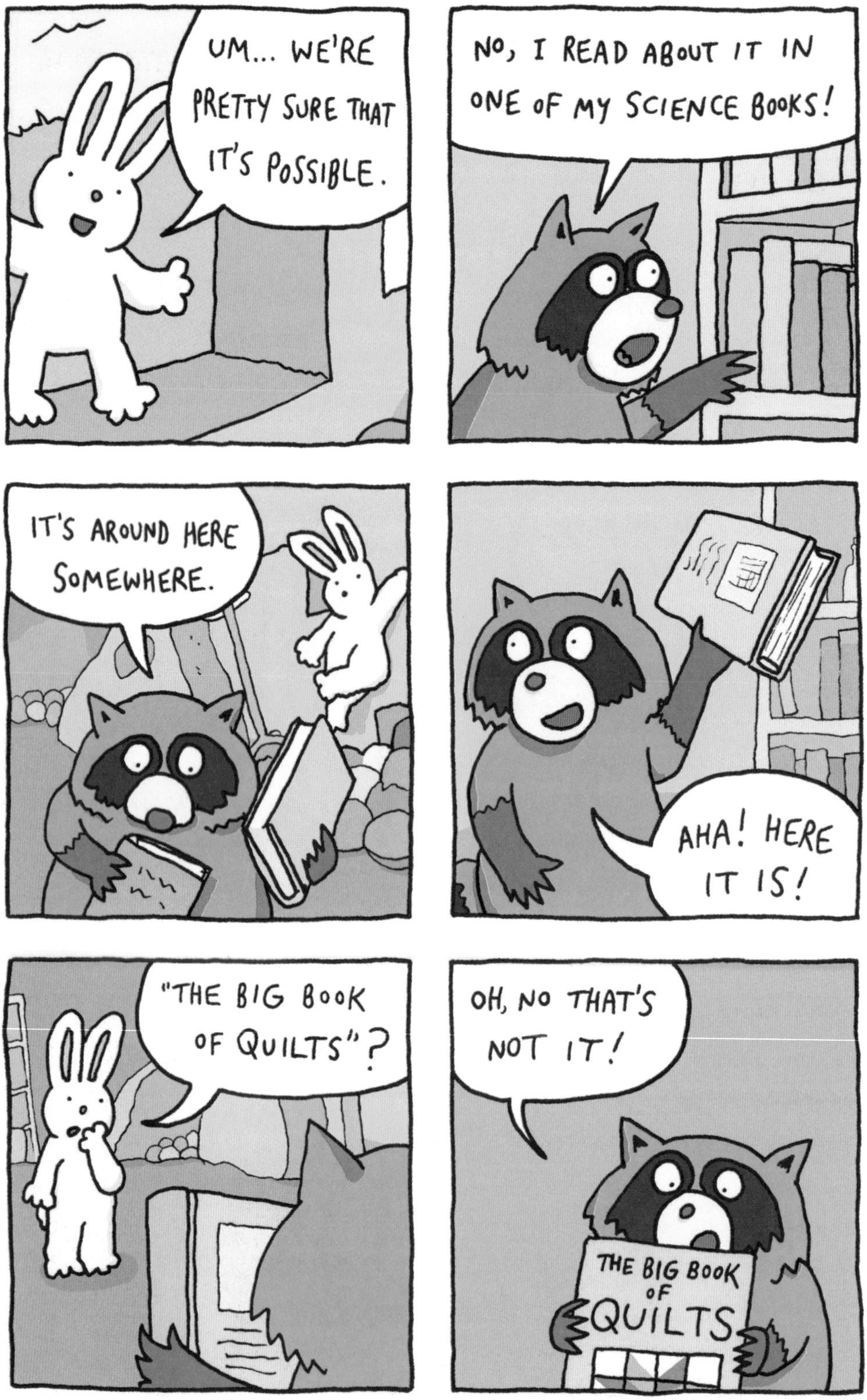
UM... WE'RE PRETTY SURE THAT IT'S POSSIBLE.
NO, I READ ABOUT IT IN ONE OF MY SCIENCE BOOKS!
IT'S AROUND HERE SOMEWHERE.
AHA! HERE IT IS!
"THE BIG BOOK OF QUILTS"?
OH, NO THAT'S NOT IT!
THE BIG BOOK OF QUILTS

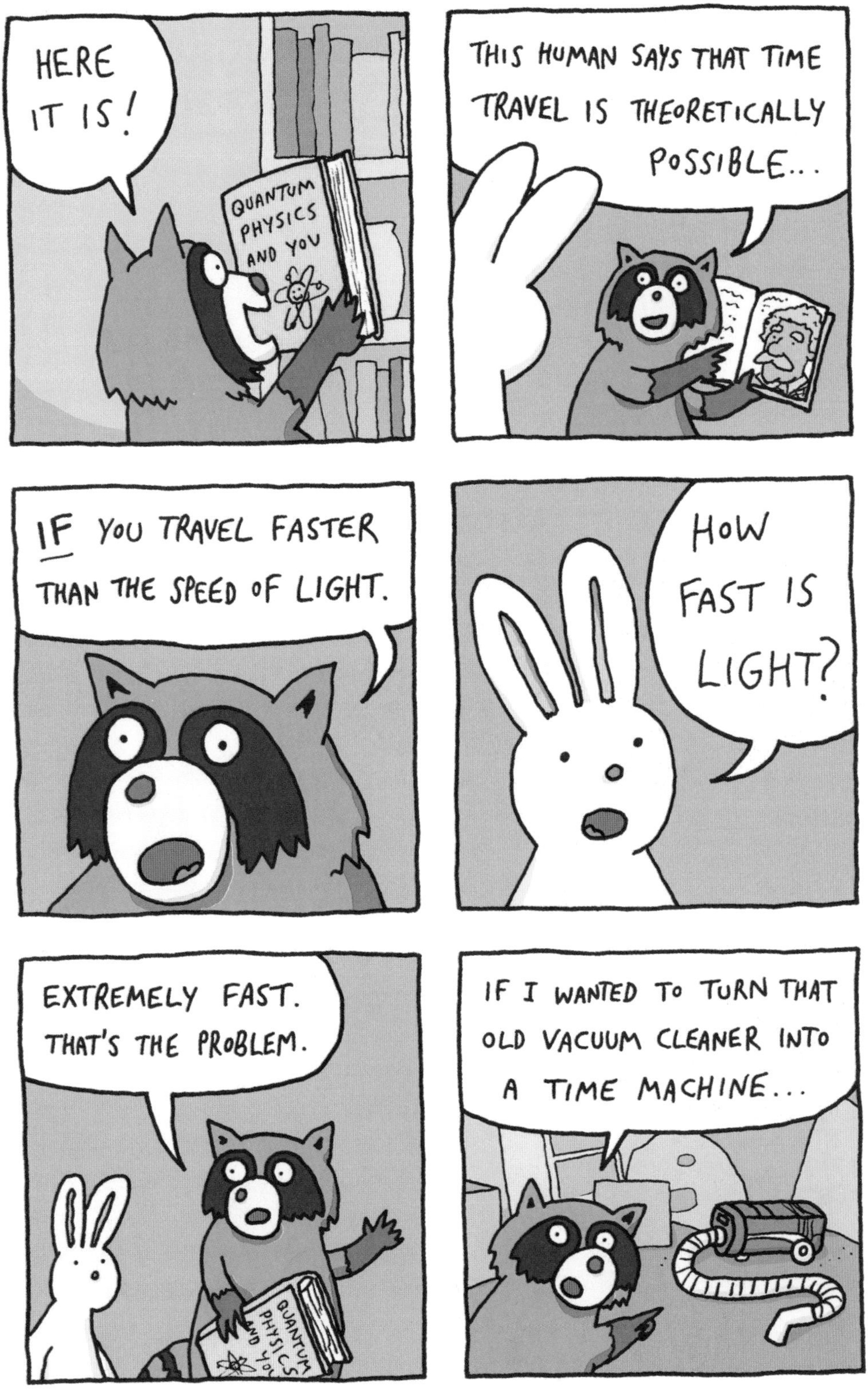
HERE IT IS!
QUANTUM PHYSICS AND YOU
THIS HUMAN SAYS THAT TIME TRAVEL IS THEORETICALLY POSSIBLE...
IF YOU TRAVEL FASTER THAN THE SPEED OF LIGHT.
HOW FAST IS LIGHT?
EXTREMELY FAST. THAT'S THE PROBLEM.
QUANTUM PHYSICS AND YOU
IF I WANTED TO TURN THAT OLD VACUUM CLEANER INTO A TIME MACHINE...

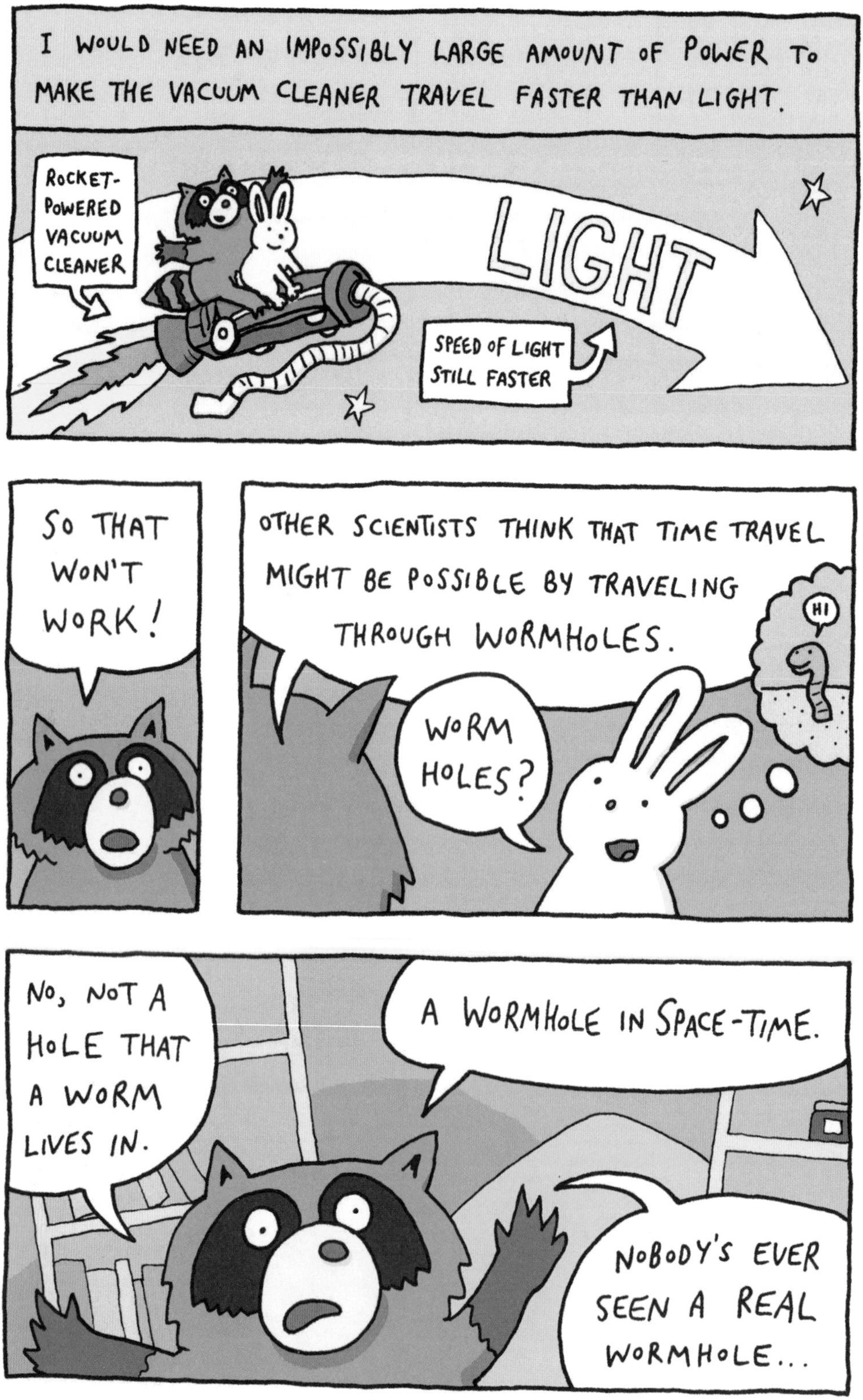
I WOULD NEED AN IMPOSSIBLY LARGE AMOUNT OF POWER TO MAKE THE VACUUM CLEANER TRAVEL FASTER THAN LIGHT.
ROCKET-POWERED VACUUM CLEANER
LIGHT
SPEED OF LIGHT STILL FASTER
SO THAT WON'T WORK!
OTHER SCIENTISTS THINK THAT TIME TRAVEL MIGHT BE POSSIBLE BY TRAVELING THROUGH WORMHOLES.
WORM HOLES?
HI
NO, NOT A HOLE THAT A WORM LIVES IN.
A WORMHOLE IN SPACE-TIME.
NOBODY'S EVER SEEN A REAL WORMHOLE...

BUT PEOPLE SAY IT'S LIKE A BLACK HOLE THAT CONNECTS DIFFERENT POINTS IN SPACE, AND MAYBE EVEN IN TIME!

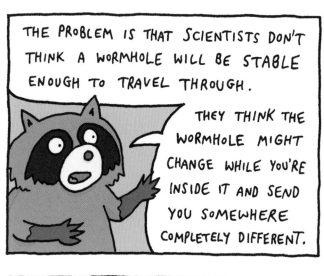

A

WHEE!

NORMAL LONG, BORING PATH FROM A TO B

WORMHOLE SHORTCUT FROM A TO B →

B

THE PROBLEM IS THAT SCIENTISTS DON'T THINK A WORMHOLE WILL BE STABLE ENOUGH TO TRAVEL THROUGH.

THEY THINK THE WORMHOLE MIGHT CHANGE WHILE YOU'RE INSIDE IT AND SEND YOU SOMEWHERE COMPLETELY DIFFERENT.

I GUESS THE FUTURE PEOPLE WILL FIGURE IT OUT!

YES, I GUESS ANYTHING IS POSSIBLE IN THE FUTURE.

EVEN ALIEN INVASIONS!

ALIEN INVASIONS?

DON'T WORRY! I'M SURE EVERYTHING WILL TURN OUT FINE!

141

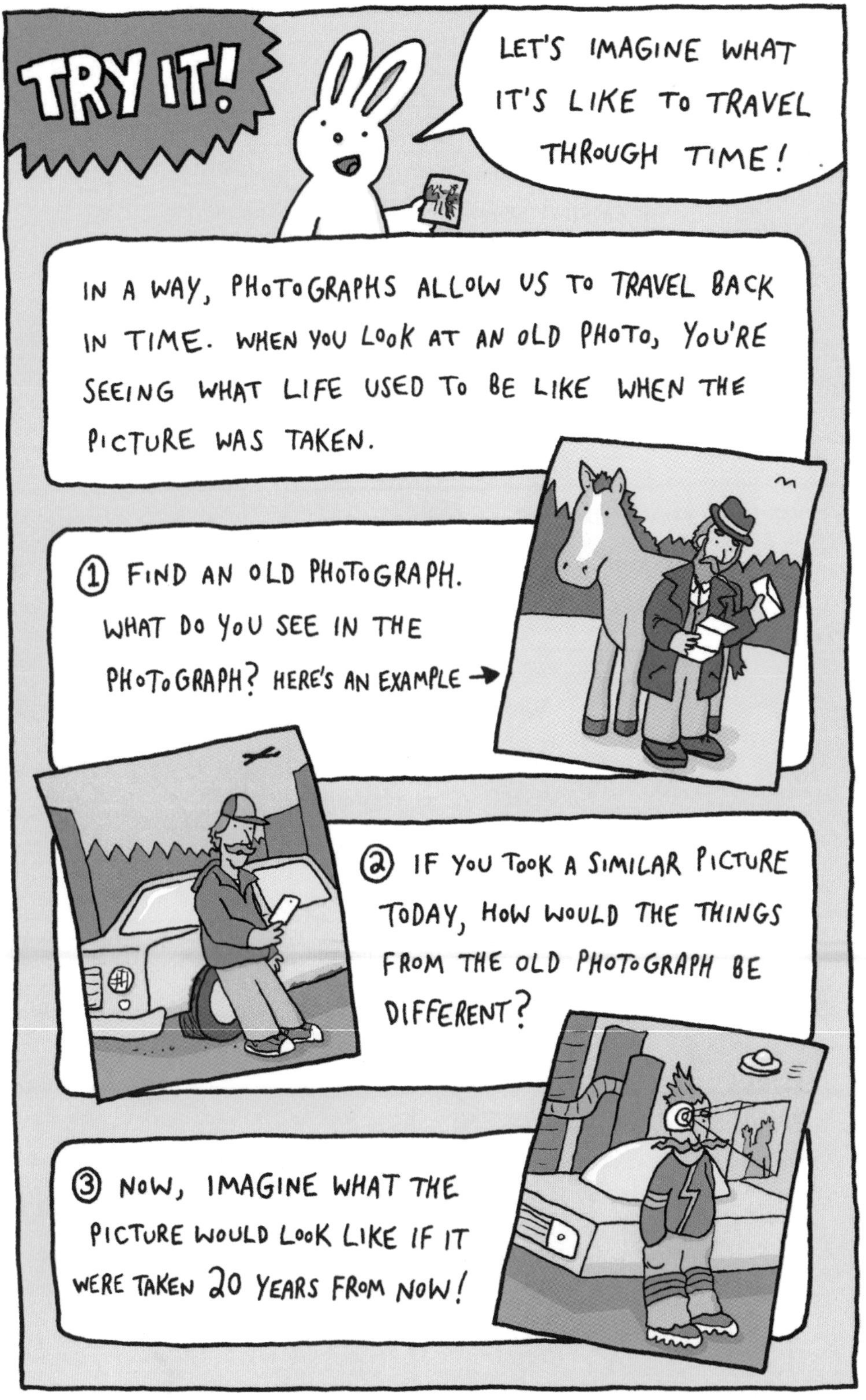
TRY IT!
LET'S IMAGINE WHAT IT'S LIKE TO TRAVEL THROUGH TIME!
IN A WAY, PHOTOGRAPHS ALLOW US TO TRAVEL BACK IN TIME. WHEN YOU LOOK AT AN OLD PHOTO, YOU'RE SEEING WHAT LIFE USED TO BE LIKE WHEN THE PICTURE WAS TAKEN.
① FIND AN OLD PHOTOGRAPH. WHAT DO YOU SEE IN THE PHOTOGRAPH? HERE'S AN EXAMPLE →
② IF YOU TOOK A SIMILAR PICTURE TODAY, HOW WOULD THE THINGS FROM THE OLD PHOTOGRAPH BE DIFFERENT?
③ NOW, IMAGINE WHAT THE PICTURE WOULD LOOK LIKE IF IT WERE TAKEN 20 YEARS FROM NOW!